The
COMPANY
Daughters

SAMANTHA RAJARAM

The
COMPANY
Daughters

Bookouture

Published by Bookouture in 2020

An imprint of Storyfire Ltd.
Carmelite House
50 Victoria Embankment
London EC4Y 0DZ

www.bookouture.com

ISBN: 978-1-80019-176-1
eBook ISBN: 978-1-80019-175-4

For my parents.

"Everyone knows that the male sex cannot survive without women. And yet it seems that Your Excellencies have planted a colony without wishing to. To make up for the lack we have looked for funds and have had to buy many women at high prices…"

−1609, letter from Governor-General Jan Pieterszoon Coen

Prologue

From the stern of the *Leyden* I listen to the slow drum of the sea. I have heard this music for so long now, it has found its way into my sun-toughened skin. I think when we finally arrive, I will know the sound of this ocean better than my own voice.

A flock of seagulls drifts overhead like a great arrowhead, hovering in the air, on their own journey elsewhere. I wonder where they will go.

Maybe they, too, seek Batavia?

I say the name of our destination throughout the journey, whenever I tire of the rotten potatoes or the worm-filled bread. As though I may understand this place if only I repeat its name, and make it familiar. No other word I have spoken or heard resembles it, its secrets and promises, frightening for its newness but still pulling me closer.

The ocean rolls itself out before me, boasting its silver trough, its bone-white crests—the whitest thing we see, now that we are dun-colored from sweat and dirt. But I never tire of this view. If I were a man I would be a sailor and live out my days on this gleaming, changing surface. But I'm neither man nor sailor. Only a female. Unmarried, poor, orphaned, wearing a stained dress and scratched *klomps*, and carrying a threadbare pouch holding two guilders and some bits of colored glass.

The seagulls cackle and disperse in the sky, and I force myself to leave the deck and return to our quarters.

The rest of the Company Daughters will be waiting for me.

Part One

Chapter 1

Amsterdam, 1620

Three knocks on the door. I use the knuckle of my forefinger, quiet but distinct.

Tap.

Tap.

Tap.

Theirs is the same dark green door of the other houses in the Herengracht. Black shutters on the windows and small, red bricks. Unlike the others, cheerful, blue crocuses line the doorstep. The blooms slant toward the sun, opening like little mouths to the light, reminding me of my sister Hlaska when she was hungry for *havermout* and milk in the morning.

When I see such flowers in our gray city, I think their planting is generous. Color to break up all this dimmed sky. The petunias in boxes at windowsills, hyacinths and hydrangeas in pots outside doors. Little gifts. To beggars and fishmongers and soldiers and sailors trudging the streets, surviving.

To girls like me, seeking escape.

My stomach growls, and I hope it quiets before I speak to the owner of this house. I've not eaten in two days. No wild sourgrass here in

Amsterdam and I'm too ashamed to beg from the merchants, afraid of what they may ask for in return, afraid of being imprisoned in the Spinhuis for begging.

My neck is still bruised near my nape. Blue thumbprints on my hips. I feel scraped out from my hunger, and my bones pull like dull blades against my skin.

Unhurried steps approach the door.

The lock turns, and the door opens halfway.

A woman answers. She is around my age—seventeen or eighteen. But otherwise, nothing like me. She wears a lace collar and a pearl pendant at her throat and in the faint sunlight angling onto the step, the loose hair above her ear gleams like candle fire. I feel even smaller and uglier with my unbrushed, mud-colored strands, hastily braided and tied low at my neck to cover the bruise.

"Hallo?" she asks. Her voice is lower than I imagined. Pretty girls often have high voices and I have wondered if they train their voices to be so airy, not more than whispers, or if they are born that way. Predestined for beauty as the Calvinists claim they are predestined for heaven.

I take in a quick breath.

"My name is Jana Beil. I'm looking for work." I slow my words. She can't know this is the eighteenth door upon which I've knocked three times. If you are too hungry, they think you will steal.

I force myself to continue, though my stomach rumbles from emptiness and I'm sure she has heard it.

"I can clean and cook. Everything—rearrange your bureaus, scrub the step and rugs. Polishing work, too. Silver and wood."

She glances over me quickly, my frayed, spotted apron, scuffed *klomps*, stained stockings. I fold my hands across my middle so she doesn't see the black arcs under my nails, the pin I've used to hold my skirts together now that they are torn at the waist.

Few in Amsterdam use house servants, except for people in houses like this—three stories, with a long hallway stretching far back. Despite this, Amsterdam is full of women seeking such work, sleeping on doorsteps and alleys, dreaming of servants' quarters and a hot meal.

"Tonight I'll work for just a meal," I continue, my words out in the world before I can think them, for I'm so hungry. "You can see how I work." The idea takes form as I recognize the fragrances from inside. Warm *hutspot* and the sweetness of *appeltaart*, which we had in the Bos a few times each summer when my sister Helena and I picked enough wild apples.

The girl looks over me again, but now with less distrust. She must know I'm hungry. I'm too hungry even to feel ashamed at her pitying glance. "Well, we did just lose Gerta," the girl mutters to herself. "Wait here and I will ask Fader."

"What is his name?" I ask, hoping to impress him with my greeting.

"Pieter Reynst," she answers, straightening her posture. "And I'm Sontje." She turns to fetch him while I wait on the doorstep next to the blue, open-mouthed crocuses. Hungry, just like me.

Chapter 2

Pieter Reynst is very tall, perhaps the tallest man I have seen, even in Amsterdam, where our Dutchmen are hands taller than the Spaniards and Jews who work at the docks. His dull, yellow-white hair falls to his shoulders and he has sad, blue-gray eyes lost in fine wrinkles. His skin hangs a bit loose on him, as though he lacks enough flesh for the skin to stick to.

I look at his long, graceful hands made for quills and ink. Careful hands. I have learned to look at men's hands first, trying to determine if their hands are the kind to clutch or pummel, to pinch or remain safely folded.

His look safe enough.

"What is your name?" he asks. His voice is very soft, even for a Dutchman.

"Jana. Jana Beil." I repeat my offer—a day's work for a meal.

"Perhaps you'd like that meal before we talk about employment?" He smiles and his sad eyes brighten. "You look nearly the same age as my daughter. I would not have her go without food. You should not, either."

He invites me into the house as Sontje watches, unsmiling.

I enter and note the small paintings in the hallway, the fresh-cut tulips in the vases. Not too much clutter to require dusting, and the furniture is spare: a few cupboards, benches in the main sitting room—the *zaal*—mats and rugs on the floor. A rectangular mirror stands in the hallway and I glance at my own reflection. I'm smaller and thinner than I imagined, with a hardness around the eyes that my sister Helena would not recognize. A year has passed since she died, and I'm relieved at least that she is spared from knowing of my difficulties.

The back of my mouth stings at the warm smell of *hutspot*. My stomach roars again, and I press my fist against my middle to silence it.

"Our cook Hilda left for the evening, but we will fix you a plate," Pieter Reynst says and asks me to sit at the table. Sontje stands in the entrance to the dining room. He looks at her expectantly. "Go on and fetch her a bowl." She walks off toward the stairwell. The kitchen must be downstairs in the cellar, and I wonder at the size of this house, which is nothing like the one-room cottage I grew up in with Fader, Moeder, Helena, and baby Hlaska, though Helena and I had the entire forest for our games. Some houses here even have a privy inside, so no chamber pots requiring emptying. I wonder if this is such a house.

Master Reynst interrupts my thoughts. "Looks that you need some regular feeding. Hunger is good motivation. You can start today. We have an attic room where you may stay tonight if you like."

Sontje returns with a plate of food, distracting me by the smell and sight of it. *Hutspot*, as I guessed, but so many other things too. My stomach is sour with hunger, like it may turn in on itself.

"Let's leave her to eat in peace," Pieter Reynst says. Sontje looks like she wants to stay and watch, as though my grating hunger might provide entertainment.

"You probably haven't had this before," she says, after her father leaves the room.

I'm not sure what she means—*hutspot*? Or this quantity of food? Either way, the words are barbs aimed at my low condition, or perhaps she enjoys making me wait to eat my meal.

I say nothing, just imagine what I will taste first. Perhaps begin with the rye bread to settle my stomach, then the *hutspot*? I must eat slowly though I wish to swallow the entire meal, even the dish, simply to fill the hole in my middle.

Sontje lingers a moment, but then she leaves to another room. Maybe she realizes I will not taste anything until she's gone.

I don't even think of the strangeness of this meal, that they have offered me the bounty of their own supper without knowing anything about me. I think only of the food and how I would describe it to Helena. *The bread is warm and flavorful and I use extra butter because you would do so if you were here.*

I eat until my stomach is tight against the waistband of my skirt and my mouth aches from chewing. The rye bread and *hutspot* with prunes, an apple, stewed sorrel, a piece of cumin cheese the size of my fist, *koeken*, two roast potatoes, and, at last, a slice of *appeltaart* better than even Moeder could make. I describe each thing in my mind. The prunes stick to the top of my mouth. The cumin cheese tastes like smoke scattered outdoors.

I should leave something on my plate out of politeness, but I'm too hungry even for my manners. If there is good food on my plate, I shall not waste it.

Sontje returns and looks in on me before I'm finished.

"That's more than I've ever eaten in two sittings," she remarks at the scraps remaining, and my skin burns at her observation.

"It's delicious." I think of the remaining *hutspot* and how I cannot waste it.

"Bring the dishes back to the cellar and I'll show you to your room."

She gathers up the silver, all but my fork because I'm still using it for the last remaining bites.

Chapter 3

The next morning, Sontje approaches as I scrub the entryway floor. She stands in the doorway and I cannot help noting how the sun settles into her hair from the high window. I'm jealous of her unripped dress, the silk ribbons in her gold hair, the cleanness of her fingernails, the whiteness of her skin, barely marred by sun or poor sleep or chapped by the cold night wind. She has never eaten sourgrass for a meal or slept in the alleys or under trees.

"Did you know you screamed when you were sleeping? I could hear you from my room." My small, attic bedroom with its sloping ceiling lies directly above hers. A warm, dry space from which I can hear the pigeons making their nests in the rooftops.

"I did? I'm sorry if I woke you."

But she ignores my apology. "Why did you scream?" she asks, leaning against the doorframe.

I keep scrubbing, back and forth with the boar bristle brush so I make a design of alternating triangles on the wood. I'm still tired from the days before I arrived here, the sleep which is not sleep at all, but a half-awake panic that battles fatigue. My body aches from yesterday's work—knocking on doors, and, finally, the two hours spent before sleeping, when I swept the entire house of all cobwebs, shined up the stove and its crusted grate, and scrubbed out the pots from the meal

I ate too quickly. My stomach swelled and gurgled from the shock of so much food.

"A bad dream," I answer. My knees will be bruised from kneeling on the wooden floor, even though I've folded my dress beneath me.

"What about?" She watches as I scrub another triangle into the floorboards.

"I don't remember." But always, it is the same thing—an abandoned tobacco pipe, playing cards. Sometimes a candle's flickering light against a dingy wall. A howling scream deep inside myself, but fear locks the scream within. I can sometimes force myself to wake, or wrest myself from the memory.

Sontje twirls a bit of her golden hair behind her small ear. She waits for more of an answer, but I refuse to provide it. She shrugs.

"When you're finished with the floors, I need help moving my bed to face the window. My best friend Sussie—her father is a burgher whose house is even bigger than ours—says the sunlight in the morning brings better dreams at night."

Chapter 4

Two weeks pass and I soon find a comfortable routine at the Reynst house. Washing the steps in front of the house early each morning, dusting on Wednesday, polishing on Monday and Tuesday as well as shopping for the meals, which stout, plain-faced Hilda cooks in the evenings. Thursdays for scrubbing. On Fridays, I clean the kitchen and cellar, my fingernails blackened by the week's thick cake of grease and my knuckles dry from soap by the end of the day.

I know every room. The foyer where Master Reynst receives merchants, the *zaal* with its walnut table, highbacked armchairs, and gilt leather tapestry. The fireplace, which spews smoke through the house so I must keep the bedroom doors closed. The bedsteads and backhouse. And of course, the attic, whose ceiling is so low I must bend down when I'm inside, and I'm not nearly so tall as Sontje. As I had hoped, they even have a *secreet*, a cupboard-size room with a hole on a bench through which you do your business. In the end, I prefer our methods in the forest, where the must of leaves and mosses and earth overcome the stench.

Today, I'm cleaning Sontje's room. She is having tea with Sussie, whose wide-set eyes seem to run from each other to the far edges of her face. Sussie never looks at me, just hands me her cloak when she enters. I know it will always be this way with her. Such women need their servants to be invisible.

Their laughter from downstairs sounds like seagulls arguing. Louder than I expect from Sontje, since she speaks so quietly. Surely, they are discussing Sussie's possible betrothed, a wealthy landowner's son named Johannes—Sussie speaks of little else.

I dust Sontje's cupboard, a massive oak and ebony piece with deep scrollwork and thick, grooved bun feet that collect grime. Her bedroom is otherwise simple—the cupboard and small bedstead, a trunk in the corner, a tapestry decorated with thin, pale green vines covering the bed.

Hearing their laughter, I try to recall when I last laughed so freely. When Helena and I were young and could run far from the cottage to play, tripping over our bare feet in the grass. We learned to hide our laughter when indoors. Fader hated the sound of it, said the noise hurt his head. If we laughed at the table, he slammed down his thick, knobby hand, shaking all the crockery. Laughter could not be trusted. It came and went so quickly, like our Dutch sunshine. Instead, we allowed ourselves quiet smiles. Only baby Hlaska was permitted laughter because she did not yet know better.

I approach Sontje's trunk and run my hands over the top of it, smooth so it can serve as a bench. Vines carved on the outside, similar to the pattern on her bed cover. A trace of dust remains on my hands, so I clean the top using the cloth kept in the waistband of my dress.

I flip the latch up and pull open the lid.

Inside, her dresses lie neatly folded. Most of us have only one or two dresses, but she has four. I reach in and extract a Bible, and inside its pages find a long, black feather which I run over my palm and brush across my cheek. I push the dresses aside after returning the Bible. A sewing kit with a ceramic thimble rests between the layers, along with two pairs of gloves and a hand mirror with a bone handle.

I'm not thinking when I take the top dress from the trunk. Moeder said I was always this way, listening to some other voice inside myself when I should know better. Fader, before hiding me (which was often), blamed the Devil himself for my curiosity, and accepted the grim task of beating Satan from my bones.

I run the back of my hand against the dress, having never touched silk before. I smile, imagining little silkworms hard at work on a spinning wheel. Gold embroidery spills over the puffed sleeves and openwork— more stitching than I have ever seen. Nothing like my simple white cotton blouse, long skirt, and apron. I untie my own skirts so they fall, and pull off my blouse. Naked, I step into the dress, pushing my hands through the narrow sleeves, yanking up on the bodice so it fits over my shoulders.

The fabric feels heavy on my skin from all the embroidery and openwork and I realize that wealthy women walk as they do—slowly, stiffly—because they are freighted down by their wealth. Their gold earrings, ruffs, thick corsets, layers of petticoats, and embroidered dresses must burden them. I feel a surprising pity, that they, too, must sometimes feel trapped, though in a different sort of cage. Wealth for women requires slower movements, just as poverty requires a quicker pace—to finish tasks, to arrive early, to rush to the market when our employers run out of eggs. And for once, I feel some small advantage in my own poverty—at least I walk at my normal speed as long as my *klomps* remain comfortable on my feet.

I wonder if such a dress could make me beautiful like Sontje. I walk to the mirror on the opposite wall beside the bureau. I'm not tall, so the bodice is too long, but I become someone else in these clothes. Not quite the "ugly little speck" Fader sometimes called me. Not Jana escaping from the Bos or the Ringhouse, or Jana in my shadowed dreams.

The overlong sleeves end mid-forearm instead of at the elbow. The shoulders sag. But my skin looks almost lovely against the rose fabric. I unwind my hair and gather it at the top and turn left and right, inspecting myself, noting my left side looks better than the right. I have a small mole near my eyebrow that I have never noticed. I'm not given to seeing myself closely in mirrors. There is never enough time for it.

I release my hair and re-tie it, trying to rub out the hard, small, deepening line between my eyes. I step closer to the mirror, to see how else my face may have changed since leaving the Ringhouse. Brown eyes. Fader's eyes. I have never liked them. Moeder's eyes are blue, like Hlaska's. Like Helena's.

When I was young, I wondered if the world looked different depending on the color of one's eyes. Did the world through Helena's eyes look slightly blue? Perhaps my own dour expectations of the world are owing to the muddy color of my eyes. How would the world look to Sontje, who has her father's gray eyes?

I unhook the front of the dress, unused to its closures—only the wealthy have time for such complications. I observe my nakedness, for I have only ever seen my face in a mirror. I open the dress, allowing my breasts to peek out. Open the fabric further still. I have never given my body much thought, but now I imagine seeing it as someone else would. A body that could move one to desire. Round, high breasts, red nipples the size of *stuiver* coins. I cup my breasts in my hands, for the first time aware of their softness, the dull sting of them when I squeeze from underneath, pushing aside thoughts of the Ringhouse.

"Jana." Her voice is sharp and startling.

Sontje stands at the door.

Chapter 5

I have not seen her angry before. Her lips are pursed. Eyes narrowed. Her features shrink in displeasure, and for the first time, she does not look beautiful. I tuck my breasts into the flap of cloth but the dress remains open so I cross my arms.

"What are you doing?"

A stupid question meant to embarrass me further. I think of Moeder chiding me for my curiosity and how it always brings me trouble. I should be grateful to have work at all, but I can't silence my desire to know answers. And then I find myself in tangled knots I wish I could undo.

"I'm sorry." I wish to remove the dress but not with her watching, which brings to mind other memories.

"That is Moeder's dress." Her voice lowers in accusation. "I have never even worn it." A familiar sting of shame returns, for I can smell my own wild odor from my hours of labor and infrequent baths. "Remove it and put it back, Jana." Though her voice remains beautiful even in her anger, she says my name like it is an ugly, rotted thing.

I wonder how I may excuse myself, return to some ten minutes earlier and leave the trunk and its fluted silk dresses alone with my reputation unmarred. But, of course, I'm locked in Sontje's room, half-dressed, and flushed with shame.

Sontje turns. Her hand grips tight to the door frame.

"Now I will have to wash it," she adds, before shutting the heavy door behind her.

Chapter 6

For a week she does not talk to me. I spend hours in my bed before falling asleep, wondering if she has told Master Reynst, who remains distracted and kind, or if she is waiting to tell him, and why.

The memory of her gaze as I stood naked in front of her wall mirror burns me with humiliation. At first I'm relieved by her avoidance. But days pass, and I grow worried by her silence, and afraid of what will happen when Sontje tells her father of my misdeed. I did not think of her much before, but without her usual pleasantries and the questions she asks without genuine care for my answers—You slept well? You ate breakfast?—my work here grows suffocating. Such empty conversations lighten the day, allowing me the luxury of believing I belong in the Reynst house, washing their floors and dusting their furnishings.

I might lose my work, my bed, regular meals. If only I could go back to that day, somehow scrub myself clean of whatever urge compelled me to open her trunk and to pull on that dress. I have often wished to wash away all my wrong-headed impulses. And my darkest memories.

My shame makes me wish I could afford to leave this house altogether, except there is cream-porridge and roasted hen and quince cakes and *veldhoenders* with sauce, and a bed in the attic with only dreams of the flickering candle. And not the candle itself.

I imagine myself abandoned to Amsterdam's damp alleys again. When I first arrived in the city, I only wished for escape, but now that I'm at the Reynst home, fed and sleeping indoors, I'm loath to lose these comforts. But having lived through so much upheaval, I doubt I will ever know the full taste of safety. I'm forever assuming some future disaster. Readying myself to flee.

It's Friday so I clean the cellar, a hateful chore for the darkness and grime and stench of burned food from the *jambless*, and set myself to polishing the hinges and outside doorknob of the Reynst house so I can have some time in the sunlight. Since the Ringhouse, I'm always searching for it.

I wipe the hinges so their brightness crackles against the grayness of midday. I splash boiling water on the step and kneel to scrub it clean of bird droppings and the wind-strewn leaves stuck and flattened to the surface.

Travelers remark on Amsterdam's cleanness. All day, street cleaners shovel the horse *poep* and scrub down the brick, as though our battle against filth is against Satan himself. But the filth is more than dust and droppings. It is also our sick-headed, our beggars, our pox survivors left blinded and riddled with pits. And in this desire to rid the world of evil, other evils are committed. Like those committed in the Ringhouse, hidden just outside the city, and others committed in the city itself. Just yesterday, Master Reynst remarked that a ten-year-old boy was decapitated in the House of Correction for committing a murder. Master said it was a shame indeed, but no ten-year-old should be killing. I wonder who the boy murdered. I wonder why, and what was done to him.

As I'm thinking of that unfortunate boy and scrubbing a white streak of bird droppings on the corner of the step, Sontje approaches. My stomach twists.

"Hallo, Jana," she says, smiling. I'm unsure how to read her smile. Has she forgiven the incident with the dress? Is she simply being polite?

"Hallo, Mistress Sontje." I look up for a minute before working the brush over the step again.

"You're very thorough," she says, watching. "You're a hard worker, Jana."

I'm confused by her compliment, so I simply nod.

"It's been strange between us," she says.

I wait for her to say more.

"I would like to forget it. Promise never to go through my things again."

I nod my head, my breath lodged in my throat. I wish I did not look quite so low, kneeling on the step in front of her, scraping off its muck.

"I have just one question," she continues. "Why did you do it?"

I stop my scrubbing, and stand up to face her.

"I don't know." I wish I had a better explanation, but with her gray eyes staring into mine, I can only be honest. "But I regret it." I feel shame like thick oil on my skin.

She nods and sets her mouth in a prim line. "I keep her things because they are all I have of her." She then takes in the whole of me, a quick glance from my stained *klomps* to my *hollar* cap. "That color was unbecoming on you. It looks better on a fair skin and you are quite dark."

I glance down at my old *klomps*. Moeder often pitied me for my complexion, brown from the sun because I hated wearing a bonnet.

"If I told Fader he would remove you in an instant," she continues. "We have had thieving servants and he has no patience for that."

I wonder if he would think trying on a dress amounts to thievery, but I remain quiet, worrying about my employment.

She pauses. "What did it feel like? I cannot yet bring myself to wear it."

A strange question, but at times Sontje is more thoughtful than you'd think. Helena asked such questions—*if summer was a color, would it be red? Why does the grass feel soft together, but sharp alone?*

I pause to consider her question and close my eyes a moment to remember.

"Heavy. And it didn't smell like you."

"What do I smell like?" A crooked, amused smile I haven't seen before.

"Lavender." I pause to think. "Sunlight."

"Yes, lavender water. I purchase it at the Dam market—the florist makes it." She looks pleased, and gazes at her crocuses, which look brighter on this drizzly day. "The crocuses are Moeder's. Fader said they were her favorite flowers."

"They are beautiful. I noticed them when I first arrived."

"Sometimes I think I may like tulips more, but then I tell myself these are better. It's odd how we learn to like certain things because we are expected to. Makes me wonder sometimes if I truly like anything I think I like."

I have thought the same thing. Everyone wears decorative aprons over their dresses, but at times, I find them ugly, even ridiculous. And then the thought is overpowered by the belief that I must like them because everyone else does.

"She died during childbirth. I nearly died also," Sontje says in a quiet voice.

"I'm sorry." Such tragedy is not uncommon, even in the cities. Childbirth is a mess of gore and blood. I've seen it. "Your father didn't remarry?"

"No. I think he wants to believe he loved Moeder too much to remarry, but Sussie's mother told her that Fader was not especially nice to Moeder. Absent. You know, he is mostly living in his thoughts."

"I've observed it." But I have a fondness for this trait in Master Reynst. It makes him seem harmless, a bit like a child.

"I sometimes think he refuses to remarry because he feels guilty." Sontje pauses, lost in some thought or another. "Jana, I'll tell you a secret." I marvel at her straight, healthy teeth, all nearly white. Most women cover their mouths when they smile or abandon the expression altogether for fear of revealing unsightly gaps and rot. But she can smile openly, and knows it. "I think I have a beau," she whispers, and I wonder why she's telling me this. Perhaps out of pity? Remorse for her earlier cruelty? Or because Sussie is gone for the week? "His name is Hans. His father owns one of the wealthiest shipping businesses in the city. Sussie says it would change our standing here altogether. No more poor, motherless Sontje Reynst. I would be the wife of Hans Luiken."

I smile at her revelation. This is the Sontje I know, and I'm relieved to see it. Her earlier seriousness worried me. Not only must we servants scrub and boil and scrape and polish, we must maintain a steady, neutral tone with our employers, caring neither too much nor too little. Any shift in our employer's favor means we will lose our work.

"It's still early," she continues. "But he said he thinks of me all the time. Of course, 'with sweet words are hearts broken'—as Sussie often reminds me. But I do think he likes me. The way he looks at me. As though I'm the only girl in all of Amsterdam."

"How did you meet him?" I'm eager to chat with her, to begin again and wipe the slate clean of my earlier errors. And this idea of courting, I find curious. I've never been courted myself. Indeed, I can't imagine having the leisure or desire for such things.

"We first met at the *kerkhof* after church service. Sussie's friend introduced us. And then we went as a group for a picnic. I noticed he always sat beside me. Kept looking at me." She smiles. "Do you know how your skin feels different when you know someone is watching you? Almost like an itch?"

I nod, remembering, though I wish I did not.

"I could feel him watching me the entire time—" she drops her voice to a whisper and lowers her eyes "—and I did not mind it at all."

"He's handsome, then?"

"He looks sharp enough. And he has good manners. When we walk, he stands between me and the road so I can tread undisturbed by the horses and carts. I feel protected."

How strange it must be to feel safe with men, when I have always felt more afraid.

"Perhaps you could accompany us when we go on a walk? Then I won't tell Fader about the dress." At this, my face burns.

"As a chaperone?" Though women are free to walk through the city with men, wealthy young women sometimes have a minder, but I'm not much older than Sontje myself.

"Well, yes. Fader is traditional and he would find it unseemly for Hans and I to walk alone. And he is too busy."

"If Master Reynst approves…" I say, though I have no desire to do such work. I'd prefer polishing the most ornate silver pieces or scrubbing this step all day, when I can be alone with my thoughts and unconcerned about making some error. But at least chaperoning will be easy work, and will ensure my status with her.

"Thank you, Jana," she says. "I'll talk to Fader." I step aside so she can enter the house.

I continue with my washing, satisfied with this exchange. Now she will need me at least a bit longer.

This constant vigilance around the employers and my need for usefulness reminds me of when Helena and I would climb the rotting trees in our Bos. The balance and care required for it.

You keep climbing and hope the branches will hold.

Chapter 7

In my two months with the Reynsts, I have learned to read my master and Sontje. The girls at the Ringhouse said any good servant must. If you read them well, you know when you can request money for a new bonnet or a guilder's increase in pay or a free Saturday to roam the markets. When in high spirits, Master Reynst taps his fingers against his hand as though listening to some pleasant melody no one else hears. He remains distant, his thoughts elsewhere, but the thoughts seem to be of a brighter sort than he normally entertains.

Sontje notices and softens also. I'm hanging two of her dresses, smoothing the pleats, as she arranges her hair for afternoon tea. She uses black lace ribbons like the ones Sussie wore on her last visit.

"Fader is well today," she says, and I'm glad that she speaks to me. "I think he's investing in an important voyage," she adds. "If all goes well, we stand to make a good fortune."

This is a rare confidence—wealthy people seldom act as if they care much for their money. I have observed this at the market, overhearing the wives of burghers and businessmen share stories of "coming into" their fortune, as though their riches simply waited for them like expectant guests.

"We are well enough off, but if we had a greater fortune, there would be no question at all about my marrying Hans," she says, more to herself than me. "It helps that I'm beautiful, but status always matters more in this city. Especially with the Company people."

She means the Dutch East Indies Company, or V.O.C., which sponsors voyages to the colonies and earns great sums in such trade, but I pretend ignorance. Sontje is eager to educate me and if my feigned ignorance improves her own self-regard, I'm content to play the role. In this, her need for approval differs little from patrons at the Ringhouse, who enjoyed sharing their expertise about rasps or woodcutting or the best cows for milking. Her eyes brighten, and I can't help but smile at her excitement and interest in impressing me.

"It's why Amsterdam is growing so quickly, how we've moved so many of our Dutch citizens off to the colonies, and have made a fortune in the spice trades." She smiles, unable to conceal her pride. "Fader was a master shipwright for those early voyages. He used the money he made to invest in later voyages and the bounty they brought back. It's a gamble, but the Company only invests in the best ships and crews."

"I didn't realize." Indeed, it has never occurred to me to wonder how the wealthy obtain their spoils. I have always assumed they were born with their riches, like Sontje with her beauty.

"The Company intends to make a capital in one of the ports very soon. The British East India Company would like to best us, but they will not. Fader says we have the better ports and trade routes. And ships," she adds. "Fader is consulting on the construction of their largest one yet. When it sets off to the colonies, it will be able to bring back thrice the usual load of spices. It will be a huge success for the Company. And Fader."

I have finished hanging her dresses but move slowly so Sontje may continue talking. After the incident with the dress, I feel it necessary to listen to her prattle so she knows I appreciate her forgiveness. And I'm surprised she knows things about the city that I don't know myself.

"The ship should be finished in a few months. It must be perfect because it is the first cargo ship of its kind. Fader just found out he could be an investor—first they only offered him shipwright consultation." She whispers now. "It's like a secret society, who they let in as investors. Sussie says Hans's father is one. I only hope Fader does well with it. But I'm sure he will. He's always thinking about his ships."

This makes sense; when Master Reynst is daydreaming he gazes into the distance, as though waiting for some vessel past the far horizon to come into view.

Chapter 8

"Fader approves," Sontje says as I clear the breakfast table the next day. I could easily devour the half-eaten cake she's abandoned on her plate—I had only buttermilk porridge this morning—but I restrain myself.

"Of what?" I ask as I puzzle out how to carry everything—teacups, Majolica dishes, salt cellar, serving platter, utensils, and napkins—downstairs in one trip. I start with the dishes, piling each piece on top of the other.

"You acting as chaperone for me and Hans, of course."

Of course. She assumes I have nothing better to do than worry over her beau. I pull the stack of dishes and linens and crockery onto my arms.

She leans back in her chair and smooths down a wisp of her bright hair. "I was thinking of a walk today with Hans. Down the main canal. Or maybe to see the ships."

"It's the second Tuesday of the month."

"What do you mean?"

"When I do the polishing and linens. And Master Reynst is receiving someone tonight for dinner." I hope she doesn't notice my irritation.

"Oh, you'll finish it. You work quickly. And the house looks clean enough. We can purchase some lilies at the market which will look nice in the *zaal*." Sontje stands up and leans toward me, and gently adds her teacup to the pile of crockery in my arms. "You are the best house servant we have had, Jana."

I note her shrewd praise and ready smile. "What time shall I be ready?" Perhaps I can squeeze in a few more tasks first. No use in being angry. At least Hilda will be making a pear *taart*. I heard her mention it to Sontje last night.

"I told him noon. We will walk to Dam Centre."

"That gives me only an hour to finish polishing and wash the linens." My heart quickens with the tide of tasks I must now complete before evening, and which I should complete first. I'll need to fire up the *jambless*, boil the water and make a bath of lye for the linens, and buck them on the board for drying before I leave. And without much wind, the linens will require more time to dry. Perhaps I should do the wash now and then the polishing? Though the polishing will take some time as well. The deep engravings on their best silver require extra rubbing—tarnish collects in those small cracks and clefts. I try to work out all these tasks in my mind, feeling myself grow numb with the impossibility of their completion.

"Thank you, Jana," Sontje says in her slow, even voice. "I'm eager to see Hans today. You can tell me what you think of him, and whether we make a good couple. Sussie says we do, but maybe you will think differently." I'm annoyed with my own small satisfaction that she would seek my opinion of her beau. I know she won't care much what I think of him, but hope her confidences may ensure me a long term in the Reynst home.

I carry the teetering pile of ceramic and silver down to the kitchen, thinking of what tasks I can do in the next hour, and worrying how I will get through the rest of them later.

*

Hans Luiken arrives at noon, as promised. He wears a white shirt with a large collar, a black coat, black boots, and a broad-brimmed black hat that seems more fitting on an older man. He is very tall, with limbs too long for his body, as though he's unsure how to control the range of himself. His small teeth hide deep in his gums, and his long nose is slightly crooked, which makes his long face look longer. He may grow into his body, but for now, he has an awkwardness I would find endearing, if not for the arrogance beneath it.

He smiles at Sontje, pursing his thin lips over his little teeth.

"You are looking pretty as always," he says to her, offering his elbow as I wait behind them.

She turns to me and smiles. "This is Jana. Fader said she could be our chaperone."

Hans nods, a gesture he seems still to be practicing, as though he must concentrate to show the proper amount of superiority.

I keep two paces behind Hans and Sontje, not sure how close I must be. I'm not trained for this work, and I try to restrain my resentment that I cannot be at the Reynst home finishing the linens or sweeping the *zaal* one last time. I like finding routines in my cleaning, gauging my speed and thoroughness as I work.

I decide to observe rather than think of all the tasks I'd prefer to be doing. Moeder once told me, when I complained about some chore or another, that we must make the best of things. I wondered at the time if the task she made the best of was of mothering the three of us.

The heel of Hans's boot is smeared with mud or *poep*. A rusty-brown. His gait is long and confident, and he stands very erect, as though afraid he will slump at any moment. He rubs his short beard as he speaks, as if reassuring himself that the scruff remains in place.

Sontje's waist is small and delicate, but curiously strong. I think of a lily's sturdy stem. She is that wispy sort of woman who is ethereal in her form—no flesh in excess, everything simple and neat. Even the mole on her neck looks perfectly formed. I would envy her, but she seems so different from me altogether, I can only admire her beauty as though she is one of the fine Delft vases in the Reynsts' lacquered cabinet.

"Fader has promised me his trade. Even if my sister Beatrice marries next year, he only needs to provide a dowry. The family business is mine," Hans speaks loudly, as if wanting every passerby to hear.

Sontje nods her head. I know she smiles because I can see the lifted curve of her cheek.

"I want to buy a proper horse carriage," Hans continues. "Not the plain ones on our streets. They use a different sort in Sicilia—the *carretto*. Sometimes I tire of our Dutch need for plainness, as if we must feel guilty for our wealth. Why? Has God not given it to us freely? Why not celebrate it?" Sontje nods again and I wonder if she is listening to him at all. "The Italians know more about beauty. Freshness. We just clean everything. That's what any visitor remarks upon first. Amsterdam's peerless streets."

"You have been to Sicily?" Sontje asks.

"Two years back. Fader and I went to look into shipping silks there."

"And you enjoyed it?" Sontje twists a loose tendril of hair behind her ear so he will notice its fine shape and the glow of her hair.

"Yes. Everything is full of passion. Not like our Dutch, who want to keep all our passions in a tight box. It bores me sometimes, all the restraint. One must *feel* things. Be moved by beauty." His voice softens. "Sontje, I'm moved by *your* beauty."

Sontje glances back, blushing, as though checking to see if I've heard, but I stare down at my stained *klomps*, trying not to laugh. I'm embarrassed for the both of them.

"Thank you, Hans. That is kind of you to say."

"Everyone thinks you are the most beautiful girl in all of Amsterdam. You must know that." And it's true, for even now, everyone else on the street looks dull and burdened and small when compared to her.

"I did not know and find it hard to believe," Sontje says, but she sounds very pleased.

We pass by the Spinhuis, where Amsterdam sends the city prostitutes of Haarlemmerstraat and Boomssloot and Nieuwendijk and the petty thieves after they've been flogged or punished on the pillory. All part of the city's efforts to clean us of our sins, though the sin of poverty offends them most of all.

Though of course, the Ringhouse lies outside of the city, away from any inspection.

The gray Spinhuis building is so large it looks belched from the earth, and not built by human hands. Master Reynst once said that the female convicts spend their days spinning yarn and sewing to absolve their crimes. I feel an immediate panic, seeing the queue of ragged women, wondering if any of them might know me, and hoping we can walk at a faster pace.

Instead, Hans slows his steps. He stares at the female convicts, chained together as they wait at the Spinhuis gate for their punishment. The women wear fancier dresses than mine—likely loaned to them by the proprietors of their houses, thus creating more debt for them to repay. One young woman—short and lumpy like a stack of plumped pillows—has the telltale divots of smallpox on her cheeks. Another has gray, mottled skin like an old woman, though she cannot be more than twenty-five years old.

Hans watches them coldly, as though they aren't human at all, and I shudder, for I, too, have been studied this way.

"Look at that one," he leans toward Sontje and whispers. "What's wrong with her face? As though she has cobwebs on it?"

"Shh." Sontje says, smiling through her nervousness. "What if she hears you?"

"What indeed?" Hans says, shrugging, and quotes an ugly verse I've heard before, though I can't recall where: "'They tie them up. Kill them dead. So they won't commit their crimes again.'"

"That's cruel, Hans." Sontje says quietly. "The Bible tells us not to kill."

"It's their own fault," Hans replies with the authority men use when they do not wish to be contradicted.

"Most of them are just poor," I can't help but say, but they cannot know my own shameful story. "I've heard many of them come to Amsterdam to become seamstresses and lacemakers."

Escaping from other lives, like me.

Sontje looks back at me and laughs a small, rabbity laugh that makes me hate her a little.

"I'm sure they've done *something*," she insists, but sounds unsure.

"Of course they have," Hans says, with a dismissive glance toward me.

I feel like a dam overflowing. "How would you know?" I ask him, emboldened and suddenly weary of them both. Only in the wave of my anger do I feel the surge within me and realize my efforts to blockade my feelings all this time—about Fader, the Ringhouse, the nights I've spent cold and afraid, awake in the itchy darkness with rats and roaches scrabbling around me. "Have you ever fallen asleep so hungry your stomach feels like it's eating itself?" My voice grows louder, so one of the women in line at the Spinhuis gate looks at me. "Have you slept in an alleyway listening to the rats? They chatter, you know. You start to know the sound well. You even imagine their conversations."

Sontje looks at me, with a flash of anger in her eyes.

And worse. Pity.

"I'm sure these people could have found honest work," Hans continues. "We all have choices, and it's our duty to choose God's path." Hans pauses. "You're a perfect example—Sontje mentioned how hard you work, how well you do. Any of these criminals could have done the same."

He seeks to quiet me, but his words only enrage me more as he flatters and uses me as evidence for his own small-minded beliefs. I purse my lips, willing myself to stay quiet.

"I'm sure you are both right." Sontje blinks when she's nervous, and speaks more quickly. "But enough of such dreary topics. I'd love to see the wildflowers on the banks. Sussie says they are finally in bloom."

I resent her efforts to change the subject, to use me as her chaperone so she may one day marry this ignorant, small-toothed, muddle-minded young man, whose voice now grates like the scraping of a heavy knife on a porcelain platter.

I glance back and recognize a girl from the Ringhouse. Lotte from Haarlem. She stands behind the cobweb-skinned woman. I didn't notice her before. She looks very thin and wears an angry bruise on her shoulder.

Lotte opens her mouth as if to speak to me. I shake my head, motioning for her to stay quiet. Sontje's thoughtful eyes catch our silent exchange, but she says nothing.

My cheeks burn with panic. Hans is occupied with the sight of other unfortunate women, now dressed in their Spinhuis uniforms, and faces scrubbed clean of powder. I take a deep breath, minding my place so I will have somewhere to sleep.

"Yes, I noticed the flowers on the way to the market a few days ago," I reply, hoping my voice sounds even. "You should see them, Sontje. It's a short walk from here."

Hans raises his chin, assuming the posture of someone older than himself—a burgher or councilman, not the spoiled child he is.

"Shall we continue?" I stammer, eager to leave. Lotte stares at me, and I worry she will speak. She often irked the customers with her tactless questions about their wives.

Thankfully, Hans says nothing more. He takes Sontje's elbow, like she is a pretty pet to be owned. The gesture causes some strange sensation in me I cannot name. Perhaps there is no word for it. Worse than unpleasantness. Just a feeling I revisit as I hurry through my remaining chores for the day, like a question I cannot answer.

Chapter 9

"You don't like him, do you?" Sontje asks at breakfast the next day while I gather her plates to take to the cellar. I'm not thinking of Hans at all, and resent his mention so early in the morning, when I was content thinking of what to buy at the market for Hilda and what route I could take to get there. I'm always looking for new streets to explore.

"Hans? He seems a good match for you." I balance saucers on plates, cups stacked on them, the silverware nestled in the cups. I'm getting better at stacking them, though I must laugh at myself for thinking such skills are useful for much.

"It sounds like a criticism of me, to say we are a good match." Sontje sounds irritated.

"Not at all. Only that he is tall and fair and wealthy, like you."

"We aren't as wealthy as the Luikens." But Sontje is flattered that I think otherwise, and her sour expression softens. "Perhaps if Fader's ship goes well, then we may end up wealthier. But as you saw, Hans has travelled. He knows much about the world."

"One world, anyway," I cannot help but say.

She pauses. When she speaks again, she is quieter. "Jana, that woman at the Spinhuis kept looking at you. Do you know her?"

Dread presses into my throat, and I lose all thought for the dishes in my arms, which shift in my unsteadied grip.

"No, of course not," I say. "I must resemble someone she knows."

Sontje is quiet, studying my face which I labor to make as expressionless as possible. The edges of the plates bite the inside of my elbows. I focus on the uneven seam of the wooden floorboard pressing into my stockinged feet.

"She looked eager to speak to you," she says, but when I remain silent, Sontje abandons the subject.

My heart knocks inside me as I imagine what Sontje would think if she knew of my time in the Ringhouse. No respectable family would keep me in its employ.

"I listened to what you said to Hans," Sontje begins again. "And it made me think. What is it like to be poor? To wear such old, ripped clothing? To have to look so plain?"

At first, the innocence of her question surprises me. I wonder if she's ridiculing me and my temper flames.

"How do you think it is?" I answer. "Haven't you seen the orphan children clamoring for *stuivers*? The old men with long clumps of hair and ripped boots with their toes exposed, the grime covering their arms?"

Sontje purses her pretty red lips. "I see them. I just pay them little mind."

"Why?" I ask, though the dishes feel so heavy in my arms.

"It's poor manners to stare. And I can do nothing about their plight."

She confirms what I have always believed the upper classes think of us—that we are unworthy of their concern.

"I often try to imagine what it must be like for them though," she continues. "Not knowing what they'll eat each day, having no hope other than to survive another miserable night."

Sontje purses her lips again and I wish for nothing more than to disappear from the room. "Have you lived that way, Jana? I mean, before you came to us?"

The plate rims etch red lines into my arms as I hug them closer to me. For once, I long for the dim cellar, to scrub and wash in silence. And yet, I also want her to understand.

"Yes," I admit, feeling pinned to the floor. "I have not always slept in your warm attic or eaten your good food." I smile, hoping to look grateful, allowing the silence to fill in the space so she will not ask more questions.

She nods, as though understanding she shouldn't ask more. And for this, I'm thankful.

"The dishes are heavy..." I say, glancing toward the tower of porcelain in my arms.

"Yes, of course, Jana," Sontje says. I feel skinned by her gaze, and eager to leave before she asks more questions. "You should go."

Chapter 10

I'm irritable today, having my monthly disease. My back and thighs throb and the shorn wool I wear inside myself to staunch the blood itches and shifts. I wish I could remove it. Some poor women, lacking *stuivers* even for bits of wool, simply trail drops of blood onto the sidewalk. Even at my most penniless, I was too ashamed for that. I would tear a bit of my underclothing and roll it into a wad to push inside myself to collect the blood.

When I first started my bleeding, Moeder told me the blood could cure the bites of mad dogs and ward off agues, but I never believed her. I find nothing magical or powerful about my monthly illness except that when bothered by a man, my blood will fend him off. Today I would like nothing more than to lie curled in my cot like a dog. But instead I must go to the market for a capon, turnips, and rusk, and then scrub the *jambless* because it is Friday. If it's not scrubbed often, the smoke is thick and sour, and makes us cough upstairs. But it remains hateful work. The wood fire blackens the inside of the *jambless*, reminding me of a cave. I can't help but think of poor Helena in its suffocating darkness.

Sontje enters the cellar where I'm washing the dishes.

"I wanted to tell you, Jana." Her eyes bright. "Fader has approved of *kweesten* with Hans. This means I'll be married to him soon. And when it happens, I will have you to work in our house. You could help me with our children."

Kweesten doesn't exist in the Bos, but I have heard of it. The woman leaves her window open at night to receive her lover, who then peers through the window, declaring his love. Such a silly practice. I try to imagine Hans during *kweesten*. Will he whisper her promises of Italian horse carts late at night? I swallow my laugh at the thought.

"Hans pays me many compliments. He notices how I wear my hair in different styles and how I tie my apron."

"That is kind," I reply. But does love require only that a man notice a woman's beauty? Especially when it is so obvious? Sontje's beauty floats to the surface like fresh cream on milk. More impressive if Sontje were plain, which would compel a man to understand her and search for her beauty. Though I have not loved anyone before, I have felt warmth for others—a kind word, or admission of some weakness. Ada at the Ringhouse, for example, whose face was pitted with pimple scars, sometimes bought me licorice balls with her pay and told me stories about her childhood in Rotterdam. In time, I found her beautiful for her large, dark eyes and generous heart.

Sontje chatters on about Hans. "He praises everything I do, and for so long I have felt invisible. You know, Fader is always thinking about his ships and whatnot."

"He is thinking those things for you, though." I can't help but defend Master Reynst, who has grown thinner and drawn these past weeks.

"But that's his obligation," Sontje replies, then hastily returns to the subject of her Hans. Her voice softens when she speaks of him. I prefer her regular voice.

"The other night, he kissed me," she continues. "The kiss felt very strange, but then, I started to like it. Not too much, of course," she adds, blushing prettily.

"How odd." I've never felt what she describes. Only the man's tongue plunged in my mouth like a wriggling, digging creature, and I was its dark little den.

"If he kisses me, then he *must* marry me, don't you think?"

I'm not sure what to say, thinking of our stretching wombs, which trap us in lives no one wants. But I know Sontje seeks reassurance. "He seems honorable. And he's told you that you'll be married."

"Yes," Sontje nods, comforted. "That's true. He is very romantic. He acts one way around others, but with me he's much softer."

I think Sontje has created a story in her mind of Hans and of the life she wishes to have with him. I even manage to feel a little sorry for him, for he is only an instrument in it.

As she is in his story. Just another Italian horse cart.

"I'm happy for you," I say, and indeed I do feel happy for Sontje, despite my distaste for her beau.

"We will likely be married in a year," she continues. "He's just now learning his father's business." She smiles widely. "Oh Jana, I'm so eager to look at wedding dresses and such. He will want something quite grand."

I think of her mother's dress, the one I have worn and she hasn't. "You won't wear your mother's gown?"

"Ah, no, it's old and out of fashion." She looks at me and shrugs. "You said yourself it was very heavy."

For a moment, we are both embarrassed thinking of that time, which now seems long ago.

"Yes, it was," I say, recalling the softness of the silk, the crispness of the embroidery against my fingertips. For that moment, at least, I felt the possibility of beauty in myself. And with the event far behind me, I even savor my past disobedience, though I hurry to distract Sontje from the memory. "Once Master Reynst's ship returns to harbor, you can start a whole new part of your life."

Sontje looks off, daydreaming about her beloved Hans. "A new life." She smiles, her lovely teeth white and square. "I will welcome it. I'm so very tired of this one."

Chapter 11

The next day, I prepare the mid-morning meal—*poffertjes* and jam since Hilda is arriving late. I bring the meal to Master Reynst in his study.

"Good morning, Jana," he says. His eyes are red and his long hair is uncombed. A smell of restlessness rises from him, a sour odor. "The *Antwerp* is leaving today so I'm doing a last review of the navigational charts." He speaks more to himself than me, but I like how he thinks of his manners around me. Most men don't bother. They belch and scratch and snort without a thought for anyone. "My mathematical skills are not very sharp," Master Reynst continues. "The problem is determining distances over *kromstrijk* so I can verify an estimate for arrival and return."

"*Kromstrijk?*" I have not heard this term before, but I suddenly regret asking. It's not my place.

Master Reynst looks up from his charts. Smiles. "Curved direction. The Portuguese wrote about it in the 1500s. *Kromstrijk* completely changed how we navigate the seas. And then Gerardus Mercator drew a world map spacing the latitudes so the *kromstrijks* are a straight line. Makes navigation easier and more accurate. Sea captains and sailors taught me over the years. Not the sort of thing a shipwright learns, but half my head is thinking of the ocean at all times." He pauses.

"Sontje never asks questions about my work. I'm sorry I'm not very accustomed to explaining it."

He turns his map toward me as I stand across from him at the table, my arms full with the tea set.

"See how the lines are spaced differently?" He points a finger toward the map. "They are called rhumb lines so the angles on the map are equal to angles on the earth. A navigator draws a straight line on the map to find the bearing for the course."

"Bearing?"

"Using the curvature of the earth to get to the destination."

"How will you know when your ship has arrived at port in the Indies?"

"We may hear from other ships making the voyage back. Otherwise, we wait."

"It's a long wait," I say.

"Yes. Ten months, hopefully less. But it's a good day when a ship leaves port. So much goes into the voyage. I try to contain my nerves about it and feel accomplished. Makes for a better voyage to think good thoughts. We'll drink a bit of wine tonight to celebrate the launch— I've been saving a Burgundy for the occasion. You should join us, Jana. If all goes well, in ten months' time, we will have a good fortune."

"Thank you," I say, surprised by his generosity. Ten months. It is a long time, and I think of Sontje and her own dreams of ten months' time.

Ten months until Hans asks for her hand.

Chapter 12

In the end, only three months pass before they are engaged.

The families plan an engagement dinner and Hilda and I must race from task to task, preparing for the grand meal.

I'm nearly finished scrubbing the floor of the *zaal* when Sontje approaches.

"Jana, can you lace me?"

She stands in the square of waning sunlight that enters through the high window of the *zaal* and in the shaft of light, small motes of dust flicker and dance, reminding me of fireflies in the Bos.

She holds her bright bundle of hair in one hand.

"I'm nervous. So many important people will be there," she says. "Company merchants, burghers, businessmen. I won't know any of them."

"You will make a good impression," I reassure her.

My childhood memories and the beauty of the sunlight, Sontje's bright hair, and her long and graceful back compel my heart to start sounding deep within my chest. I feel both surprise and confusion, reminding me of the first time I saw flowers bloom after a pitiless winter in the Bos.

I remember the flowers. Azaleas.

I place my hands on her warm shoulders, turning her so she stands straight in front of me. I reposition the corset on her narrow hips.

"Turn back?" I ask and pull the laces from the center, tightening her stays. "Suck in a bit." I note her narrow, graceful waist, which I have observed on our walks these past months. Why does it fill me with sadness now?

A golden herringbone weave of downy hairs trails down her neck, ending at that shy, round bone at her nape. On Sontje the stays must be pulled very tightly to suggest the rise of a bosom. The abundance of her hair is a surprise when the rest of her is so slight. "Like the handle on a broom", she has complained of her slender body, her lush hair.

I pull the strings, but not too tightly. I have seen her become faint from the press of whalebone, her color fading, her forehead suddenly glowing with sweat. I knot the laces into a single bow below the stays.

"Your knots are the best, Jana. Better than Sussie's. They hold fast but come out easily when you need a full breath."

"It is my one talent." I regret the woeful bitterness of my tone.

"Not at all," Sontje replies.

I suddenly wish to trace my fingers along her neck, which smells of warm milk and the lavender water Sontje dabs behind her ears with two fingers. Tying her into her little prison, I feel strangely jealous of the stays and whalebone, though I can't say why. Is it her recent kindness? The ceramic thimble she gave me last week? That she will be a married woman soon? My heart quickens again as she inhales, the blooming bosom rising just below her white throat.

"That dark blue color is becoming. Brings out the pink in your cheeks," I say.

She smiles and now I see it. All the haughtiness disappearing and her sadness, like mine, a blue-gray shadow under her eyes.

"It's odd," she says, smoothing her bright hair. "All my life I've wanted this, to marry a wealthy man who pays me many compliments. And now that I have it, I feel somehow empty."

I feel a curious sensation myself, which I can't name or pack into any sort of box. Not sad, not happy. Not resentful, either. A heaviness. Perhaps I'm catching the *rhume*.

"Master Reynst looks well. He is talking more than usual," I say, after a moment. "At tea, he spoke of being a boy in Maastricht, escaping the fields of his youth for Amsterdam."

"It's true, he's said more today than he's said in weeks."

I have a desire to defend Master's silence— his aloofness makes our one discussion of ship navigation more dear, as though Master Reynst sees me as more worthy of conversation than others are.

I finish tying the stays and Sontje turns around, a bit paler for her corset. What happens next is a surprise.

"You have been a good friend to me." She wraps her long arms around me, pulling me close with surprising force.

I have never been so near to her. I smell lavender and clover and smoke from the *jambless* that creeps into the *zaal* when Hilda is cooking. I feel myself stiffen in her embrace, though I wish for time to slow itself, and to feel more at ease in her arms.

"Thank you," she whispers to me. "I didn't like you much when you first arrived, but I have come to think of you differently."

My words feel shut up inside me. Sontje's long hair tickles my cheek and despite the whalebone, I sense the warm softness of her flesh and the blunt bones of her shoulders against me and I suppress an unexpected desire to weep. I have not received such an embrace since Helena's passing. The pawing at the Ringhouse counts for nothing—the opposite of an embrace. Even now, I try to scour its memory from my skin.

She releases me and turns to glance one last time in the long-framed mirror at the side of the *zaal* before leaving.

Chapter 13

A sudden change has come over the household in the two weeks since our embrace. I find myself watching Sontje more closely, hoping she will reach for me again. Instead, she appears nervous, her movements more rushed and uncertain than before.

Master Reynst behaves differently also. Now he leaves for the taverns in the evening, and returns late at night, banging against the walls, even forgetting to lock the door behind him, so I must wait until he's settled and then creep downstairs to secure it. Sontje provides no reason for the change in Master Reynst and pretends as though nothing has changed.

But when Sussie arrives for tea in the afternoon, I try to learn more. I'm worried for the Reynsts, of course, but also worried for myself, having no other work than this.

I stand in the hallway, listening at Sontje's bedroom door, cracked open enough that I can see inside. Her voice sounds clipped and strangled, as though she cannot breathe well enough to speak. As though she has been weeping.

"I don't know what to do." Sontje sniffles and coughs, a pitiful sound.

"Try not to worry," Sussie says, with a sweetness I've not heard from her before. "Perhaps he's not lost everything."

"I can't even ask. He's at the taverns all day. Such an old man to be cavorting with drunken stable boys. He staggers home late in the evening and stinks like a horse when he wakes the next morning."

"It must be difficult for him. Having had money for so long…" Sussie fingers the new enamel pendant at her throat, a gift from her intended.

"Fader invested everything in that ship." The bitterness is clear in Sontje's voice. "I knew it was a risk all along."

"But it's beyond your station to counsel him."

"Yes. I know nothing of such things."

"Johannes tries to explain his family's business to me, but it's all very dull and I soon lose interest," Sussie says. Newly engaged herself, she is always mentioning this fact, as though she, too, cannot believe it. But her Johannes is no great prize. Round like a cheese and he laughs too loudly.

I peer at them through the opening in the door, hoping Hilda doesn't come looking for me to go to the market. "Does everyone know?" Sontje asks as Sussie reties her braid, appraising herself in Sontje's mirror. Sussie's shoulders are too broad, as though her head belongs to someone else's body.

"Well, for its size, Amsterdam is still a small town," Sussie answers brightly, as though excited to be trusted with Sontje's problems.

"Yes," Sontje says sadly.

"I won't say a word." Sussie smiles at her reflection and straightens the new pendant at her throat, ready for a change of topic. "Johannes says this pendant is the newest design from Italy. Very popular there, but I'm the first to have one in Amsterdam." She smiles again, revealing her small, pointed teeth. Like the fangs of a wolf cub.

Chapter 14

Days later, Master Reynst calls me into his study, a small room full of maps and books stacked on a square desk away from the high window.

"Miss Jana, I'm not sure if you have heard." His eyes seem even more downcast than usual and I feel my old fear creeping in. The sensation had receded in these past months, though it still stalks me when I sleep. "The *Antwerp* was lost." He speaks in a whisper now, as though too ashamed to admit the loss. "And with it, all my money. I have no choice but to let you go. And I have come to regard you as something like family, so it is no small thing to me."

I wonder if Hilda knows about the ship. She seemed nervous yesterday, forgetting where she kept the salt, dropping the ladle twice as she stirred the soup.

He looks at his maps. "I have told my associates about you, Jana. Your hard work. I hope you will find another position soon. I would offer you your room for as long as you like, but we will soon have to take a boarder."

I nod, numb to his words, imagining what will come next, and embarrassed that I allowed myself to believe my life could offer anything more than an escape from one nightmare to another.

My mind races to Sontje and then I feel ashamed. She won't care if I leave, when her Hans crowds her thoughts.

But I will miss her. And Master Reynst as well.

"I'm very sorry, Jana," he says. "I took too large a risk. I'm sure Sontje will be sorry to see you go also. Please visit us whenever you want. You and Hilda are like family."

I pause for a moment. Panic forces my thoughts to come to me in gusts, like our autumn gales.

"Master Reynst?" I say, keeping my voice as calm as I can. "What if I could remain as your boarder? I can find some other employment." My voice cracks a bit at the end, to ask him such a favor. Servants are their best when invisible, speaking only when asked some question. "I have grown fond of my little attic bedroom." Indeed, the coos and warbles of the nesting pigeons in the morning lessen the drudgery of each day, though not as much as the sight of Sontje, whose company I seek between my many tasks.

Master Reynst rubs his sparse beard as he sometimes does when deep in thought. "We will need at least five guilders a week," he says. "I feel badly asking that from you."

"I will start looking today," I say, sounding more confident than I feel. Five guilders is a large sum. "Thank you, Master."

Master Reynst smiles sadly, perhaps thinking of how his fortune has turned. His eyes look rheumy and red, and he trembles in the morning now, once so much he dropped his teacup. The store of wine he keeps in the cabinet is gone, though I've not seen him drink it. Still, he's nothing like my father, whose drunkenness came on like a raving storm. Master's drunkenness is quiet. Full of defeat.

And though I feel sad for him, my mind clicks into survival mode. I'm already thinking of my next steps to stay in my little attic room with its sloped ceiling. Close to Sontje.

Chapter 15

After I've finished washing the pots and crockery for Hilda, who is red-eyed and sniffling following Master Reynst's news, I hurry off to Dam Centre. Adelheid the baker might know of someone requiring my services.

As I walk along the canal, I pass my favourite rowhouse, painted a vivid, bright blue with white trim unlike any other rowhouse I've seen. Like the pigeons above my bedroom, the blue house gives me some joy to lessen the monotony of my daily tasks. It remains stubbornly cheerful on even the grayest days, reminding me to keep my own spirits hopeful.

I look for Adelheid's stand at the market, but her daughter—a miniature Adelheid herself with the same round cheeks and dark eyes—tells me her mother is bringing a fresh supply of *brezels* from her kitchen.

"Should be back in an hour's time," the girl says, only a little irritated that I don't purchase anything. I promise I will buy the fresh *volkorenbroden* when Adelheid returns. Sontje likes the loaves warm and fresh, like sleeping babes.

In the meantime, I go from stand to stand asking about work. The cobbler, the leathermaker, the fruit stand, and flower stall. I ask the other servants, gathering herring and vegetables for their employers, if they know of anyone who needs a cleaner, a seamstress, a laundress, a governess.

I even ask at the butcher's shop. I'm good with a knife. Fader taught me to skin a deer when I was only seven years old. *Pull the skin with one hand, lay the blade against the flesh with the other.* On that day, I saw the deer before Fader did. A doe, he told me later. The doe stood behind a spindly downy birch, her pretty head bent down to the leafy ground. I gasped at her beauty—red-gold fur and delicate lashes. Her round black eyes wide apart, her pink flaring ears. Innocent as morning and I thought I loved her more than anything, even more than Moeder, who had scolded me that morning for tripping on my *klomps*.

"Good girl," Fader said. And then before I could breathe, he had killed it with his crossbow. How odd it was, to see the deer so alive, trembling behind the tree and then suddenly dying before me, the blood glistening on the leaves, turning the dirt black. Its insides gleaming, purple and red, before Fader gutted it. All left as a shiny heap on a pile of oak leaves. "Now, come here." Fader had pulled me to him, I thought—foolishly—to embrace me. But instead he pushed my face into the cavity of the hollowed-out deer. Its ribs red with bits of white coming through. Dark like a cavern and smelling of blood. The heat still fresh and I realized warmth is how you know something is alive.

"You're a hunter now." Fader's wide fingers gripped my neck loosely.

He then grabbed my knot of mouse-brown hair and pulled my head back. I was still reeling from the metal smell of fresh blood.

"You don't want to boast of this to others, though. Not the kind of thing girls should be doing." Only then did I smell the sour *jenever* on his breath.

Fader carried the doe on his back and the flies hummed around him as we neared home. Moeder cooked her in a *hutspot* with rye bread and rusk.

I ate the doe's flesh. But only because Fader would have used the lath on me if I refused.

I return to Adelheid's stall at the market and thankfully, she is there, arranging *brezels* in a basket. I purchase four of her fresh *volkorenbroden* for Sontje and a *brezel* for me to eat now.

"Madam Adelheid," I say when she hands them to me in a parcel, "I'm looking for work. Do you know anyone seeking a servant?"

She must see the hunger in me, and smiles kindly.

"In fact, Elsa told me earlier this morning that the De Graafs need a maid. Theirs is the biggest house in the Herengracht." As Adelheid speaks, she wipes down the stand and rearranges the *brezels*. I've heard others call her husband a lazy *traag*, but she makes up for it with her tireless industry. "It's getting late today, but go there early in the morning tomorrow, and tell them Adelheid sent you." She wraps up one more *brezel* for me, smaller than the others, but I'm grateful for the kindness and unused to it.

I thank her and turn to leave before she stops me.

"One more thing," she says. "Watch yourself with the master of the house. I hear his hands are…" She pauses, searching for the word. "Greedy."

I nod, ignoring the familiar blackness in my stomach. I tell myself it is my usual hunger, roused by the fresh breads now filling my basket.

I have the evening open to me, so I return to the Reynsts' to leave the parcels from the market and then set off again for the docks. I so rarely have a free moment, and the sun shines warm and welcoming on my skin. I'm eager to have more time with it.

One can live in Amsterdam and yet forget the sea. Some weeks I have been so weary from working I forget even to look at the sky on my walk back to the Reynsts' house in the evening. Then I suddenly remember. I look for the moon and I'm comforted by its beauty. A bit like Sontje's loveliness—both round and slim, veiled and clear. Changing. How many moons have I passed without looking? Sometimes I see a particularly beautiful moon—low-hanging, orange—and wish she were near me, so I could show it to her.

And even once or twice I have imagined us lying beneath that silver sphere, my lips on her white clavicle, tasting the lavender water on her throat.

Such thoughts arrive, unwanted guests, in a blaze of shame. I try to imagine a man instead—Isaac Jacobs, who sometimes drove Master Reynst's carriage to Company meetings and always smiled at me. His gray-blue eyes are a similar shade to Sontje's, but his chin juts out like a ledge. I have not seen his neck, and while I'm sure he must have a collarbone, I have no desire to see it or feel it against my lips.

By the time I arrive at the docks, the weather has changed. The clouds are thick, the color of used bathwater. But a ship is in port, preparing to leave for Batavia, our colony in the East Indies, and I enjoy looking at the great vessels, wondering where they have been. I try to imagine the sky in other places. Bright blue, cloudless. Less talk of King Philip, this slow-boiling war between the Protestants and Catholics. I care for neither of them, though Moeder was a Protestant. Growing up in the woods, we went to church but once a year, and Moeder led the prayers each morning in front of a stump of candle at sunrise.

I have felt God in church only once—the sunlight making a pattern on the slate floor of the church at De Wallen as the minister spoke of redemption. But I sometimes felt some spirit fierce and lovely within when I walked in the Bos. On one of these occasions, I was a young girl escaping to the woods after one of Fader's beatings—even after the bite of his meaty hands and the roar of his voice, I still longed for him. *Make him love me,* I asked the trees. And though he never did, I felt an unexpected lightness under those branches that day as the wind blew across the forest, and the brittle orange leaves fell upon my hair like a blessing.

"Full load today?" An old man with freckles on his balding, sun-burned head addresses a younger man walking off the pier.

"Ay. Cargo full of spices," the other man says, who looks to be in his thirties. He carries crates off the dock and unloads them alongside me.

"Pardon me, my dear." The man addresses me. His skin is darker than a Dutchman's, but his eyes are blue. "Just arrived with a cargo of spices and cannot see over my load." He smiles, his eye teeth turned inward, pleasantly so.

This brief escape from my worries, watching the ships and imagining their journeys, gives rise to curiosity I don't usually allow myself. The younger man's friendly expression emboldens me as well. "Where did you just come from?"

"Batavia. Paradise, I should say. Sunshine every day. You can do what you want. No need to worry about those ten pennies and *taes*. And the fruits there—things you've never seen. Mangoes were my favorite. Slippery and sweet, full of syrup, with a texture I've never found in any of our native fruits. You pick them off the tree and eat them right there if you're hungry." He chuckles. A nice sound, like wood blocks sliding together. "But I've never been one for table manners."

"It's not dangerous there?"

"Ay," he nods. "It is. And the journey can take many months. This last was a monster. We ran out of food. Teeth just fell out of some sailors' mouths. I managed to keep all mine," he says, smiling again. "And once you get there, if the heat doesn't kill you, the diseases will."

"I didn't realize," I say, trying to imagine the teeth falling out of my own mouth.

"But at least the blacks can't do anything to us. They don't have guns, just knives and spears. We make them work for us. And they work hard. They talk even less than our Dutchmen." He looks at me square, slows his words. "The women aren't as pretty as our own, though."

I smile. It is always a risk—conversing with men. Ask a few questions and they expect you to open your legs for the answer.

"I'm sure a few were satisfactory?"

"No, not for more than the occasional roll." He arches his brows. "Me, I'm partial to girls with light brown hair, wide hips." He's still smiling, but his look is pleasant.

"You should buy me a meal," I say to him, surprised at my own boldness. I've eaten only a *brezel*, and the sun is setting early. Or am I feeling guilty for my earlier thoughts of Sontje?

"I can do that," he says. "I'll need to unload these boxes first."

"I can wait."

"Well then, sit over here, Miss." He points to a crate beside us, brushes it off with the palm of his hand, and gestures for me to sit. "My name is Tobias Levy. And you?"

"Jana. Jana Beil."

"Well, Jana Beil. It will be an hour or so. Meanwhile, you can tell me why you're at the harbor. Not many women here, not like you." He looks at me differently now. Smiling as though we share a secret.

*

In that hour waiting for Tobias Levy, I begin to doubt myself. What will he expect from me? But each time I resolve to cancel our shared meal, some reason prevents me. I enjoy our flirtation. Feeling desired.

And I'm curious about his travels. Batavia. The word sounds so strange. I say it in my mind again and again, trying to make it mine. *Batavia. Batavia.* What is it like to live in a place where there is so much sunshine? Where one need not seek it out as I do, finding a small beam through a window and placing my arm in it, simply to feel a bit of warmth?

As I sit at the docks with some rare time for my own thoughts, my mind wanders to Sontje. She is this to me. Sunlight through windows, through clouds. How she wears a ribbon one day and an enamel comb the next, changing herself. How she laughs and teases Master Reynst for forgetting his hat or for the gaping waistband of his trousers. But she also reminds me of Helena in her seriousness at unexpected times. Perhaps it is only her beauty that moves me. And her wealth, which allows for her brightness and beauty and glow. Still, so much of my childhood was spent in the winter of my father's rage and my mother's ringing fear. All my desire collects toward warmth, light, and summer.

A muddle of dread and confusion follows as I watch Tobias drop another pallet on the dock and then lean backward, rubbing his neck. I am beginning to have a slow understanding of myself.

"Ready for you, Miss Jana," Tobias Levy says, interrupting my unsettling thoughts. "Let us get a good meal."

Chapter 16

Tobias Levy takes me to a tavern not far from the docks. An old brick building smelling of *zware shag*, tobacco smoke, and vinegar. He finds a table near the corner that rattles against the uneven floor when we use our knives, so he folds a kerchief from his pocket and places it under the table leg. The small gesture lightens my misgivings.

"I've been to Aden, too," he says, chewing on a chicken bone. He talks with his mouth full. A black grain of pepper is lodged in the space between his front teeth. I stare at the speck instead of his eyes so I will be less nervous. "You know, in Agra, if a man dies, his wife joins him in the fire. They call it *sati*."

"You've seen this?"

"No, I've not been to Agra. Heard it from a soldier who witnessed it himself. True love?"

"True rubbish. The wives must feel compelled."

"My thoughts also. Probably greater rewards offered to them in the afterlife or some rot like that." He smiles even as he chews. "Eat up, lass. No need for manners with me."

I eat the *sla* and stewed meat. The meat is overcooked, nearly like a paste, but I relish its rich flavor. I feel a bit guilty even asking for this meal, for I saw Tobias's thighs wobbling with fatigue as he set down the last boxes.

"You never miss Amsterdam when you're gone?"

"My people are nomads. Sephardic Jews. We've never had a home. Shadows, shade. The entire world is our home."

"Have you lived in the woods?"

"Ay, I have. Something magical about sleeping under the stars— stare at them long enough and you start to think you could be one of them."

Helena once said the stars were like eyes watching us, winking like old friends. I always thought the stars protected us, and reminded us that darkness is never complete.

After our meal, Tobias walks with his hand at my elbow and guides me along the harbor streets. His boarding house is not far from the Reynsts'.

We both smell of wine and roasted meat. I'm surprised that I enjoy the sensation of his thick arm at my waist, the warmth of him on this cold night.

"Look at the moon, Miss Jana."

It hangs low, only a sliver is gold but lit from beneath so the rest of the orb is visible.

"It's an interesting name—Jana. Hebrew."

"Is it? My mother named me for a girl she once knew. She liked the sound of it."

"It means paradise."

"Then it is not fitting to me."

"I disagree." He smiles, and heat rushes to my cheeks.

"What do you most miss about the sea?" I ask.

He pauses. "One thing is the moon on the water. Some nights you stand on deck and all you see is that fat bauble in the night and the rippling maw of the sea. Makes you almost believe in God."

"You don't?" The few Jews I know wear the Star of David at their throats. They close up all their shops on the Breestraat for Sabbath and fill the synagogue on the Houtgracht instead.

"Not anymore. I learned Hebrew, and I keep the Taleth with me. I take it on every voyage, but I've seen too much to make any sense of God. When I was a boy, I watched King Philip's soldiers murder a Jew from my neighborhood. Most devout man I ever knew. He prayed all the day long. And they didn't think twice that he was an old man. It's an image I'll grow old with, Abraham's look of surprise as they gutted him with a musketeer. It's why we left Spain when I was a child. We knew what was coming." His blue eyes look black. "If I had my way, I'd be a Greek. Worship Poseidon. God of the sea." He looks beautiful to me in the moonlight, with the thatch of lines at his eyes and his long forehead. "I've never been back home. But I smell orange flowers in my dreams sometimes, and I know I'm missing it. We used to smell them in the springtime."

We've entered an alleyway. A man and woman embrace in the shadows. Probably a prostitute, judging from her naked shoulders and loosely tied hair. The man is stocky and short. A bald circle at the top of his head reflects the moonlight. He groans like an animal.

"Worth every guilder," the stout man says.

The woman sighs, but I'm certain she pretends. I'm ashamed at the sight.

Tobias removes his hand from my elbow, and I'm grateful.

We walk silently through the alley and back into the open moonlight, and I grow troubled, thinking that he may expect the same of me. But he's different from the roughnecks I've known. I like his high forehead, dark brows, and those open, bright blue eyes. He's stronger than me for certain, but he is not the type to enjoy roughness. I've learned to spot them quickly. They have a wildness in their eyes, even if they're wealthy.

Tobias looks at his boots for a moment, smiling.

"What is it?" I ask.

"I was thinking that you looked so young and lovely in this light. You're an interesting woman, Miss Jana. Full of thoughts. You have the look of someone living some other, hidden life."

At this I'm silent and gaze at his wide, high boots instead. The worn laces, the bindings frayed. I cannot imagine him purchasing something as ordinary as boots. The style is popular among merchants, flagging at the top.

"Do you wear shoes when you're on deck?"

He laughs. "I thought we were discussing your many thoughts."

I blush, as I often speak before thinking. Fader used to cuff me for that. "Spinny-headed *meisje*," he would call me.

But Tobias addresses my question with a seriousness that warms me. "Boots on deck? Not always. Especially when we get closer to the islands. Gets hot like a forge in that sun. Some of us strip down to our breeches just to feel the sunshine on our skins. By the time we make it there we're so tired and hungry, the sun is all we have."

"You must be eager to go back there," I say.

"Ay, but I have work to do. I'll stay here a few days and help with the cargo, make some contacts with the merchants and managers I know. They forbid us Jews from joining the guilds, but even the smaller merchants can do well enough."

"And after that?"

"Off to Bruges with some of the cargo. I have contacts there. I prefer the sea to gravel roads, but this, too, is part of my work."

We come to a brick building with a quaint turret.

"This is where I stay," he says.

We stand before the building, and I feel embarrassed, unsure of what to do.

"Thank you for your company," he says, without touching me. I'm both surprised and confused, having grown used to others expecting much more for far less of my time.

I wish him a good night and hurry back to the Reynst house. It's late, and I must wake early to see about work at the De Graafs'.

Later, once I'm finally lying on my uneven cot in my little attic bedroom, my thoughts return to Sontje. I imagine my lips on her skin. My hands holding her slim hips. Winding her long hair around my index finger. From where do such thoughts arise? I have never been told they are evil thoughts, but I know they are.

Nothing is said of women loving women. Only of men and men (a grave sin), or women and men. The church condemns lust and pleasure, but still the brothels flourish at the outskirts of Amsterdam. The proprietors take in girls just past their first bleeding to do their work for two flavorless meals per day. Esteemed grandfathers grunting like donkeys, smelling of ale.

Instead, I think of Tobias. His mouth, his hands. But the images escape me, disappearing like sunlight behind the morning fog. I return to Sontje. Her white fingernails peeking over the tips, a strand of her fair hair hanging into her eyes.

I have not wept in a long time, but a sweep of sadness rises from my stomach, and causes a humming in my ears. I think of starlings swirling above. Unfolding and folding in that way they do every autumn before they leave Amsterdam. That is how my sadness feels.

I'm only a maid, hardly even a friend. The Reynsts could replace me tomorrow if they wanted, if it weren't for their sudden misfortune, and with any of the starving girls roaming Dam Centre in search of work. And still, my feelings are an unyielding stain I cannot wipe or scrape or scrub out like a mud splatter on the floor.

Chapter 17

The De Graaf family lives off the main canal, in one of the houses reserved for merchants, landowners, and regents—the grandest in the city. These houses are even bigger than the Reynst residence and have multiple floors and rooms, brick exteriors, green doors, and roofs of bright red tile. Even children have their own rooms. The kitchens at the back have a full built-in cupboard. Potted tulips, the most expensive of flowers, line the windows and lend some cheer to the grayness of our skies, made darker by the smoke from all the peat burning into the air for warmth year-round.

Though I would have dreamt of work at one of these wealthy houses before, now I regret having to spend so many hours in this new place, with unknown employers, and without the easy chatter I now share with Sontje.

I arrive at the grand entrance of the De Graaf house. The door is taller than the Reynsts' door, with long windows that stretch across the face of the building. Such uncommon windows must be shipped in. To have so much light is a luxury in gray Amsterdam.

Before I can knock, the door opens.

"Yes?" The woman must be Madam herself. She is little and round with shiny, pink cheeks and a pinched mouth.

"Adelheid sent me. About servant work?"

She looks me over, top to *klomps*, without hiding her directness.

"You've done this work before? And you work hard? I won't abide laziness. 'He becometh poor that dealeth a slack hand.'"

"Yes. At the Reynst home."

"Well, let's see how you do today. I have a late tea this evening with some friends and the silver needs polishing. The last girl left so suddenly."

As Madam walks me through the house, I look at the art on the walls. A full-length painting of what must be Master De Graaf hangs in the center of the main *zaal*, displayed at eye level. He stands with his feet crossed, head cocked over his shoulder. A compass sits on the table behind him, next to an atlas and white pitcher. Most cannot afford such paintings, which cost some four hundred guilders.

Another painting hangs in the hallway, different from the others. I only get glimpses of it as I walk back and forth between rooms. If I stop to admire it, Madam may deem it laziness. In the painting, a skull rests atop a small pile of books. A feather quill, an extinguished candle, and overturned *roemer* beside it. A warm, tawny light gleams from the skull, making even its few protruding teeth look beautiful. I wish to linger and make sense of the painting's arrangement, the source of its light, so I move closer toward the hallway.

"Start with some polishing," Madam says, and shows me to the dining room where the tarnished silver rests in a heap at the center of a great wooden table decorated with intricate carvings. I resist the urge to trace the etchings with my finger.

"The polish and cloth are inside the cabinet." Madam tips her round head toward a dark wood structure that spans the entire length of the dining room's far wall. "I want the silver its brightest for tonight." She permits herself a tight smile that makes her look like she may be ill.

"I can pay you twice whatever you were paid before." She pauses. "As long as you are dependable and thorough." I tell her my price, adding a guilder more to twice my rate at the Reynsts' to cover my lodgings, and she agrees. I feel a small victory in this negotiation.

And so the morning passes quickly—the first day is most important for showing your value. After the polishing, I spend the day scrubbing the privy outside, then the floors and the long windows, requiring me to use a stepladder. I wipe every crevice neglected by the last servant, digging my index finger into the cracks to remove all traces of grime. Corners of bookshelves, sills of the high windows, even the small ledges at the top of the drawers where dust collects if the drawers do not firmly close.

It is late afternoon when I meet Master De Graaf. He resembles his portrait only a little. His hair is well past his shoulders, a dreary blonde going gray, and not nearly as thick or golden as the portrait suggests. And no record of the pox marks on his face exists on the painted canvas, nor the dome of his belly. Funny how the wealthy are all as big as *Lakenvelders* but wish to look thinner, while those of us who work for them can hardly keep flesh on our bones.

I can tell from the first that he will give me trouble. His rheumy eyes linger at my bosom.

"Nice and lush, you make them, Miss," he says as I fluff the pillows.

Though he's wealthy enough to afford several baths per month—unlike the rest of us, who must be satisfied with one or two—he has a ripe odor of rotting fish and sour milk.

I must be careful not to bend forward to sweep the dust from the floor and hearth. He's exactly the sort who will take such opportunity to pinch and bump up against me.

It makes sense, now, my pay. Madam surely knows about her husband. Perhaps he is the reason for the last girl's departure. I learn from the sour-faced cook, Elsjen, that Master's fortune is owed to Madam's family. He lost most of his own in a failed business years before. Madam's dowry saved them from ruin, but she seldom lets him forget it. Perhaps that is why his eyes travel elsewhere, though I have known such men, and doubt any single woman could please them at the best of times.

I smile at Master's compliments, as expected of a servant, but resolve to be vigilant in his presence.

I manage to complete the day's tasks without running into Master again. My knees and thighs shake from climbing up and down the two flights of stairs, and my shoulder aches from all the polishing and scrubbing, but Madam nods in approval when I've finished, and tells me to return the next morning as I leave.

I enjoy the evening air as I near the Reynst house, glad that the walk is not too far. I force myself to stop thinking of Master and his greedy looks. I'm eager for some rest and Sontje's company. I even feel some pride in my new wages.

I let myself into the quiet house. No one comes to greet me, though I scold myself for expecting it, being a mere boarder now. I walk through the *zaal* and find Sontje sitting at the dining table, her face in her hands.

"Is something wrong?" I ask, and she looks up. Her eyes are red and swollen, her irises an unmatched blue. I go to her, sit next to her at the table.

Her voice is small, almost a whisper. "Hans has broken off the engagement. He found out we lost everything along with the *Antwerp* and called it off. The coward refused to come and tell me himself. Just sent me a message through his coachman." Sontje inhales deeply. "And Sussie says he is already set to marry some other girl. From Delft. She comes with a sizable dowry. He'll not even have to work. I'm sure he's content."

Contentment. It's a strange word. Sontje uses it often. We Dutch cannot be happy, cannot express joy, not as adults anyway. But contentment is possible. The idea that a quiet life is enough. That aspirations end there. Sometimes I think of something beyond contentment. But there is no word for it. An idea without name. As though I must be elsewhere to know what it is.

"*Helaas,*" she sighs. "Who will want me now? Everyone knows we were to be married. Now I will be Hans Luikens' castoff girl. Unwanted. A spinster living with her father forever. Even Sussie will not wish to be my friend now. You know wealthy people only like you when you are prosperous as well." At this, she surrenders her restraint and sobs into her hands.

"I'm sorry, Sontje," I say. "You are certainly more than Hans Luikens' castoff girl. And if Sussie cannot be your friend now, then she doesn't deserve you. What is friendship if you can't share such disappointments?"

Sontje wipes her cheeks with the back of her hand, and sniffles.

"I didn't know you loved him so much," I say, feeling some bitterness.

"I did not love him exactly. But we would have had a nice life. I thought Fader could hold things together for longer. But I'm sure you see he is not himself, coming home drunk, escaping to the taverns to avoid his creditors. And I have no sense of what to do. I keep burning everything I cook because Hilda is gone. I never learned how to use the *jambless*."

"I can make something today," I say, though I feel so tired I could nap right there on the unswept floor. "How is Master?" Though I know the answer. I've smelled the ale on him, sour on his breath and skin when he returns home in the evenings.

"He is lost with his ship," Sontje says with a sigh. "At the tavern, hatching ever more absurd ways to recover his fortune."

Sontje emits a sob. The sound is new to me, animal. Not Sontje at all. Even when Master Reynst first lost their fortune on the *Antwerp*, she didn't do this. I hold her hand now, which is so soft I can't help but marvel at it. No callouses at the thumb from scrubbing, no ridges on the inside of the palm from carrying buckets of water and chamber pots each day. Even the knuckles of her hands are smooth, soft like her damask bedclothes.

My arm winds around her shoulder and I pat her back. I would kiss her bud-pink ear if I could.

Sontje rests her head on my shoulder. Her scalp smells of honey. I worry less about Master De Graaf, feeling her delicate breaths a-flutter in my ear.

"Hans." Sontje says his name as though for the last time. I think back to the months I spent walking with them through Amsterdam's streets, listening to his boastful statements and cruel judgments of the poor.

I will not miss him at all.

Chapter 18

Madam De Graaf is not home when I arrive the next day, but the cook, Elsen, tells me I must mop the floors. I start with the halls, then the *zaal* and bedrooms, and I save the study for last, because Master De Graaf is there.

I wait as long as I can, hoping Madam will arrive, but she doesn't. I knock on the door of the study.

"Yes, come in," Master says.

He sits on a highbacked wooden chair, busying himself with a scroll map. He turns it this way and that. Coughs.

He looks up as I enter.

"Go ahead and wash the floor. Don't mind me," he says.

I nod, hoping he doesn't see my cheeks redden. In a house such as this, you are most vulnerable on your knees.

"We want the house spotless. I'm hosting some of Amsterdam's wealthiest merchants tonight," he says. "Captain Hooghe just came on a fleet from the Indies." I wonder if he seeks to impress me. Mostly such men pinch and pat, no pleasantries necessary.

Bram wanders in. Madam took her time with babies—she's older than most mothers. Perhaps because she knew what was required to get them.

He is a quiet boy. He looks at me, then at his father.

"Bram, say good morning to Jana."

"Good morning," he says, in his father's cheerless tone.

"Do you need anything?"

"I can't find my hat and it's raining outside."

"Yes, your mother will be angry if you come to dinner with wet hair." Master looks fondly at his boy, but I see his impatience. "Go and look upstairs."

I don't know which is better—to scrub with my hips up in the air or with my bosom hanging down in front of him. I decide it is safer to scrub toward him. Some men prefer bosoms to backsides. Others like both. I'm not sure which Master prefers and if I knew, I'd choose the other.

"You grew up in Amsterdam?" he asks from behind the map.

"I grew up in the forest, sir." A spot on the floor requires that I lean forward to remove it. "Outside Amsterdam."

"Amsterdam Bos…" he says slowly. "Such beautiful trees."

Something in his voice makes me look up before I have time to regret it. He has folded his map and stares. I can see the movement inside his breeches.

The door opens and Master returns the map to his lap, gazing downward. It is Madam, here at last, distracted by a book she carries.

"Ah, hello Jana," she says, glancing toward me. "Yes, the floor does look better. I'm sure Master De Graaf mentioned the dinner party tonight?"

"Yes, Madam." I keep scrubbing. It's always best to remain industrious. We must never give the impression we have a moment to breathe.

"After you finish with the floor, you'll need to prepare the table. We'll be having a boar for dinner."

"Bram is searching for his hat," Master says, looking up from the map.

"It's in his room. The boy forgets everything. He's worse than his grandmother."

How they can switch on and off, these men. It's as though their minds contain little locked rooms, and the doors never open.

"I'll check on him myself," Madam says.

Master returns to his map as though I'm not even in the room.

"If you like, I could use some help tonight. I'll pay you extra for your service. You can start by helping Elsjen," Madam De Graaf says later in the day, as she sits at her dining table counting out her silver. Spoons and knives and even forks, which I've never used before, though I have pressed their tines against the palm of my hand at Sontje's house.

"Thank you. I'm happy to." Master De Graaf cannot do much to me around his esteemed guests, and I'm eager to earn extra guilders.

I head down to the kitchen, still shaken by Master's behavior, and wishing to be far away from him. When I arrive, Elsjen is lifting the roast boar onto a platter.

"Can I help you?" You cannot assume with Elsjen. She has thrown out servants who presumed to know how to fill the tea pitcher.

"I'm doing well enough."

"Madam asked me to help with the fruit."

"Polish the apples first," Elsjen says. What a strange name, *Elsjen*. A name for someone prettier and wealthier than Madam's pinched-face cook.

I take an apple from the basket near the *jambless* and polish it with a muslin cloth I've tied to my waistband. I bring the apple to my nose and smell. A bit like clover. Springtime.

"Have you tasted one?" I ask.

Elsjen arranges peeled parsnips on a roasting tray. "No, of course not. I only arrange them in bowls for Madam or bake them in an *appeltaart*."

"I didn't mean to suggest—"

"Well, then, don't," she says testily.

As I wipe the apples, I think of the Bos, when Helena and I once found an apple tree so laden with fruit we must have been the first to discover it. We raced there, not believing in the bounty of shining red fruits hanging thick from its branches. We took turns climbing and picked every apple and dropped them to the ground. Helena wanted Moeder to make an apple sauce for baby Hlaska. I wanted them for ourselves.

We held those apples like they were stars from the heavens. We sat under the apple tree and counted to three before taking a bite at the same time. My teeth sunk into the polished skin and the juice dribbled into my mouth.

But the apples were chalky as though made of glue mastic.

Helena coughed and choked. We spit and sputtered. We gathered our saliva and swished and spit some more, the frayed apple bits collecting beneath the tree.

Such a bitter taste.

Helena was silent all the way home.

I'm serving dinner to Master De Graaf's guests, all burghers, clerks, merchants for the Company, carrying their self-importance on their puffed-out chests. And then I see Tobias.

He is the last to arrive, and if he is surprised to see me, he makes no show of it. He dresses more like a gentleman now—his work boots replaced by low shoes, a doublet, and new garters. He looks handsome in this dress, though I prefer him in his simpler clothes.

I, too, pretend I have not met him, though I also think of the evening we shared not long ago, and my face warms with the memory as I hurry off to the kitchen. How odd it is—I know the almond smell of him, the feel of his rough hand resting on my arm, and now we are strangers to each other. I resolve to speak to him only if he addresses me first.

"I need some help, Jana!" Elsjen calls to me from the hallway.

She has plated the boar on the largest of the De Graafs' silver platters. Unlike other meats, which look so different from the animals they come from, roast pig looks like the animal itself. I cannot help but feel sorry for it. We each take an end of the platter and place it on the far end of the table, waiting to be summoned to refill wine or *passglasses*, or to bring more food. I'm careful not to look anywhere but at the boar's face, which bears a woeful expression, as though surprised at its misfortune.

"Excellent meal," one of the men says. Bits of meat stick in his teeth as he chews, and breadcrumbs litter his shrubby beard.

"Mmm," Master De Graaf replies absently, gnawing at his own bit of boar's flesh. "Much to celebrate. The market in amber and sappanwood is flourishing. We have achieved a monopoly. Opium, camphor, cloves, thanks to the Western and Eastern quarters."

"The English are always complaining about our ships—green timber and poor measurements—but look what we've done with them! Bringing back a fatted calf every time," the bearded man says.

Tobias has yet to touch his meat.

"My own Anna purchased a tortoiseshell box the other day. I told her she wouldn't have it without us," another guest says. He wears an elegant doublet and polished boots.

"Indeed. All of Europe is in our debt." Master leans back in his chair. Picks his teeth with his forefinger.

"But remember the *Narrenschiff*," a sickly man croaks from the corner of the room, raising a long and crooked finger. I heard the story of the ill-fated ship as a child—the Ship of Fools, a German poem warning of foolishness and pride.

"Rutger, you are a dour one," Master De Graaf says after a hearty belch into his hand. "Let us celebrate our multitude of victories—trekkers in the veldt of South Africa and the riches of Batavia! Much to be praised."

The man named Rutger moves his roasted parsnips around the plate, and remains silent.

Tobias's low, stately voice rises above the din.

"I agree with him. Every storm followed by a calm and vice versa. Better to be cautious than proud. The *Antwerp* was only just lost, and now the directors are trying to save more money. I hope that doesn't mean fewer provisions for our ships or shoddy construction." Tobias takes a gulp of wine.

"That's why we have the orphans," Master De Graaf laughs again. He is in high spirits, being at the center of this company. "No relatives, no money, no real ties to anything. They're a ready lot of laborers for the colony. And if they die on the journey, no one will care."

"Yes, we all know how you favor the orphans. Especially the pretty, female ones," the bearded one says, and Master flushes, but says nothing more. Elsjen tells me later the bearded man is a burgher, with many connections to the Company.

"Perhaps a toast for the orphans is in order?" the bearded man continues.

The men laugh, all but Tobias, who glances at me instead. And then they raise their goblets and drain them clean.

*

"Jana," Tobias says, lingering in the dining area after the other men have wandered into the *zaal* to look at Master's newest paintings. "I'm surprised to see you."

I'm relieved I'm not some forgotten, castoff girl to him. "I'm surprised as well—I thought you were leaving to Bruges." We both speak quietly, aware my reputation might be tarnished by talking to a man outside my station.

"I received this invitation and decided to postpone the trip by some weeks. These men are much wealthier than me, but they all owe me favors, and soon I will be starting my own business bringing their wares to the markets in Bruges." He smiles. "I didn't expect to find you in attendance."

"Hardly in attendance. I will be polishing your dishes and sweeping the crumbs you leave behind."

Tobias nods. His eyes grow serious. "He seems to like you, De Graaf."

"What do you mean?"

"Just be careful. I have heard much of his misdeeds."

"Misdeeds?" I stiffen, thinking of earlier today.

Tobias sighs. "Rumors, but I don't doubt them. That he is rough with the servant girls, and has paid a few of them to leave, girls younger than you who bore his children." He lowers his voice to a whisper and I must lean closer to him, noting the bitter smell of wine on his breath. "In truth, I've seen the Company ledgers. He's paid at least three of these girls out of the Company's accounts so Madam won't learn of the whole ugly business. So, watch yourself, Jana."

I don't know what ledgers are, but I, too, can imagine the truth of these stories. "No need to worry about me," I insist, pretending more courage than I feel. I set the dishes upon a silver tray, all the utensils to the side, stacking as much as I can while keeping the tray steady.

"May I walk you to your lodgings tonight?" Tobias asks, his kind eyes a warming sight among all the other guests, who treat me as though their dishes and forks and goblets and *roemers* carried themselves from the grand dining table after their meal.

"I will be here late, helping Elsjen with the cleaning."

"No matter, Jana. I will stay here as long as De Graaf will have me, and after I can wait for you outside. I know a tavern not far from here where I can linger, if need be." He pauses. "I feel I should take the tray for you. It will be heavy."

I laugh at the thought of Tobias in his fine dinner doublet and dress shoes carrying the tray to Elsjen in the cellar. And though I'm tired from today's chores, his kindness, and its rarity in this house, persuade me.

"I suppose I can meet you in two hours," I say, deciding I can safely carry only four of the eight goblets. I nod to him as I grasp the tray firm in my hands and head for the cellar.

I will have to return for the rest.

Chapter 19

I hurry through the sweeping and washing and drying and replacing of items in Madam's cabinet, afraid I will take longer than two hours. A *roemer* nearly slips from my grasp as I scrape dried wine from its bowl. I must pay more attention.

"Daydreaming about a beau?" Elsjen asks as she places the fruit basket and butter jar into the cupboard. She offers a rare smile and her face softens with the uncommon gesture.

"Too busy for all that," I say, though I feel my cheeks flush and look back down at the dishcloth, as I work over the glass.

Tobias waits at the near corner, just as he promised, and I feel relieved to have his company on the dark walk home.

"You must be tired," he says, offering his arm.

"Not any more or less than every other day," I say, placing my hand on his forearm. "Though these parties can be tiresome."

"For me as well. So many old men praising and comparing all at once. It makes me dizzy."

"Or maybe that's the wine," I say. "I noticed your glass was empty. More than once."

He laughs. "You notice such things?"

"As much as I can while I finish my tasks. Makes the long days go by faster, and the short ones seem less like they've passed me by."

"What else did you notice?" He looks at me as though my words deserve hearing.

I wait, thinking. "The old man at the dinner. How he was nearly as invisible as me."

Tobias nods. He stays on the street side to protect me, and I recall Sontje praising Hans for doing the same. "Men like De Graaf never listen to caution. But old Rutger is in the right. Our riches cannot endure forever. Though we like to pretend otherwise."

I worry he will be offended, but I ask my question anyway. "Does it bother you? To work for such men?"

He pauses in thought. "Does it bother you?"

"Yes," I say, thinking of Master's display today. "But I have no choice."

"I feel much the same, being a Jew, always aware of how they could turn against me on a whim. But when I'm in Batavia, I can forget it for a while. Get lost in the newness and wildness of a place so different from here."

We walk in silence, the dark lit only by candles in the rowhouse windows, Tobias's warm arm resting under my raw hands. Though I feel happy in his company, and enjoy the sight of him, too, I cannot deny my stronger pull towards Sontje—our growing friendship, and how each new day holds the promise of more of it.

In my conversation with Tobias, I am also reminded of my talk with Master Reynst about ship navigation. Rhumb lines and Gerardus Mercator. And how unaccustomed I am to being heard, especially by men, so I feel surprised in those rare moments when they listen.

We arrive at the Reynsts' street. I do not wish to go too close, for either of these worlds to know each other.

"Thank you for the walk back," I say, wondering again how best to say farewell.

"It was my pleasure." He doesn't drop his gaze to my bodice or venture a touch. "It is as I said before, you are a different sort, Jana. A world unto yourself."

He holds both my hands in his. They feel strong around my own. Dry and warmer than mine. Though other men have seen the full measure of my skin and flesh, this gesture feels more exposing.

"You should come with me to Bruges," he says suddenly, his kind face catching the half-moon's light. "You could get away from the De Graafs, start a new life in a new place. Amsterdam is not an easy city."

"Bruges is not far enough from Amsterdam to be very different," I say. But I'm also thinking of Sontje.

He releases my hands, and for a moment I miss his hold on them.

"Well, if you ever come to Bruges, please ask around for me," he says.

"If I ever do, I will."

I turn and head toward the Reynst house.

An emptiness enters me as I leave Tobias Levy on the street, for I doubt I will see him again.

When I arrive late at the Reynsts', I expect everyone to be asleep, but Sontje greets me at the door, as though she is waiting for me.

"Oh Jana," she says, her hair hangs loose at her shoulders. It's wild, in a way I've not seen her before. I feel panic in my own belly, sensing her own unease.

"What is it?" Her face looks different, as though shaped by some new emotion that it was protected from before.

"It's Fader," she says, her voice tight and small. She dabs the inside corners of her eyes with a wrinkled kerchief. "He is dead."

Chapter 20

I stand dumbly before her, thinking of when I last saw Master Reynst. I recall his clear blue eyes. Sad eyes full of apology that he could no longer afford me. I brought him tea out of habit, and was happy to do so, seeing his weathered face.

"He passed at a tavern last night," Sontje explains as I remove my *klomps* and shawl. "No one bothered with him. I went everywhere looking for him after you left early this morning. Thought I'd been to every tavern, but I didn't remember the one across the canal. Probably the worst of them all, with *daub* coming out from the walls, and the floors covered with old ale and hay. The whole room smelled of urine. And that is where Fader took his last breath."

Sontje sobs again and I suppress a desire to kiss the top of her hair. Her lips pinch at the corners and a deep line forms between her eyebrows. She blinks and wipes her eyes with the back of her long hand.

I want to taste the tear that rolls to the tip of Sontje's nose.

"I haven't been able to sleep. I'm so tired," she says. "Who knew death required so many errands? I hardly have time to think of what to do first. And he still has creditors... The shipwright's guild should provide me with a stipend and assist in the burial, but I have to inform them and produce a certificate of death. I will have to sort through Fader's things to find the guild membership in case they don't have the record."

"How about your mother's family?" I ask, wondering why she never spoke of her people before.

"After Moeder died, they disappeared." She pulls her shoulders back and straightens herself for a moment, but slumps down again. "Have you ever felt hopeless, Jana?"

"Yes, I have." But I don't wish to say more of that, of my time in the Ringhouse or Fader's beatings. "But if I think of things that sadden me, I will only be sad."

"That's true. But I can't help but think we feel a thing for a reason. If God gave us the ability to feel sadness or fear or hopelessness, we should feel them, no?"

"Or perhaps He gives us the ability to realize that our feelings change over time. So we can trust that we need *not* feel that way forever."

She smiles, with her lips barely upturned. "You sound like a philosopher. You are very smart, Jana. I have always thought so. Smarter than me."

"Not smart. Just one who wishes to survive."

Sontje nods. "I'm not sure where to begin."

"I'll fix some tea," I say. "Sometimes the warmth is a comfort."

The tea calms her and she resolves to talk to the guild first. She leans back in her chair and smooths down her untidy hair, then takes in a deep breath.

"Jana, have you ever wanted children?"

I'm surprised by her question, and pause before answering. "No. I don't think of them."

"Never? I mean, when you see a young mother with her beautiful baby?"

"No. I can hardly survive on my own. And I saw my mother give birth to my sister Hlaska. It terrified me."

"You saw it?"

"Yes. I delivered her from my mother's womb. Sometimes I think I can still smell the blood on my hands."

Sontje flinches at the mention of blood. "Oh, Jana. I'm so sorry. How old were you?"

"Ten." I imagine the dank, sweaty smell of our cottage, and Moeder panting and wailing like a dying animal. "I was so scared they would both die. When Hlaska cried, more like the bleating of a goat, I felt such relief. But then I thought Moeder would die."

Sontje looks like she might cry, and I feel badly for burdening her with my own wretched stories. "Where was your father?"

"Who knows? He came a few hours later, so drunk he cried because he'd missed the birth. Said it was a good thing I was there to catch the baby. But it didn't feel like catching. I don't think I breathed the entire time. I was so afraid."

Sontje is silent for a moment, perhaps stunned by my tale. "Well, you've distracted me from my own sadness," she finally says. "I suppose I should remember that Fader was not the best father. Hardly noticed me. Frittered away my inheritance, left me nothing but this house."

"He was the kindest master I have had," I reply, thinking without wanting to, of Master De Graaf. "I will miss him. And at least you have stories."

"No, I have no stories."

"Master never told you about your mother?"

"No. Everything I know of her is from Madam Pelgraff." Madam is a thin, old neighbor with watery eyes. "She told me that Moeder had a weakness for *appeltaarts*." Sontje presents a weak smile. "Like you. But now I have neither parent."

Wishing to draw her from more sad thoughts of her dead parents, I ask a different question. "When was the first time you saw something beautiful? Do you remember?"

She closes her eyes in thought, then blinks them open after a moment. "Once when I was a little girl, I walked down the street into the old forest nearby."

"The one by the church?"

"Yes. I had always found the trees there frightening, something about their nearness to the church. But I decided to walk into the forest, and I saw rocks covered in thick green moss, like fur. As if the stones had turned into magical creatures."

"And that was beautiful?"

"No," she laughs. "I had just forgotten about them. Rocks like little furred animals. The beautiful thing was the sky between the tree branches at dusk." She looks directly at me, and I wish my face was less plain, so she could see something lovely within it. "The trees were in silhouette, the leaves were starting to fall off so they looked like long, old-woman fingers, and the sky between the branches, just at the edges, seemed the loveliest, most beautiful blue."

Chapter 21

The next morning, before dawn, Sontje knocks on my attic door then enters. She holds a candle, burned nearly to its wick.

"Jana, I cannot sleep. I keep thinking how the creditors will ask for repayment. They already came by yesterday evening, not one day after he died. I'm lost for what to do about it. I don't think even selling everything in the house would extinguish the debts."

I sit up in bed, rousing myself. I, too, worry about the arrival of Master's creditors and their demands, and returning to the alleys with their filthy, scrabbling rats. But I try to reassure Sontje instead.

"You cannot take up sewing? Your needlepoint is good."

She sits next to me on my little bed, and I take her boldness as proof of our growing friendship.

"Some hemming and darning? Enough women already do such things and all with greater skill than mine." She looks out the small attic window as if she might find the answer to her troubles outside. "I would be so sad to leave this house," she continues. "The last place Moeder lived." Her golden hair falls across her cheek and something magical occurs between the straightness of her hair and the roundness of her cheek. Circle and line. "I have this worry that if I lose the house, I will lose her all over again."

I think back to our embrace of many weeks before, the delight and memory of it still with me.

"Then we must do our best so that will not happen," I say.

Sientje holds her hands out in front of her, studying her slim fingers, the ovals of her nails. "Useless hands. Meant for holding teacups and pulling on dresses."

I look at her unmarked hands in silent agreement—too smooth for washing pots and stoking fires or scouring clothes against the washboard. I'm sorry for her suddenly, realizing how childlike the wealthy are, with no taste for having to survive.

"My hands were always very soft," she continues. "They were one of the things Hans most admired about me. Said my hands felt like Lamb's Ear, those plants with the furred leaves," she says, both sad and triumphant.

I take one of her hands and before I think on it, I bring her palm to my lips. Her eyes widen and she pulls her hand back, as though she's touched a hot kettle.

I've forgotten who I am, and where, though I know of no place in this world where I could have such desires.

"I'm sorry. I just felt sad for your lovely hands."

"No, it's… sweet of you, Jana." Sontje looks back at her palms, as though they are no longer hers.

"I've always admired your long fingers and delicate wrists. My fingers are short and scarred from burns and lye."

She looks at my wrists and nods in agreement. "But they tell a story, your hands. That you've survived and worked hard to do so."

"That I have."

"Mine tell no stories at all. I've had it too easy."

I pull my hands back, afraid I have shown her too much.

Chapter 22

The week passes, and Sontje busies herself with Master Reynst's accounts, seeing about his guild rights and creditors. We take our meals together, but we remain distant. Master's passing has left a rawness in us both. And still, I am not sure how much longer I can be a boarder in her house, though she is happy to take the guilders I bring from my work at the De Graafs.

I'm at the De Graaf house now, having swept the front room and bedrooms, and I'm polishing the silver in the dining room when I feel Master De Graaf watching me.

He stands in the *zaal*, a faint smile on his thin lips.

"Looks as though I've secured another contract for goods. I'll get a good sum for the imports with all my contacts at the Company. Real demand for vanilla and cinnamon now," he says. "I should make a killing on the next fleet. We are planning a trip to Bruges as well. They've a taste for cinnamon."

I work on the curlicued etchings on the handle of a spoon, not wanting to encourage him. I must scrub the handles hard to remove the tarnish. I press my thumbnail between the grooves, busying myself.

I must mop up the *zaal* next, but there is only one exit from the dining room and he stands blocking it.

He walks further in, continuing his chatter.

"It's very interesting, my line of work. You're in the middle of everything. Where all the exploration occurs. Every new expedition brings new discoveries—do you know they have lizards in the Indies the size of cows? Nearly like dragons? And snakes that can crush a person to death?"

He stands beside me now, at the shorter end of the long table.

I study the scrollwork on the spoon while imagining a cow-size lizard, feeling frozen to the floor.

"Such a pretty neck you have," he whispers, stepping behind me. "White as cream."

Though I've not often seen the back of my neck, I expect it's ruddy like the rest of me, not creamy at all, and quick to brown in the summer.

But I also know this fact of my coloring makes no difference.

His thumb brushes my skin, traces the hairs at my nape. I study the long rosewood table in front of me, Madam's most valued furnishing, its top thickly carved with vines and flowers, and a pattern of smaller flowers and intricate leaves trails around the table's edge. What flowers? Tulips? Roses?

The pile of Madam's silver lies in front of me, blemished by tarnish I have yet to remove.

My heart pounds and I feel I may vomit. I recall other hands, other men, but in these moments, they all feel the same.

"You are a temptation," he whispers into my neck as the blackness enters into my skin, both slick and sticky at once.

The candle. The cards.

I turn to him, the constellation of pitted pockmarks covering his chin level to my eyes. I smell sour mackerel on his breath.

His hand cups my breast. He squeezes it, clutches it like an apple, and I gasp.

"Madam will be home soon." I use a softer voice, not my own, and move away from him, around the edge of the table.

He narrows his hungry eyes, and I rush to draw some space between us. I force the ice from my body and scoot myself around the table.

"I must sweep the floor now, Master," I say, hating the pleading sound of my voice. But the table now lies between us. Its curving petals and leaves swirl around me, like the fallen leaves on the day I left our cottage in Amsterdam Bos.

Not tulips, but amaryllis and roses.

He studies me a long moment.

Then, thankfully, he leaves.

Madam returns soon after, and asks me to go to the market. Only when I close their grand door behind me and walk to the next street, do I feel welcome air filling my lungs. My stomach stays twisted from the morning, full of my shame.

I take some time after the market, not wishing to return to the house.

I stop at the canal.

Clouds fishtail through the blue sky, and I'm finally comforted. Sunlight slices through the elm branches. The low branches of a maple tree tremble, and I note the ready consolation of leaves and stillness. Trees have thus served me throughout my childhood.

A pair of *meerkoets* float on the water, one after the other. I come here sometimes to watch the waves lapping against and sliding toward each other, like hours into days.

"Jana!"

I turn around.

Sontje.

"What are you doing here?" I ask, happy to see her.

"The brisk weather is good for me. Forces me to think." Her cheeks are bitten red from the chill air. "What are you doing out?"

"Went to the market, and now, watching the birds."

The *meerkoets* bob on the water. Sooty black feathers and stark white bills. One flaps its wings, revealing gray feathers underneath before it resumes swimming. Lazy and free. Sontje's eyes match the gray of the canal water.

"*Helaas.* Not a care in the world, those silly birds," she says. "Must be nice to float on the water with so little effort." Her expression remains deadened by her grief and worries.

Looking at the gray water, I also think of Tobias Levy and his stories of sailing on the ocean. The vastness of it, feeling part of something so large and powerful you can only submit and have faith in it.

"Funny how the water rolls off their feathers. Like magic. Nothing sticks," she says.

"I've often envied them—how they can both swim and fly."

Sontje clasps her hands together and stares at her crossed thumbs. "I have some news." She fixes me with her gaze and I wait for her to explain. "Jana, I'm just returning from Company headquarters. I'm leaving Amsterdam."

A blackness enters me again, though I'm cheered by her sudden bright smile. I have not seen it these past days.

"You have some relatives in Den Haag. I remember…" I say. Den Haag is not so far.

"No. To Batavia."

"Batavia?" The word sounds so strange in my voice.

"Yes. A new ship, the *Leyden,* leaves in two weeks. They are looking for women for the settlers to marry. The Company will pay the dowry and cost of the voyage there, and even provide some new dresses." At this, she looks embarrassed. "I can't stay here. I'm afraid every time I leave the house I'll see Hans with his new wife. Even Sussie calls less and less, though we've known each other since we were girls. Without Fader, there's nothing for me here."

I try to imagine Sontje in paradise, ignoring the twisting sensation within me.

"Does one apply for this?" I ask, not knowing what else to say.

"General Coen himself met with me." She plucks at the grasses with her fingertips. "They want women with no ties to the homeland, so we cannot return. I've never been outside Amsterdam—not even to Bruges or Den Haag. This is all I know. Batavia sounds so far away. And there's sunshine all year round."

Her eyes brighten. "Everything would be different. No one I know. No one snickering at my misfortunes. Poor, unmarried, orphaned Sontje. No possibility of seeing Hans with his rich new wife from Delft. No reminders of the house I will no longer own, and all its pitiful memories." She blinks quickly, eyelashes fluttering. "Imagine it. Blue skies, not gray. Ocean. Trees."

"We have trees here." This is all I can say. I'm too full of sadness, and jealousy that she will journey to this place I can only imagine. Batavia. Still a word from another time. Like the memory of a dream I cannot recall. And then some disappointment that I'm no consideration at all. But why would I be? I have brushed and washed her floors with boiling water, even as my face burned and my legs shook with fever. I have laundered her linens in lye that has coarsened the backs of my

hands, so even beef tallow cannot penetrate my toughened skin. I
have comforted Sontje on her mother's death anniversary and cooked
sugar with egg whites and rainwater for the plum preserves she likes
at Christmas.

"Yes, yes, we have trees," Sontje says with impatience. "But the
trees in Batavia are nothing like the small kindling trees we grow here.
There the trees have roots that hang from their branches and sweep
the earth. Birds of every color, not our insignificant sparrows. Parrots.
Have you seen a parrot?"

"I have not," I say, trying to steady my voice, though I feel the
stinging threat of tears and blink them away.

Just then, a sparrow alights on the branch of a nearby elm. I've
always loved sparrows for their sharp black beaks and slim legs.

"Good, strong, hardworking men—soldiers—waiting to marry
us. Someone will fall in love with me, don't you think?" She smiles,
waiting for my compliment.

"Of course," I say, as the sparrow climbs into the gray sky.

Sontje blows a strand of her sunlit hair away from her eyes.

The *meerkoets* follow one another down the canal. Just black shapes
on the water now. The sun gleams on their black feathers. Makes them
as beautiful as an ugly bird can be.

Sontje turns to me and takes my hand.

"Jana, why not come with me?" Her eyes shine. "You can start
over, like me."

I savor my coarse hand in hers, and in that gesture recognize the
impossibility of her words. We are nothing alike—Sontje with her
silk bustle, her training in tea pouring and manners. I'm not what
the Company seeks in its daughters—plain and toughened by lye

and washboards. I have only my single faded dress and scratched, uneven *klomps*.

The *meerkoets* glide further off, headed under a small bridge, trailing the rippled water behind them.

"Think of it, Jana." And Sontje squeezes my hand again, stroking my palm with her thumb. "There may still be time."

Chapter 23

I will be late back to the De Graafs'. I walk as fast as I can in my long skirts.

The Company's grand headquarters face the shipyards—the largest building I've ever seen. Soaring walls that close up around you like you are a bauble in a box. But the varying red and white bricks and the numerous windows lighten its grand presence.

I've walked by it many times, but I've never been inside.

I pass through the gate, nodding to the guards at the front. Pass through the courtyard where well-dressed merchants in fine leather boots and plumed hats laugh and talk.

"I'm looking for Master Coen. Do you know which office is his?"

The merchants look at me, appraising in the way men do. I wait for it to be over. My plain brown hair, solid build, clear skin. Smear of mud across the toe of my *klomps*. The unraveling hem of my dress. Passable, if I weren't a servant.

"Master Coen is on the second floor. The last office at the end of the hall," the taller one, with bushy reddish hair to his shoulders and a weak mustache, says. "I imagine you're arranging for a Company dowry?" He smiles and winks.

"Thank you." I pretend not to hear his question.

"I hear the ship is full," the tall one says and laughs. The other man is smiling.

"Thank you, Masters." I walk quickly, their eyes upon me as I go, like pins in my backside.

My *klomps* clack on the stone floor inside the building. I try to slow my steps to the end of the hall.

His office door is half-open.

Master Coen is an old man. Balding. His red, flaking scalp gleams in the light through the window. I smooth down my dress and rub the dried mud off my *klomps* with my thumb before knocking.

"Yes?" He looks up at me, squinting.

"Master Coen? I'm here to ask if I can join the women on the next voyage to Batavia."

He looks at me like the others, as if I'm a cow for slaughter. "Come in." Now he stands up like a proper gentleman and waits for me to sit.

I rarely see such old men. Most die too early to reach Master Coen's advanced years. His body shakes as though rattled by an invisible storm. Though he has only a fine floss of hair—his wig rests on the chair beside him—a coat of white dander flours the shoulders of his doublet. I can see what death will look like on him.

He opens a leather book on his table and takes his quill. "First, tell me your name."

"Jana Beil."

He scratches this information into his book.

"And your family? Where are they from?"

"My people are from the woods outside Amsterdam."

"Do they approve of you leaving? You won't miss them?"

"I've not seen them for some years." I will not tell him why.

"And what sort of work do you do?"

"Cleaning. Housework. I was the maid for Sontje Reynst, who is going to Batavia on the *Leyden*."

"Oh yes, Miss Reynst." He smiles. "You are close?"

"Yes." Though in truth, I'm not sure.

"Good. Batavia can be a lonely, wild place. It's good if you know someone. But after ten months on a ship, you'll know the other passengers better than your own mother, I suspect."

"Ten months? I expected a shorter journey." But then I recall Master Reynst's words—*ten months, sometimes less.*

He laughs, seeing my surprise. "Sometimes longer. Sometimes shorter. Depending on weather and navigation. It's an adventure."

"You've done it?" I cannot imagine someone in his state anywhere near a boat, even when docked at harbor.

"Ah no. But my son has—Karel. He's there now. His letters are like adventure tales. Accounts of the natives and their un-Christian rituals. Storms at sea. Sailing alongside a whale, even."

Master Coen presses his fingertips together, leans toward me, and looks in my eyes. I'm surprised by the spark I see within him, for, a moment ago, he looked like a different, wearier man.

"You understand you cannot return for at least five years? That you will meet your husband when you arrive, and if you ask to return you must repay us the dowry as well as the cost of your passage or be detained in a pauper's prison? It is no small thing. And life there will be very different from here."

"I do. Yes." Though I had not known of these consequences before. He's trying to frighten me, but I resist being afraid, like it is a winter wind I must endure. Fader used to say the wind cleared our thoughts. If you wanted to figure out some problem, you must stand outside in the gale until it sends you the answer.

Master Coen purses his papery lips and nods.

"Well then. I have no space on the *Leyden,* but I will put you on the list for the next voyage."

"When will that be?" Despair settles inside me. That I will be without her, and will have to work at the De Graafs' longer.

"Six months or so. Once the *Leyden* girls are settled."

"And there is no space on the *Leyden?*"

"No. But I can assure your place for the next one."

I nod. *Six months. She will forget me by then.*

But as I leave the V.O.C. building, I cannot help but look upon Amsterdam as though I'm leaving it. How different it seems. The gray, seamless skies, flat streets, and narrow alleys inspire protectiveness. No longer the indifferent city that spits me out when it's run out of servant work, but the place that welcomed me after I escaped from the forest and the Ringhouse with nothing but my clothing, memories of Helena, and a few trinkets wrapped in fresh poplar leaves.

But Sontje is right—there is nothing more for me here. I want nothing else than to be on the *Leyden* with her, but how can I make it so?

The houses look small and dreary, now that I'm thinking of ten months at sea, and Batavia.

I arrive late back to the De Graafs', but Madam is busy drinking tea with her wealthy friends and, thankfully, Master has left for an appointment. I lengthen out my chores, waiting for him, even as I feel my chest tighten with each passing hour.

Chapter 24

I'm fortunate. Master arrives before the ladies have finished their tea in the upstairs tearoom. He hastens to his office and takes no notice of me.

I follow behind him and stand at the door.

"Yes?" He looks at me blankly, this morning's misdeeds forgotten. I'm less than the pitted marks on the tile floor.

"Master," I say, ignoring the pounding of my heart, wishing to erase the shaking in my limbs. "I have a favor to ask."

He brings from his pocket a lens to read the sheaf of papers in his hands.

I ignore his look of annoyance, thinking instead of how he came up behind me, and the blackness I felt under his greedy hands. A flame of anger grows inside me.

"You mentioned you know many Company people. And I'm trying to get on the *Leyden*. To go to Batavia." I feel his gaze on my collarbone and recall his mackerel whisper in my ear.

"Batavia?" He laughs. "Whatever for? Full of heathens and disease."

"I wish to leave Amsterdam. The Company will pay the dowries of girls willing to live there with a settler."

"Ah right, the Company Daughters. Too many men in Batavia settling in with the blacks and natives there. But you know you cannot return? The journey is terrible."

"I understand all that." I cannot hide my impatience.

"You'll not know which man you'll get."

"Master Coen says there is no room. I want you to ask him on my behalf," I continue.

"And why should I do that? And deprive Madam of your good work?" A smirk draws over him.

I feel anger harden in me, gathering in my voice.

"Because if you refuse, I will tell Madam of your misdeeds. I know you need her money, and that you lost your own fortune. And I know of the other girls who left, too." My heart drums so hard inside me, I can hear it. "And then I will tell anyone else who asks. Everyone. Adelheid the baker will vouch for it. She told me she would." I hope my voice sounds convincing. My hands tremble, so I clasp them together.

"You have no evidence against me." Master's eyes narrow, and he looks even more unsightly. "Who will care what a silly, worthless servant says?"

"I know you've paid for them out of the Company's funds. I know of the..." I strain to remember Tobias's whispered words from the dinner party. "I know about the ledger. I have it, in fact." I try and still my face, and keep my eyes trained on his, so he will not doubt me, though I've never seen a ledger, and don't have it, and only recently learned the word.

Master pauses and scratches his weak chin, but I can see he is afraid. "You ignorant, little *kut*," he says quietly after a time, and I cannot help but flinch at his foul language. I lock my knees to remain straight and as tall as I can, even as my anger and fear battle inside me. He closes his eyes, perhaps imagining the next girl—fairer than me, maybe younger. And then his posture softens. "I will talk to Coen. But I make no promises." He pauses, as if to say something, but then thinks better of it. "I think you will find yourself on the *Leyden's* manifest. Never return here. If I see you, I will make certain you will regret it."

"Yes," I say. But I refuse to call him Master now.

A wolfish smile crosses his lips. I know the look from my Ringhouse days.

But if De Graff serves me properly, I will never see him or his hateful smile again.

Part Two

Chapter 25

Blue. Nothing but blue. The blue sky. The blue sea. Sometimes a grayish cast on them and then sky and sea melt together. I expected to see fish or even a whale. Birds overhead. Instead, water surrounds us and nothing else. Only the sloshing of the sea against the keel of our ship, the jangling of items onboard all day and all night from the rocking. Our own tiresome voices.

So many new words I have learned at sea: carracks, caravels, galleons, and frigates. In those first days, I am entertained by the grand *retourship* itself, having never been on such a vessel. The red lion of Amsterdam hangs at the *Leyden's* prow, and I'm taken by her crimson deck and green-painted masts. Her immense sails. Long planks of wood cover the decks and I try to imagine the trees they came from. Oak, most probably. The *Leyden* was the largest ship at port and carries some eighty of us altogether. I could not help but feel proud as I boarded the ship in Amsterdam while so many others watched, and children waved to us.

One girl who, for a moment, I mistook for Helena.

On the *Leyden* I wish to be someone else. Without a history. No Helena or drunken Fader brandishing his lath, no fearful, silent Moeder following another of Fader's tirades. No Ringhouse or scrubbing the front step of the Reynsts' home only to end up at the De Graafs' for a handful of coins. Sontje also says little about our earlier days back in Amsterdam, as though she, too, wishes to be someone else. And so our shared desire to reinvent ourselves draws us closer. I think little about the end of our voyage, when I will marry some stranger who works for the Company. When I find myself wondering about the future and all its unknowns, my thoughts cause a surge of fear and worry within me, and I head to the deck and draw myself back to the shimmering ocean, the fine, blue line at the horizon. I think instead of the days I've spent with the other Company Daughters, and most of all, with Sontje. Ten months is a long time, long enough for me not to think this will end anytime soon.

We are only five weeks into the journey, with no land in sight. Adelheid gave me a dozen *brezels* before we left, and I shared mine with Sontje. We ate most of them the first two days. Otherwise, we eat biscuits and dried figs and apples. Some salt beef, herring, dried peas, and rice. At the Reynst residence, I came to expect regular meals. I miss vegetables after the first week, especially carrots. The crunch, sweetness, and juice of them. Everything we eat is salty and dry. I overheard the skipper Albert say the food now is the best we'll have during the voyage. Fresher than what we'll be eating in a few months' time.

"If we're lucky we can catch some gulls for fresh meat," he said. The idea of eating those seabirds repulses me. But I've eaten worse things.

The *Leyden* hosts seven women on this voyage; the Company makes conservative investments. Just six daughters, as one, Maritjen, is already married—to the captain, a hulking man named Gerhard, whose fingers are thick like *worsts*. Maritjen acts as our caretaker. She is around my age but acts much older, advising us on our hygiene and clothing. Never smiling or joking with us.

For the remaining six of us, Albert assigned us our berths. At first I was disappointed not to berth with Sontje, but now that I know the closeness of these quarters and the sharing of chamber pots and such, I'm glad of the distance. Sontje's berth-mate is the youngest on the ship, twelve-year-old Madaleen, who has watery gray eyes and thin, yellow hair. She still sucks her thumb when she thinks no one is looking. Her mother remarried after her father died and was eager to send her off. The girl carries a yellow-haired doll whose name is Drika. Hard to imagine little Madaleen married, with her fawn legs and runny nose.

Catherina and Agatha are orphan sisters. They only talk to each other. And that too, in whispers. Sontje jokes that the only way they'll marry is if twin settlers in adjoining cottages live somewhere in the colony.

My berth-mate is Griet from Utrecht, the skipper Albert's seventeen-year-old niece. Albert took her in after her parents died of the plague, and he wasted no time casting her off to the next man as a Company Daughter. She is plain like me, with small blue eyes, scant eyebrows, and her pale skin is spotted with reddish patches that darken when she blushes, which is often. She reminds me of the little Dutch mice, who, like Griet, are splotched in color and seem always in a panic.

During those first two weeks, everything caused Griet shame, from the listing of the ship which upsets our movements to the boorish cries of the sailors on deck. She spent a good portion of the day apologizing for her lack of balance, and I wondered how she did not tire of excusing herself.

"I'm not any more able to walk than you," I finally said in frustration. "Do you not see the bruises on my own arms?"

Even so, I'm careful to change my clothing only in darkness, so she will not see the scars across my back from Fader's hidings, and others since. I do not wish to explain any of it.

Between the surprise of my new surroundings and my daily seasickness, I think less often of Sontje. The journey stretches out before me and sometimes tricks me into believing we will always be on this ship, toppling over this great stretch of water. My visit to Master De Graaf changed something in me, like a pin being turned in a lock and a small, hidden door opening. A sharpening clarity of my purpose. For once, my motives have no basis in guilders. And unlike the other Company Daughters, I did not board the *Leyden* for the promise of a dowry.

I came for Sontje, and more besides, though I am not yet sure what. But I feel closer to contentment. I'm reminded of the feeling I had as a child when I discovered those bits of colored glass in the tree hollow as I walked through the Bos.

Blue, rose, amber, green.

A growing sense of expectation, that perhaps I can have more than the meager life intended for me.

Chapter 26

My berth-mate and I speak only a little in those first few weeks of the voyage. I spend most of my time with Sontje and Madaleen in their berth instead. I'm shy around Sontje in this new space, unused to sitting about and chattering the way wealthy women do, but wishing to spend time with her. And I have a great fondness for shy little Madaleen, who hangs on our every word and gesture.

For hours each day, Griet sews lace on a bit of cream fabric, fixed to her stool in our berth. I try not to watch her. I never liked when people watched me work, as though my labors existed to entertain. When I'm in our berth, I clean. The uneven wood floors, my little hammock. Even the planked walls, which I smooth down with a rasp I found on deck.

Over time, the boredom of our surroundings and my own frustration with our confines cause in me a deepening irritation at Griet's presence—her serene expression as she inspects her needle and sucks on the white thread, working the needle along the fabric. The silence feels thick around us, only interrupted by the sounds of our industry—water sloshing in my bucket, the clink of Griet's thimble falling on the floorboards.

Today I cannot endure the silence.

"How can you do it?" I finally ask, my voice sounding foreign and rough in the stillness.

Griet looks up from her fabric as if coming out of a dream. Her panicky habits soften when she works at her lace.

"You sit for so long, just smiling away at your bit of linen. Isn't it maddening?" Perhaps I'm envious, for I lack a hobby beyond cleaning, which is still work.

She blushes at my question. Two mismatched spots on either cheek and another pink streak down her neck.

"When I'm making my lace, I'm not here at all," she says.

"Where are you, then?"

She resumes her sewing, making small loops around the fabric, her thin fingers move with quickness and grace even as the boat sways.

"Back in my parents' little cottage. Practicing the lute my father gave me. I was never any good, but it's a comforting scene to remember. Even with my awful playing, my father looked upon me with pride. And I find if I wander back into my memories, I can better tolerate this journey."

I'm surprised at her words, first that she says so much at once, and second, that I believed, until now, her silence marked an absence of thought.

"Moeder taught me lacemaking," Griet continues. "She learned from an old Italian woman. We Dutch women make chrysanthemum lace, but *reticella* is quite different and unique." She furrows her brow, inspecting some problem in her work. "Moeder hoped to teach me bobbin lace—much faster than *reticella*—but the tools are expensive. I like to think Moeder knew I would find myself on a ship one day, so she made the choice for me. I require little else but a bit of fabric, thread, and my needle. Much easier on such a journey than bobbin lace." She returns to her sewing. "Each little knot builds on the other. One dropped stitch permits time to think on my errors."

A curious statement, but I'm happy for our conversation and some pause to our lengthy silences. "What errors have you committed?"

She counts stitches over her fabric before speaking. "I do not know, but I must have committed them, since my parents are gone. Good Uncle Albert readily took me in and I'm grateful for that." She looks up at me, still flushed. "If you like, I will show you my sewing technique."

"Yes, I would like to learn," I say, hopeful such activity will entertain me as it does her.

I have more questions, but a quiet knock on the door of our berth interrupts our conversation. I open the latch that keeps the door from swinging open and shut with the shifting waves.

Sontje. This is the first time she's come to my berth and I thrill at the sight of her, that she has come to see me. She offers the familiarity of my life in Amsterdam and still something unknown and new.

"I was going mad in our berth. I'm tired of dressing Madaleen's old doll." She enters and sits on the other stool nailed to the floor. "She's a sweet thing, but so little. I feel like her mother at times."

Griet retreats back into her sewing.

Sontje glances at my berth-mate and for the first time since boarding the ship, I see a bit of the woman I knew in Amsterdam—the haughtiness of having beauty and wealth.

"You're like dear Jana, always keeping busy," she says to Griet.

Griet smiles. "'He becometh poor that dealeth a slack hand.'"

Sontje scowls at the remark, and I suppress a smile. I remember Madam De Graaf saying the same to me, and how long ago that seems now.

"One cannot just sit and sew all day," Sontje replies. "It can't be good for one's health."

"I'm sewing the ruff for my wedding dress. I'm hoping to finish it by the time we arrive in Batavia," Griet replies.

"But they give us our dresses," Sontje says. "As part of the contract."

"I wanted my dress to remind me of my mother, who taught me this art," Griet says.

"Griet is quite skilled," I say, wishing to smooth over whatever tension is growing between them.

"Yes," Sontje agrees, with some reluctance.

"Do you sew?" Griet asks Sontje.

"A little, and I have some skill for it. But I prefer painting and writing. I never had the patience for those silly needles." She turns to me where I sit on my low hammock. "Jana, the wind is perfect. Let us go to the deck."

I think of inviting Griet and feel a moment of guilt, but I wish to spend time alone with Sontje. And so we leave Griet to her needle lace and silence.

"I don't know why that girl gives me an itch under my skin," Sontje says when we reach the open air. The men crowd the decks, and we feel uncomfortable being around so many of them. They eye Sontje. A few of them smile at her, and she turns her gaze to her *klomps*. The older ones glance at me, but I keep my eyes steady on the long ocean before us.

"She hardly spoke when I first met her," I admit, savoring the feeling of our old closeness, just before we began this voyage. "But she's more interesting than I expected her to be."

"You're impressed by her lace," Sontje says in jest. "And I have no skills to offer."

"I knew you before I knew any of them," I say, shrugging.

Sontje smiles and her eyes brighten. "I finally hung some things in my berth. A painting of Moeder Mary that Fader gave me one Christmas. And for the first time since I came to the ship, I looked over Fader's old atlas."

"And the pressed flowers?" She had shown me her pressed crocus blooms when I helped her pack for the voyage.

"No. I'm not yet ready for them." She holds her hair back against the stiff wind, looking out at the gray-green water. "I wonder if I'll ever see those flowers growing again."

"Perhaps not, but I think the flowers in Batavia will be even more beautiful."

For a moment she takes my hand, and I'm reminded again why I chose to be here, on this ship.

"If only all these men would disappear," she says and slips her smooth fingers between mine.

Chapter 27

I adjust to the *Leyden*, its smallness and sounds. This is a skill of mine, to learn to like what I have, even little things. At the De Graafs', I made a point of stopping by their paintings, especially the painting of the skull and stacked books. I noted the fine strokes on the canvas. A *vanitas* painting, Sontje later explained. The books for knowledge, the extinguished candle represents life. A reminder that nothing lasts—early ripe, early rot. Gazing at those paintings, I claimed a moment for myself, to feel a bit less owned. I sometimes imagined myself inside the De Graafs' landscape painting of cows lowing on a field, and could almost feel the sunlight on my neck, the cow's warm breath on my palm.

I spend long hours on the deck and think less and less of Amsterdam, or even land, busy exploring the vessel. *The Leyden* has four decks and three masts. Like most *retourship*s, the hull is covered in skins. I asked one of the sailors the reason for the coverings and he said the skins protect the hull from shipworm, which burrow into the wood from stem to stern. Over time, the skins will rot off the hull and fall into the sea.

The four decks have different purposes, and in this the ship mirrors Amsterdam itself. Full of little divisions that tell the world your worth. The wealthiest passengers enjoy the quarters above deck. The carpenters and cooks stay in the gun deck, in berths that offer far more space than ours. The biggest berths belong to the officers. And though I've not seen their quarters, the sailors often complain about their berths in the cow-deck, with low roofs requiring them to bend over when inside. They all come out for breakfast rubbing their lower backs and moaning about their knees.

Livestock roam the second deck, mostly pigs but a few cows for milk as well. This was a surprise to me, and the stink of the animals stings my eyes. They groaned and grunted the first days of the journey but by now are too stunned to make much noise. Maritjen mentioned the livestock will die either by disease or slaughter halfway into the trip and thereafter we will have to survive on salt pork saltier than the seawater used to soften it for eating.

I have come to love the swaying of the ship. Its stew of sounds. The shouts between the crew members, the way the shifting boat causes people to reach out to things for safety—the guardrails, the walls, even other travelers. In such gestures I'm reminded we require one another, at least on this voyage. Some evenings we hear rough singing from the soldier's quarters, songs I have heard before but cannot name. All the world diminishes into its smallest speck of life, and we are all that speck. Tossed about on the water together, whatever divisions we have created on this moving surface are of our own making.

At times I think I could live like this, on this ship, surrounded only by open sky and lapping waves for all my days.

Tobias Levy said the heathen Indians believe we lived other lives before this one. If I believed in such a thing, I might think I was a sailor in another life. The waves, their constant movement, their differing shapes and patterns, their shimmer and gloss, fill me with joy, and I'm grateful for a quarter hour to hold onto the deck pole and watch them move. On the *Leyden* my helplessness sharpens, but it becomes everyone else's helplessness, too.

I watch the men working the rigging and the immense sails under the skipper Albert's firm instruction. Hard to imagine such fabric being cut and sewn together. As though only giants could do such work. The men's constant motion back and forth with the rigging reminds me of my own industry in Amsterdam. Always working. No time for stillness.

Over the din of the sailors, I hear Albert speaking to Captain Gerhard.

"I have some debts, but the Reverend told me the girl, with her skills, would fetch me a good sum. He knows an old man willing to pay two hundred guilders."

"They don't pay us enough to do the hard work needed on the ship, or for the risk in doing it," Gerhard replies. "We have to take what we can. No sense in charity when you're sent out to sea."

Albert doesn't notice me standing so close. And when he finally does, he looks embarrassed and quickly greets me. I'm wondering what payment he speaks of, and if the girl he mentioned is Griet.

He is a grizzled man—white hair to his shoulders, long, blackened thumbnails like claws. He smiles easily. "Thank you again for the *brezel* you gave me when we started the journey. I may not have another for some time." He doesn't look at me in the lustful way of Master De Graaf, and I consider that a kindness.

"What do you eat in Batavia?" I ask, when Gerhard leaves to take over instructing the sailors.

"Rice. Prawns and fish. Different spices. Everyone complains about the food, but I like it. After months at sea, I can eat anything. This is my second journey, so I know what to expect. I keep thinking I'll make a fortune but I'm finally starting to see the Company doesn't reward the men who actually risk their lives retrieving its bounty. That's how they lure you in." He looks out into the sea, shakes his head.

"I thought all the sailors make a good fortune on these voyages."

"Not when you consider half of us never make it back alive. We've lost one ship already, just last year."

"Yes. I know about it." I avoid telling him the *Antwerp's* sinking brought me here. He may find my presence on the *Leyden* a bad omen.

"They don't make a show of it—the Company needs to keep up appearances."

His bitterness surprises me. To the rest of us, the Company is the jewel of the country, bringing us nutmeg, pepper, silver, making the wealthy even wealthier. Hans Luiken once mentioned that a man amassed a fortune of over fifty thousand guilders working for the Company. I've not had more than two hundred guilders total in all my life.

Albert continues. "Each time I come outside it seems you are here, watching the water. I would say you are wistful for land, but it seems you are more interested in the waves."

"I do love to look at the water. Its many patterns and colors. Sometimes I spot shapes beneath—some sort of fish."

"You sound like a sailor. We are always more interested in the water than the land."

We pass some moments watching the waves, their shifting colors and light.

"What fish is that?" I point to a dark shape moving below.

The skipper looks closer, leaning over the port. Narrowing his eyes.

"Ay, men!" he calls out suddenly. "It's a shark! A demon fish!"

A clamor follows. The sailors run toward us. One carries a stick with a hook at the end. I hurry out of their way.

"I've seen these creatures swallow a man whole!" Another man shouts. "Opened the demon up and a man's arm was inside, still wearing his sleeve!"

"I've seen it too!" another sailor says. The men smell of sour wine and sweat.

I take another step back.

"Use the net! Let's capture him first!"

They hold a long net of jute and wood over the deck. I walk further toward the edge of the deck to see. A black shape moves beneath the water, graceful as liquid.

"Look at its fin!" a sailor shouts. "A big one!"

The fin slices up through the churning water and I wonder at the purpose of this upright triangle—to direct the creature? To serve as a warning?

"Now!"

The sailors throw down the net while another plunges his rusted harpoon into the thrashing creature and red plumes appear in the water, so much red I can hardly see the fish anymore.

They pull up the net with a black shark writhing within it, so big that the four men pulling the nets look exhausted from their efforts. The creature is nearly the length of a man, and it puts up a great fight. His tail slaps Albert on the side of his face.

"Devil's own child!" Albert cries, pulling up the net. "We'll teach him!"

They throw the shark on the deck, its blood a darker red than the deck paint, which is peeling and fading from the salt and sun. The blood spills onto the sailors' bare feet. One sailor slips onto his backside, and I cannot suppress a laugh.

"Here, let me have it." Albert takes the spear and pulls it out of the shark. The beast thrashes, and thumps the deck wall.

At that moment, little Madaleen arrives on deck for air.

She takes my hand.

"What are they doing?" she asks, her gray eyes wide and afraid at the pool of blood.

"I'm not yet sure, but I pity the creature." I regret having brought it to Albert's attention. I pull Madaleen closer to me and she peeks out from behind me.

"Take out its eye!" another sailor says, his own eyes ablaze in a way that makes me wish, for the first time, to be off this ship. Madaleen is shaking.

They plunge the spear into the shark's eyes as it writhes. Seawater sprays on us, even from a distance. I taste the salt on my lips.

"It's a mighty beast indeed! This will be a story for when we arrive at the Cape!" The men slice off the shark's fins in quick strokes using the blades they carry in their pockets, in a deft movement that surprises me in its boldness and cruelty. How the creature must feel, lashing about on these foreign decks, suddenly stolen from its life?

Blood mixes with water and spreads across the deck. I wonder how I will return to the berth without blood staining the sandals I have made from fabric and rope since my *klomps* are useless on the tilting *Leyden.*

"Throw it back into the water!" Albert yells. His eyes look maddened, too. "Tie a barrel to it first. Let it suffer 'fore it dies." A barrel is produced and tied to the great fish, who still thrashes against the deck and slaps another sailor with its powerful tail. I cannot help but admire its dark length of sleek muscle, its steadfast will to live despite its wounds.

They somehow tie a barrel to the poor creature and then drop it back into the water. The men cheer and clap, watching the shark bang against the side of the boat, blood blooming into the sea.

"The demon fish wishes it had never come to the *Leyden*," one of the sailors claims proudly. "Too bad it's poisonous or we could have feasted a fortnight on its flesh!"

"No sailor stew for that demon fish!" another sailor yells. "Bring out the ale for a celebration!"

"No alcohol on deck," Albert says, but gently. "Let's go inside and have a proper celebration." They peer over the port, but I can't look.

Madaleen still clings to me, her fingernails digging into my waist.

"They didn't even kill it for food," she says sadly.

"This wasn't about hunger," I reply. "Not that sort of hunger, anyway."

"I found the demon fish beautiful," she whispers from under my arm.

I imagine the animal sinking into the water, disappearing forever after such a mighty struggle. No praise for its labors.

And for some reason, I think of Griet, and Albert's words to Gerhard. "I did, too, Madaleen," I say, and kiss the top of her unwashed head.

By nightfall the blood dries to a red stain. The crew scrubs the deck so only a faded blot remains the next day, as though none of this ever happened.

Chapter 28

After four months at sea, sleep is a surprising boon of this voyage. The movement of the ship permits me to sleep longer than I'm used to, and Griet is a quiet sleeper, mouse-like even in rest. Perhaps my body seizes sleep like a hungry creature now that I have some time for it, after so many years of privation.

Over the past weeks, Griet shares her knowledge of lacemaking with me, and I have a new appreciation for her talents. The sewing and building of knots one on top of the next proves challenging, especially with the rocking of the *Leyden,* but Griet is a patient teacher and with time, I gain some skill in her art. Over the course of her lessons, we become friends, sharing stories and observations, but also long spells of quiet. I learn to appreciate our mutual silence, where once it grated on me.

"I had such a dream," Griet says this morning, waking me even as sun streams between the plank walls.

"What about?" I ask, looking across to her in her hammock.

"Food, Jana. So much food." Her voice softens. "Candied pears, groats-gut pudding, and quince tarts. And green things. Chicory roots and onions and hops salad and sorrel." She pauses, as though savoring each word. "And fruit. Grapes on a silver tray. Dark purple and shining like little gems. I picked one off and bit down. The grape cracked between my teeth." She pauses, remembering her vision. "I can still taste it."

My own mouth stings and waters at her description. We all dream of food. We eat nothing but hard tack and salt fish. Milk from the cows, but none of us want it. We all yearn for green things.

"I used to make a summer salad. Purslane and lamb's lettuce," I say. The Bos fed Helena and me when Moeder could not.

"Tell me," Griet says, as though preparing for a gripping tale. I have come to enjoy this quality in her. Plain, quiet Griet who listens well to my stories.

I describe the salad and add to it other ingredients, making it more extraordinary than anything I have actually prepared. Fresh tomatoes, blue borage, and orange calendula flowers. I tell her of Elsjen's asparagus with butter and nutmeg, my only fond memory of my short employment with the De Graafs.

"I could weep for that salad," Griet says. "I hated such things as a girl and how I desire them now."

We lie still in our hammocks, remembering past meals, our stomachs gurgling and roiling in protest. I feel irritable at the memory, though. I wish not to be reminded, for this longing for good food forms the noise of all my thoughts.

"Jana," Griet says in a lower voice.

I wait, still lost in my memories of asparagus. Warm and tender with its curious herbal, sour flavor. I wonder if such vegetables exist in Batavia.

"I've been feeling so tired of late." I hear her own shame at this admission. "Even my lacing tires me."

I, too, have noticed a weariness about her, but thought it boredom. And our diet is so poor now. Some sailors tried to grow a small garden on deck, but the high waves made quick work of their efforts.

"And…" Griet continues, her voice quieter. "I have purple spots on my legs and arms. I don't believe they're bruises. My teeth feel loose in my gums."

At this disclosure, I become afraid. We have all heard of the "sickness." Swollen limbs, purple flesh, rotten gums. And we know the whispered stories of one sailor or another falling ill, only to disappear from the ship altogether. We don't ask questions, though. The sailors refuse to speak about all that can go wrong on such a long journey—the flux, typhoid fever, not to mention everyday accidents and, of course, storms at sea.

"I'm sure it will pass," I tell her, but decide to observe her closely.

Chapter 29

The weeks wear on. Griet swears me to secrecy. We observe the sailors' numbers thinning, and hear, on occasion, a splash louder than the sound of large sea fish. But now that she has shared this fact with me, I find myself frozen with uncertainty. I worry I will catch her sickness. I worry she will die. I've grown fond of Griet, her long silences, her industry, her stories of childhood in Utrecht—which become more and more fanciful as our voyage lengthens.

I notice her smell now. A rotten odor, both sweet and sour, that forces me to spend more time out of the berth. Her dreams become more vivid, so she spends long hours in bed recalling them to me. Full of colors and food, and scenes from Utrecht—services at Dom church and walks along its canal.

"Please, Griet. Let me consult the medic."

"They will throw me overboard," she says, her small eyes wide in panic and I'm reminded again of her mouse-like resemblance. "I will pray harder. I must think more on my errors and ask forgiveness."

I lack the heart to tell her otherwise. Pious little Griet, whose uncle sees her as just another avenue for profit. I think of telling him, but she begs me not to. And I wonder if he would only help her to see his two hundred guilders.

"Moeder and Fader will take care of me," Griet adds. "They watch me from the heavens. I see them in my dreams."

I take to the decks for fresh air and to escape from my worries. The waves on the water, the steadiness of it, soothe my conflicted thoughts.

I'm on deck looking into the water when Maritjen, the captain's wife, approaches. Her brown hair is coiled in heavy braids around her head like a crown.

"You spend as much time on deck as the sailors," she says, as though noting some weakness of my character.

"Just getting some air."

"Gerhard says females must take the air in moderation. It's too much for our weaker constitutions."

I say nothing, hoping she will leave.

"I know all the sailors on this ship, so if you have any questions about the voyage, you can always ask me. Gerhard and the skipper are very close. Have to be. The captain and skipper are the most powerful men on the boat."

She wants to say more so I wait, listening to the sloshing of waves against the gun hull.

"Your friend, Sontje. You mentioned you knew her before?"

"I have known her for some time." I will not say she was my employer.

"She is very pretty, not plain like the rest of the Company Daughters," she says without apology. "How is she not married already?"

"I'm not sure." I'm certain Sontje would not want Maritjen to know of Hans Luiken.

"Gerhard finds her beautiful." I'm about to interrupt, but she raises her hand. "No, no, it's fine. We have a very honest marriage, Gerhard and me. It's good he tells me."

I cannot imagine such a thing, so I stay silent.

"He's always liked skinny little things. I was like that at first, but marriage puts flesh on a woman." Maritjen smiles and pats her plump middle. "Though I suspect at the end of this journey I'll be back to my marriage weight. Gerhard says the food gets worse and worse."

I nod, relieved to be speaking of a different subject. "I'm already tiring of biscuits."

She snorts, which make her appear even more piggish than before "He says by the end, we will even fight over the hard tack." She peers into the water, as though wondering what I find so arresting about its movement. "I haven't seen young Griet in some time."

"She's resting," I say, resenting having to think further of her predicament.

"Catherina thinks Griet might be ill."

"She is busy with her lacework. Almost finished with her sleeves." Indeed, the lace is beautiful and delicate, as though spidery snowflakes cling to the fabric.

"Her industriousness impresses us all," Maritjen replies. "She will make a good wife."

Not wishing to stay with Maritjen, I excuse myself. I've learned to stay away from women like her, always seeking out some rumor or another. Such women find their only joy in making others feel poorly.

Chapter 30

Two weeks pass and the smell of rot fills our berth now. I hardly sleep and retch at the odor.

"Can I tell Albert?" I ask Griet, who can do nothing but lie in her hammock now.

"He will throw me overboard or leave me in the hold with the others." Her voice tightens with despair. By now, we all know of the handful of men left in the hold to die. We hear rumors of rats eating their flesh as they wait for death.

"You're his niece. He wouldn't treat you like the sailors."

Her eyes are bloody where they once shone white. Her black gums grow over her teeth and I must cover my nose and mouth with a kerchief for the putrid odor.

"He cares nothing for me. He never looks in on me. I hoped it would be otherwise, thinking that because he and my mother shared a womb, he must have some affection for me. He only meant to make a good sum off my betrothal."

I admire her keenness even in her dreadful state.

"Jana, isn't the sky beautiful?" she asks, suddenly, though little sky appears through the planks above. Her feeble voice turns bright and strange. "How it glows so orange and rose? Like smoke rising from a chimney? Have you noticed?" She smiles, revealing her repellant gums.

Some teeth have recently fallen from her mouth, just as she predicted in her dreams weeks ago.

"Rest, Griet," I say, afraid for both of us. I can't share her berth anymore, but feel loyal to her, and I do not trust Albert. My guilt and memory of the demon fish and its horrid death at my hand prevents me from telling Albert of Griet's illness. But I also fear he will blame me.

I can't think of that now. I'm once more Jana of the Ringhouse, thinking only of surviving.

I find Sontje in her berth after Griet has fallen asleep. Madaleen is playing draughts with Catherina and Agatha in their berth.

"Jana," Sontje says. Though she is thinner now and less radiant for our poor diet, she remains beautiful and tidy in her appearance. My warm feelings for her are still there, even more so because I have come to rely on the constancy of her presence. She studies me. "What's wrong?"

"Griet. I think she's dying." Though I told Sontje of her illness, I've refrained from saying too much, meeting in her berth or on deck in recent weeks.

"You must tell Albert."

"You know what they've done to the others."

At this, she's silent. We all wonder if we will have men enough to reach the Cape.

"Can I stay with you and Madaleen?" I ask, timid at my need for her help. "The stench is too much for me."

"Yes, of course. Untie your hammock and we can fix it here."

We work in shifts caring for Griet. We take her rations of hard tack and dried peas since hunger plagues us all, and Griet's gums have overgrown her teeth so that chewing causes her agony.

We wash her face and apply a salve to her lips and listen to her ravings about the church in Utrecht and her father's old lute.

I worry Sontje won't be able to tolerate Griet's pitiful condition, but she proves to be a devoted nurse, combing back Griet's limp hair, holding her purple, swollen hands, keeping the berth as tidy as possible despite Griet's piss soaking through her clothes.

I think of Sontje in Amsterdam, and how little of that carefree girl remains.

"What a horrid death," Sontje says, when I relieve her from her duties late one evening. "I can't bear it. I feel ashamed for being annoyed with her before."

"You were both different girls then," I reply.

"I felt jealous of her closeness to you." Sontje looks at her *klomps*, now blackened and scuffed.

I don't know how to respond, so I take my place near Griet's bed.

I'm sitting beside Griet at dawn. The grayish light glows between the wall planks and Griet's small, puffy eyes flicker open.

"I'm dying," she says simply.

I prefer to be truthful than to reassure her now. "Yes," I answer, and hold her hand. "I'm sorry. I'm so fond of you, Griet. You have been a good friend and berth-mate to me."

She smiles and even her terrible odor and decaying teeth fail to diminish my warmth for this courageous girl. I know I'm changed for our months together on the *Leyden*.

"The only thing that has helped me in this," Griet says as tears roll down her face and into her hair, "is the memory of being loved. My mother and father tried their best even as they were dying of the plague. They begged Uncle Albert to take me so I would not get sick myself or have to watch them die. And so they passed without me beside them. Alone. They didn't see my face as they left this world. But I recall how they looked at me that last time, when Uncle Albert came for me. And that is all that helps me now. Not even prayer. Just knowing I was loved."

I squeeze her hand and cannot help but weep myself, for I've never felt such love from my parents, but I felt it from Helena and miss her daily.

"I think it's here for you," Griet says, though I'm unsure what she means.

She grits her teeth as a painful spasm passes through her frail body. Exhausted by her efforts, she closes her eyes.

"My ruff. The lace. Take it. Wear it on your wedding day," she whispers.

Some hours later, her body stiffens. I listen for her breath and hear only silence. Such a different and dreadful silence than the ones we shared these past months.

Chapter 31

I worried Skipper Albert would blame me for Griet's death, but I think he was so humiliated by the loss of one of the precious Company Daughters, he said little about it to me, beyond expressing how sad it made him. Albert attended her funeral on deck with the rest of us and, with three other sailors, helped to bring her wasted body up from the berth before whispering a quiet prayer and tipping Griet over, and into the waiting sea.

I cannot stay in our old berth, so Sontje is my berth-mate now, in her cabin. Madaleen stays with Catherina and Agatha, preferring their larger berth now that I'm here.

Though we room easily enough, we bicker. Since Griet's passing, I'm more direct with my words, less afraid of Sontje.

We argue over the chamber pot, and who shall empty it. We have one each in our berths, loosely fastened to the wall. A common latrine lies at the head of the ship, but we don't use it, foul as it is from the men. The piss sloshes about in our berth's chamber pail and spills onto the planks. Sontje rarely remembers to clean it. I have to climb a ladder holding the pail, and then release its contents into the ocean. The foul stuff splashes onto my clothes and I stink of urine while Sontje still smells of lavender and milk.

"Sometimes you could empty the chamber pot," I tell her.

"I have."

"When? I haven't seen it."

"The piss sloshes about on the floor, and when I empty it, my dress gets soiled."

"The same happens to me." My anger surprises me, how it changes my voice and I'm suddenly embarrassed. The days of seasickness and boredom and my sadness over Griet have made me impatient. "Perhaps I should get some fresh air. But you know, Sontje, I'm not your servant anymore."

She looks at me, surprised. "Yes, of course you're not." She smooths the pleats of her dress, since the humidity makes everything wrinkle. She sighs. "I suppose in some way I think you still are. But then I have always treated you more as a friend than servant."

I think of the times in Amsterdam when she scolded me for being minutes late from the market on rainy mornings or if I forgot to purchase some item. And still, I can't entirely blame her. She has known only her own easy life.

"I'm sorry, Jana," Sontje says. I allow her apology to hover between us. She has never apologized to me before.

"I will return soon," I say, enjoying having the last word, and I leave for the deck to be free of Sontje for a spell.

Hours pass before I return to our cabin. I watch the sea from the decks, observing the gun ports, exploring parts of the ship. The cow-deck with its low beams, the expansive bow and cabins of the high deck, where the captain lives.

I knock on the door of our berth. How well I have come to know its two blackened hinges, the metal handle that I must push down with both hands and the door on which I lean the full weight of my body to open.

When I enter, Sontje is sitting on the trunk, her face in her hands. "Sontje?"

She doesn't answer. Her hair hangs unraveled around her shoulders, which I've seldom seen, since Sontje prefers neatness. Everything tucked and hidden.

"What's the matter?"

She stays silent. I hear the sounds of our berth, sounds so familiar to me they feel like they are part of my body now. The creaking of the walls as the ship sways, the bellowing, faraway voices of the sailors.

"I was thinking of poor Griet. What if we never arrive there? What if we end up like her? I have dreams my teeth turn black and my flesh swells and rots like hers did." She sniffles. "And I miss my old life. The main canal, Dam square, the house most of all. Even if it wasn't mine anymore, if I had stayed I could have still seen the house sometimes."

Of course she misses her wealth, her Hans, her dresses, her servants. Roasts and banquets and tea parties.

"That life is over Sontje. Better you accept it now than keep wishing for it forever."

"It's cruel to say that." She looks at me, her red-rimmed eyes glinting in the sunlight beaming through a knothole in the wall. "We've endured so much these past months."

I confess I enjoy being her equal in this moment, but I remind myself to be patient. She doesn't know much of my own life—I've shared only the smallest scraps of it with her because I don't want her pity or understanding.

"I'm only saying acceptance is the easiest way to move on. Memories always seem better looking back."

"I remember being happy," she replies. "I *was* happy."

I shrug. Happiness is a luxury. Like Sontje's feathered quill and silk apron.

"I've eaten better on this ship than I ate in my family's home in the Bos at times," I tell her. Indeed, I've heard the sailors say the same. "In those first months, at least. Hot groats in the morning with butter, bacon, and stockfish. I was accustomed to one meal a day and here, I have three."

This silences her. She forgets at times that she has had so much. But the ease of her life has not prepared her for anything. I have learned to expect little from the world and remain surprised by its rare generosities.

"I must seem very spoiled to you," she finally says while studying her thumbnail, dark gray with grime. She always kept her hands very neat back in Amsterdam, and this dishevelment must trouble her.

"We only know the life we have." I have been too harsh. I try to imagine what this voyage must be like for her. To go from her comfortable two-story house in the Herengracht with a cook and servant, and where she has lived her whole life, to our small shared berth with its low ceiling and foul chamber pot nailed to the wall. And now rationing water and bread and wondering about the uncertainty at the end of this voyage.

"What did you see on the decks?" she asks.

"I saw the captain's quarters—from a distance."

"Are they as nice as everyone says?"

"Definitely larger than ours. But I feel badly for the soldiers. Crammed into the gunports and hatches. So dark and dank in there. They must be miserable. And always I note the ones who are missing."

She grows silent, surely reminded of Griet, as I am.

"I miss things, also," I say. "The taste of apples most of all. I didn't have them often enough after I left the Bos. Now the salt pork and biscuits make my eyes water."

"Also the plums," Sontje replies. "What I would not do for one of the black ones. The tight, tart skin and all that soft, wet, flesh underneath." She sighs. Complaining about the saltiness of the provisions is a pastime second only to playing draughts. One night we did nothing but spend the time comparing the ration of salt pork to the saltiest thing we'd ever eaten.

Saltier than a goat's salt lick.

Saltier than the sea.

"I miss different things every day," Sontje continues. "The common starlings. Some mornings I miss their songs so much I could cry. The next day, the musty bread smell of the *zaal.* I used to keep the window open in the spring and summer to get rid of the dankness, but now I miss that smell. And Fader. I even miss him snoring at the dining table because he was too drunk to walk the stairs to his bed."

"I don't miss my father," I say. "He is not nearly as good a man as yours was."

"What did he do?"

I worry I've opened myself up to more questions that will take me back to the Ringhouse. So I quote Isaiah, one of the few passages I know. "'Forget the former things; do not dwell on the past.'" The most memorable verses are often the most difficult to follow.

"Yes," Sontje nods. "But… is it bad to miss the things you love?"

"I did not love my father, so there is nothing to miss." It's the first time I've confessed this aloud. The admission hangs in the air, heavy like the musty smell of Sontje's *zaal* and I regret raising the subject of Fader again.

"He was unkind to you?"

"At times, but it could have been worse." Though I cannot imagine how.

"You never speak of your family or life before you came to work for us. It's as though you sprung out of the earth without any history at all."

I stiffen. "I've told you of my sister Helena."

"How many sisters do you have?"

"Two. One, now."

Sontje doesn't ask further "Tell me about the Bos."

"I used to go for long walks in the woods alone." I imagine the woods as I tell her. The linden trees, the columns of speckled birches, the way the air smells wilder and cooler under certain trees, as though the trees have cast magic in their own shadows. "I used to gather the autumn leaves in my apron and then release them upward and let them fall on me like snow. And it was my habit to peer into the trunks of trees. Sometimes I found a store of acorns or pinecones. Sometimes a nest. I never touched them. Once I saw Fader raid the acorns from a tree and I wondered if he was starving the squirrels who had done the work of storing them." *Better they starve than you, my* sukkel *daughter.* I recall Fader's crooked, mean smile, like when he gripped a hand around Moeder's bony hip when he desired her. "After that, if I found acorns on the ground I'd place them in tree holes as an apology."

At this, Sontje smiles.

"On another of my walks I saw a small pebble of blue glass in an oak tree," I continue, lost in memories I've not shared with anyone since Helena. "I called it God glass. I pressed it against my forehead. Smooth and cold. As I walked I saw more of them. All different colors—blue, rose, amber, green. One speck of glass in every tree. I thought they were gifts from the squirrels."

"That's very sweet. I wonder who put them there."

"The squirrels," I smile, remembering. "I took each one. Kept them in my apron pocket. I thought to leave them for the next person to happen upon them, but I believed they were mine, and I did not wish to refuse a gift, having received so few in my life."

Blue, rose, amber, green.

I have them still.

"I would have taken them, too, and I have had many gifts," Sontje says. And I have a sudden wish to hold her hand, for sharing that kindness.

"And then? Where were you before you arrived at our house?"

"In the Bos," I lie, feeling my cheeks flush with her questions.

Sontje pauses, considering my explanation. "The first time we walked with Hans and we passed by the Spinhuis, I noticed a woman there. One of the convicts. She seemed to know you."

"I told you, I didn't notice her," I say, sounding false even to myself, and surprised she still remembers.

"She stared at you for some time. I didn't say anything. Hans and you were already arguing and I felt too nervous."

"I don't remember it," I lie again.

Sontje looks deeply into me and I force myself to return her gaze, knowing that if I flinch she will see my dishonesty. But I say nothing more and she, mercifully, abandons her questioning.

"Perhaps someday we will even miss being on this old boat," Sontje says after a time.

Chapter 32

After six months at sea, the *Leyden* has changed us all.

I'm turning brown from my time spent on the deck. My forehead peels and tightens, but the discomfort hardly bothers me. The beauty of the moving waves, the action of the crew draws me to the deck for hours each day. The expanse of sea glimmering in all directions marks as close a resemblance to freedom as I have ever known.

I remain unsure of my place with Sontje, my confusion a clinging vise around my chest on some days, but at other times, outside tasks consume me—washing the linens or playing draughts with Madaleen. In moments when I think less of Sontje, I wonder at my foolishness, being on this journey for her sake, when my own feelings change like the movement of the waves. But the feelings for her always return, a desire to touch her skin, to smell its lavender. I am this new Jana, but still drawn to Sontje, pushing from my mind thoughts of what awaits me at the end of all this. And so I hold to my belief that I have some purpose here on the *Leyden,* to be someone other than the young, hungry girl waiting on the steps of the Reynsts' home all those months ago.

Sontje, too, gives me occasional hope to believe she might feel the same. A smile when I recount a memory of my girlhood, praise for my resourcefulness when she complains of boredom and I devise a game of storytelling where we each make up some tale about each object in our berth.

"Jana, you are ever a surprise," she says one day when I fashion a spinning top for Madaleen from a loosened nail and bits of cloth to resemble a miniature replica of her doll, Drika. And then Sontje touches my hand, leaves her palm resting there. Into this gesture I pour my desire. I count the times she touches me in a week, reading into her movements desire or revulsion. *Silliness*, I chastise myself. But sometimes she looks at me, a sidelong gaze, and I think she reads my thoughts and even welcomes them.

Our time together on the *Leyden* has changed Sontje also. She now takes out the chamber pot without complaint. She washes the floor, though not very well. I do not criticize. I know each time she must do these chores she is reminded of her old life being stripped away. When she does such work, she never hums or laughs or speaks. Just finishes the task quickly.

And another shift as well—Sontje now disappears for periods at night and doesn't tell me where she has gone. I wonder where she leaves to, but feel embarrassed to ask, aware she doesn't wish me to know of it. She walks barefoot so I won't hear. She unlatches the door and opens it only wide enough to exit sideways. We seem to have entered some secret agreement, where I pretend I'm asleep, so she can believe she safeguards her secret. In such moments I'm reminded of myself as a child when I would feign sleep as Fader climbed on top of Moeder, grunting and groaning like a dog.

This evening, Sontje sits atop her trunk, reading her Bible while I lie back in my hammock, looking at the knotholes in the wood ceiling, imagining they're eyes. What do they see? Jana in a sooty, blackened dress, loose at the waist and arms, and Sontje forever returning to the contents of her trunk, as though expecting something new to appear?

"I never knew you to read the Bible so often," I say after a time. I never learned to read and have always wished to.

Sontje looks up from the page. "I never used to. Church was a habit, like combing my hair. But maybe these habits have a purpose. They provide some feeling of being home."

"Is there a verse you like? A story?"

She licks the tip of her finger and turns some pages, looking. "I keep searching for the proper verse. Just a comfort to read words I know."

"Read some to me."

She places her finger on the page, tracing the words. A strand of hair falls forward and she tucks it behind her ear.

I feel close to asking her about her nightly departures just then. I think of how I would ask the question, but somehow, I'm afraid to know. Afraid of what she might ask in return. Afraid to take from her this one secret, since we have so little privacy anymore.

"I like Psalm 23, like everyone else," she says, smoothing down the page. "'Thou preparest a table for me in the presence of mine enemies.'" She laughs to herself. "Perhaps because I'm hungry all the time."

"Read it to me," I say, hungry for continued conversation. "I'm not sure I know it."

She begins. I wish to listen to her low, quiet voice for all my days.

"I'm not sure I believe it," she says after reading the psalm.

"I suppose that's its purpose. That one must have faith the table will be prepared."

We both fall silent with our thoughts. *Our tables and enemies.*

Later that night, she leaves again.

Chapter 33

Maritjen has invited us to her captain's berth for tea and because we are so starved for social functions, we make a great event of it.

Two days prior, we discuss the sad state of our frocks and meager possibilities for their improvement. I make some effort to participate, though my single, plain cotton dress inspires little discussion. Maritjen has sewn a bit of lace to hers—a yellow silk with matching apron.

We've all collected saltwater in tubs to wash our clothing and we hang a clothesline to dry our frocks on the deck. We wring our many layers—petticoats, skirts, aprons—in the saltwater, adding drops of lavender oil and lye and beating them against the floors to clean them. We hang only our outer clothing on the outside line. Our drawers and chemises dry in our berths for modesty and drip water on the floors. I've already heard the sailors laughing at our dresses hanging gaily from the line and even I'm embarrassed at the excess of Sontje's lace and brocade and ribbons swaying in the breeze on this creaking ship.

"How will you wear your hair?" Madaleen asks Sontje as we sit in our berth, since it receives the most breeze. As we sail southward the air has grown stiflingly hot, so much so that the sailors sleep on the deck. Sontje and I often have visitors seeking reprieve from their own stifling quarters—Madaleen most of all.

"I haven't thought of it," Sontje says.

"You should wear your hair loose," Madaleen advises. She spends hours braiding Sontje's hair, brushing it with her own bone hairbrush.

"We have some ribbons," Catherina says. She and her sister Agatha are never without their sewing. They sit on small stools they've brought from their berth.

"I'll do a single braid around your sweet face," Sontje says to Madaleen, cupping her chin.

Madaleen smiles. "My cousin used to braid my hair. She's younger than me but could braid anything—the stems of flowers, blades of grass. Her brother never let her braid his hair, of course, so when she wanted to braid, she was kind to me."

"Otherwise she wasn't?" Sontje asks.

"No. Especially after my uncle died. He was Moeder's brother. As long as Uncle was alive, he treated me like his own child, but after he passed, my mother remarried." Madaleen grows quiet, looks at her hairbrush.

I forget at times that she is only a young girl. Too young to marry. Only twelve. But the settlers want girls they can easily mold, and she's tall and pretty, even if weakened by all the salt pork and lack of fruit and vegetables.

"I have enough ribbons to trim two, maybe three, frocks," Catherina continues.

"And I have some whitening cream. And pot rouge for our cheeks," Agatha adds.

"Sontje doesn't need whitening cream. She still blooms like a rose," Catherina says. They are sweet girls. Unattractive with their red noses, long foreheads, and narrow shoulders, and not especially interesting. I soon run out of things to discuss with them, but some people are that way.

"She will be swept up as soon as we bring the boat to port," Agatha agrees. We have been told little about our marriages, other than that the men themselves will select us. We rarely speak of the true purpose of our journey—marriage to strangers in a distant colony. It seems somehow tactless. Conversations center on pleasantries—foods we miss, happy memories, sewing projects.

These younger girls are taken with Sontje's beauty and refinement, and eager to follow her example, that, for her charms, she will likely marry before the rest of us. Of all the girls, I come from the most modest background. The others were middle-class but for some misfortune—dead parents, jealous stepmothers—they ended up on the *Leyden*. Sontje still trails the remnants of her wealth in her intricate clothing and the cool distance she preserves between herself and the rest of us. And so the girls follow her. Walking on their toes like she does. Expressing boredom by placing an index finger between their teeth. Cocking their head to the right when lost in thought.

"Jana, do you want a bit of ribbon for your hair?" Catherina asks.

"Yes, Jana!" Madaleen says. "Wear a bit. Your hair is the same each day."

"You should," Sontje says, probably relieved to no longer be the subject of their conversations. "String it through the braid. It would look so lovely in your thick hair." She smiles. I have not seen that in some time.

"Yes," I say, flushing at Sontje's compliment. "I suppose I can wear a little."

None of us have been to the boatswain's quarters before, which remain separate from everyone else's. Order is the center of life on the ship.

The Company levies harsh consequences for sailors who defy their superiors—tying them to the keel and dragging them in the water, amputating limbs, even nailing sailors to the prow of the ship for a day as punishment. I've heard the wicked sound of the lash in the gundeck more than once already.

Maritjen's berth is smaller than I expected. I imagined it grandly furnished, a bit like the De Graafs' study. I imagined shelves. A desk with unrolled maps. A small lamp for candles. A tapestry and even paintings nailed to the wall. Mosaic floors, though I know the impossibility of such things on our ship, like chandeliers with candles because of the threat of fire.

I'm surprised the boatswain's berth is only slightly bigger than ours. Their hammocks are wider. A bit of caulking stops up the gaps in the wood. Bits of fluff and twine collect in one corner—Maritjen is not a natural housekeeper. She's scented the berth with dried lavender, but I can still smell the sour stink of the chamber pot.

Gerhard leaves as we arrive in our finery. He presents a tight smile to each of us, lingering a moment longer on Sontje, who blushes and looks away. We wear our paltry finery and I feel absurd—like a tropical bird—in my corset and mules, ribbons in my hair. But the other girls chatter with excitement. Maritjen opens the door to the berth, and she, too, wears a newer frock. A heart-shaped, gilded pendant on a thin gold chain hangs around her short neck, and large enamel earrings stretch her small earlobes. Sontje must feel an ache of envy. She always loved such adornments but sold hers to pay off Master Reynst's remaining debts.

"Welcome," Maritjen says grandly and ushers us in.

We sit at a table that has been moved inside the berth. She offers a pot of tea and a plate of dried fish. Crew members enjoy larger rations of food—butter, dried peas, beans, and ale.

"Madaleen! Your hair looks lovely," Maritjen says, as though she did not just see her hair arranged in this way earlier this morning.

Madaleen beams, playing along. "Sontje fixed it for me."

"Very nice," Maritjen replies. "Sontje, you're looking well. A nice frock you have on." She inspects Sontje further. "But the ruffle is bent. You didn't notice? I know it's so difficult to keep one's clothes in order on this ship."

Sontje blushes, for she has always prided herself on neatness.

Maritjen continues. "At least in Batavia we will have slaves to do all that work for us." Madam De Graaf said the same of me during the party when a drunken Company agent spilled his wine on the floor—"It is no trouble, our Jana will clean that up." How it irked me to be referred to that way, as though I belonged to her, like an agreeable house cat.

"I think the moisture has wrinkled it," Sontje says, in a quiet voice.

"Mmm." Maritjen nods in sympathy.

"Maritjen, what a spacious berth you have!" Catherina interrupts, meaning to flatter her.

"Being the wife of the boatswain has some advantages." Maritjen smiles. "The wood still creaks, the rains still leaks in, but Gerhard has done a bit of helpful caulking."

"Our berth is terrible when it rains. I've woken in the night with my bedclothes soaked," Catherina says.

"Yes, I realized how it must have felt like to be a child who wet the bed," Agatha adds.

Madaleen giggles uncomfortably. She has wet her hammock once or twice but only Sontje and I know this.

Maritjen passes around rolls in a well-woven basket, stained dark brown. She must have brought it new for the voyage, because the fibers remain unfrayed and the color is uniformly dark. The rolls look hard and dry, heavy like doorknobs, and unworthy of their basket.

"I've checked them for maggots," Maritjen explains of the rolls.

"I ate a roll the other day that tasted so bitter from the worms." Agatha winces at the memory.

"I hardly notice it anymore. Hunger removes taste," Catherina adds.

"I used to love the bread rolls at a bakery in Delft," Madaleen says. "Always so warm and soft."

I'm the least wistful of them. For me, the sight of light skittering over the waves tastes as good as Adelheid's *brezels*.

"I miss a good *myheen* sausage. And fresh *stamppot sla*. I liked it least of all back home, and now I crave the cold leaves under the potatoes. I even miss the carrots catching between my teeth," Agatha says, and Catherina nods in agreement.

The basket is empty. We spread the sour butter thickly to cover any maggots nestled inside.

The feast is better than I expected: salt pork, of course, and bread, but Maritjen has somehow found fruits that are not completely rotten. The apples are soft and we cut around the worms, though worms no longer disgust me. They are just bitterness and a dry, cottony texture.

"Gerhard told me as we get closer to the Cape, we must save the fruit. On one voyage here he said half the men lost their teeth. Some of them even died. He thinks because they ran out of fruit. But the surgeon says fruit has nothing to do with it—it's the sunshine and air and buildup of bile." At this, we cannot help but think of Griet and allow a respectful silence.

Madaleen swirls the juice around her mouth, as though that will protect her.

"It's a good thing your Gerhard knows so much about this voyage," Agatha says.

"Indeed," Catherina agrees.

Maritjen nods primly. "Please, take another."

She passes the basket around.

"You came from Amsterdam?" Maritjen asks Sontje as we nibble on our soft fruit, to make the eating of them last longer.

"Yes."

"Where in Amsterdam?"

"Not far from Singel. The center of the city."

"A nice area, I've heard. I have some relatives in Amsterdam."

Sontje nods and I know she wishes Maritjen would speak to someone else.

"How are you here, then? Why are you not married?"

"I was engaged," Sontje says after a pause.

"And what happened?"

"What was his name?" Madaleen interrupts.

"Hans." Sontje's eyes redden, but only I notice.

"Was he handsome?" Madaleen asks. "He must have been. You are so pretty."

At this, Sontje smiles and pats Madaleen's hand.

"He was tall. Blue eyes. A good build. Always kept his sleeves turned out." She says this as though she is trying to remember him herself. "Jana knew him, too." She looks at me, her eyes bright.

I never found Hans handsome, even in his velvet jacket and felt hat. But I sense she needs me to say otherwise. "He was handsome enough," I offer.

"Did he die?" Madaleen asks.

"No."

"Then what?" Maritjen raises her eyebrows.

"He broke off the engagement," Sontje replies.

"But you're so beautiful!" Madaleen looks indignant. She crosses her arms. Maritjen cannot conceal her smirk.

"My father lost all his money. And then he died." Sontje purses her lips. She fixes her gaze on the knothole in the far wall— a hungry, open mouth. Everyone is silent, perhaps reminded that most of us are here due to some misfortune or another.

I wish to rescue Sontje from the women's questions.

"But now we will make other fortunes," I say, "and live in new bungalows with fruit trees in the back."

"I'm sure your settler will be better than that Hans," Agatha says and we nod, even if we have our doubts.

Chapter 34

Sontje still leaves the berth at night. Maybe once or twice each week, less than before. She waits until I've stopped moving in my hammock, but I feel the change in the air as she walks, and hear the planks creaking despite her light footfalls. She holds the ropes of her hammock as she tilts herself onto the floor, her skirts raised so they won't brush the floorboards. She steps over the fourth board that is loose and turning green.

The cape she wears is her mother's old bed cover. Time on the *Leyden* has muted its colors, softened its fibers, made it ugly as it has made all of us uglier. The garment becomes a different thing upon her thin shoulders than when draped across her eiderdown.

She has mastered opening the door in the nighttime, the moonlight entering only briefly as she exits. I always wait up for her return. The sound of her footsteps, so light, as though she is half-ghost. The hammock sings a *slaapliedje* as she turns toward the wall and settles back into sleep.

Tonight when she returns to her hammock, she is crying. I can tell because she sniffs and moves in the hammock to muffle the sound. But still, I'm afraid to ask where she goes.

Or why.

*

Sontje has been hiding illness the last few days, stating she is tired from the journey. She waits for me to leave for the deck, and as I depart I hear her gagging into the chamber pot. At night, I hear her stomach roiling. Sometimes she asks me to leave the berth so she can relieve herself.

"Sontje, you are ill."

She lies in her hammock and turns her pale face toward me. "It's all the maggots in the food. The saltwater."

I put a hand to her forehead. Her body shakes with cold, though my woolen blanket covers her on top of her own.

"Your skin is very hot."

"Your hand feels so nice on my forehead."

"Sontje, you need to see the medic."

"Maritjen? She is useless," she says with surprising vehemence.

"There is a surgeon onboard as well. I can get him."

"But Hans, you always said that you would care for me." She smiles and puts her hand on my cheek. I'm anxious hearing her address Hans in her fever, as though I'm eavesdropping on a conversation, and yet my own sickened curiosity compels me to listen. She continues. "Remember that night we left the house and sat in the wet grass? My skirts were damp but I didn't care. You told me about your father. That you'd seen him with the servant girl, her skirts up to her waist. You thought for a moment he was biting her." Sontje giggles. "Like she was a bit of *boterkoek*."

She grows silent just as suddenly. I hold her hand. Her fingertips are dry and blackened, the skin wrinkled and loose on the backs of her knuckles. "You told me I was your little tulip. Many colors—yellow and white. You asked me to lie down in the moonlight and you opened my dress and kissed me from throat to waist." An unexpected sob. I know every sound of her breathing—as she first falls asleep, the deep drone of her breathing when she dreams—but not this gasping sound. "I have been alone for so long."

"Sontje?" I say, unsure.

Her eyes widen.

"No, Hans. You cannot see me like this. You will not love me this way."

"Drink," I hold a goblet to her lips again. She grabs my wrist with a ferocity that gives me hope for her recovery.

"Don't leave," she says, and even in her state, paste rimming her lips, her complexion deprived of its bloom, her sickly, bloodshot eyes, my heart quickens. She is still here.

"Drink," I whisper, and kiss her pale, sticky forehead.

Sontje's voice softens. "I'm missing my house. The black shutters. Gerhard says I'm too bright to be a flower. I'm bright like the *noordster* blinking in darkness." Her voice trails off and she is wracked again by tremors, and I feel jealousy and fear creeping into my gut.

But I'm too worried to dwell on her raving confessions.

"Sontje, I will return in a moment. Let me get the surgeon. Say nothing more about Gerhard, please."

Sontje is placed in quarantine the same day. Since Griet's passing, Albert shows more concern for the rest of us, perhaps worried the Company could lose more of its investment on this first journey carrying females to the colonies.

I busy myself with cleaning our room, rearranging my few items so I feel the berth is my own. I open Sontje's Bible, left on her hammock, and I stare hard at the inked marks on the page, as though my efforts could somehow reveal their meaning.

Madaleen visits me later that day. Her cheeks look raw and red, her eyes wide.

"Your skin is dry, Madaleen. I have some wool oil." I take the salve from my trunk and scrape my fingernail across the jarred ointment. She tilts her chin up at me and closes her eyes as I rub the grease into her skin. She looks younger than her twelve years, savoring my ministrations. Her face upturned, eyes closed, I think suddenly of Helena. An ache in my stomach that is not this listing ship.

"Are you well?" I close the jar and place it in my small trunk.

She nods but her lip trembles.

"What is it?"

"Sontje."

"She is ill, but she will get better," I reassure her.

"No. Not that." Madaleen hesitates and looks down at her *klomps*. A blue flower painted at the toe of one of them. Red on the other. "I overheard Agatha and Catherina."

I wait. That is usually the best way to invite someone to talk.

"They say terrible things about her."

"What things?"

"I don't want to tell." She glances up at me, then back to the flowers on her *klomps*. "That Sontje leaves at night. To see Gerhard."

I have learned to hold my face quite still. Fader taught me how. I found if I showed no fear, no sadness after a beating, he would stop, too frustrated to prove his power over me. Too lazy to convince even himself.

I use that skill now.

"It's not true," I say and I flatten my voice. "Best not to say anything to anyone, though. You know how those two hens gossip."

Madaleen nods, relieved, for even at her age, she knows the wrongness of coveting another's husband. The men are always blameless, simply acting on their natures.

"Can we play dolls?" she asks. She keeps Drika in the pocket of her apron and pulls her from it now.

"Of course." I'm relieved to have the distraction, though my mind returns again and again to Madaleen's words. Sontje never looked at Gerhard when we saw him on deck. And Gerhard is so different from Hans—black-haired and thinly bearded, though he has a haughtiness around his eyes when he smiles. Another one not to be trusted. Before her illness, Sontje said nothing of Gerhard. But always, she retains some secret part of herself. As though she possesses another world within. Indeed, her secret self is what draws me to her.

I recall Tobias Levy said the same thing of me.

Chapter 35

When Sontje returns from quarantine two weeks later, she is thinner, even more pale. Her skin hangs loose from her bones and her cheekbones protrude, but her eyes shine as before. She bears the quiet triumph of someone who has won a hard battle. Even Maritjen regards her with new respect—few survive the fever. Strangely, Sontje's hair has grown thicker in these weeks and she piles her flaxen locks in a plump bun at the top of her head, wraps a strip of old muslin around it, and no longer bothers with the intricate braids and knots the other women labor over, taking short breaks between braiding to rest their aching arms.

She insists on resuming her share of the chores, so I finish them as she naps. She sleeps hard now, like an old dog. Her body thirsts for rest. I empty the chamber pot, sweep the rat droppings and dust the floor with a broom whose handle comes loose as I sweep. I clear the spider webs and fetch seawater to wash the floors.

She wakes when the ship sways and my mopping pail topples over.

"You seem to sleep better now," I say, as she sits up in her hammock.

"I've earned it," she says, rubbing her eyes. "The fever freed me. In my delirium, I felt as though I was drifting further and further away from my old life in Amsterdam. I stopped missing everything, and thought only of getting better, battling this fever, keeping the water in my body. There is nothing like illness to wrest you into the present." She pauses. "It was a terrible sort of gift. I'm thankful to be back."

"Thankful to be back here to empty the chamber pots? To eat more salt pork and rock-hard biscuits?" I put away the pail and sit down in my hammock to resume my sewing. I'm making a dress for Madaleen's Drika, using a bit of cloth Albert found and gave me on one of my visits to the deck.

"Yes, even that," she says, presenting a weary smile. "I'm toughened now, like our hard tack. Now I know I can survive."

She cannot love me, not as she loved Hans. I know what I am. Poor and plain with scars on my back and hands and skirts blackened and threadbare at the knees from spending so many hours kneeling on floors. But I can show her kindness. Kindness and generosity are my only charms and I lavish them on her.

I put down my sewing. "I saved these for you," I say, pulling from my trunk four dried figs I received from the cook. I give the knobs to Sontje, though my mouth aches with hunger for them.

She takes the figs and chews one, closing her eyes to enjoy the sensation of something different than our usual provisions. She swallows and looks to me.

"Why do you do so much for me?" she asks suddenly.

I cut my sewing thread with my teeth so I have a moment to consider my response.

Some part of me wishes to confess my feelings, but I'm afraid. "Your father was kind to me when no one else was," I say instead. "And I have the habit of being in your service."

"But remember how you once scolded me for not doing my chores?"

I smile. "That is true."

"You pity me." Her face hardens.

"No."

"I could not stand it if you did," she says. "I already feel so different from everyone else on this ship. I have felt closer to you than the others because you see me."

"I try."

"Then know I cannot stand pity. Yours most of all, when you have been a good friend. Give me tasks to do. Chide me for my laziness." A fierceness enters her gaze I've not seen before. "I'm stronger for the fever, for Hans's breaking of the betrothal, for Fader's shameful, drunken death. It took me so long to realize it, but now I know."

I think of my own trials. The Ringhouse and Fader and De Graaf's lesser violations. I envy Sontje her strength. "I'm glad for that, Sontje. You sound stronger than I've seen you."

"I feel stronger," she says. "The things you've endured. Do you feel stronger for them?"

I feel a lightness now that she is back in our little berth. I imagine myself with her in her hammock. She is so close. And still, I'm fixed in place.

"No. They have only made me more afraid." Though I wish I could say otherwise.

Chapter 36

Seven months. We are rationing the water now. One half-cup of water per day. The water teems with small worms, but we are so thirsty we drink it anyway. Food is also in low supply and hunger makes us irritable. The bread is more maggot than bread. We have no fruit. Just a bit of salt pork and those merciless biscuits. The hunger remains with us always, like a companion we wish to be rid of. In my sleep, hunger invades my dreams, so in the middle of some childhood vision of the forest, I see a clawed animal in a tree, then realize the same animal is in my stomach, scraping from inside.

Sontje grows distracted at times, lost in thought, and my old jealousy returns—she is thinking of Hans or Gerhard. Colored by my envy for these men, I find fault with her constantly. The delicate curl of her fingers around the water cup seems forced, unnecessary for the roughness of life on the *Leyden*. The sound of her breathing, which I have always loved, now grates on me for its steadiness and quiet. Her natural grace reminds me of my own deficiencies—my heavy steps, my awkward ambling on our vessel. Her occasional cough sounds needlessly loud and guttural. Such is the problem of the required closeness of our journey—my desire for her remains along with a buried, abiding resentment as well.

But now, I'm too hungry and tired even to remember the names of those I saw every day in Amsterdam. What was the name of the butcher's apprentice? The fruit peddler with the long yellow hair and horse's face who never showed her teeth when she smiled? Amsterdam feels like another life, and the person I was when I spoke to those forgotten people retreats, as though readying to disappear.

One night, when I am particularly impatient with her complaining, and after a quarrel over the chamber pot, we ready for bed and lie back on our hammocks.

"Sontje, do you feel you know yourself?" I ask out of frustration, but also curiosity. I often look forward to these nightly conversations as sleep weighs down our eyelids and we talk of things we would not discuss in daylight, or among others.

She is quiet. I like knowing her only by the sound of her voice. Being a plain and unremarkable child, I often wished we could be only bodiless voices, unattached to our imperfect forms. But then, I reasoned, our voices would become the source for our appraisals, and my voice is as unexceptional as the rest of me. A voice that sounds like many others and can hold only the simplest of tunes.

"No," she says after some time. "I don't think it's possible. I know I like *olykoeks* on Sunday mornings and yellow tulips and rose-dyed silk dresses. And I revile loud men in alehouses and people who walk too slowly in narrow streets and this godforsaken ship where we must waste so much time. But still I'm often surprised at my own thoughts and actions. Especially now."

"Which actions?" And I think maybe she will tell me something of her nightly departures or Gerhard.

"*Helaas*, this journey has made me do things I don't understand. Or perhaps it was Fader dying or Hans marrying that Delft girl. Or knowing I'm set to marry some stranger in a place I know nothing about. Who knows what compels our actions in the end? But I often feel restless. As though I'm trying to feel everything I can now, because life will be so different when we arrive in Batavia."

She grows quiet again.

"I worry I have committed great errors," she says after some time.

"What errors?" I recall Griet's belief that her parents' deaths owed to her faults, and think of finally asking Sontje directly about Gerhard. But I feel afraid. Some part of me still does not wish to know.

"I have done things Sontje of Amsterdam would never do. But Sontje of the *Leyden* is a different girl altogether. Hungrier, I suppose."

"It is all the hard tack and lack of water," I say and she laughs. We listen for a moment to the sloshing of waves against the hull. A friendly sound now after so many months at sea.

"Do you know yourself, Jana?"

"I've never had so much time to think about it. I was always working. But on this ship I think of it more."

"And? Who are you?"

I pause, wondering how to answer. I have thought on this, but have been afraid to share with anyone. "I think I'm the waves when they are calm and the *meerkoets* in our old canals and a lost *klomp* I once saw in a bush and the demon fish the sailors slaughtered all those weeks ago."

"Jana, you are a strange one." But I know she is smiling because her voice lightens.

We recall life in Amsterdam, a time I made candied quinces but used salt instead of sugar, and how Master Reynst tried to spare my feelings by praising them nonetheless. Soon our voices trail off into sleep.

She leaves later that night, though. And when she returns, she is limping.

"Sontje?" I whisper into the darkness.

But I hear no reply.

Chapter 37

"Sontje, you must bathe. I will help you."

For days after that night, she remains in her hammock, her back turned. She refuses to face me or to change her dress. She has stopped crying, which was not even sobbing. Too quiet for that. Just a silent, steady tide of tears for days. She still says nothing. Doesn't bother to tie up her hair. She pisses through her dress, until her urine dribbles onto the floor. The stink is so terrible, I finally ask the cook for a copper pail to place beneath her.

I pull her from the hammock. Her eyes are still dead and vacant.

She is awake, but her body remains listless. I pull her foul dress from her body, then the petticoats, which are stained and sticky. I recall the bright petticoats nestled in her trunk when we first embarked—she was so particular about her undergarments. Now I'm cleaner than she.

I can't help but observe her long body, which I have never seen stretched out this way. She says nothing, just looks at me as I survey her skin. A mole peeks above her breast and I note the gentle slope of her ribs to the deep hollow of her white stomach. Even in this condition, bruised and frail, I wish to kiss the tops of her shoulders, to taste her skin from neck to knee.

I fill another copper tub with seawater, which is warmer than I thought it would be. Sontje winces as I walk her to the tub. She sits in the water, eyes still empty. I sponge her body with a torn bit of my bloomers as she squats, mute and indifferent.

The bruises bloom like black roses on her shoulders. On her back. The water drips onto her caved stomach. Someone's fingerprints are stamped bruises on the back of her neck and I'm reminded of the thumbprints branded on me when I first arrived at the Reynsts'. Rage fills my body, a desire to bring such roses to her assailant's skin.

"Now I will wash your neck," I say, keeping my voice steady and soft, in spite of my anger. "Now I will wash your back." I explain as I wash each part of her, as though by my naming efforts I can help her reclaim what he, or they, took.

"I'm washing your elbow, Sontje."

"I'm washing your breasts."

Even covered in bruises, her body is beautiful. White beneath the bruises, graceful and long-boned. Slim-hipped. Her waist narrowed from the stays. I would trace my lips across her shoulders, simply to replace those scratches with tenderness. To remind her she is more than the bite marks imprinted at the top of her right arm. I feel a swell of protectiveness and awe at her nakedness, every bruise and crusting scab proof of the body's desire to heal and reawaken. We all have this hidden seedling desire to survive.

Though I have never sung to anyone but Helena, I sing to Sontje now. My voice is low and tuneless. Fader called it the howling of a she-wolf when he once heard me singing to the trees.

The girl plays with little things
That will serve in her kitchen.

Moeder taught me the song. I thought nothing of it then, just simple words. Did not think how she meant to prepare me for a life of serving others, and only scant play. With little things.

I remove the words and hum only the melody for Sontje.

And then I dress her wounds.

Madaleen tells me later that she ventured to the upper deck to see the stars on that clear night. Then she heard the men's drunken calls and jumped into the nearby rescue vessel. Peeking out from the longboat's cloth tarp, she heard Sontje first. Then saw her in the moonlight, how the men clutched at her elbows, moved her to a darker place on deck.

"I couldn't watch. Only heard them grunting and tussling with her. But I knew it was something terrible. I saw at least five of them. And she is so weak now, since her fever." She looks at me, ready to cry. "I was so afraid. She will hate me for being there and not doing anything."

"You're just a girl, Madaleen. You can't be expected to do anything. Do you know who they are?"

"No," Madaleen replies. "I didn't see their faces." But I know she is too afraid to remember.

For the days following her attack, I can't help but imagine the details of that night. When I'm washing the floor of our berth, or looking at the glittering waves, even when I'm recalling some trivial detail of my old life to Agatha, who is forever asking tedious questions to pass the time, the images interrupt. The men pull up her skirts. Their eyes glazed, hungry. Seven months at sea. The salt pork almost gone, the water nearly finished. But here is a hunger they can feed. Sontje's faraway gray eyes, too frightened to cry. The men arguing over who goes first. Whether it's best to be first or last and whether she'll last long enough for all of them. They probably decided on rank in the end—the Company has trained them well. The boatswain. The steersman. The second steersman. The third. The fourth. The fifth. Perhaps two cabin boys at the end, to prove their budding manhood.

Only Madaleen hidden in the longboat and a sliver of moon to bear witness.

Chapter 38

Maritjen and Agatha chatter outside Agatha's berth as I head for the deck. The breeze sends me their words, and I stop to listen.

"They are always together in their berth. They don't even ask us to be with them," Maritjen huffs.

"They've known each other so long. Even before the *Leyden*. I'm sure they don't mean anything by it. And they are also close to Madaleen."

"You don't think it odd that they spend so much time alone? Sometimes I see Jana looking at her in a way that seems... too devoted. Even for the best of friends."

"Whatever do you mean?" I imagine Agatha furrowing her brow. She looks sour when she is puzzled. "Really, Maritjen. You should have been a *rederijker* the way you concoct stories."

"Except they don't accept women."

"That's true of most things. We're only good for cleaning and birthing and cooking." I'm heartened to hear such bitterness from Agatha. Perhaps she was always like this, and the discomfort of our journey has brought her anger to surface.

"Tying ribbons in our hair. Darning stockings." Maritjen laughs.

"Gossiping," Agatha replies. At this, I smile. She is not often so needling. A wave of gratitude at her loyalty fills me, and Maritjen grows silent.

*

"Better that Sontje remains in the berth anyway," Maritjen says to Catherina as we play draughts in the evening. "She's been sick for so long. She's fortunate she has such a devoted nurse in you, Jana. One could not hope for such a generous friend. Like sisters. More than sisters."

Maritjen looks at me in challenge, but I persist in playing as though nothing has happened.

"I can't imagine she wants anyone to see her, after the incident," Agatha whispers.

"What do you mean?" I ask her. I did not realize they knew.

"She was attacked by the men," Agatha says, unable to hide her pleasure in sharing the secret. Catherina nods in agreement. I have the sudden desire to lash out at these two simple, tittering girls but I'm not certain what I could say that would hurt them most.

"How do you know?" I ask.

"I heard it from someone." She casts a sidelong glance at Maritjen. "But that would explain why she won't see anyone." Agatha sniffles, a frequent and unbecoming sound that makes me glad I'm not her berth-mate.

"She brought it upon herself." Maritjen snorts and lifts her brows, looking uglier than usual. She has lost a tooth on the voyage, and now covers her mouth with her hand when she smiles.

The sisters nod.

"Unmarried women are always a problem," Maritjen continues.

Now the sisters are silent.

"I don't mean you, though," Maritjen adds quickly, "but marriage tames our wilder instincts. I know it's true of me. 'A wife not proud of her high birth/Yet from a line of solid worth.' My friend back in

Haarlem told me that one." Maritjen is smiling again because she has covered her mouth with her hand.

"And the men are always blameless," I can't help but say as Catherina moves her piece. I'm tired of these women, their rumors and stories, and weary of pretending to be like them. "They are allowed their lusts and cravings, while we must have the virtue of Ruth. It has always seemed an injustice."

The sisters look at me and then at Maritjen. But I've not eaten properly in days, and I have stopped caring what they think of me.

"Oh Jana," Maritjen says with mock frustration. "Always so angry. Your husband in Batavia will have some work to do."

Chapter 39

Sontje lies in her hammock at midday, staring at the knothole above that permits the moonlight at night. She opens and closes one eye at a time.

"If I close my right eye and look at the hole with my left, the sky is more blue," she says, finally. She blinks her eye open and closed. "I've never noticed that before."

It's the first time she's spoken to me in many days, so I say nothing and wait for her to say more.

"It's a little gift. If I want to see a grayer sky, I can look out my right eye. If I want a blue sky, I look out of my left."

I sit next to her on her hammock, so I'm under the knothole too. I haven't been close to her like this since I bathed her weeks ago.

I cover my left eye with my hand and look out the oval hole.

"It looks the same color to me." The sky is a blue I saw maybe twice growing up in the forest. A summer-blue.

"Maybe that is my magical spell," Sontje says. "When I was a girl, I heard a story about the winter witch, and I believed we all had a magical spell or power. Every night I would pray I could discover mine. Maybe I could travel into the past and meet my mother. Or maybe I could use a spell so I could fly. I prayed and prayed, but I never found it. Never found my magical power." A tear rolls from her eye and across her left temple.

I smell the sweetness of her along with the sharpness of her sweat. Sunlight glows on her cheek. She wears only her sleeveless underdress because the air is sticky and warm, like a suffocating, unwieldy blanket. The bruise on her shoulder heals slowly from poor food or her pale skin, but has finally faded to a faint yellow. In the circle of light through the knothole, Sontje remains beautiful. Even lovelier than the sea.

I don't even think.

Or perhaps I don't allow myself to think.

I'm tumbling into this moment without thought. And I'm always so full of thoughts, as Tobias observed. But so close to her, I become someone else. Someone whose thoughts follow after. As a maid, I'm accustomed to keeping my reactions inside.

Yes, Madam, I will polish the silver.

Yes, Master, I will scrub the floor.

Now my mouth finds the faded yellow patch on her shoulder. Her skin feels moist and warm, and smells differently up close. Like something new. I kiss her again, just below the bruise. She remains still, but tears roll down her face, gathering in her loose hair. I kiss her skin down the length of her still-bruised arm. Every part smells a bit different from the last. Closer to her neck I smell the tang of her underarms, at the inside of her elbow I smell a sweetness that reminds me of Early Dutch honeysuckle. The inside of her wrist smells of clay. The crooked tip of her little finger smells of the saltwater we use to clean the floors and linens. I kiss this part of her, cold and brittle against my mouth.

"Sontje," I say, moving my face toward hers, and speaking softly into her neck.

She says nothing.

Turns her lips to me.

*

Later at night, we lay our bedclothes and whatever sheets we can find to cover the floorboards. Petticoats and old dresses, double-folded blankets. I find scraps of old canvas that I've sewn together and we lay them one on top of the other, on top of everything else. Anything to mask the unevenness of the wood pressing into our backs, for in our hammocks we can only hold one another's hands.

The sea is still and the moon shines a shy beam through the hole so only a bit of silver finds us. In the light, Sontje is gold and silver. Treasure and bounty. We are kneeling on our self-made pallet, wearing only our underdresses.

"Your bruises are nearly healed," I say.

"You just can't see them in this light."

"Then I prefer to see you now. Like this."

"I look horrid in daylight."

"You are always beautiful." I brush her cheek with the back of my finger. She smiles a sadder smile than any I have seen before, even sadder than when Hans left her, or when Master Reynst died.

"Thank you, Jana." She weaves her fingertips through mine. Our knees touch and I feel as I did when I was a child, on the first day of spring when the sun would wake me. A warmth enters my skin and moves upward like the trilling skylarks from the grasslands of the Bos.

She takes my hand. "So cold."

"Always," I say. "My sister complained about them, but welcomed them on her forehead when she was sick with fever."

Sontje's fingertips are soft like the daisy petals Helena plucked and showered over my head. *See, now you've made it rain.*

She traces my jaw, my neck, my shoulders, the shallow slope of my breast, the stirring nipple.

My hands follow hers, upon her. Tracing and tracing. Sontje's sharp collarbone. Sontje's gentle shoulders. A shudder between us.

Now we are shaking.

Now we can't breathe.

"How is it that I feel both cold and hot?"

"I feel the same," she says.

We kneel in front of each other and I've forgotten everything. This swaying ship. Helena. The dreary tasks of my life before this journey—the *passglasses* to be polished. The stew meat to cleave from the slick, bleeding bones. The *volkorenbroden* to deliver in Adelheid's uneven basket, and chamber pots to empty. The water to carry and heat and use sparingly to avoid unnecessary trips to the well. Only her lips on mine, searching. Only our breathing. Our closed eyes. Our shared tongues.

We move slowly. I'm careful of Sontje's hidden bruises and I wish to taste her again and again. The skin of her neck, her sharp ribs, the trail of moles along her thigh. She is softer than anything I have known.

The inlaid tulips and leaves, the flickering candle. The crumbling stones.

All disappear.

Even time.

Chapter 40

In the morning, I breathe into Sontje's neck, warm from the shaft of sunlight through the beams. *Will she hate me now? Feel ashamed of what we did?*

She keeps her eyes closed, but when I take her hand, she tightens her fingers around mine.

"Sometimes I try not to open my eyes. Pretend I'm still sleeping," she says, stretching against me. I inhale the lavender water on her neck once more. The flask is near empty, so she uses it sparingly.

"I always open my eyes with a start, thinking of everything I have to do that day, every worry I have."

"What worries?" Sontje asks.

"What it will be like in Batavia. If I'll wish to return home." Though I try not to think of the point of this journey and simply live each day as it comes, I can't help but worry about the husband I'll meet at the end of this. Especially now.

"Best not to consider it a possibility."

"True, and I don't really. I think I'll love it there, the newness of it, at least."

"You do? What do you know of it?" She kisses the underside of my arm and I'm flooded with relief.

"I met someone before we left. He sailed there a few times. Told me of the trees, the sun, the fruits, the ocean. Strange insects and animals. Lizards that change color to match the trees."

"Someone? You haven't mentioned him," she says. "A beau?"

"Just a man," I say and kiss her long neck again.

"I've never seen a lizard."

"I've seen snakes. But only common adders. Mean things, and small. Once one crawled into my *klomps* when I left them outside."

Sontje shivers. I stroke the top of her arm and she presses herself into me.

"This thing we've done… it's a sin, isn't it?" she asks. "After all, our bodies belong to our future husbands, whoever they may be."

I kiss her thin shoulder. "Maybe… but we hurt no one by it." I can't help but feel bitterness—the fact of my body's ownership passing from hand to hand—my father's pummeling, the other men with their pawing and leering, as though I existed only for their gaze. All the exacting employers who have required tireless labor from me. Only Tobias gave thought to my own wishes. And since Griet's death and Sontje's attack, I care less about our sins, when the men commit ones much greater than ours.

Sontje sighs, once more stretching her body against mine. "And yet, I feel a lightness I've not felt in so long." She takes my hand before falling back to sleep.

Chapter 41

We will soon port at Table Bay. Everyone is merry. Relieved we've made it this far. Maritjen keeps her hand over her mouth more than usual for she is smiling so much. Madaleen stays with us in our berth, asking so many questions. What do you think the Cape looks like? Do you think it will be difficult to walk on land again? What are you most looking forward to eating?

The men tell stories. So accustomed to my presence on deck, they no longer make any effort at politeness around me. They talk about the "bonny savages," raising their eyebrows and smiling. Slapping one another on the backs.

"I hear they will do whatever pleases you for a broken lice comb and some tinsel."

"They don't even know it's broken. Just bring some bits of metal and they'll be ready."

"Ugly little things, but they'll do. Backsides like nothing you've seen before. Good if you like a woman with flesh. Just don't look at them or you'll go limp."

"Think of them as livestock. Feed them and do what you will." The men snicker and nod their unkempt heads.

"I was never this desperate back in Naarden."

"I've heard otherwise!" More laughter.

Table Bay is so called for the flat-topped mountain we see in the distance. On that final day I stand on deck as long as I can, but we must take turns because so many of us want to see. The water near the Cape is an otherworldly blue. Richer, bluer than mere water, and evokes in me both melancholy and joy. And then I recall where I've seen its familiar color— it's the same hue as my favorite cheerful turquoise-painted house in Dam Centre.

A flattened cloud stretches over Table Mountain, its edges like long fingers pulling us forward, beckoning. I'm surprised to see two other ships in the harbor and I wonder if our *Leyden* looks as worn as those, with their patched sails, chipped and splintered hulls.

The land looks dry. No trees, just shrubbery in greenish patches in the distance. But we laugh and smile, taking turns watching the land come toward us. I can hardly remember what earth feels like underfoot. To walk without holding on to anything, without having to bend my knees at all times.

Madaleen takes my hand as she watches the shore approach. Her palm is moist in mine, and with her other, she holds her little doll Drika, now missing one eye and patches of hair. The doll's dress is now gray where it was once bright yellow. Sontje has tied a small scrap across Drika's missing eye and calls her Pirate Drika to make Madaleen laugh.

"We are almost to land, Drika," Madaleen whispers. "See the mountain with the strange flat top? That is where we will be." She releases my hand to point out the jutting form in the distance, then recovers my grasp.

"No," Madaleen whispers to Drika. "It isn't the end of the journey quite yet, but it will be a safe place, and we can finally walk on land."

*

Those first steps on the sand feel so odd. My feet are used to the *Leyden's* irregular wood planks, the blunted square nailheads underfoot, and relentless swaying of water. The giving of the sand feels almost like the ocean, but nothing else moves. I wait for the mountain before us to bob up and down as though nodding its head. But of course, it sits still, and I wonder at the miracle of its stillness when I used to know little else.

We kick off our *klomps*, which we've donned for the first time in months. Press our toes into the sand, feel the grit under our overgrown toenails. The unmoving earth surprises us all.

"I keep waiting for it to move," Sontje says, taking my hand.

I squeeze her hand in reply but quickly release it, thinking of Maritjen's gossip. We've spoken little about our nights together on the *Leyden.* What's the use in discussion? We belong to each other only in our berths.

Outside, I feel no safety with her.

The Cape Station is nothing at all. Just a bit of beach, some dusty traders and natives without teeth or proper clothing. The trees are bigger than any I've seen back home, with gnarled trunks and waxy, oblong leaves. Milkwood, the sailors call them. Sugar bushes—ugly, spiny flowers with small petals, like overgrown thistle. Nothing like our full-blossoming tulips and roses. One small building made of mud where we can get supplies of fresh vegetables and water and where traders bring their loads and haggle over what they have brought.

Small tents and huts surround the main station. This is where we will stay for the next two weeks to unload cargo, make repairs to the *Leyden,* and rest. Sontje and I share a cabin with Catherina and Agatha here, and I miss our little berth, and the bed we made there.

"How nice it is to get off that *verdomme* ship," Agatha says. She has already traded a half-used jar of face cream for a basket of fruit and a small terracotta cup. I've never heard her curse before, but she has learned from the sailors.

"Just to smell something other than rotted fish is a miracle," Catherina agrees.

Though I miss the *Leyden,* I can see it at port, looking smaller than the two other *retourships*. On our first morning on land, I leave our tent to gaze upon it—the pocked hull, patchwork sail, and great mast puncturing the sky. A beloved place where I felt some freedom for being so enclosed. I'm sad to see it from this vantage point when I have been part of it for so long.

On that humble vessel I have left everything I knew before, except Sontje.

Sontje avoids looking at the *Leyden,* never speaks of it. After her attack, she spent most of the journey in our berth. The sailors treated the rest of us with greater formality and politeness, too, and I wonder if Albert chastised them or if their own blackened consciences compelled their better manners.

She is afraid of the other travelers, also from Amsterdam, who embarked on the same journey sometime after us but arrived earlier, and could hear gossip from the other *Leyden* passengers.

"Some of them may know of me," she says. "Of what happened that night on the *Leyden.*"

I try to reassure her. "No one will speak of it because the men know they can be punished for what they did. The Company is strict about such things. I overheard some of the sailors discussing an incident at sea that was punished here at the Cape. A boatswain was whipped and stripped of his title for his sinful acts." The act itself the sailors failed to utter, but Sontje raises her eyebrows in question. "And what happened to the... other person?"

"That I don't know. But try not to worry, Sontje. No one will say anything. You are the same beautiful woman who first boarded the *Leyden* ten months ago." But even as I reassure her, I know this not to be true. I'm not the same Jana Beil who boarded the *Leyden*, after all.

"No," she says sadly. "I'm a different creature altogether. As you said when we first started this journey, it is better not to remember that other life."

We have time to explore the area as the men unload the *Leyden*. I'm surprised at how difficult freedom is at first. So used to the cramped spaces of the ship, the outside seems too vast at times, too easy to get lost in. The great trees here are fuller in their leaves and branches, and throaty, fearless birds hide within them. They make our own little Dutch birds seem like timid insects.

Weep weep. Weep weep. The birds command. But we can't see them for the thickness of the tree cover.

In the evening, the sun lowers and the air cools. The men retreat to their cabins for meals and entertainment, which consists of draughts and singing, and most often, women. They bring the native women back to their tents—stocky Khoisan women who wear scant clothing. I have never seen skin of such colors—the color of clay or wet beach sand, or a warm red nearly like earthen bricks. I must stop myself from staring at all the colors. We Dutch must seem a tiresome array of pinks in comparison.

The native women wander around the camp, many with infants—some curiously light-skinned—bound to their backs, others carrying outsized bundles of grasses for thatching or clothing to be laundered.

They have the same weariness I recognize in myself from my days as a servant—a sense of surrender to the day's boundless tasks.

The men yell and grunt so loudly from the tents, so joyful at the fulfillment of their primal desires, we cover our ears in embarrassment. That is when Sontje and I decide to leave the camp and explore further afield.

Sontje glances back at the men's tents as we leave. "I feel sorry for the women," she says. "They must think us vile."

"Not us, only our men. I have heard the sailors themselves say there are no Ten Commandments south of the equator. Here, they act as if no reckoning exists."

Sontje shakes her head. "They must resent us. For not attending to our men."

"I doubt they think of us at all." The women look at us without curiosity or pity. Their efforts are sharpened only on the task of surviving; all other emotions become flies to shoo away. I have known that life myself.

On the second evening of our grounding, Sontje and I walk to the watering hole just beyond the settlement. Few people bathe at this time. The air is cooler and the mosquitoes rise up in great humming clouds, but here we can be alone. We invite Catherina and Agatha, knowing they will refuse. They are taken with the few other Dutch women who arrived on the other two ships and they visit each other's tents and prattle on about the homeland.

At the banks of the small lake we remove our clothing. I watch as Sontje unties her stays and removes her petticoats, the shadow of tree branches glancing off her body.

"How lovely you are," I say.

"You, too, Jana."

But I laugh. "You are blind to say so. I'm your opposite—dark where you are fair, short where you are long, broad where you are slim."

"I love the brownness of your skin, how strong you are." She takes my hand and places it on her warm breast.

We wade into the pool. The coolness is a gift.

We stay close to the banks because we don't know how to swim. Slick grasses brush against our skin and wind around our ankles. We hold hands as we wade deeper into the water. Past our hips. Past our lean, underfed bellies. Just to our nipples, which harden in surprise. We splash quietly. Look at one another and say nothing. With Sontje there is no worry. She has spent so many silent days with me in our berth. We have no need to speak anymore.

The moonlight widens its beam over us. The long cocksfoot grasses at the banks become black silhouettes. The darkness emboldens the surrounding insects and birds. They chirp and screech and hiss and whistle, claiming this place as their own.

"Gerhard told me a story about how he became a sailor," Sontje finally says. We have never spoken of him before, not since her feverish ravings on the *Leyden*, so her words are a revelation. "He was walking home one night when he was a young boy in Delft, and he met an old fisherman. He said the man had a face like a demon's. Long, black teeth and red, trembling hands. He said it was the most awful scare, but the fear he felt is what made him want to go to the sea—a sense that the world was more magical than he had thought."

"As children even frightening experiences can seem magical," I reply. And then I ask her. "You were seeing him, Sontje?"

She waits a moment, as though unsure whether to tell me. "Yes, at night. I resented Maritjen with all her boasting about her dear husband Gerhard, and he flirted with me from the start. I missed that feeling of being desired. All my life I've felt like an inconvenience to Fader, and then Hans came and paid me such compliments. I was hungry for more of it." She sighs. "I was a stupid girl. As though it is such a wondrous thing for a man to want us. Now I feel it a curse."

I think of my own long-buried desire for her, but say nothing.

We stand still, chest-deep in the water, listening to our breaths.

"And you, Jana. You've been ever faithful. You're even on this horrid voyage across the world with me. And why? You could have moved to Bruges or Leiden or Haarlem. Why go on this journey?"

"I wanted something different," I say, and feel the moment has come to confess my feelings. That I have desired her for so long. That I am on the *Leyden* because of her.

But I'm afraid.

"But there are so many places in Europe. And then you could return to Amsterdam if you didn't like them. No need for a ten-month journey and endless suppers of worm-filled bread."

"I worried something might happen to you."

"That is far beyond what is expected of a domestic." She smiles, her teeth a bright flash in the moonlight.

"Yes," I admit.

We remain in that tight silence, allowing the water to enclose us and for the darkness to make us different people. In the night, our clothes become unsoiled, our hands lose their cracked appearance from the dryness and salt. Our nails become smooth, clean, trimmed, not ragged and blackened with dirt that embeds underneath them and in the whorls of our fingerprints. Our skin no longer smells of the salt we eat and breathe. I lick my fingertip to see if the dream is true.

I taste salt.

I now know the hungry sound of her breathing in sleep, as though her long breaths demand more space than the rest of her. She laughs in her sleep and sometimes even speaks in nonsense sentences. Her voice in sleep is higher, happier than when she is awake.

"I have thought your feelings for me were strong," she finally says. "That perhaps I was the reason you came."

I try to ignore my sinking heart, the sick feeling blooming within at my exposure. But after all she has endured, how can she bother with such treacly sentiments? She is like an injured animal nursing its wounds in a cave, to be drawn out slowly and with tenderness. I fear making a declaration, for the burden Sontje might feel knowing I came on the *Leyden* to be with her, and that I worked so hard for it.

My thoughts change shape, circle to square to rectangle, as I imagine her reactions. Will she feel disgust? Will she wish never to see me again? Or wish she had not asked me to join her?

But pleasure lies in the possibility of her response. That I could reveal something so close to my own heart, when for all my life I have hidden my feelings under the cumbersome need to survive. Men shoving my head into the pallet as they entered me, or pawing at my shoulder, or caressing me gently when I did not wish to be touched at all, or forcing their tongues in my mouth, so I choked and coughed. I have not had the strength to refuse others' desires, nor the fearlessness to declare my own.

This feeling of love or lust or whatever it is, shameful and consuming, also permits me to see myself in a new way. Jana Beil, who can now feel a swell of joy at the wind moving through trees, or a flock of unknown birds alighting on a rooftop. I feel alive in a way I haven't felt before, noticing beauty in the smallest and most unlikely of things—my own reflection in a silver pitcher, the light reflecting off the waves when the sea is calm.

"I came on the *Leyden* to be with you," I finally say, as a ripple of water kisses my collarbone, but I am more afraid of my confession than of the water so close to my face. "I had to threaten Master De Graaf to get me on the ship, because Master Coen said the ship was already full." I wonder if she can hear my heart, through the gentle lake's tide between us.

Her hand encircles mine in the water. "I'm not as afraid as I thought I would be," Sontje says of standing in the lake, though she holds strongly to my hand.

I wait for her response. I don't wish to force an answer, when so much has been forced on her already. "In our months on the *Leyden*, we have come to know water, if nothing else."

We slide closer together, and that is answer enough. Our skin slick and cool, as we hold one another against the feeble current.

Listening.

Afterward, we lie upon the banks. We gather one another in our naked arms, and I feel free with Sontje under the cover of tree branches and darkness. I'm surprised and happy she's so forward, as though we are on the *Leyden* again. We kiss. The slick, coarse, circle, stink, stone, flower, white, seashell, blossom, blush, pit, bone, straw, fire, line, snow, meat, air, breath, and bruise of one another.

Chapter 42

We lie still in the copse by the lake for some time on the banks and then some creature moves in the darkness, crackling against the brush. I turn closer to Sontje, still naked and cool from the water disappearing off our skin in the breeze. And then we are kissing for so long I think I've stopped breathing, when she turns away from me for a moment. Disappears within herself as she sometimes does since her attack on the *Leyden*.

"You are thinking about that night, aren't you?" I ask.

She is silent.

A cricket's rhythmic summoning sounds nearby.

"I think I understand it a little." I'm full of nerves, and worry I may vomit if I tell her. But I force myself, to show her this ugliest part of myself because it may help her. "It has happened to me. Before I worked for you and your father. And it nearly happened again thereafter."

Still, she says nothing. And I feel myself tremble. Perhaps she will be disgusted or will pity me.

"I had nowhere to go. I had lost my sister and could not return home—I was afraid of my father, could not tell them what had really happened to Helena. So I decided to walk and see where it led me. I slept out in the forest. Ate whatever I could find. Growing up in the

Bos, I knew where to find sourgrass and apples. Sometimes I'd come across a traveler or spinster living in the Bos and they would give me food…" And here, I falter. Afraid of how she will react, and if she will think differently of me.

Sontje's hand covers mine.

I continue.

"One traveler I met on the road from the Bos to Amsterdam promised there was work nearby. He offered to take me. He seemed nice enough. Gave me food he brought with him—*worst* and a cheese *taart*. I can't bring myself to eat either of those now. I often think, *if only I had not taken his* worst *and cheese* taart. He didn't bother to tell me what the work would be, but I followed his advice and I believed he was kinder still to take me to the building, a half day's walk from where he found me."

"You had no thought he could be dangerous?" Sontje asks, at last. I have asked myself this question many times, thinking I deserved what happened afterward for all my girlish innocence.

"If I did, I was too desperate to trust the thought. I felt so alone after Helena died… and in the Bos we knew only the few families living around us. We had no reason to distrust anyone but our useless father. I have turned this over and over in my mind and I try to find one moment where I could have chosen differently, but the girl I was then… I would have made the same choices."

"You are so different from her now. I can't imagine such a thing happening to you again."

"But it did," I say, thinking of the man, whose name I've forgotten, though I will never forget the cheese *taart* nor my stupidity in trusting him.

She says nothing to that. "And so he brought you to that place."

"Yes." I return to that dark memory. "And the proprietor was a woman, which I believed a good sign. Madam Aad. At first, I just cleaned the kitchen. I thought it was a boarding house, and I would save up so I could go elsewhere. I had no plans, only a desire to leave the Bos behind.

"And then one day, Madam Aad asked me to go to clean one of the upstairs rooms. And I went and knocked on the door…" At this memory, my voice feels strangled inside me. I'm unsure I can say more.

Sontje's eyes redden. She looks distant again. Her mind is probably back on the *Leyden,* on the deck with those men. I know because some part of me is always in that upstairs room of the Ringhouse.

"A man opened the door. He pulled me inside." I wish my voice would not shake, but it does. "I was too surprised even to exclaim or scream. Stunned like an animal. I wish I had screamed, so at least he knew how I hated it. But I was too afraid. And it would have made no difference."

Plump tears stream down Sontje's cheeks. They are not for me, but I feel I must finish.

"He was a heavy man. Coarse, dark hair all over him. He tore off my clothes. Madam Aad would give me a different dress after. One with lace and frills I had to repay her for. It's how they keep you in debt. Perhaps that is why I wore your mother's dress. Some part of me wanted to wear a dress with lace and ribbons and good stitching without thinking only of that time."

Sontje wipes her eyes. "Now I wish I had never scolded you for it. I'm sorry, Jana." But that is all in the past, so I say nothing more of it.

"He had a belt. He had fists. He had twine and leather cord. They make it as awful as possible first, so everything thereafter feels tolerable." And as I explain, I see each object. The hairy twine. The cord binding my wrists. His tobacco pipe on the night table. "He kept me for two days, to break me."

The flickering candle.

His great, hairy arm across my middle. Not an embrace. Another cage.

A cage within a cage within a cage. And still other cages ahead.

She waits. The crickets trill again.

"I stayed for nearly two years. Worked off the dress. And then one day, a girl went missing and Madam Aad left with her roughneck handlers to search for her in Amsterdam. I waited until night and escaped out the top window after a customer attacked me." Those were the thumbprint bruises on my hip and neck when I arrived at the Reynsts' green door days after my escape, the steps with their hungry crocuses. But I do not tell Sontje this. She did not see my bruises. "I nearly died that night. I felt more animal than person. Some small part of me wished to live. Even now, I'm not sure why."

"And then there was more after you left us?"

"When I worked at the De Graafs', Master De Graaf tried to, but I left before he could… take me." Even now, my employer's name feels like rotted meat that I must spit out.

A breeze. The leaves whisper and we listen. Sontje's hand in mine and inside us all our ugly, hidden feelings.

"It is a terrible thing. Like there is something hateful inside me I can't root out," Sontje says.

In the darkness, I can only vaguely see her eyes. I continue, though my heart strikes hard inside me, as though punishing me for all I've finally revealed.

"I can scarcely remember the Ringhouse now. My mind will not permit me. But I still have dreams. Objects on the floor, an abandoned tobacco pipe, playing cards. A feeling like I can't breathe. But I can't remember more than flashes of it."

"I feel that way sometimes now. Just a thought here and there, and then I'm hollowed out inside. Like every good feeling I've had is lost forever."

I nod. "It fades over time."

"How much time?"

"I do not yet know."

She laughs. "It's good you understand. I feel no one does. Like I'm all alone and every man I see is guilty."

"That doesn't end. The loneliness. The feeling of being hunted."

"Yes," she says. "Hunted is how I feel."

And somehow, even in this shared darkness in ourselves, we feel desire. Our mouths become all of us. Each other's tongues. I taste the lake water on Sontje's skin. Mineral, sour, faintly like the canals. I kiss down her leg. I press between my lips the hard tendon behind her heel and she laughs.

And then a sound.

"Did you hear something?"

"Yes." I kiss her once more and gather our clothes beside us. But we take our time dressing ourselves—if it were a man, he would have spoken by now.

Petticoats, stays, aprons. We tie each other into these layers of fabric.

Suddenly, a native woman stands behind us, holding a torch. A *strandloper*. Beachwalkers, the sailors call them because when they first encountered the natives, they were walking on the beach. So dark in the night I only see her outline. Short and thin. Her face all angles. Her eyes narrow like they are almost closed. Lips so thick I think of the plums I gathered in the forest. She stands still like one of the broad baobab trees growing nearby. As though she will never leave.

Sontje smooths down her skirts so they cover her knees again. I move slowly.

The woman waits for me to finish dressing. Fixes her small eyes on us. Sontje nods. Smiles. The woman's expression doesn't change.

She says something to us. A clicking sound. At first I feel the same revulsion toward her that the others feel toward the *strandlopers*, but then I wonder, is that *my* revulsion? Or is my distaste for her simply what I have learned from our men? As my eyes adjust to the darkness where she stands, I see her eyes are not small like pig eyes at all. They are thoughtful eyes. Eyes that see. Her voice is ugly in that stuttering speech of theirs, but then ours must sound just as strange. I try to imagine how Dutch must sound to her. Menacing? Absurd?

"I'm sorry," Sontje says, crouching down to her small stature. "We can't understand you."

But the woman hardly looks at Sontje. She watches me instead. Gestures for us to follow her into the darkness of the groves. She makes another series of clicks with her tongue.

"I don't think we should." Sontje rubs her collarbone with her thumb. A nervous habit she acquired on the *Leyden*.

"I think she's safe."

"But they'll be looking for us."

"No. They won't. The men are too drunk to care."

Sontje has no reply. She knows it's true.

We follow the woman into the groves. Different sounds surround us. Night sounds. Strange birds, groaning frogs, and the bare keening of animals I do not know, will never know. Above us, a stirring in the trees suggests the presence of animals overhead, larger than anything

I have seen in the Bos. Everything about this place feels menacing, but also, enchanted. If one must perish in a forest, this would be a forest fit for it. To be surrounded by such mystery at the end is a gift.

A giant insect darts across our path and Sontje gasps.

I take her hand.

The woman moves more quickly than we do on her small, unshod feet. But perhaps she can feel the path beneath, whereas we can't.

I'm pulling Sontje along past the bamboo and then through trees I don't recognize. Trees with great trunks and small, spindly branches with hardly any leaves. Trees full of spines that catch on our clothes. Orange flowering bushes, white cup-like flowers looking ghostly in the weak moonlight. Trees that mutter. Trees that moan. Trees that seem to follow behind us.

"Jana, we should go back," Sontje whispers.

But I ignore her. Something pulls me forward. Not a voice, but a feeling. I have felt this before. The time I found a bird's nest that had fallen from the branches, and Helena and I cared for the naked birds, wrapping them in moistened cloths, feeding them drops of water from Moeder's thimble. A quivering feeling within. A sense that I am where I should be.

The click-woman takes us to a red rock, a bit of green shrubbery outside. The forest retreats here, like the rock has pushed it away. She nods to us and ducks into the hole.

I stop at the entrance, just ten ells from the shrub.

"We should return to the camp," Sontje says again.

I say nothing. I can't move. Memory fixes me to this place, like the spider Fader once impaled with a stick. Just like that. He was always doing such things. Destroying simply for the joy of it. How the spider wiggled, confused, for moments earlier it was itself and alive, as it had been yesterday, the day before, the moment before.

The memory was not the spider. It was Helena. The spider impaled by the stick. Helena buried by the cave and then, finally, giving up.

Sontje pulls my hand. "We don't know her."

Helena held my hand when we entered the cave, and a memory emerges that I had forgotten. Only Sontje's hand in mine at this exact moment, at the entrance to this red cave, could stir up the memory of Helena's hand, sticky with tree sap because she never refrained from touching the trees as we walked, feeling for their different roughness, the smoothness or spiny needles of their varying leaves. *This is how I can remember them*, she would say.

The click-woman stops. She waits for us. Turns to see we are behind her. She clicks again, but not to us. It is as though she is speaking to the trees or the air. She seems to argue. She sighs, then continues forward.

"We don't have to go," Sontje says, full of doubt and fear. This is how she must have looked that night on the deck of the *Leyden*—forehead wrinkled, eyes wide.

"No, we must." I squeeze her hand. "Both of us."

The shrubs move. Something stirs inside them. She holds my arm with her other hand. Swallows.

"Jana—" she begins.

My heart beats quickly, like it is a separate creature from me. A few paces inside the cave and the outside world disappears. The walls look damp and alive, as though we are inside some slumbering creature. Sontje's hand grasps tightly around mine. Cold. The woman walks slower, continues to speak to air, the walls, the torch she holds.

"I wonder what she says," Sontje whispers.

"I think she is asking questions."

The click-woman scans the walls, and her flickering torch reveals figures painted on its craggy surface. Some appear to be animals, others both human and animal. One with the head of a cow or goat. Other human figures appear to be dancing, holding spears. Nothing like our paintings, all statements of wealth, plenty, prominence, or piety. These tell different stories. They seem to come from somewhere beneath the cave wall, and then to disappear.

I can't see the end of the cave. We walk slowly because the floor is uneven, full of slippery gravel. The woman seems to know where to take us. All the while she speaks in those curious clicks.

We pass handprints stamped on the walls, paintings of horned animals. Thin figures running in a line, holding pointed spears, and half-man half-beast creatures that recall our own stories of centaurs and harpies. How odd that these people have them, too. Is it human nature to imagine such fantastical creatures? Or perhaps such creatures once existed and then disappeared. Circles within circles, triangles, and straight lines in different patterns flank those human and animal figures. Hunting scenes not unlike our own. Figures gathering around a large animal.

I'm reminded of our paintings of fruit baskets, grazing cows, lace-making and lute-playing. All speak of different lives doing the everyday tasks that provide rest from our darker thoughts below the surface. I think of the small painting in Master De Graaf's study—a farm boy napping with his dog while sheep graze nearby. The lives of the poor made decorative, a way to announce one's wealth in Amsterdam. But here, the everyday becomes magical. Unchanging but hidden, as though their open display might rob these scenes of their force.

The air smells as though it has never been breathed. The click-woman stops. Turns to the wall. *Click.* She points a long finger at the figure. Nods as if to say, *This one.*

Three figures. Women. Those same rounded buttocks and stomachs. They stand in a line, facing us. Holding hands. Outside of this cave I would think these drawings primitive, childlike. I would recall Master De Graaf's painting of the skull and find it superior—how like reality, how meaningful in its symbols. Skulls and books and maps of the discovered world...

But in the silence of the cave, the darkness carved away by the click-woman's torch, these figures are more beautiful than any painting I have seen in the tasteful homes where I have cleaned, washed, dusted, folded, and tolerated others' abuses.

The women come alive. I think of some ancient hand that put them here. Why? Why this interior portion of the cave?

They look at us, waiting.

Sontje tightens her grip on my hand. She feels something also. Her tears come free. They drip off her chin and yet her face doesn't look sad. Nothing like her face during the weeks following that night on the *Leyden.*

The click-woman stands beside me. I'm between her and Sontje. The figures entrance the click-woman, too, as though she has not seen them before. In the flickering torchlight, the figures appear to move, as though they wish to speak to us.

The click-woman takes my hand and for a moment the flames still. Her hand is smooth. Cool. Her fingers curl around mine and I realize with shame at having denied the fact before: *Yes, they are human.* I had regarded them as something animal-like. The simple fact of their uncommon darkness, nakedness, and their strange language were all we required to make them something else. Something not us. But her hand is just like mine. More beautiful. Softer.

In this darkness we are the same.

I think again of Helena's hand, back in the cave, where we hid from the rainstorm. I left to find us some food when the storm eased, but when I returned, the cave's entrance had collapsed. I screamed for her, a voice I had never heard from myself. Emptiness and dread. The more I plunged my hands into the rubble, the less earth I managed to move. The linden berries I had picked for her lay strewn far afoot, soggy and abandoned. Only her hand in the rubble. I can see it now. Black dirt in her nail beds. The hangnail Helena pulled from her thumb, which left a bit of crusted blood.

I'm afraid, Jana. Her feeble, muffled words. She had been waiting for me to return, and this desperate, fearful plea was the last of her voice. She held on only long enough to make another command.

See everything, sister. All the things we wished to see...

Not even goodbye.

But in this cave so far from Helena, I feel closer to her than I have felt since she died. I've not permitted myself to cry over her, or for any of the cruel events that happened since she passed. But I do now. My tears feel hot and ragged on my skin. They slip over my cheeks and dampen the collar of my dress.

I do not wipe them off. I hold tight to Sontje's hand. And the click-woman's.

I don't know how long we stand in the cave, watching the three female figures watch us. Their hands becoming our hands. Our breaths becoming one breath. We find a rhythm for breathing without even trying.

The click-woman clicks to us. Gently loosens her hand from mine. Turns around and walks toward the entrance, this time not speaking to the cave or the wind or herself. Only the sound of her feet pat-pat on the cave floor.

We follow her out.

Part Three

Chapter 43

We dock in Batavia tomorrow after another two months at sea. Our last night on the *Leyden* and I lie with Sontje, for what may be the last time, savoring the swaying motion of our *retourship*, the glow of moonlight through the knothole we now know so well. I feel an early homesickness for this now-careworn vessel and the history we will leave here: the shadowy blot on the upper deck marking the demon fish's slaughter, the plank of wood in our berth where Sontje marked each passing moon—nearly three hundred nicks in neat rows. I wonder about the people we will become in Batavia, for I did not think of the people we would grow into on the *Leyden*. We made a life here. A small life, but one with beauty enough.

"I didn't really think about the end of this journey. It just went on for so long, it's as though I forgot its purpose," Sontje whispers to me. We never sleep in our hammocks now but on the floor, under our piles of castoff clothing and unraveling covers.

"We were different people when we began."

"Yes." She grows silent, remembering the differences. "Jana, what if no one wants me? If they can tell I've been... spoiled."

Her question hurts in the quick of me. That she believes she is ruined for those sailors' crimes. That she will be someone else's, and she's not lost sight of that purpose.

"Nothing about you is spoiled. You survived," I reassure her. "And I will always want you."

"But we can't live together. And we must marry. That is our entire value here."

I resist thinking about this future even now that it is nearly our present. In Amsterdam, I thought little of what lay ahead, my energies so absorbed by the requirements of each day's survival. I note another difference between us: Sontje has had the luxury of being able to dream of the future—to imagine her wedding ribbons and Three-Kings-Bread for Epiphany and things I never thought to dream of. I can't help but resent her constant worrying over the future. Such worry itself seems a type of wealth.

I look at her squarely and trace an invisible line from her ear down her neck, until my hand rests at her hip.

I can resent her bleak conclusions even as I love her.

"We will live near each other. The town is not so large," I say.

Sontje rises to her elbow and her lovely face finds the moonlight stolen through the knothole of our berth. "Jana, our husbands will dictate our nearness. We have no way to know. Even Sussie, who I've known since I was a child, went from seeing me each week to visiting once a month after her engagement."

I kiss her, hoping to distract us both. "Well, Sussie hardly seems like the type to assert herself."

Sontje gives me a look. An arched eyebrow that makes me smile.

"She'll have a good enough husband. I doubt he'll drink often or beat her."

"A fine husband indeed." I can't help but smirk. "But yes, that is all we can hope for."

She says nothing more, but wraps herself around me as we fall asleep, so I dream I'm tangled in vines and wish never to be free of them.

Chapter 44

"The Company Daughters have arrived!"

A heavy, shapeless man, one of the few wearing a wig like our men back home, announces our landing as we steady ourselves down the gangplank on to the beach sand, curious to know this new place and its settlers. A small crowd greets us. Men thinner and ruddier than any Dutchmen I have seen. Their rough skin reminds me of cured leather, and shines red like roasting meat. How unattractive we must look to the people who have always lived here, who are accustomed to this climate, whose skins don't protest this sunlight as ours do. I think of the click-woman, who looked like a gold statue on the day we left the Cape. She stood on the beach as Khoi men pushed our ship into the waves and she raised her hand to Sontje and me. An unexpected happiness followed her parting gesture.

Before docking, we scrubbed our dresses and skins, polished our teeth with driftwood we had gathered at the Cape and rationed over the remaining weeks, wishing to make a good impression on these men who will become our husbands. Agatha kept a tin of rouge and we all applied a thin film of red to our cheeks and our lips, not too much or we would look like harlots. Just enough to suggest we could still blush. But seeing the men, I think we should not have bothered with such efforts.

I see the other girls' disappointment as they scan the men who have come to greet us. All older men, many missing teeth and hanks of their sun-bleached hair. One man limps toward us and, for a moment, I expect him to ask for alms. Another has great, red, cracking sores on his face that make my own face ache in pity. A few of the men do not bother even to wear tunics or sandals. Their misshapen, calloused feet resemble blocks of wood. And they watch us like we are hot *stamppot* after a long winter.

Madaleen holds my hand tightly. Hugs Drika close.

Unlike the other girls, the displeasing condition of our greeters surprises me, though it shouldn't. They have endured the same journey, after all, and without the civilizing vigor of females, they have no reason to wash their faces or mend their trousers or rub tallow into their cracking skins. And the debauched men we met at the Cape should have prepared me for this welcome—the disheveled, hungry-eyed men who gaze upon us now. So instead, I think to the unexpected gifts of this place—its smooth sweep of untouched coast and the dense forest beckoning just beyond the settlement.

"Welcome to Batavia!" the man who announced our arrival calls out. His name is Henrikus Falks.

I learn later he is the Reverend who will perform our marriage ceremonies, and this motley group of men will soon be our husbands.

Chapter 45

Batavia lies at the mouth of the Tjiliwong River flowing to the sea. Reverend Falks explained the Governor-General chose this site on the northern coast to bypass the Strait of Malacca, a site of skirmishes between Dutch and Portuguese traders, and to monitor ships passing through the Sunda Strait.

A narrower, brown arm of the river flows through the center of the colony, smelling of fish and rot. Its murky stillness reminds me more than anything that I'm not in Amsterdam, whose waters move in cheerful ripples, small and polite, as if they exist to apologize for the city's constant fog.

Here, a thick haze settles over the town in the morning, but burns away after some hours. Narrow, silted canals surround the main town, made up of two long rectangles of land. Fields and streets fill the western side of the establishment, while the residences and public buildings—the church and town hall in its modest square—lie to the east. Aside from the river and canals, the language is what stands out to me first. I expect to hear more Dutch, but everyone speaks Portuguese, ugly and full of vowels. Even the Dutch traders and merchants have learned it. The natives—slaves—speak their own language, too, Malay mostly, some Sundanese. But Portuguese most of all.

After a meal and some rest, Reverend Falks takes us around the settlement. I'm eager to see our new environs, but dislike how he parades us around the colony, how the men stare and even hiss as we walk past. One even makes a scene of beating his black slave in front of us, as though hoping to impress.

Sontje shudders beside me as we walk in twos behind the Reverend. "I never saw such things in Amsterdam," she whispers.

But I think of the water cells where we drowned thieves, or the Spinhuis where our brothel workers wore out their days spinning thread, tucked away from the supposed virtuous dwellers.

"They only hid it better back in the homeland."

As we continue, the Reverend points out the modest rampart encircling the settlement, speaking in a booming, sermonizing voice meant to attract the attention of passersby. "Notice the Company models the settlement after our own Dutch towns. The same grid-shape as our city streets, the same gabled roofs and narrow rooms. It's nearly as good as being back in Amsterdam." He beams as if he designed the colony himself, though I wish the buildings looked different, and not like our Dutch had simply rebirthed Amsterdam's sameness here.

The stone churches and the castle dominate the settlement. The stone churches, of course, resemble ours at home—thick, white walls and a sloping, blue-tiled roof—but the structures look absurd somehow, even uncomfortable, here in this unyielding sunlight.

As for the castle, the settlers built it on top of the old city, named Jayakarta, razing the city's native structures to the ground. When Falks turns away, droning on about some Company achievement or another, a slave empties his nostrils near the castle wall, giving no mind to us women.

"Part of your work here—your civilizing efforts—is to keep the slaves obedient," Falks explains as we approach the center of the settlement, clearly enjoying this task of informing us of our new homes and responsibilities. "You'll each be given sticks or ropes to keep at the ready."

"For what purpose?" Catherina asks, and her eyes widen as he touches the rattan stick looped through his breeches.

"To strike the slaves, of course." The Reverend loosens the stick and hits the air to demonstrate. "These slaves are all prisoners of war, or driven to us by droughts and famine. They still need some reminding that they are ours now." Sontje looks at me, her eyes round, and I know she feels the same as I do, wondering how we'll ever use such instruments.

"And what sort of work do they do?" I ask, to distract myself from the sting of a blister on my perspiring feet, now trapped once more in my *klomps*. Later, the Company will present us with sandals, better suited for this climate, though I sometimes wear my *klomps* out of habit.

"All things." He replaces the stick back in his breeches, finished with its display. "They work as honor guards and valets. They build the canals and roads, fire the forges to make nails for the Company's new buildings. They carry bricks and wood for construction." Here, Falks nods toward the pitiable slave bent over by the great load of wood he carries on his narrow back.

"And they are the island's natives? The slaves?" Agatha asks, also worried by the rattan stick which we now notice all the settlers carry.

"Not so many of them," Falks says, relishing her question. "The Company brought some from India and our other colonies. Some are from the Cape, as you may recognize in their peculiar features."

"Why bring slaves when so many natives live here?"

"It's easier to control slaves taken from their homelands," he explains. "And this way we need not engage too much with the local kings and such, who will want some of our profits in return."

We grow silent, considering our new home as we walk. I did not expect slaves here, stupidly believing our own men would perform the work to make the settlement. But as we make a slow circle through the colony, the slaves continue to pull my attention. Their gleaming skins are darker than that of the Khoi and they wear their hair long. Their bodies are slight and bony, seeming too weak for their labors. I learn later that the slaves live in battered bamboo huts or in servants' quarters with their masters within the rampart walls, and are divided into four groups—household slaves, craftsmen, the *kulis*—or unskilled slaves—and the chained slaves, who live separately from the others. The chained slaves dig and dredge the narrow canals meant to resemble our canals back home, and when I see them, I think of the ropes used on me in the brothel, and can't help but tremble at the memory.

I'm overwhelmed by the newness of this place. I try and make sense of the settlement, imagining myself living here, even picturing with distaste the possibility of some female slave walking behind me like the slaves follow the male settlers now, carrying their betel boxes. It appears everyone chews the sweet, fragrant betel leaf, staining their teeth orange, and spitting its red juices into the dirt.

Some of the female slaves wear our Dutch style of clothing and look awkward and weary in our many skirts in this thick, humid air and scouring sunshine. The widows wear their native blouses, called *kebayas*, and long, simple skirts, called *kains*, wrapped around their slim waists.

As for the Batavia natives, they look entirely different from any of us, or the Khoisan and Indians, for that matter. They stand much shorter, with dusky yellow skin and fine, small hands and feet. Their upturned eyes disclose very little of their thoughts. Around us, they are quiet and serious. Hardworking. But later that first night, I hear laughter and singing from their huts beyond the town wall. Louder voices than I have heard from them in the day, as though they become different people once the moon rises and they retreat to their own homes.

I learn later that the brothels here, too, resemble ours. They lie outside the city walls like the Ringhouse, or, like De Wallen, close to the shipyards where soldiers and sailors work. And this is why the Company brought us here, after all. To curb the swell of half-Dutch children, lawlessness, and venereal disease. But I only learn of all this later. For now, they keep us ignorant of our daunting purpose.

We are only a few poor and sickly girls, stumbling on the still ground after so many days at sea.

We are kept in a compound of white buildings close to the church, since we must attend morning and evening services. Other than a chaperoned walk with Reverend Falks, we exit the compound only for services. We sit in the front rows of the church and feel the men's eyes upon us. They bring us to the church not for God, but for appraisal.

I miss my shared berth with Sontje. Maritjen's suspicions on the *Leyden* now make us cautious. I wait for some reason to touch Sontje's arm or shoulder, remarking on some meaningless thing or another, creating reasons for closeness.

I miss her neck under my tongue. Our shared sleep.

As promised, they give us new dresses for becoming Company Daughters. Plain, identical white frocks with single-stitch lace caps.

Nothing we would covet back in Amsterdam. But by now we are sickened by our old clothing, tattered and stained to a dull brown from our voyage, trailing threads that catch on branches and splinters. We exclaim over the whiteness of these simple dresses. Madaleen gathers violet flowers and ties them stem to stem with thread and wears them around her neck. Against her white dress, the flowers become vivid and change the color of her eyes from gray to blue. We praise her prettiness, at which she smiles.

The Reverend has arranged for the native women to bring us food twice a day. They will not look at us, but stare at their sandaled feet.

"They seem nice," Sontje says to me after we receive our breakfast of fruits and boiled rice from a native woman assigned to us. "They remind me of the woman back at the Cape."

"She wasn't a slave, though." I recall again the click-woman's soft hand in mine.

"These here are slaves?"

"Of course. They don't receive payment for their labor." Sontje's innocence annoys me. Has she not noticed the lash marks on the back of the old woman who brings us the afternoon meal? The slave men who empty their noses or piss outside the Dutch buildings when their masters look away?

Sontje continues as the other girls admire the colorful fruits stacked in a bowl for all of us. "But the women smile when they give us food. And you hear them at night. Singing and clapping from their huts."

"It's how they survive." I, too, smiled at Master De Graaf and the other men, hoping that kindness could prevent further abuses. I, too, hummed tunes as I hung the aprons, collars, and linens to dry, to distract myself from the ache in my shoulders and back or the numbness in my wrists. To stay awake when I arrived to work in the wintertime, before the sunrise. Or to remind myself I existed even if I was invisible to everyone else.

Sontje uses a spoon to loosen the sticky rice in her bowl. "The men don't tell us very much. When everything will happen."

"No."

"In that, we are not so different from the slaves. Taken from place to place, fulfilling destinies others have ordered for us."

"I doubt the slaves think so," I say, as Sontje passes an orange to me, knowing how I love its sour juice.

"The men don't even know that our dresses are no longer fashionable."

"I suppose we don't know that, either." I smell the fruit, eager to taste it.

"In my old life, I would never have worn this simple dress. A dress for a farm girl. But now I'm relieved to wear something other than the rags I wore on the *Leyden*. These days, I hardly envy myself my old life. It seems so empty and innocent. These people wouldn't even imagine the old house with its cathedral ceilings, the extra *zaal* with Fader's paintings. I can scarcely imagine it myself anymore." Sontje takes a dainty spoonful of rice into her mouth. Chews. Swallows.

"The extra *zaal* was ever a nuisance to me. More sweeping and washing."

Sontje laughs. "We only used it when Fader received important men. Otherwise, the only guest it received was the day's dust."

"Yes, always a frequent visitor." I feel a sting of bitterness at the extra *zaal* and all the dusting it required, but I push aside those memories and finally taste the wedge of fruit Sontje passed. Its tartness stings my cheeks and jolts me from my memories of dust and Amsterdam.

The rice birds trill outside as though laughing.

*

How many more days? No one tells us. At sunrise, the Reverend gathers us for morning prayers at the castle. We bend our heads and ask for forgiveness. For what, I do not know.

Our evening walks are the high point of my day, other than the sparse moments of closeness with Sontje. Reverend Falks marches us around the compound like a herd of lambs, past the unfinished ramparts with Portuguese a braying noise around us. He tells us the Governor-General is full of plans to build and fortify the colony.

I watch all of it, hungry for the outdoors, the unnamed trees, the calls of strange birds and strong, cloying smells I can't recognize. To understand this new home. I observe as the slaves lay brick for the houses, and carry still more to reinforce the city wall. They haul bamboo sticks on their backs and balance bricks on their heads. They sweep and wash the streets of the compound using brooms made of unfamiliar twigs and grasses. They do not look at us, but keep their eyes on the ground, making themselves invisible, as I once did. Only the native children smile and laugh, and gather around us to touch our hands, in awe of our color. The children are beautiful. Even Agatha, who finds the natives ugly and says they resemble clods of dirt, can't help but love the children here.

"They look so much happier than our own somehow," Sontje says of the children as we follow behind Reverend Falks.

"It must be all the sunlight," Agatha replies.

The settlement men mostly greet us with empty smiles, pretending we are not women who will bear them children, clean their chamber pots, and watch them die in their pallets years from now. But some look at us hungrily, gazing directly. Not even a smile. Not even curiosity. Only impatience.

I wonder which of us they will get.

"What we need in these colonies is a helping of virtue," Reverend Falks declares as we walk. He can't help but sermonize in every conversation, as though he has forgotten any other way to speak. When he has some very important lesson to impart, he turns around to address us, walking backward. In that manner he once tripped on a passing slave carrying bricks, and released such a tirade against the poor soul that I could not relish the scene of Falks stumbling over himself.

He continues. "Or, as I've heard elsewhere, 'the spirit of Sarah, the virtue of Ruth and the humility of Abigail.'"

I puzzle over Abigail, who I've not heard of, but I'll not admit my ignorance. The others nod their heads in agreement, even Sontje, though she seems to be smiling at her *klomps*.

The Reverend turns to face us, and I'm nervous for another mishap with one of the slaves. He speaks in a low voice, as though sharing a secret. "These men have been away from civilization for months, even a year or two. They have forgotten our…" Reverend Falks pauses here, searching for the proper words. "Softer ways. It is your duty to remind them. Cleanliness in your homes and in your hearts. Chastity at all times. You will be protectors of home and hearth. You are as much a part of this endeavor as the settlers to whom you will be married."

We listen and nod in agreement.

We wait. We have nothing else.

Chapter 46

"Jana, let us escape," Sontje whispers to me from her cot on our seventh night in Batavia. "We can leave now and return by morning."

I hesitate, then note with some sorrow how obedient I have become.

"I feel like the caged parrot Sussie's mother purchased in Dam Market. I stopped visiting her house because I felt so sad for the poor creature." Sontje rests her face on her propped hand, and I wonder how many nights we have left to speak to each other this way.

"Is the door locked?" I did not even think to try opening it.

Madaleen, Catherina, and Agatha sleep soundly as we move off our cots. We have only thin robes to wear over our underclothes, and I'm again thankful for Batavia's warm climate, even at night.

We carry our *klomps*, afraid of their sound on the clay floor.

Agatha stirs in her hammock. She sighs. I wonder what she dreams of—her future husband? Some boy from her past?

We stop at the door.

Sontje unlocks the indoor barrel lock, gently working the latch back and forth while I watch the sleeping women. I hold my breath, hoping the outside lock remains unbolted. I enjoy this feeling of thwarting Reverend Falks's orders, of stealing away from the others.

The door opens. The rusted hinge may creak if opened too wide.

"Open it just a little."

Sontje squeezes through and I follow.

At first we stand outside the door, unsure of where to go. We drop our *klomps* and press our feet inside them.

"I want to go into the forest." Sontje crosses her arms, rubs her shoulders for warmth. "Falks always parades us around the same route through the settlement. I want to see something new."

I delight in Sontje's adventuring spirit, when she once sought the comfort of rules.

The full moon permits us to see the branches and brush, so we walk toward the row of teak trees behind the cottage. Not far from the trees lies the surrounding unfinished city wall, and the dark thatch of the forest waits for us beyond. Reverend Falks has cautioned us not to explore the area, describing to us insects as big as rats, rats as big as dogs, and reptiles as large as our Dutch belted cows.

I hesitate. "Are you sure? It's still quite dark."

Sontje kisses my cheek, squeezes my hand. "You pulled me into the cave back in the Cape, and you were right about it. I have the same feeling you did then about this forest. I have a sense we should go there, and see the sunrise together."

I kiss the knuckle of her hand in reply.

"Our freedom is disappearing day by day, Jana. We must grasp it while we can."

We arrive at the wall, just higher than our waists. We remove our *klomps* and throw them over the wall, then hoist ourselves over the structure. Even this small feat—passing over a short wall in our nightclothes and bare feet—excites me.

"Let us see these cow-sized lizards," Sontje says, reaching for my hand.

*

The birds announce themselves as we walk—the night herons, finches, peafowls, bulbuls, and storks. Amsterdam's *meerkoets* and sparrows seem only the approximations of birds for their feeble chirps. I imagine their shame if they saw these giant, spanning creatures with their *donderbus* cries.

"One of the girls at the Ringhouse told me that birds kept in cages, given food and water every day, without any threat of being eaten or attacked, still live shorter lives than birds that go free," I say to Sontje as we walk over vines, still holding hands. I think how natural it feels to speak of the Ringhouse to her now, like a great darkness in me has cleared.

"I understand that feeling. Even though I'm afraid here, I feel excited somehow. Excited to be afraid. Everything here is different. The people, too. In the Cape, the people were one way. Here, another. If we had remained in Amsterdam, I would never know that."

"Does that make it worth it? Leaving?"

"I don't know." Sontje says. "But I miss our old ship. Our leaky, cramped berth. Even the stupid chamber pot we always bickered over."

We find a clearing after some time. The sky lightens and I feel myself growing anxious. Soon the others will wake. Our adventure will be over.

Sontje walks under a tall tree standing alone in the clearing. "Look at this." She runs her hand down the bark, which is colored in streaks of blue, violet, red, yellow, and green. "It looks painted. I've never seen such a tree."

"And there are others like it." Further away, I see smaller, thinner trunks, also seemingly painted. "Reverend Falks said he's heard stories of the natives burying their babies in the trees."

"I never know what to believe when he speaks," Sontje says with surprising harshness. She looks up through the branches. "And if they do bury their dead in the trees, I think they must have good reason."

We stand in the silence of the tree and like Sontje, I can't help but place my palm on its smooth trunk, tracing its colors.

"I love how the branches slice the moon into pieces," she says, looking upward.

I stand next to her, worrying for a moment about tree snakes and insects, until she leans over and kisses my neck.

I hear a rustling sound in the canopy.

"We shouldn't waste too much time looking at the moon," Sontje whispers and turns to stand in front of me. Her hands slide into my clothes and I lean back against the tree as she unties my thin robe, kisses me as though devouring my skin. I'm unused to such lust from her, having always regarded myself as her pursuer.

The tree canopy hums above us—birds waking or some variety of insect.

I ignore the fear rooting in me and feel triumph in this. Even in our captivity, we've found each other. Seized at whatever joy we can find.

I open Sontje's robes as we kiss. I'm again thankful for the mild climate. Her pale skin, the sweep of her ribs, the hollow between her small breasts.

We use our robes to prepare a makeshift bed on ground. I try not to think of what creatures surround us. I recall our shared bed made of old rags and clothes, and I'm on the *Leyden* again, only the moonlight covering us.

"Sometimes I think it looks lonely," Sontje whispers to me against my cheek, and her fingers trace the jutting bone of my hip.

"What do you mean?"

"The moon." She kisses my collarbone and moves her lips down. My stomach twists at her touch, hungry for more of her, and I think back on that first day on the Reynsts' doorstep, a different sort of hunger. "Alone in all that darkness," she says. "I think that will be me." But then her mouth is upon me and I lose all thought for what she means.

We arrive back at the compound at dawn. The girls remain asleep, and our adventure is all the more precious for their slumber through it. Sontje's taste lingers on me, the smell of her skin on mine as I return to my hammock and pretend to sleep.

Later in the morning, the old slave woman, Dewa, brings us breakfast on a teakwood tray. Her face is full of deep lines, wrinkles that nearly obscure her eyes and ripple over her forehead, crisscrossing her cheeks. A brown mole rises on the side of her nose. I can't help but stare.

Dewa places on the table a pot of sticky, congealed rice, salted fish, a bowl of papayas, guavas, and a round, yellow fruit whose name I do not know.

"What is this fruit?" I ask her.

She doesn't answer, but slices off a quarter. Presents a yellow-orange wedge to me in her open palm.

I smell it before tasting it. A deep, rich, sweet fragrance. The skin is thick and smooth, too tough to bite through. Dewa shows me how to eat it, taking the whole piece into her mouth and scraping out the fruit while pulling the skin against her few teeth.

I touch my tongue to its flesh first. Sweet and sour, like nothing else I've tasted. After our months on the *Leyden* without anything fresh, I savor cool, wet, foods. I pull the flesh from its skin and chew. Juice and fibers and a sweetness stranger than any sugar or honey I have tasted.

I suddenly recall Tobias Levy's description.

"Is it good?" Sontje asks, watching me.

I close my eyes and taste again the heavy tang of the fruit, its clinging, surprising sour, like an idea beyond my grasp.

"Mangoes," I reply.

Chapter 47

Sontje is claimed first.

As we all expected, and just ten days after we've arrived. Reverend Falks informs her in front of us. He does not deign to take her aside and let her settle into the fact of it, but announces the betrothal using the deeper, booming voice he reserves for his sermons.

"Mistress Reynst," he declares. "Someone has asked for your hand."

We are sitting in the rattan chairs—Catherina, Agatha, Madaleen, Sontje, and me—finishing our breakfasts of sticky rice, fish, and fruit. Catherina holds a mouthful of guava seeds and looks like a squirrel. She thinks it inelegant to spit them out in male company and instead collects them in her cheeks.

"What is his name?" Sontje asks with her typical coolness, as though the Reverend has merely announced it might rain.

"Willem Brouwer. A good man." Reverend Falks pauses, seemingly convincing himself. But he looks down at his gray shirt sleeves and I know he is lying.

"When?" Sontje asks.

"The wedding will be in two days. Just a simple service in our church. I apologize we can't give you a more elaborate ceremony. But we will serve a supper for everyone."

"Will I be meeting him before the wedding?" There's an edge to her voice, but only I hear it.

"He will be taking you for a walk this evening. He's busy at the moment, loading the *Leyden* for its return trip without you ladies. On the voyage back your vessel will stop in China. The English tried, but I think we Dutch will be the first." Reverend Falks can't conceal his pride. The empire spreading its robust limbs ever outward.

Sontje says nothing but purses her lips.

"And how are you all this morning?" The Reverend continues without further thought to the matter, and the girls chatter on about what they miss about the homeland, welcoming Falks's clumsy attempts at conversation. He is a longtime widower himself and unpracticed in talking to women, but he seems to enjoy our company.

"I long for *metworst*," Catherina explains, savoring Falks's attention. "But otherwise, it's quite lovely here."

Reverend Falks smiles, and his eyes linger on Catherina's full breasts.

Willem Brouwer arrives in the evening. His face is lined from the sun and he smells of ham and woodsmoke. His odor enters the room before the rest of him, and shoves aside our feminine odors of lilac, lavender, and the roses we have placed in glass bottles around the room.

The toe of one of his scuffed boots is peeling back, revealing a grimy corner of his stocking. His red nose is large and fleshy, pitted with large pores. But his small hands are scrubbed clean, the nails even. I imagine his hands on Sontje, and revulsion climbs into my throat. That she will have to wake up with a stranger's face beside her in the morning. That he will soon know the sound of her breathing, the taste of her mouth, the shape of the mole on her neck.

"Here for our walk," Willem Brouwer says in a deep and jovial tone, more a frog's voice than a man's. He looks hard at Sontje head to foot, then nods in approval. He presents his arm to her, triumph plain on his rough face.

She glances at me before she leaves.

A pitiful look I have not seen before, but imagine Madaleen witnessed that night on the *Leyden*.

"He smells of rot and *worst*," Sontje whispers to me after everyone else is asleep. "And he kept on about lions—that they live in the jungles here, he's seen them at night and heard their growling. That's all he could talk about. Oh, Jana. How will I share a bed with him every night?"

I stretch out my hand and find hers in the darkness.

"I can't refuse," she says. In the darkness I can see only the outline of her face. I smell her, though. Lavender water and the buttery smell of her sweat.

"No. You can't."

"How do they decide who selects first?"

I have wondered the same thing. "The way they decide everything else, I suppose. Favors, influence, money. You are the prettiest among us, so it's not unexpected." A tightness grips my chest—my sadness at losing her? Or some last, stubborn jealousy of her riches from our Amsterdam days? Or my fear for her?

Perhaps all these things.

For a moment she is silent. "Well, at least I know what to expect on the wedding night. It can't be worse than the ship. I already know what I'll hate about his face—I did this with Hans, too. I knew his little teeth would be my fixation when he angered me. That I would have to swallow my disgust in such moments." She looks at her apron, probably thinking of Hans and his rich wife from Delft.

"And with me? What do you hate?"

She smiles in the half-light. "I can't think of anything, dear Jana." The outline of her face changes. "I tried. The things I thought I wouldn't like I just loved more in time. The way you wrinkle your forehead when you are talking seriously about something. Your nervous habit of rearranging items on a table."

"I didn't know that."

"You have always done so. In Amsterdam, you rearranged tulips and whatever objects Fader left on the display table. And here, you fiddle with the Bibles." She returns to the topic of her betrothed. "For Willem, it will be the way he looks when he makes a joke, this look of expectation, as though he's asking—*I'm humorous, am I not?* And then he laughs so loudly at his own stories, barking like a dog."

"And he talks as well."

"Yes, constantly. I'll learn to ignore it. Fader did the same at times. It's like they must keep talking to remind themselves they're still alive on God's good earth."

This is a surprise to me, for I only saw Master Reynst's reserve.

Sontje swats away a mosquito near her neck. "His hands scare me," she whispers. "They don't match the rest of him. Too elegant and unmarked. I don't trust a man whose hands don't match him."

"I thought the same."

"I try to imagine those hands on me."

A flame of jealousy at this thought. "Best not to think of it."

"I prefer to plan. To know what could happen. Expect the worst and be surprised if it's better than expected. A lesson from our days on the *Leyden*."

The inkling of that night causes my stomach to sink. This Willem Brouwer from Rotterdam who knows nothing of Sontje. Who has never seen her garden of crocuses.

"I wonder if he will have heard about what happened before…" Sontje's voice is so quiet I can hardly hear her.

"I doubt it. The Company wants a return on its investment."

"Yes. No point in sending defective goods."

"You have no defects." I reach across to cup her cheek in my hand.

Sontje laughs an empty laugh. "No. I'm beyond repair. You only remember who I was before."

"No. I love you now. This Sontje. She is so much stronger, and more herself."

Later that night, as the others sleep, as I sleep, Sontje's cool fingers wander under my thin sheet, whose sole purpose is to confound the ravenous mosquitoes. Her fingertips crawl underneath my hipbone as I lie on my stomach, like the touch of a ghost. My face is turned toward her and I open one sticky eye.

She whispers so softly, I almost think it a dream. "I have admitted it to you before, when you were asleep. But you should hear it awake, Jana." She brings her face close to mine, so I can hear better. Her eyes show a wildness I've not seen in her before. "I am set alight by you, dear Jana." Her fingers creep along my hip and stomach. If I look away, if I blink, this thread between us breaks.

Outside the lorikeets call.

Weep. Weep.

The owls answer.

Who.

I lift my hips and her fingers enter, slick and purposeful and, for the last time, mine.

Chapter 48

I have no choice but to attend the wedding. Sontje said I should not, but everyone else will be there and Reverend Falks expects us to attend such functions together. The other women laugh and chatter and compare waistlines and braids and their reappearing whiteness after weeks spent indoors. They wonder and gossip over who will be next. They have forgotten the day when we first arrived, that their prospective husbands are men they have already seen. Pockmarked, heavy, bald, sweating, limping, aged, sun-roughened, and loud.

I sit in the back of the church. Madaleen sits beside me, hiding Drika under her petticoat. Maritjen sits at the front of the church with her Gerhard, chin up, pretending she knows none of us.

Sontje. She stands at the nave of this humble, humid church. Light has found her, as always, and with her hair lit up she is Sontje in all her beauty—in the window light of her house in Amsterdam, in the shaft of moonlight on the *Leyden,* sleeping in my arms.

She is thinner after our journey, and so she looks even taller than before. She stands very straight, wearing a black velvet gown and satin underskirt which peeks out from the hem—the Company loans out the same unwieldy wedding dress for each of us to wear. Pearl buttons on the bodice. Willem stands beside her, thick and ruddy from the sun. Smiling like he's caught a prized pheasant. He fluffs himself up and emits mighty coughs during Reverend Falks's greeting. I think the two men do not like each other.

She glances at me. A brave smile. My heart a crisp apple, crushed.

Willem Brouwer clutches Sontje's elbow as they walk slowly past me. I can't help but imagine him with her only hours from now. His mouth on her fragile, white skin, his strange hands. He will taste her lavender and sunlight.

I shudder.

"You can't be cold?" Madaleen asks, seeing my reaction.

"No." I wrap an arm around her.

At the last of the sacraments, the couple faces us. Willem Brouwer's hand lies upon the small of Sontje's back. This back I have kissed and traced beneath my fingertips, and scratched with my nails. Sinew and softness that I have loved.

A mixture of sadness and jealousy—I have felt it before.

"I hear Falks owed him a favor," someone whispers behind me. "A considerable debt. That's how Brouwer got the prettiest one."

Chapter 49

A month passes before I see her again.

I fear Sontje has forgotten about me, then berate my selfishness—she is trapped with a man she hardly knows and who has a low reputation even among these rough men. At night I think of her, and our time together seems like a vanishing dream. The taste of her throat, her breaths when my fingers slipped inside her and how she kissed me as her fingers entered me as well. My disbelief and awe that in our nakedness we felt only joy, never violation. In the storm of my loss, I think the only remedy would be to moan like a bereft mother or a new widow.

But in the compound, I'm not allowed even this.

"I wonder what she is doing?" Madaleen remarks, combing Drika's little tuft of hair. She misses Sontje nearly as much as I. Though the town is small, Willem Brouwer's cottage lies on the outskirts, and as we are not permitted to leave our compound, Sontje may as well be back in Amsterdam. I keep hoping to see her on my secret morning walks, but I never do. Only the slaves are out so early, hauling and digging and washing the streets before the sun blazes over everything.

"Probably setting up house," I say. But I know she is most likely slaking her husband's thirst for a woman. We have heard stories—men who keep their new wives in bed for days. And not so they can rest.

"I wish we could visit her."

"They must settle first."

"Dewa doesn't seem to like Willem much. She winces when she hears his name." Dewa made a sour face when I once mentioned Maritjen, and from then on I knew she could be trusted.

"I don't think she likes him, no." I pat Madaleen's hand.

"I've heard he has other children. Children with the native women. Have you seen those children? Fathered by the men here? Some are so beautiful. I saw a young girl just yesterday walking toward the forest. Her skin looked like gold, and she had green eyes. I smiled at her, but she didn't smile back."

"Their lives are unhappy," I say. Reverend Falks explained to me on one of our walks that the orphans belong to no one. They can't be accepted as Dutch but the natives reject them also. They live in an orphanage at the edge of the compound—a sad thatched roof and box of a building, not yet painted, that receives little breeze. A few older, pious townswomen sometimes take them in for short periods, but if they are anything like the older, pious women of Amsterdam, those children will grow unloved and become little more than servants or prostitutes, turned out at the age of fifteen.

"It's like we're being plucked off a branch, one by one," Madaleen says, toying with Drika's hair.

"Yes." I can't make the effort to convince her otherwise. My heart is heavy in my chest.

"Like fruit or scraps from a heap, I'm not yet sure." Madaleen holds Drika close.

I give her a quick embrace. "All depends on who is plucking."

*

We find out later in the evening that Agatha is next.

Her intended husband, Jacob Merkus, is a wealthy senior merchant. Though Master Coen told me we would marry soldiers upon arrival, it seems some of our future husbands have higher positions in the Company. I think back on Skipper Albert's intentions for Griet and wonder if they have already bartered each of us away.

"At least he's wealthy," Catherina says to Agatha at tea, who, for all her earlier eagerness to marry, now appears bewildered by her approaching wedding.

"Maybe you'll have a grand house like the Governor-General," Madaleen says.

"And slaves to do all your work," Catherina adds. Some of the houses use slaves to do all manner of work, from cleaning to gardening to washing and cooking. But we also know of Dutchmen who take on the slaves and father children with them, like the natives here who keep multiple wives.

"I only hope he is a decent and godly man," Agatha replies, perhaps thinking of Willem Brouwer. She pauses. "As a girl, I always felt I would have some say in the matter of my own marriage."

"We would have, sister, had Fader lived," Catherina says quietly. For the first time, I behold the labor required for the sisters' bland cheerfulness. Like all of us, they find ways to conceal their disappointments, but the pain abides despite their efforts.

I think of my own losses.

Sontje will attend the wedding. And that is all I care about.

Chapter 50

She walks into the church holding Willem Brouwer's elbow, and wears a new dress, no doubt a gift from her husband. Simple lace edging on fabric the same light blue as the shy veins that show through the whiteness of her neck and chest. She has parted her hair in the center and pulled it tightly back. The clean line of her scalp draws in me a sweep of tenderness. Her skin is so white and exposed.

Sontje looks thinner still than the last time I saw her. The sharp bones of her face emerge more plainly. She often claimed she looks like an old woman when she loses weight. That is what Master Reynst told her. Said it was the same with her mother when she was too nervous to eat.

She glances up and scans the rows until she sees me. The simple fact of her gaze is a relief. A smile only I can see.

I watch her as long as I can, trying to determine the reason for her changed appearance. Something about her movements, all arranged around Willem Brouwer's. She takes slightly smaller steps. Her shoulders slump forward so she appears shorter than she is. In Amsterdam, her posture was always so straight. She never sought to hide her height.

And then I realize the difference.

She looks owned.

I don't recall the Reverend's sermon. The usual blathering on about the promise of rainbows after the rain. The rain has forever meant more to the Dutch than other weather. The floods at Delft that killed hundreds, the monsoons here. So much of our lives indebted to suitable rainfall. Rain means repentance and reckoning, and, for me, reminders of Helena. The roar of earth giving way.

Willem Brouwer guides Sontje to seats at the front of the church. Diagonally across from me. I watch the back of her head, and when she turns, a glimpse of her small ears and delicate chin quickens my heart. She does not look back.

The shimmering, invisible rope hangs between us, fraying a bit for we have been apart for too long and I know nothing of her life in this past month. If I could be with her, I would ask her questions. *Are you well? Is he kind to you? Do you think of me at all?* Because my own love compels a hunger for reassurance, a distancing when that reassurance is denied. In the beginning, every time I reached for her hand I felt exposed, ready for her rejection. And at some point, our touches became equal, no requirement to remember who touched whom first because we were each other. All day we would talk while all the others faded like colorless portraits hanging on damp walls.

The imagined rope is thicker at my end than hers. I know this when Sontje, at last, turns back to me. Just a quick glance, and I'm aware of her at the rope's thinner, fraying, end.

I sit next to an old man who taps upon the pages of his open Bible, making a crackly sound with each tap. He looks over at me, never turning his face, only sliding his gaze toward me. Perhaps I've applied too much rose water. His sidelong glances remind me of a buzzing housefly, too irritating to ignore completely, but I'm studying Sontje.

Her bandaged index finger—what is its cause?

The shining part in her hair.

I feel his leaden stare upon me, but I try to ignore it.

One week later, I'm his wife.

Chapter 51

My name is no longer Jana Beil but Jana Haffner. Madam Haffner, someone called me the other day, and I only later recognized Madam Haffner as myself. This name sounds round and prosperous. A plump woman with many children, clear blue eyes, red cheeks, and a bosom falling to her waist. Nothing at all like me.

My husband, Mattheus Haffner, is an old man. Sixty years. He has lived many lives already—as a farmer in Kessel, a banker in Haarlem with three children (now grown and living in Delft and Breda), and an Assistant Resident at the Company. I watch him as he sleeps like something dead, exhausted by the day's activities, and wonder how it is to wake up in such a weary body with sagging skin and loose flesh. He sleeps so deeply I can peer at him closely, even blow across his furrowed face and he does not stir.

He asked the Reverend for my hand after the church service. His request surprised even the Reverend, for everyone assumed Mattheus was too old for marriage. The Company reserves its "daughters" for young men. But he has influence here—his best friend is the new Councilor-General.

"Ideally, we seek wives for our younger settlers," Reverend Falks informed me. He could not hide his annoyance, as though the request was my fault.

"Whatever the Company prefers. I'm its servant," I replied. In fact, I was relieved at my suitor's advanced age. His anger would be rare, requiring too much effort. He would treat me more like a house spaniel than a wife. Perhaps buy me trinkets, ask me to wear my hair in schoolgirl braids to look even younger than I am. I've noticed this about older men with younger women. They are more in love with their own youth and memories of it, willing to settle for its approximation in someone else.

I observe his habits in those first days of our marriage. Mattheus wakes late—nine in the morning. By then I have already been up for four hours. At first, he insisted I stay in bed with him, my body repulsed by his curling yellow toenails, the white hairs dusting his shoulders since he sleeps without a nightshirt, holding me as he falls asleep.

But he is kind enough. Now, some weeks into our marriage, he permits me to wake early so I may do all the cleaning: sweeping out the *zaal* and washing the floor and watering the rosebushes he planted for me—the standard red, and then a curious grayish yellow rose smelling of mustard seeds. I then go for my walk around the compound, passing the natives' huts, hazy with smoke from their cooking, past the whitewashed church where three of us have been married so far, and as close as I can get to the port, where I can watch the sea. For some reason my memories emerge with a vivid crispness when I'm watching the dancing of the waves.

Another benefit of this marriage—Mattheus doesn't want children, and for that I am glad, having seen Moeder suffer with us. And unlike many of the other girls at the Ringhouse, who found ways to rid themselves of unsought pregnancies, I never had such problems. I consider my barrenness a small mercy for everything else I've endured.

I think of Sontje's wedding day, how she searched for me. Fear and sadness and loss shooting between both of us, but did I also see resentment? Disappointment? An unsaid accusation, that I couldn't save her, that she would now belong to Willem Brouwer and not to me. Or herself.

Sontje missed my small wedding, and save for her absence, I hardly remember the day. Some old skirmish between Mattheus and Willem Brouwer prevented her attendance.

"I'm not surprised," Mattheus said when I mentioned their absence. "Willem Brouwer is a difficult man. You are close to his wife?"

"She is my best friend. I knew her even before the *Leyden.*"

He nodded and patted my hand with his rough, veined, and wrinkled paw as though he understood. Or perhaps to comfort me. He was a stranger to me then and I had not yet learned the language of his gestures.

"We will have a good life together," he said after our wedding ceremony, taking me into his house. "I'm older, and can offer some wisdom other men can't." He explained his work, brokering agreements between merchants and the Company. He showed me the rooms of his bungalow, one of the larger houses, whitewashed, with a red-tiled roof. The latrine outside, three small bedrooms, a clean kitchen at the back and larger room for guests. He was business-like and polite, and I wondered how I would ever share a bed with him, remote as he seemed.

But even at his age, we consummated the wedding that first night.

"Jana, my wife," he said, as though reminding himself as he unpeeled my simple wedding dress, only Griet's lace ruff as its adornment, staring at my unblemished skin—I did not show him my scarred back, hided by Fader and the Ringhouse. His papery hands trembled over my hips, my stomach, my thighs, and I lay still, compliant, thinking of Sontje. Her mouth instead of his, her butterfly hands. I hardly felt him as he entered but his groan of pleasure gave me some contentment—I would have some power, at least, over him.

But on our wedding night, his breath upon me smelled like decay.

Chapter 52

We live on the eastern edge of the settlement, not far from the *stadhuis*, the center of the colony. The bungalow's many open slats in the walls freshen the flow of air and reduce the oppressive, fishy smell trailing from the canals. Fortunately, my husband has modest tastes like my own, and unlike other Company executives, who live in large houses filled with statues and paintings, and gardens with pergolas and newly dug ponds, our house is simply furnished with native teakwood and rattan furnishings. I keep fruit trees in the back, which grow much faster than the flowers and trees of Amsterdam.

So far in my marriage, I have learned the condition requires idleness and a maddening restraint. Mattheus, perhaps owing to his age, observes all the Dutch marital traditions. He expects me to serve him breakfast, and then sit with him to watch him eat it. He follows me around the house as I tidy the rooms. In this way, the work of being a wife burdens me in new ways. And then, I must tolerate his bony hand on my hip without warning, or his dry lips brushing against my cheek at any moment. His embraces, most of all, cause a great cavern of loss to open within me, for Sontje's kisses felt wet and full and alive on my skin, where his remind me of dust and dry tree bark.

I learn to be more still than my nature allows. On the *Leyden,* I worked lace with Griet, or played draughts with the other women, and spent hours on the deck, delighting in the changing movement and color of the rolling seas and the lively work of our sailors. No one especially cared about my activities, perhaps too burdened by their own boredom or worries. And later, I felt a new freedom in sharing a berth with Sontje.

But my husband hungers for my company, and seeks to relieve me of as much work as possible so that he may enjoy it. He says I have worked long enough already, and that his greatest joy is seeing me at rest. What he considers rest feels like a heavier boredom than I ever felt on the *Leyden*. But I do not tell him this, of course.

Like all respectable settlers' wives, I have slaves at my disposal as well, which further confounds my need for work. Candra and Aini are a widowed mother and daughter, living in the nearby *kampung* with the community of other widows, or *beguines*. Aini is slightly younger than me, though she doesn't know her exact age. She is slim with unusually round eyes and small, graceful hands. Candra is slope-shouldered and dour, except when I give her the licorice balls Mattheus offers me as a gift. Then she brightens with a wide, toothless smile. Aini laughs when she sees me carrying water from the well. I have the sense that both think I'm a curiosity at best, a fool at worst. Though they understand my commands (requests, really, I will never feel comfortable commanding anyone), they never respond in Dutch.

I should fall upon these slaves for work—I should exploit them gratefully, for how Batavia has changed my state in the world. But I am not accustomed to having chores done for me, and I dislike the dependency created by slavery, that I might forget where the broom is stored or how to wash my own pots. And so the slaves and I engage in a silent battle. I wash my own clothes and hang them to dry, only to have Candra take them off the line and re-wash them. They clamor for the plates and utensils, eager to clean them, to make themselves useful. They inspect the crockery and forks, wondering at their use. Aini presses the tines of a fork into her cheek, grazes a knife blade against her finger and holds the flat of it against her forehead, exploring.

Having slaves changes me. I'm troubled to think I might grow into a Madam De Graaf against my intentions. Once, I misplaced one of the pearl-drop earrings Mattheus presented to me on our wedding day. For an hour I fretted over its loss and the slithering thought occurred: *maybe the women took it.* Shame filled me—this is how Madam De Graaf regarded me. I was no better than her with my baseless suspicions, expecting the worst of people who did my bidding all day.

Perhaps such is the cost of having more than others—you expect from your inferiors your own worst impulses. And of course, I found the missing earring under the bed and felt a fresh wave of shame pass through me.

Since that time, I give Aini and Candra coins when I have them.

I'm sweeping the tile floor of the kitchen when Aini calls me to the door. I know she is vexed by my sweeping and would prefer that task to greeting visitors.

"I was on the way back from the market and thought I would pay you a visit," Maritjen huffs from under a very large bonnet to protect her fair skin. The bonnet darkens at her forehead from sweat. The Batavian sun spares no one. Our thick frocks look absurd in this heat and often I envy the natives with their lighter clothing.

She doesn't wait for me to invite her inside. "You look well settled in your nice house," she says, appraising my walls and furnishings. "Lovely roses in the front." She sits down on one of our simple rattan chairs.

"I'm settling in well enough," I say, stiffening in Maritjen's presence. I had forgotten this feeling of having to watch myself with her.

"This isn't a social visit, Jana," Maritjen says, her mouth a thin line. "The slaves are saying you pay your girls. Is this true?" And before I can respond, she continues. "You must stop. They are telling the others and it causes jealousy among them."

"They deserve a wage. They work hard, as I did when I was a house servant," I reply. Maritjen still acts as though we are on the ship, wielding power she now lacks here on land.

"This isn't Amsterdam, Jana. You ruin the enterprise like this. It is our duty to maintain the order of things." Her cheeks redden with indignation, or perhaps from the heat. "At the very least, tell them not to boast to the others."

I must do a quick calculation. Maritjen's gossip could harm Mattheus. In marriage, one must always take into account the husband. Such a consideration is new for me, and yet I'm surprised—and saddened— at how quickly I have adapted. A lesson I learned young from my own mother. "I don't tell them to boast of anything. If they choose to speak to the other natives, they will do so."

I will talk to Mattheus about Aini and Candra later, but I won't give Maritjen the satisfaction of knowing I've accepted her advice.

"You must have a firm hand, Jana. This will not reflect well on your husband, either."

Candra comes with a plate of guavas and tea, but Maritjen is already standing up.

"I must go, but thank you for the offering," she says, waving away Candra. "Gerhard and I must meet with a senior merchant this evening. I'm surprised your husband was not also invited."

"I do not ask about his every appointment," I reply. At this, Maritjen reddens further, and I gladly see her out the door.

When I raise Maritjen's complaint that evening , I'm disappointed that Mattheus agrees with her.

"She has a point, Jana. If they feel they are equal to us, we can't rule them."

"It's our household. And they deserve payment."

"Why? So they can purchase goods the others can't? So they are resented and despised and the subjects of others' jealousy in their *kampung*? So they can buy some useless trinkets and cause unnecessary trouble?" His voice, usually low and feeble, grows louder. Often I have observed this, men using their voices to overpower us. Fader did the same.

"No, so they can be acknowledged for their labor." I think of Moeder, who always grew silent during Fader's tirades. How angry I felt watching them, though I did not realize it then. At Fader's power, and Moeder's ready weakness.

"Pay them less and tell them not to inform the others," he says with finality. His temper is a rare occurrence, but in such moments I resent him mightily because he relies on the same power as our own colony—the power of tradition. Because he is a man and my husband, I must obey.

"Yes, husband," I reply. But I make no effort to keep the chill from my voice.

Later that night, I wait for Mattheus to fall asleep, snoring as loudly as my drunken father did long ago, and wrench my shoulder from under his hand. I go to my trunk, part of my payment upon arrival, and look through its contents—old clothes from the *Leyden,* heavy with memories I can't bear to abandon. A patch from the *Leyden's* sail after we docked. I chose to wear one of my own simple frocks as my wedding dress, with a bit of Griet's lace edging sewn to the sleeves.

I touch the crisp and delicate stitching, and run my finger over its furls and knots, the delicate pillow laces, hearing from deep within my memory, Griet's soft voice. *We Dutch women make chrysanthemum lace, but reticella is quite different and unique.*

I look into its intricate weave. *First a knot here. Pull the thread, but not too tightly, to make a small loop.* For hours, I watched Griet with her sewing. I recall all the time she spent teaching me her craft because the days wore on so long.

I find a pattern in the lace and gather my needles and thread. I sit at the table and practice by candlelight. Like all Dutch women, I know sewing and my skills have improved over the years. Without the shifting of the *Leyden*, the work moves faster than I expected. I work late into the night in our sitting room, lighting a tallow candle beside me, listening to the night birds, and Mattheus's intermittent snorts from our bedroom. The knots and passes relieve my mind of its restlessness and anger, and I search for a rhythm to my stitches, recalling how I created little games for myself as I worked as a servant back in Amsterdam. Stacking as many dishes as I could before walking down to the cellar, scrubbing triangles into the wood floors, folding the linens in identical rectangles. All attempts to forget myself and my condition.

Though I try not to think of Sontje, my mind returns to her as I work the thread and guide the needle through picots and bars. I recall our last nights on the *Leyden,* wading into the lake, the click-woman's flickering torch and the cave where I finally said goodbye to my sister. I will never see that beautiful place again. Sontje is all I have left of it, and even she recedes into her marriage to Willem Brouwer.

And so I return to those old habits and games, realizing they gave me something to hold to when I felt most afraid and alone.

Chapter 53

Four months have passed since Sontje's wedding, and at times I fear the loneliness and boredom will drive me to madness.

I have been alone before. Most of my life, interrupted briefly by Helena then Sontje. Here or there, even more fleetingly, with others like Tobias. But after Sontje, the loneliness is unendurable. The simplicity of our brief life together in our berth, leaning against one another, sharing stories into the night, seems a miracle.

I go for my morning walks, feeling passing happiness at the breeze blowing red blossoms from the trees, the great blue and green dragonflies hovering overhead, but beneath these observations, I ache to speak with her.

I work on my lace, perfecting my stitches, and spend long hours in my garden, measuring time by the growth of the baby limes on our new tree. Bees alight on the roses and I regret that I failed to tell Sontje of the time I clapped one between my hands as it buzzed around baby Hlaska. And how Hlaska followed me, crawling on her awkward, baby knees, as if I were some fearless god.

They are not important stories, but having shared so much with her, I wish to share more.

*

Sunday. The procession to church has become a pageant. The women wear strands of pearls in their hair and newly purchased velvet gowns, trailing uniformed manservants and female slaves hoisting parasols over their mistresses. They look solemnly ahead, following their owners' example.

The Company men complain about the display, but can't conceal their pride.

"My wife," sighs Cornelis Claesz, an older administrator who arrived with his wife before us. "She insists on wearing jewelry even to the market. I keep buying new slaves. At this point, she could hire someone to breathe for her."

"Yes, mine is the same," Gerhard says. He nods his head toward the three knob-kneed native boys marching grimly behind Maritjen. One holds her velvet purse. "Just last week I purchased two new boys for her retinue."

Mattheus asks me to wear nicer dresses, to use the slaves more. But I hardly know what to do with Aini and Candra as it is, and I resist having more people in the house, disturbing the quiet. And I enjoy the sun on my arms as I scrub the dishes and pour hot water on the front steps while the crows chortle and argue in the trees.

At dinner, he insists again.

"You should use them, Jana. That is their purpose." He chews his chicken like a goat chewing tough grass. "I don't understand why you do not. Why not make life easier for yourself?"

"It is easier for me to do what I know."

"Just watch how the other women are with their slaves."

"I have. It seems unnatural to me. I enjoy my chores. What else would I do? I prefer work to sipping tea and conversing about so-and-so's petticoat length."

"Jana, as a senior official of the Company, it looks odd if I do not have more slaves than those below me."

"Then you approve of today's parade to the church?" I'm aware I tread close to the thin boundary belonging to wives and their opinions, but I feel reckless and disappointed that I did not see Sontje today. Nearly the entire settlement attended today's service, and I thought I would see a glimpse of her.

"Of course not. They looked absurd, showing off their slaves like prize cattle. But we must adapt to the expectations of the colonies. These little displays are how we demonstrate our power."

"It's not enough power to refuse paying them for their labor?"

He gives me a hard look. A warning. But I push on. I have said worse to Fader and been hided for it. It isn't even the fact of the slaves. It is my own shattered heart. My irritability with my helplessness, my unmet desire to see Sontje that I'm pouring into this matter of the slaves.

"Do not ask me to do what I can't," I say.

"Jana, if you insist on this stubbornness, I will restrict your spending money. I've never asked for much of an accounting from you before."

I say nothing to this, gnawing on the rage entering my middle. I have worked for money all my life, and now I realize even in my poverty I enjoyed greater freedom than I have now.

"I forbid you to pay the slaves," he says, his eyes heavy on me.

An idea comes to me, that I may use this argument for another purpose.

"If you insist that I use slaves and not pay them, at least let me earn some pay of my own."

"What? So you can pay them without my permission?"

"No, so I can feel I'm earning my own keep, as I've always done. I feel useless just ordering Aini and Candra around when I'm perfectly able to sweep floors and wash the linens."

"What do you mean?" He looks puzzled at my words and I think how marriage has yoked together two such different people—me with my need for purpose, and my husband with his thirst for naps.

The idea forms just as I begin to speak, and even I surprise myself. "I want to try and sell my lacework."

"Lacework? But I thought it was a hobby. Something to entertain yourself."

"I do it well, better than just a hobby. I learned on the *Leyden* from my berth-mate who died on the voyage. Madaleen admires my work, and says she thinks others would pay for it." Indeed, she said it once, but that was back on the *Leyden* and I had just mended her dress.

Mattheus shakes his head slowly, and looks very tired. "Whereas all the other women want nothing more than to sit on their highbacked chairs and be fanned by the slaves, my wife wishes to engage in business and make her husband look like he can't provide. And all I want is for you to enjoy yourself. To rest."

"You provide as you should," I say, seeking to appease his hurt pride. "But I'm not fit for such idleness." I straighten myself, hoping he will see my determination. "I've worked all my life, and I crave it now." I recall Madam De Graaf's favorite proverb, hoping to convince him further. "'He becometh poor that dealeth a slack hand.' It's how I was raised."

He looks at me, still as stone, thinking.

"Jana, my wife. You are a bit much for me in my old age. But I see how you suffer with your restlessness. I think I understand. Growing up in Kessel, I, too, became accustomed to labor. Perhaps the work will do you some good. Tire you out so you'll spend more hours with me in the evening." He smiles, and I attempt a feeble smile in return, wondering what sort of favors he'll later require, but too relieved to worry about it.

Chapter 54

An uncertain peace stretches between us over the next weeks. We are polite to one another, and I tolerate his arms around me at night. I try to summon thankfulness that my husband allows me the possibility of earning some money for myself, but working is all I've known, and I resent having to ask for permission where I needed none before. My indebtedness to him feels like a new cage. Now I must make more elaborate meals, which demands more planning, more trips to the market, more help from the slaves, and less time for sewing. Already, I force myself to stay in bed those first mornings after our agreement, because he desires such closeness. I gather my moments of freedom like crumbs—a quick walk around the compound, quiet hours of lacemaking when he leaves for the day.

I work for hours in his absence, busying myself with stitching. Mattheus even brings me thread from the markets, and in such moments, I warm to him, and my heart lightens a bit in its yearning for Sontje, and my worst fear—that I may never see her again. Every tangled knot forces me from my memories, returns me to the task of unraveling and fixing. I make my stitches more intricate, adding some design of my own. Sometimes my patterns turn out well, other times my efforts result in gaping holes and uneven forms. But I continue. My labors lessen the ache of Sontje's long absence, and Aini and Candra welcome the opportunity to get back to their work. My attention to the lace means I hardly supervise them, which suits me anyway, as I find the role a discomfort to me, after my years of toiling for others. The two women show some curiosity at my efforts, and once, I even noticed Candra tracing her own small fingers over the lace when she thought I had left the room. I said nothing of her interest, not wanting to steal the moment from her, and recalling how I often lingered in the De Graaf hallway to look at their paintings and make some meaning of them.

By the end of three weeks, I have three different lengths of lacework to sell. Enough for cuffs or a small collar. Not much, but I can show it to the other women and see if they may order more.

I wait until mid-week to go to the market. I bring my lace in three rolls and place them in a new bamboo basket. I wear my cleanest dress—the plain whiteness of my dowry frocks quickly soil from my sweat and the dust of the village that rises in great clouds when I walk outside.

I can't help my pounding heart as I walk to the market in the main town square. Not only for my nerves at selling my lace, but also because every trip to the market or church brings the possibility of seeing Sontje.

In Amsterdam, this market would hardly merit traffic for its small size. Just two rows of stands. But here, slaves and servants and wives arrive in a steady stream. I walk just past the spice merchant's stand, housing great clay bowls of cinnamon sticks and cloves and pepper seeds. His stand attracts the most customers for the unknown items overflowing his baskets, so I stand next to it, holding my handbasket, hoping to attract customers as they leave. The spice merchant nods at me and I smile, hoping he will not mind my presence. He looks regal in his turban and long robe even in the midday heat—the clothing of a Muslim. His skin is a dark, reddish-brown, a shade I have not seen before and again I feel glad to be here, to see people I would never know of had I remained in Amsterdam.

I have some small hope that perhaps Sontje will pass through, but I have yet to see her in town.

My feet feel heavy in my sandals and I'm unsure how to stand with my basket, whether to smile or look serious. But then I think of all the times before when I have needed work and lacked the luxury of feeling embarrassed by my poverty or hunger.

"What are you doing here, Jana?" Madaleen approaches with Maritjen, who trails two slaves holding her betel box and sun *paraplu*. Madaleen married an ambitious young clerk named Tomas soon after my own wedding to Mattheus. I've not seen her since, and my heart lifts at the sight of her, even if I am disappointed to see Maritjen.

"I've been bored doing nothing but ordering the slaves around, so I thought I'd try to sell the lace I sew." I nod toward my basket, and Madaleen looks inside.

"Your work is getting so much more delicate." She takes one roll from the basket and studies its length.

"Your husband doesn't mind you working?" Maritjen scowls at the lace, which filters the sunlight, making it glow yellow.

"No. He admires my industry." I allow some defiance to enter my words. Maritjen's cheeks droop downward now, and her skin is red and shiny, as if stretched too tight against her bones.

"First he lets you pay your slaves and now he lets you sell at the markets." Maritjen shakes her head.

"What does it matter?" Madaleen interrupts, placing the lace back in my basket. "Her work is beautiful, and it doesn't harm anyone." She smiles at me. "Jana, I would like to buy some. But can you sew it to a dress? Tomas just purchased a new one for me, and this lace would suit it well. I'll have one of my slaves deliver it to you."

"Of course." I enjoy Maritjen's annoyance at Madaleen's praise.

"I think others will want your lace. It comes so rarely on the ships from Holland."

I smile in return and Madaleen gives me a quick embrace, winding her arm around my basket.

"I'm happy to see you Jana, and proud of your work."

And as she and Maritjen walk off toward the fruit stand on the other side of the market, I can't help but feel the same. Even my walk home, so familiar to me I know my progress on the route by each planted tree, becomes somehow brighter and more cheerful. How prettily the leaves of the saplings dance in the breeze, how lovely the light looks shining on the murky canals. I must laugh at myself, how I let the world change simply because I have had some brief success at my lacemaking. And still, I cling to this happiness, knowing it is mine, and made by my own hand.

When Mattheus arrives home, I greet him and even summon the desire to kiss his cheek, proud of the day's accomplishment, eager to share with him about my day. He remains quiet, and barely smiles, but I imagine his work has tired him, and I bring out a full meal—rice, fish, *sla*, and something inspired by the *stamppot* he misses from the homeland.

He says little as we eat, and chews slower than is his custom. In our first days together, I often looked away from him during meals, for he gobbled his food so quickly, often dropping bits and crumbs in his grizzled beard.

"You are quiet tonight," I finally say, wishing he would ask about my activities.

"Am I?" He sips his water, instead of taking his usual great gulps.

"I sold some of my lace today," I say, wishing him to ask me questions.

"So I've heard." He coughs into his fist, a nervous habit that, I've learned, usually follows with some criticism. "Maritjen told Gerhard, and he told the other men, and all had a good laugh at my expense for having a wife who sells at the slaves' market."

"They're not all slaves there." But I know my answer will not appease him.

"The Dutch who sell there belong to the guilds. That's the law."

"But is there a guild for lacemakers? I'm the only one here."

"Only guild members or natives can sell at the markets, Jana." He uses the voice he reserves for imparting some lesson to me. A voice that makes my skin prickle with anger.

"What I recall from Amsterdam is only men can join the guilds, though."

"It's true. Only men. We follow Dutch rules, and married women are particularly forbidden from selling at the markets."

I think of Tobias then, and how, though a man, he could not join the guilds for being a Jew. And a new wave of anger passes over me, for the guilds only seek to help Dutchmen who believe in our God, and confine the rest to poverty and scraps.

"It seems unfair, when we have no guild for lacemakers, and no men who know the craft."

"The Company has its rules, Jana. It's how we maintain order in this wild place."

"Order for some, and shackles for others." I can't suppress the bitterness in my voice.

Mattheus sighs. "Really, Jana, you ask the impossible of an old man like me."

I shrug, emptied of words, and stand up to clean the table and remove the dishes for Aini and Candra to wash in the morning.

That night, I tolerate my husband's bony arms around me, but only out of obligation.

Chapter 55

I am outside at dawn this morning, angry and heavy-hearted about the nonsense with the guilds and Mattheus's stubbornness, and hoping the sunrise will pull me from my dark thoughts. I can't help but think of Sontje, how I wish to unburden these thoughts with her. I hoped I would see her at the market, and imagined her happiness at seeing me with my own little stand, selling the lace Griet taught me to sew.

I ignore my inside chores and leave Mattheus inside sleeping. I walk outside quietly with a small knife to cut some roses from my bushes for a new vase. I have no energy for my lace today. It only reminds me of my confinement.

As I cut one of my rosebush stems, Dewa appears like a visitor from another life, though that life existed only months ago. The early sunshine glows on her dark skin. Unlike the other slaves, who wear our layered skirts when working in the colony, she wears the traditional *saya*, dyed in a rich purple, the same shade of the petunias I often saw in the flower boxes of the shuttered Herengracht houses, and I feel myself missing those common blooms and their boxes.

"Dewa," I say, smiling, happy to see her. I press my hands together in greeting as the Sundanese do to one another, but quickly so none of the settlers can witness it. The Company wants us to keep our own traditions, not to adopt theirs.

She carries a basket of fruit and some long green roots I have not seen before.

From her basket Dewa pulls out a glossy purple mangosteen, so clean it looks polished. Such an odd fruit. When opened, the flesh is white and plump like new clouds. She holds it out to me.

"Thank you," I say, taking the fruit. How smooth and beautiful, like nothing I would find in Amsterdam, but I have a sick feeling that I am holding my own grieving, hopeless heart.

She smiles, and presses between her cupped hands my hand holding the mangosteen. She points to the string of blue glass beads around her neck and then points to me.

"Candra," she says. I think she means Candra gave her the beads, purchased with money I paid her.

"You look beautiful," I say. And despite the creases of Dewa's skin and her missing teeth, I do not lie.

She takes my hands again, and I feel the bones under her thin skin.

"Have you seen Sontje?" I ask. I have asked Aini and Candra, believing the slaves must speak of us, but they know little. Sontje has only one house slave, named Sanne, and Aini and Candra say the girl speaks only of her little farm in the *kampung*, and which vegetables are ripe, and the number of crows she has killed because they attack her beans. Nothing about Sontje and little of Willem Brouwer either—indeed, even in the colony, few speak of him at all.

Dewa points to her hair and then the bright sun. Nods. *Sontje.* Madaleen is also light-haired, but only Sontje has that curious mix of white and yellow strands that brings to mind sunlight.

She shakes her head, no.

It is an odd thing that sometimes a person can return at a time when one is most lonely, and it is as though a heavy door opens and a warm wind enters, blowing aside the burden of solitude.

"Dewa, can I see where you live?" I think it strange I have not seen it, or the *kampung*, but the Company wishes us to know one another only as slaves and settlers. But I'm tired of the Company. Of what it demands from us.

She looks at me, as though weighing the possibility. I watch the raised mole on the side of her nose, the wrinkles of her forehead, the sagging skin on her neck, the full lips now obscured by small, etched wrinkles.

"I have two hours before my husband wakes," I say. He wakes even later now, his aging body greedy for its sleep. His wondering about my whereabouts is an annoyance I have yet to overcome, but I welcome the extra hours I gain for all his sleeping.

Finally, Dewa nods, and beckons me to follow.

We walk behind our white compound, a long dirt path flanking the surrounding wall, and then through a break in the wall to the *kampung*. The sunlight spills over the trees, and even the crude brick wall looks friendlier cast in the morning sun's bright beam. A narrow footpath passes by modest huts, and the thatched roofs resemble ragged, unkempt heads of hair. The native homes lie empty, except for the smallest children or those too old to work as slaves. Everyone else readies for their work, but the remaining natives peek out from their huts, regard Dewa with respect, nod at me without looking directly.

A longer hut lies at the end of the road, set apart from the others. Clean white walls.

And from inside, women singing.

Dewa gestures toward the entrance of the long hut. Strings of colored glass beads veil the doorway. The native children collect these beads from us, and will do nearly anything for a few of them. When they receive them, they hold the bits of glass up to the sunlight, one eye closed.

Smiling.

Flower blossoms and seashells adorn the ends of each string of beads. I can't help but hold a single thread in my hand. The beads remind me of the bits of glass I found in the trees of the Bos so long ago.

I part the veil and enter.

Inside, old women sit cross-legged on the floor. The natives are more agile than us. They easily sit on their heels, their legs supple from their work. Sweet smoke drifts in the air from some burning herb.

They begin to sing. Old voices, different voices. Nothing like our music. I have heard it from a distance. But how different it sounds up close, the sound cradling my heart. My bones fill with their strange voices.

At the end of the song, the youngest of the women stands up and walks around the circle, holding a teak tea tray. She stops at each woman, looks deeply in their eyes. Presents each of them tea in a clay bowl which they receive with both hands.

And drink slowly.

She approaches me with a bowl. Looks into my own eyes. A different brown than my own. Irises blooming yellow.

The women laugh and sing and drink their tea. I watch and though I can't understand their words, I laugh because they do. A feeling I am one of them, though I'm an intruder like the rest of us settlers.

A feeling I have not been seen like this before.

*

When I finally return home, the sun sticks warm on my skin, and Mattheus waits for me. I had hoped he would still be sleeping.

"Where were you, Jana?" he asks. He drinks tea from the yellow ceramic cup he nearly dropped yesterday. His hands shake as he brings the cup to his narrow lips. I had not noticed so much trembling before.

"I went for an early morning walk and met someone I knew from the *kampung*."

"Who?"

I resent his questions, but know I must answer them.

"Dewa. A native."

"Yes. I know of her. A *beguine*. She lives with the other widows at the end of their village."

I do not tell him I have been to the *kampung*, seen the magic of these women living together, their strong voices. I'm more myself for keeping this secret.

"They are an interesting people. Not like the *strandlopers* at the Cape—all those heathens walking about naked."

I think of the click-woman, but say nothing.

"Come, have breakfast with me." Mattheus pushes the chair out next to him. I walk to the kitchen for our breakfast first, and return, placing a dish of salt fish and fruit at the center of the table.

Though I wish I could refuse, I take my seat.

"I feel old this morning," he says, watching me as I cut the fish into small bits and eat forkfuls of the dry flesh. I'm still unused to fish for breakfast and prefer a simple plate of fruit.

"When I left our bed this morning, the bones of my feet hurt. My knees. At times, I try to say things and the words seem hidden in rabbit holes. I think back on my days as a young man—I used to run the hills back home, racing the other boys. I could run for long stretches without stopping. Didn't even feel the burrs underfoot. Youth is a kind of armor. Aging is the sudden loss of it, hour by hour." He looks rueful. "Not that you would know."

"I have felt old," I reply. "Poverty ages us. Waking every morning without any certainty you will eat that day ages you. Worrying about where you will sleep or whether some stranger will proposition you, or if you will be attacked in an alley after dusk."

"You have experienced such things?"

"Some of them," I say, not wishing to say more.

He slurps his tea, a long draught. "The more time I am with you, Jana, the less I feel I know of you."

I have no answer to this observation, so I say nothing. A memory of Sontje comes to me, of lying in our hammocks on the *Leyden* before sleep. A memory she shared of seeing a dead rat outside her house. "They disgusted me, their long, hairless tails, their narrow, cunning little eyes," she said, "but up close, it seemed so lonely. One of the stray cats had killed it, crushed its neck between its jaws, and in that moment, I felt such pity for it, and for myself, because I felt the same fate waited for me. Other jaws, but the same ending." I listened and felt the same way Mattheus must feel now—a sense we can never truly share ourselves. Limited by words and memories of words, and feelings unattached to words. But his desire to understand my past pleases me a little.

The strong sun through our small windows lights up the pink scalp beneath his white hair and I feel both revulsion and tenderness at the glaring fact that my husband of only months is a dying man.

Chapter 56

Some strange energy flows through me after the morning's visit to the *kampung*. I wait for Mattheus to leave after our breakfast. He has a meeting for the Company and will not return until evening. I savor my solitude and instruct Aini and Candra to wash the tiled floors and change all the bedding. They seem relieved by my requests, for I'm often reluctant to give them much work now that Mattheus refuses to provide me money. But I have decided to offer them goods instead for their work—crockery, clothing, vases, small trinkets I have.

But first, I will see her.

I take my time getting dressed in my simple white frock. I use coconut oil on my long hair and brush it until the sun-bleached ends shine. I braid and wind my hair into a thick coil. I even put pearls in my hair as the other women do. I wear my only necklace—a small pearl stone on a chain. Another wedding gift from Mattheus. I scrub my face with tallow and water and look at my reflection in my hand mirror.

Plain-faced Jana greets me.

But I feel some fondness for her now. A desire to claim happiness once more, as I once did on the *Leyden* and then at the watering hole of the Cape, and finally, under the rainbow tree in the forest beyond Batavia's wall.

I place some fruits in a basket—papayas, mangoes, guavas, and a small tin of tea.

"I will return in a few hours," I tell Aini and Candra.

Madaleen described the house to me. Small and gray on the western side of town, close to the canal. I hope a name placard will be on the door, as it is on all the other houses.

I find it easily enough, just as Madaleen described it. A small, gray cottage on a dirt path. The canal's foul smell even overcomes the flowering frangipani trees planted nearby. I wave my arms to sweep the humming mosquitoes from me. Their bite marks already cover my arms from a day when I did not wear full sleeves.

She has planted a pot of blue crocuses in the front, but they wilt in Batavia's potent sunlight. A dark brown stain is smeared on the wall next to the door. Sontje of Amsterdam would have removed such a spot. Or asked me to remove it.

Quiet but for the clicking cicadas, the distant shouts of slaves arguing.

Red clay and fallen leaves litter the doorstep. In Amsterdam, Sontje insisted on a swept and washed doorstep.

I place my hand on the heavy *suar* wood door, warm from the late morning sun. I imagine her greeting me. Will she be happy? Afraid? Will she smile and invite me in, or find my presence on her unswept doorstep a burden—of memories, of a disappeared life?

I listen to the breeze sweeping through the nearby banyans, the scratch of their hanging roots as they brush against their great trunks. I recall the wind blowing against the mast of the *Leyden,* a cheerful, slapping sound that became as familiar as Sontje's low, quiet voice.

I knock three times.

The minutes feel stretched and ominous. My *klomps* bite into my heels, and the sun beats on my back. My scalp perspires under my hair. Only a little breeze today, not enough to blunt the heat.

A rice bird sings.

A small rainbow tree grows to the side of the house, but its colors lack the vibrant hues of the forest tree we saw together. Still, I take its nearby presence as a good sign.

Her footfalls. Slow, unhurried steps.

My heart hammers.

Chapter 57

She stands in the doorway. Tall and straight as ever.

When I see her, I can't stop myself from speaking, as though all my words have waited inside me for too long.

"I miss you, Sontje. You have all but disappeared."

Her hands rest on her stomach, and only then do I notice the roundness beneath them.

So, he has put a child in her. The plain fact of Willem Brouwer's body within hers stings of grief in me. I imagine every touch I have laid on her erased. Replaced. My lips on the back of her neck as we slept. My fingertips on the webbing between her fingers. Mattheus paws at me once every fortnight now, digging away at me like I'm a hill to be burrowed into, but I have not thought of pregnancy, given his old age.

But Willem is young. He must want her nightly.

Her unreadable face saddens me. Where I once knew her every expression, she seems to wear a mask now.

"You should not have come here," she says after a long pause. Her voice is low and sad.

How I have longed to hear it.

"I had to see you."

There's a buzzing feeling inside me. Fear.

"We must go on with our lives, Jana. We had our time on the *Leyden*."

I look to her swollen stomach, confused.

"Are you ill?" I ask.

Fatigue sweeps over her face, softening her expression. "Yes. Always. I had no idea how hard it would be. And this heat. I feel like I'm suffocating. I can't even imagine wearing a stomacher. The slightest pressure and I retch."

I nod, jealous of Willem Brouwer again.

"When will it be born?"

"A few more months. I feel it moving inside me. Sometimes I have to press on my stomach so it will shift. It knocks against my ribs."

I look into her gray eyes and see they have lost their vigor and brightness. "Sontje. You have stopped fighting. You have given up."

She looks down at the doorstep, cluttered with fallen leaves and dust. "I have surrendered to this life," she says. "You always believed I was stronger than I am. And I started to believe you. Sometimes I'm angry you made me believe it, because I feel disappointed in myself, and before I would have accepted my fate. But I'm done with all of it." She pins a tendril of her hair behind her ear, and I recall the beloved gesture from our time before.

"Even me?" I can't help but ask.

"I need to rest, Jana." She moves her slim hand to her lower back. Stretches. "I will see you again but Willem will be home soon from wherever he goes off to and I need to finish my sewing for the baby."

I look at her, hungry for her gaze.

"Nothing has changed for me," I say. "And I'm married, too."

"Yes, I heard. I'm sorry I was too ill to attend." This dishonesty pains me, for I know of the contempt between her husband and mine. That Willem Brouwer refused our invitation.

Her voice goes quiet again. Almost a whisper. "I hope he is good to you, Jana."

"I hardly think of him at all," I say.

Her eyes redden and I wish she would cry. Some confirmation she hurts as well.

"Goodbye, Jana." She closes the door.

I wait on the doorstep. I'm not sure what to do. I look to the rainbow tree.

The hidden insects chatter, the birds call above. I listen to my own breathing, short and shallow, filling the blooming ache within me.

I'm still holding her basket of fruit and think of knocking again, but can't.

I lean down and sweep the doorstep clean with my hand. The grit of the red clay scratches my palm and the fallen petals from nearby flowering trees roll and clump together under my fingers. But after some time, the leaves move easily enough to the side.

When the step is clean, I place the basket upon it and leave.

Chapter 58

I attend church services each Sunday, always hopeful that she will be there. And the rest of the week I think of what to tell her and how to tell it. I take longer walks in the morning, spend more time in silence, sewing my lace. I seek reprieve from my sadness, but find none.

I learn to speak to Aini and Candra in their language, though poorly. I think of things to tell Sontje, things she no longer wants to know.

I have a rose garden and a doddering husband.

I still taste you in my dreams.

Once she has the child, she will love it and forget all about me. Nursing, carrying, playing with it. Singing to it the songs I sang to her when she was sick. She may even love Willem afterward. I will once again be raw-knuckled Jana who dusts the cabinet, who washes the aprons with lye, and polishes the silver so it gleams.

In the evening, Mattheus and I sit at the dining table finishing the *sla* I have attempted to prepare without cabbage or beef, using native herbs instead, so it tastes only faintly of the *sla* I sometimes made for the Reynsts in Amsterdam when Hilda was sick. He watches me and I'm shy, even now.

"Jana," he says. "How are you?"

Such an odd question for a man to ask of his wife. At first, I wonder if he ridicules me. But his eyes show concern. His trembling, wrinkled hands rest on my own.

"You seem unhappy. You eat so little." His hand grasps mine, and though I try to wrest it away, he tightens his grip. "I have lived a long time. I have lost a wife, a son, three dogs, one parrot, and everyone who knew me as a young man. I have known every kind of sadness. You need not share yours with me, but I will listen."

I look into his brown, old man's eyes, weighing his words. The servants are washing the linens behind the house and the rice finches sound their chip-chip calls in the distance. The air is heavy with the promise of rain.

"Anything, Jana. Let there be no secrets between us."

I have no words for what Sontje and I did. But the weight of my grief, its impossibility, compels me, so I tell him as best I can.

That night, though we sleep in the same bed, he refuses to hold my hand or touch me as he usually does.

I'm surprised at my feeling of rejection, a fear I have violated whatever contract I had entered into with the Company. What if he asks me to leave? Where will I go? And what if he tells others? What will happen to Sontje? I wind through such thoughts all night. I lie on my back and listen to the crickets, cicadas, and night birds. Chirps and screams and lamentations. They seem louder than on other nights, and their sounds reassure me.

Life will continue, either this one, or a new one. I have been through trials enough already.

*

Mattheus's hand finds mine the next morning. I clasp it in gratitude, my back facing him.

"Jana," he says, as he has said every morning since we were married. "I hope you had a pleasant sleep." His politeness is one of his best qualities—it reassures me that his civility is fixed. But I am always surprised by it, having grown up with a father who never once said please or thank you or inquired about my thoughts.

"I listened all night to the birds and insects," I tell him, wishing to make things better. "They make a beautiful noise. So different from our little Dutch birds."

He pauses, perhaps remembering all I shared with him last night.

"You were too worried to sleep," he says. He keeps his hand on mine.

"I was." I turn to him, look into his creased face. The liver spot on his temple, raised and dark brown like a young raisin. The lines etched around his mouth, the gray hair peeking from his ears, growing wildly from his eyebrows. This is my husband. I'm braced to him for all my life.

"You need not be." He strokes my cheek with the back of his finger. "I do not understand it, but it is in the past. She is Willem Brouwer's now, and good luck to her for that. It can't be an easy life with him." But before I can ask further, he looks at me with a hardness I've not seen before. "You must forget her, Jana. Be her acquaintance, be civil, caring, and virtuous as you women are expected to be. But forget her, and what you once had. That is how you go on."

I say nothing, his words barely holding meaning as I think of my unhappiness.

He watches me, holding his chin in his hand as he does when deep in thought. "I'll help you with the market, Jana, if it will take your mind off all this. I can talk to the administrators, see if I can find a place for you there, without the guild's blessing. But forget her. She's Willem's now." He caresses my cheek with his forefinger and I will myself not to flinch. "And you are mine," he adds.

He waits for an answer, but I have none.

"You will do that, Jana? Forget her?"

I know I can't, but he will accept only one answer.

"Yes," I tell this old man, my husband. "I will."

Chapter 59

Aini enters our little sitting room and watches as I work my lace. She puts down her broom and she rubs her fingers together, as though feeling the lace between them, as though hungry to try it herself.

"You can come and see." I smile and nod her toward me. She is shy without her mother, who is washing the linens outside. Aini has a long forehead and small, pointed chin, and the curious, bright eyes I first noticed in the Sundanese women.

She stands beside me, but I tell her to bring a chair. She looks uncertain, glancing toward the door where her mother is singing to herself in a pleasant, high-pitched voice.

"You can see better this way."

Aini pulls the chair from our supper table and sits next to me. I show her my progress, naming the materials—the tatting cotton for the outline, backing fabric, *cordonnet*, the silk thread I use for the lace, and my blunted needles. I explain how I must guess the length of thread I'll need for the couching stitches that fix the *cordonnet* to the backing fabric, and how I loop the lace thread through the couching stitches to build the lace. The knots must hold the same tension, and varying the intervals between couch stitches will make for uneven lace. When I first learned needle lace, the steadfast sloshing of the *Leyden* further vexed my stitches and knots. But with Griet's patient direction, I found myself enjoying the work, and I learned to coordinate my stitches to the movement of the sea, finding a rhythm to my own gestures that matched the lulls between waves.

A curious feeling enters me as I explain to Aini, who stares into my work as though looking for some answer in the threads. I can almost hear Griet's sweet voice as I explain the steps to Aini. The girl hardly blinks, she is so taken with the stitching. Her hands move in her lap, as though she makes invisible stitches herself.

"Do you wish to try it?" I hold the fabric out to her.

She looks down at her lap. Nods.

I give her my work, hesitating a moment, for I do not wish to lose the progress I've just made, but Aini takes the fabric with a surprising boldness, and begins building on my lace—her stitches soon bloom even and clean as my own. I'm impressed by her skill.

"You make it look easier than it is," I tell her.

Aini smiles, enjoying my surprised expression.

I watch Aini for some time, and then begin another piece of lace to match hers, which I will later join together. We sew in the quiet, side by side, until time disappears and I hear only Candra's voice, and below it, the sweet chattering of rice birds and the occasional breeze rushing through the palm trees outside. I discover a secret cadence to these sounds as I once did for the waves on the *Leyden* so many months ago, and the existence of such constant music at sea, and now, on this strange, Batavian land, comforts me. I need only still myself and listen for its sound, and can almost forget the burden of my losses and the wearisome pull of the colony's rules.

*

Later, Candra enters, finished with the linens and looking for more work to do. But the house looks clean enough, and I have little hunger for a midday meal. The Batavian heat and my stitching steal my appetite, and I can't help but remember the hunger of my days in Amsterdam, how it followed me for days, and how I believed I'd not feel anything but its constant bite.

When Candra sees Aini stitching, she scolds her, thinking the girl wastes time for work. Aini looks down at her hands and blinks.

"It's fine, Candra." I smile at Candra, who looks so like her daughter, but with the fine etchings that come with age. "She wanted to learn."

Candra stands over Aini and watches as she stitches. Aini explains the different stitches and needles, and soon Candra looks as taken with the lace as her daughter.

"You can try it," I tell her, and move so she may sit next to Aini. I give her my own work so she may learn as well. Aini instructs her mother, clearly enjoying the chance to teach her, and Candra listens, nods her head. Soon, she makes a few loops into the couch stitches and with the same daring as her daughter, begins her own stitching.

"I think my stitches are better than yours," she says to her daughter in Portuguese after some time.

"But I work faster." Aini keeps her eyes to her stitching, but she smiles.

"Not for too long." Candra smiles in return, her eyes also fixed on the fabric.

I enjoy watching them, their ease with each other, how they laugh and bicker, and for a moment I miss my own mother, and wonder about her and Hlaska and our little cottage in the Bos. A piercing ache comes over me, but I swallow it down, imagining that Moeder left Fader alone in our crumbling cottage, and took my sister with her. And that she lives elsewhere now, in a bigger cottage, nestled in the woods, listening, like me, to the wind singing through the trees.

Chapter 60

Three months have passed since I knocked on Sontje's door and in that time I have found a new pattern to this marriage. Cleaning, planning, shopping at the market. Walking in the early morning, and working on my lace. Aini and Candra take to the stitching, and soon join me for two hours a day working on the fabric. They so enjoy the work, they hurry through their errands and ask me about patternmaking and forming the dentelles and joining the pieces, the one task Griet taught me that I still struggle to perfect. With their help, I soon have multiple lengths of lace, which I roll into my little basket, for what I can't say, since I'm still forbidden from selling at the markets, and must wait for Mattheus to speak on my behalf. But more ships enter the port, some carrying still more Company Daughters, and I regret that I can't sell to any of these girls at the market, desperate as they are for some taste of the homeland, some object binding them to all they left behind. I imagine what I would say to them, what stories I would tell them of King's Day feasts and Christmas gatherings to compel them to buy my lace, even if such tales of celebration are not my own. I'm sure I could sell more of my work, and despise all these rules preventing me from it.

The day becomes a great, yawning creature for its sameness. Mattheus keeps a calendar on his desk and shows me how I may track the days and weeks, or know the arrival of ships. Outgoing voyages to Ambon for spices in October, arrivals from the Netherlands in May. Mattheus explained the smaller vessels leave during the monsoon season for the Spice Islands.

In Amsterdam, the seasons are each very different. The trees go from full foliage to naked and forlorn. Spring arrives and everyone ventures out, like the stoats and squirrels, hungry for sunshine. Here, the sunshine never leaves. Even in a burst of rain that drenches the clothes on the clothesline and causes small rivers to rush through the walkways, this stoic Batavian sun shines.

Mattheus is out with the new Councilor-General today and the chores are finished so I leave the house to water my rosebushes. I'm happy to have completed my studies at dawn today—Mattheus has been teaching me how to write, and my wrist aches from the exercises and pressing hard against the parchment. I practice writing Sontje's name on the parchment, stretching the letters, whispering her name to myself and then following it with my own, remembering our brief time together in the forests here and in the Cape, how we gathered each other together whenever we could, like the squirrels of my childhood gleaning their stores for winter. I fill an entire page with Sontje's name, and must curl and straighten my fingers after my practice to release their stiffness, and then hide the parchment at the bottom of my trunk where Mattheus will not find it.

But I can't avoid the interruption of my restlessness. I feel a loneliness both quiet and very loud that finds me throughout the day.

Aini has left a bucket of water outside for me, and as I pour a stream of water on my flowers, watching for the earth to turn the proper shade of dark brown, my mind wanders to Madaleen, who visited me two days ago.

I wonder what Sontje would say about Madaleen's wedding. Madaleen will not want for comforts, but I can't help but think of her shortened childhood, our games on the *Leyden*, and little Drika. Madaleen told me on her visit, with downcast eyes, that Tomas threw Drika into the fire soon after the wedding. And indeed, the loss of that tattered doll who traveled with Madaleen across the sea has aged her a little. She has the same resigned bearing of all the Company Daughters, including myself. I now regard my husband's aged hands, his wrinkling skin with more tenderness, because I must. The curling hair growing on his earlobes no longer revolts me. I've turned my distaste into curiosity. I feel only a little resentment when he reaches for me at night.

His raspy, dry tongue upon me evokes pity. No longer disgust.

But in my dreams, I sleep with Sontje. Our bodies pressed together like cemented stones. We slosh back and forth in each other's arms. On the *Leyden,* in the fickle embrace of the sea.

I'm watering the last of my rosebushes when Dewa approaches carrying her bamboo basket. I'm happy to see her. She walks to me and takes my hands in hers, her fingers softer than my own, her palms cool. She then holds her hands out to indicate pregnancy.

She means Sontje, and motions for me to follow her.

I hesitate, afraid of seeing Sontje again, afraid of missing her anew, but my worry for Sontje outweighs my fear of being hurt again. The memory of my baby sister's birth flames in my mind. Blood, crying, the terrifying mess of it all… Still, I leave with Dewa, pulled by some invisible hand. She walks just behind me as the slaves must, taking small, chipped steps for the narrowness of her *kain*, and holds a wide, fringed parasol over me. I must walk slower so she can match my pace, and I feel absurd at the pageantry of this walk, that we must preserve the Company's hierarchy even under such urgent circumstances.

Dewa whispers where to turn, and though I already know the way, I pretend otherwise. We make our labored way to the edge of town, toward the copse of banyan trees, toward the young rainbow tree, and the small house turning gray near the western canal.

My heart quickens—both for my desire to see Sontje again, and for my fear of what awaits me at her little gray house.

Dewa knocks on the door. A young slave woman, with amber eyes and waist-length hair hanging in one smooth braid, opens the door. The stillness of the house overtakes us. Only the sound of mice in the walls and our own breathing. Willem, as usual, is gone. The square openings at the top of the walls provide little escape from the afternoon heat or the stale smell inside, placed as they are away from the ocean breeze. Willem Brouwer gives his wife a poorly made home.

The slave motions us to the back of the house. The silence surrounds us, thick, like the humidity. Even the trees outside deny us their whispers. A sour, mildew smell and the metallic odor of blood further stiffens the quiet. The smell draws to mind such terrible memories: Moeder's knuckles turning white as they gripped the tattered wool blankets, my own terror as I realized I must bring my own sister into the world.

Sontje lies in a low bed in the back room. At first, I see only her trail of blonde hair, dampened. She so rarely wears it loose. I sit beside her but her eyes stay closed.

"Sontje." I can scarcely breathe, but I have missed the sound of her name in my voice.

Her eyes flutter open. "You came," she whispers. "Did you see him?"

"Your husband?" I feel bitter. He should be here, at least to witness how we suffer to give them children. I felt the same of Fader all those years ago when I pulled Hlaska from my mother's womb. "He is out."

"No. The baby. A boy." Sontje gestures to the slave, who returns with the native midwife. She holds a baby wrapped in a shroud of linen cloth.

"Hold him," Sontje says. "Please."

Years have passed since I last held Hlaska and I worry I have forgotten how to hold such a new one. The soft head in one palm, its rump warm in my other. It feels like a lump of freshly baked bread. Its eyes are closed and it breathes in quick bursts, like the rabbits Helena and I watched in the Bos, when we could still ourselves long enough in the shadows.

"Ours," Sontje says. "That is how I think of him, Jana."

But I'm not sure what she means. I hold the infant, looking into its small, sleeping face. Dewa stands next to me, cooing to it in her language, smiling with her remaining teeth. Sontje falls asleep and I search for her in its features, for Willem, too. But the baby looks like itself. Like neither of them. I recall Hlaska in my arms all those years ago, bloody and wrinkled and slow, and how I could not believe even then that she was my sister, and that I had pulled her from my mother with my own small hands. How my terror gave way to relief that Moeder was alive after spilling so much blood. How it stained my fingernails and, even after two days, I found brownish smears on my arms.

The baby roots with its tiny, open mouth. Searching for its food.

"I think he's hungry," I whisper to Sontje and Dewa gently grasps Sontje's shoulder, to wake her. "How long ago was he birthed?"

Sontje yawns and sits up, gathers her child from my arms. "Some hours? I'm not sure. I've been so tired." She laughs. "My breasts are big like Sussie's now. I never thought they could ache like this." The midwife helps Sontje pinch her breast and squeeze drops of milk onto the baby's lips before it takes her into its open mouth.

Dewa laughs as the baby sucks with a full appetite. Tears stream down Sontje's face as the baby suckles, his hands moving slowly as if through water.

"What's wrong, Sontje?" I worry she remains sick from the childbirth. Moeder was weak for days after birthing Hlaska.

Sontje's eyes never leave the baby as it nurses. "I'm only thinking how happy I am, and how unused to happiness I've become. I thought these last months had stolen even its memory from me."

"I'm glad he brings you some happiness." But I wonder if she is happy only for her baby, or if she keeps some fondness still for me. Her earlier words, when I first arrived, follow the delirious speech of new mothers. My own mother cried for joy with little Hlaska, but only days after, resumed her typical bearing—her lips again a tight line, her eyes dead and weary.

Sontje's eyes fix on me, at last.

"No, Jana. I'm happy because you came. My life has been a misery these months." She pauses to kiss her baby's head. "I feel no love for Willem. Not even the simplest affection. I wanted to see you, Jana, but Willem kept me home those first months. Wouldn't let me go to the market or even church. He thought every other man wanted me— perhaps he felt himself inadequate to be my husband. And then I was with child and too sick to leave the house anyway. And then you came here to see me, and it was just too hard." She looks at me now, her eyes tired and red from her recent tears. "In every way Willem is a disappointment. He complains about every minor and imagined slight by the other settlers, expects me to do everything in the house, when I have never had to before." Her old haughtiness from Amsterdam returns, as though she has forgotten why she came to Batavia at all. "He could not even stay at home for his own son's birth."

"Do you know where he is?"

"No." The baby now taps its tiny hand against her breast, as though claiming her. "And I no longer care. I have my slave Sanne to help me. If he does nothing for me, I owe him less, and can pursue my own happiness. I deserve it, after all he's done." She says no more about it, and I don't wish to press her. The birth was surely hard enough to endure.

"So I have decided it," she continues, her eyes flashing. "In my heart, this boy is ours—yours and mine—and we remain together, just as we were on the *Leyden*. My feelings have not changed. We can find ways to see one another, Jana. The colony is not so big after all."

I feel the pull of Sontje, of everything we've lived together, but I can't yet trust her. I'm too afraid.

The midwife leaves the room, as Dewa watches us with her wise, curious eyes, and I wonder if she understands.

Sontje reclines in her bed, and her pale skin looks sickly, her hair scattered and mussed as it was when she took ill on the *Leyden,* but she resembles the Sontje of Amsterdam more than when I first arrived at the unswept step of her little house.

"That is," Sontje says, smiling, "if you will have me again."

I say nothing, just touch the baby's head is it nurses, caressing its sparse, velvet hair, and try to believe her.

Chapter 61

I stay with Sontje until the sunlight through her oil shades darkens to a deep orange. Dewa leaves after an hour, and Sontje releases her slave Sanne and the midwife.

For our few hours together, I forget Mattheus. I sit next to her on her pallet, and we take turns holding the baby, and I delight in its freshness, and the way Sontje coos over its every movement.

But I must return home. The setting sun warns me. "I must leave," I finally say. "Mattheus will be wondering about me." I feel my old panic edging into me at having to explain my lateness. At times, marriage differs little from the Ringhouse. The same feeling of being trapped, though I remind myself that Mattheus is kinder than I expected, and I dislike having to deceive him.

"I'd like to see you in a few weeks," Sontje says, shyness entering her voice.

"Sontje… I told Mattheus. About us." I wait for her reaction. Will she be angry? Afraid? A stricken look passes over her.

"He saw how I was suffering after the day I came to visit. I had to explain. He has forbidden me to spend time with you," I continue.

She holds my hand as the baby sleeps against her, curled under her neck.

"Dear Jana. I thought it would be easier if we no longer saw each other. I felt so defeated. Lost with Willem and in my pregnancy sickness. I had awful dreams every night. Terrible memories from the *Leyden*. The night I was attacked. Gerhard. Griet dying before our eyes." Sadness slows her words, and I suddenly regret adding to her sorrow.

"But other memories kept saving me in my nightmares," she continues. "Memories of you, us. I would feel myself drowning in my helplessness, and some memory of you would float into my mind, stopping my sadness just as it became unbearable." Her eyes brighten, reminding me of the night she asked me to leave with her to the forest when we first arrived here. The same cheerful, lively expression. "How you cared for me after the attack, sleeping on the floor of our little berth. The night we escaped to the painted tree. At every moment when I thought I would die of my sadness, you returned, and saved me."

I say nothing, feeling distant even as she confesses this to me. In these past months, that hard pebble of my old self has returned. Sontje was the first and only person I loved in this way. The only person I trusted after Helena died. Her rejection set me on some backward course to the girl I was when I arrived on her doorstep nearly three years ago. Hungry. Numb.

She sees my hesitation.

"I will earn you back," she says. "Even if it will be harder now that Mattheus knows." She is thinking out the problem, and I recall this same calculating expression from that day when she flattered me so I would chaperone her and Hans Luiken. "Madaleen will be visiting me soon. I'll send a message through her for when we can next meet."

*

I hurry from Sontje's cottage, as I did when I worked in Amsterdam, rushing off for one errand or another. The sky darkens into a glowing violet, and I fear I will arrive home after Mattheus.

And indeed, when I arrive, he is already home.

"Where have you been?" Mattheus comes from the bedroom as I open the door. He often lies down for some minutes after returning from his work at the *stadhuis*. At least his voice sounds agreeable. "You look flushed and healthy." He kisses my cheek, and I feel guilty for the lie I must produce.

"I visited Madaleen." I surprise myself with my own quickness. I've never enjoyed lying. Some of the Ringhouse girls lied for sport, laughing when we believed their fantastic stories, but I prefer a freedom that would not require such tales and the effort needed to invent them. I hope for such freedom, though I have not known it much.

"I hear their new house is the grandest in the colony," Mattheus says. Though I've not seen the inside of it, I have passed by. Tomas built the first *landhuizen* of the colony. Two stories with tall windows and a mansard roof like the great homes in Italy.

"Yes, the house is impressive," I lie, resenting this first lie about my whereabouts, and how it has already multiplied into two. I hope Mattheus doesn't ask for the particulars of Madaleen's home.

"The pepper trade has made Tomas wealthy in a short time." Mattheus sounds wistful. "The Chinese and Portuguese merchants covet pepper, cloves, and our *sappanwood* without end. If I were a younger man, I would invest all I have in the trade. Buy you a *landhuizen* grander than Tomas's." Mattheus often mentions how he would do things if he were younger. I wonder if I will do the same in my old age. I hope not.

"We do well enough," I say, grateful for an opening to escape the topic of Madaleen's unseen house and my earlier activities. "We have meat and bread and two vegetables for tonight's meal, and a *rijsttafel* for tomorrow." I hope Aini finished the cooking. I forgot to ask her before I left.

He looks at me with a tenderness that adds to my guilt. "I have some news for you, too, Jana."

I wait for him to tell me, wondering what news he could have that would interest me.

"I talked to the Councilor-General about your... problem at the market," he says, not wanting to speak too directly of our last argument. "The Company is quite firm about its commitment to following the rules of the homeland."

I say nothing, thinking on the Company's commitment, when we have no slaves in Amsterdam, but use both natives and a growing numbers of slaves from abroad for all manner of work here, and all without pay.

"But the Councilor-General discussed the matter with the guilds, and since we have no men working lace—it's women's work, after all—and the Company wishes the wives to continue our homeland traditions, they agree to cede you a small area of the market so you can sell your lace. We can't find such fine lace here, and importing it is too costly. I argued that these small touches of home will be a comfort to our women as they are tasked with the responsibility of keeping our traditional ways." Mattheus stands taller, proud of himself for his words on my behalf.

I'm touched by my husband's efforts. Admitting to these powerful men that his wife wishes for paid work must have been an embarrassment. Men rely on such trifling points to mark their success—great *landhuizens* and wives tucked in idleness. At least Mattheus understands I'm not like the Maritjens of the world.

"Thank you, Mattheus," I say, hoping he hears the gladness in my voice. "I have some pieces ready to sell already. I'll work on a few more and will claim my little stand in the market next week."

I feel naked in his direct gaze. "I had to offer to do some shipwright work without pay, promise some other favors," he says, his voice turning cold. "It wasn't really the bargain I'd hoped for in our marriage, but I expect smoother seas between us now, no?"

I nod, imagining a record of accounts between us. Will he want more of me in bed—more elaborate meals? *Hutspot* twice a week and *koekjes* for tea? But I tuck away my disdain, partly of my wifely obligations. Instead, I think of patterns for new lace, and what I must do to prepare for my stand. My little basket is nearly full of lace rolls, and I can charge an extra fee to sew them to women's dresses. My heart beats faster as I think of having, at last, some money of my own. I dislike my reliance on Mattheus, how he provides everything I have save for my few trinkets from Amsterdam and my white Company frocks. The plainness of my dependency deepens my guilt for having spent the last hours with Sontje. But I try and ignore my shamed conscience.

"I'm grateful for your efforts for me." I smile, though the gesture feels unnatural.

"No matter, my dear." Mattheus kisses me again, but this time on the mouth, and I recognize the hungry look of him. That tonight after our dinner, he'll claim his marital rights.

Chapter 62

Weeks pass before I see Sontje again. But I'm glad for the time and embrace the distraction of making more lace with Aini and Candra to sell at the market. I need some time to consider Sontje's words, to weigh their steadfastness. I worry about Mattheus, and now regret telling him about us. My admission gave him opportunity to forgive me, so that now I feel guilt for my dishonesty and continued desire. Each time I think of Sontje, I'm reminded of my husband's generosity. Without Mattheus, I would be less than nothing here. The Company could even strip me of my plain white dresses. I could be sent off to the brothels—the only non-native woman serving the newest boatload of merchants, soldiers, and sailors. The thought of returning to such a life rouses a sick, vile feeling.

True to his word, Mattheus secures a place for me at the market. A far corner at the very end of the row that receives the least shade, but it is mine. For four hours in the afternoon, I sit on a large, overturned basket in my place with my two small baskets of lace, sewing whatever new pattern I've created. If Mattheus resents my efforts, he takes pains to conceal his bitterness. He brings me new threads and backing fabric, and even compliments my improving patternmaking. I can't help but warm to his generosity, and feel greater guilt for my deceptions.

A new shipment of Company Daughters arrived two weeks ago, all young, awed, and still stumbling about from the roughness of their voyage. Homesick, sallow, and thin. Falks has loosened his grip on this new shipment of girls, and they explore the enclosed grounds of the colony in groups, and most often our little market—the only part of Batavia that resembles home. Despite the Company's desire to recreate our Dutch towns here, Batavia remains itself. But I'm happy for how this place flouts its master's orders like an unruly slave. Or disobedient wife.

I'm couching lay thread into a square of fabric for a new pattern, lost in the snowflake shape I've drawn onto the cloth, when I hear her.

"Jana?"

Even after weeks of not seeing her, my skin warms at the sound of my name in Sontje's voice.

She approaches, holding her baby.

"What are you doing?" She glances down at my basket.

"Selling lace. Keeping busy." Her baby squirms under the muslin cloth covering him. "He already looks so much bigger than when I last saw him."

Sontje smiles, her eyes bright and happy. "He changes every hour. Wrinkling up his forehead, crossing his eyes. I can't stop looking at him. I'm afraid I will miss some new gesture." I stand up from my overturned basket, and she uncovers him so I can see.

"He is beautiful. He looks more like you now." I'm happy that not much of Willem Brouwer is in the child. Maybe just a bit of his dimpled chin.

"You should hold him." Sontje passes the baby to me, and my stomach pitches at her hands against mine, so familiar, long and slightly damp from the heat.

I hold the infant and feel his downy hair against my nose. That new, wild smell I recall from baby Hlaska. A freshness I searched for in the Bos, thinking some flower must possess that unique fragrance, but I never found it again until now. I rub my thumb against his tiny foot, soft like the leaves of a lamb's ear plant. As a girl, I would marvel at Hlaska's toes, small and perfect like new grapes. I had forgotten until now.

The baby looks at me. Red, wet lips and Sontje's round eyes, but his pupils spread over his blue irises and make his eyes look black. He takes a slow gaze at me, above me, around me, as if unsure where to look Then he nuzzles into me and falls back asleep.

"He is lovely, Sontje," I say. And can't help but feel a little jealous of Willem Brouwer again.

Only slaves linger in the markets today, haggling for items for their masters. Our women prefer the indoors at midday, and for this I'm thankful. I would hate to see Maritjen, or Gerhard, right now.

"Willem must be happy," I say with some bitterness.

"I'm not sure of that. The baby is competition."

"He's jealous of his own child?" I can't believe such a man, but I shouldn't be surprised. New fathers sometimes came to the Ringhouse. I had one or two, though I push the memories away.

"I'm not yet well enough for... relations," Sontje says, blushing. "Willem is impatient." For the first time since meeting her today, sadness enters her expression. "It's terrible to feel so trapped. I keep hoping he will change. That this baby will grow some kindness in him."

"I'm sorry, Sontje. I wish I could help you."

"Seeing you helps. And our boy in your arms."

At this I bristle with hurt. "He is not ours," I say. "He is Willem's."

As much as I wish for this boy to be ours, I worry that Sontje will change her mind once more, and then I will lose her again, along with the infant.

Sontje rubs her son's back as I hold him.

"To me, he is ours. Willem was not my choice." She kisses her baby's head, and I feel as though she wishes her caresses to be carried through him to me. "You are."

I still distrust her. I am too damaged from my life in the Bos and the Ringhouse to believe Sontje can love me after rejecting me before. And then I have my life with Mattheus— I have told him about us and he'll be angry if he discovers us spending time together now.

"He's your baby, not mine," I finally say, hating that I must hurt her so I can protect myself. "He is lovely, and I can see why you love him so much. But I see him so rarely." The baby bleats, wishing for Sontje. His cry only strengthens my words. "Does he even have a name?"

"Ebel." Her hands linger over mine as I pass him to her. "I only wished for you to love him." Her eyes redden, and I worry she will cry. She's seems quicker to cry now that she's been through childbirth. She holds Ebel to her again and kisses him. "But I understand."

I try to soften my sharp words, keeping my distrust to myself. "I only mean I can't love him so soon. After so much distance. What if you change your mind again? How can I know your feelings?"

"Then let us meet more often. Willem rarely stays home for long. Off to meetings or to drink with soldiers. I hardly know and care even less." Her voice hardens. "I feel I'm raising Ebel alone."

Her sleeve pulls up as she holds Ebel. A long, bluish bruise covers her forearm.

"What is that?" I ask, tracing my finger along her arm.

She flinches. "It's nothing."

"He did that?" Anger quickens my voice.

"I forgot to prepare the capon he wanted a few days earlier. I'm so forgetful since the birth, and so tired from waking throughout the night to feed Ebel."

I hate hearing her make excuses for Willem's behavior, which reminds me of Moeder's stammering explanations for Fader's abuses, how she pretended all was normal and in doing so, taught us to expect such treatment ourselves. Moeder's old rhyme enters my memory again, and with it, a mix of sadness and rage for Sontje and my younger self, Jana from the Bos, so full of feelings, but having nowhere to keep them.

The girl plays with little things...

I shake myself out of my dark thoughts. Sontje stands here with me, after all, and unlike Moeder, who only pitied and made excuses for Fader, Sontje defies her husband, attempts a secret life with me. And I'm no better. Even in her presence, I'm thinking of tonight's dinner for Mattheus, how much time I'll need to prepare a sauce of egg yolks, broth, crumbs, saffron, and onions for roast *veldhoenders*. Payment for Mattheus's grudging support for my little business. We all must survive as we can.

So I say nothing more and take her hand. Ebel reaches for me too, and I laugh.

For this moment, at least, we become our *Leyden* selves once more, belonging to each other, and not to our grim memories or tiresome husbands.

Chapter 63

Once a year, the Company holds a general meeting of its employees—inspectors, sea captains, clerks, merchants, and soldiers hired by the Company, too. Batavia is now the main port handling the Company's ships between Asia and Europe. The men discuss the next year's business and strategies for dealing with the threat of Portuguese pirates and the growing black market for opium. They retreat to a smaller outpost outside of the city for their meeting, away from spying slaves and Asian traders, a meeting that lasts three days.

Mattheus and Willem will attend the gathering, so I'm not surprised when Sontje arrives at my doorstep on the evening after Mattheus's departure, holding baby Ebel in her long arms. She wears one of the white dresses gifted to us for our services to the Company, her gold hair even thicker than before, now tied back with her favorite black lace ribbons.

"I thought since both the men are out," she looks down at Ebel cooing in her arms, "we could be a family for a time."

I'm surprised by her suggestion, but I'm happy to see the both of them. Ebel smiles and this small gesture thrills me more than the sight of Sontje, who I still regard with some wariness.

"Take him," she says, passing me Ebel.

I gather him in my arms.

"Is this prudent?" I hesitate, thinking of the bruise that stretched out over her slim forearm from weeks ago, and Mattheus's command that we end our friendship.

"No," she replies, a challenge in her smile. "Do you wish us to leave?"

Ebel grasps at my hair and gives a strong tug, as though in alliance with his mother.

But I'm happy to refuse her, and decide to permit this one visit. We'll have no other opportunity to be together like this. "He doesn't look willing to leave just yet," I say. "Come inside. I gave Aini and Candra leave for the next two days. They work so hard on the lace, hardly resting. And I wanted time alone. I'll never grow used to the presence of slaves. Expecting work from others without paying them fair wages. I must be cautious in secretly paying them for their lace, or Mattheus will stop me."

"It's good you are paying them, though. Whatever you give is more than the rest of us provide." Sontje enters and sits on one of the rattan settees arranged in our main sitting room. I'm not as impatient as the other wives to clutter the house with new baubles and mementos of the old country. Most houses here boast great teak curios piled with porcelain and silver, tapestries on the walls and floors, but I find the damp air hostile to fabrics, and the silver tarnishes quickly here. I prefer using the natives' materials—earthen bowls, baskets, and rattan pieces, which keep the air fresher indoors.

"Maritjen often complains about your treatment of the slaves," Sontje says, lying back in the settee, as though finally able to rest. "She is vexed by your behavior. I saw her last week and she complained also about your business at the market. Said it's unseemly for a wife, and poor Mattheus, he must be so embarrassed, and so on." Sontje laughs. Ebel looks at me with his great, watery eyes, as though waiting for my reaction.

"If it wasn't the slaves, she would find fault with the condition of my doorstep or the state of my roses. Never mind she lives all the way at the other end of the canal."

"It's me she truly hates," Sontje says. "I think she knows about Gerhard."

"It's her own fault for giving him permission to act that way by being such an unpleasant cow."

"She's just as trapped as any of us," Sontje says, making a comical face at Ebel. I can't help but laugh at her expression. "It's worse if you're plain."

"I suppose it is," I reply, recalling her past criticisms of my own appearance back in Amsterdam.

"Oh Jana," she says, sensing my memory. "I think you're beautiful." She looks at me, then. Hard. "I think of you so often. My thoughts of us and Ebel are all that keep me afloat."

Ebel makes a feeble cry for his mother and opens his mouth, hitting it against my own empty bosom.

"Nothing here, little one." I give him to Sontje and she loosens the ties at the top of her dress and pulls out her breast, full and white, so different from her delicate form on the *Leyden*. Ebel hits his mouth against her chest, hungrily, until she pushes her breast into his mouth.

"You are so womanly now," I say, watching. "Like one of those Madonnas in the paintings I saw at the De Graafs'." I saw Master staring at those figures often, imagining their plump bodies under his quaggy fingers. I chide myself for thinking of him.

"It's odd, isn't it? I've always been such a broomstick. But I like this body. How it feeds my boy."

And I agree. She looks rosy and happy, smiling at Ebel.

"You've not really seen me yet, Jana," Sontje says, a sly look to her once Ebel has settled in for his feeding. "How different I am."

Her suggestion causes a clenching within me, despite my doubts.

"Ebel will fall asleep soon. And I would like to show you."

We place Ebel in a large woven basket next to the pallet I share with Mattheus. I try to ignore the sharp, woody smell of my husband on the rough, cotton sheets as we lie down on the pallet and remove our layers of clothing, finding each other again.

Her skin smells sweet. Her new milk deepens her fragrance.

Her mouth can't have enough of me.

I think we will be heard through the open slats of the cottage, through the brittle, plaster walls. The houses are built close together with only larger courtyards behind or in front of them.

We trace with our fingers the newness of each other—the fresh silver lines crossing her middle from pregnancy, the broad, red circles of her nipples, which, months ago, were small as my own. I kiss the shallow ridge at the tops of her shoulders, her long neck and the hollow of her elbow, wishing to reclaim from Willem Brouwer these places I loved before he ever knew her.

"You've grown thinner, Jana," Sontje whispers. "I did not realize before with all our layers and petticoats. Batavia has changed you." Her hand rests on my hipbone.

"I could not eat after seeing you when Ebel still lived in your belly. I lost my hunger."

"Such a difference to when I first met you. You ate more than I'd ever seen a girl eat. I envied you, how you wanted things without shame."

I'm no longer ashamed of my hunger that day, but recall how Sontje watched me eating, and how I resented her examination. "They don't want us to desire much. Only little things. Brooches and pearl earrings and ribbons for our coiled hair. And after some time, we stop wanting more than that. But the hunger for those little things just grows and grows. Because we never really desired them, but forget how to want the things that mattered to us."

"Jana, always the philosopher. I've missed that of you." Sontje kisses me again, her lips soft and wet upon mine. "But I think I understand. That explains Madaleen with her great house, or Agatha with her fifteen slaves—did you know? She has a slave who does nothing but follow after her with a great stretched silk fan from China." Sontje laughs. "But I've also heard her husband uses two or three of the slave girls as concubines, and Agatha can't say a word about it. It's common here—some even take on slaves as secondary wives. And they can even inherit property." She grows quiet in her thoughts. "It would not surprise me if Willem had a few out in the *kampung*."

I doubt Mattheus would, and I'm again reminded of my good fortune to have an old husband, too weary to bother Aini or Candra for more than tea or sweeping.

Ebel wakes up, crying again for his milk.

"Can you bring him to me?"

I get up from the bed and take Ebel. He stops crying and looks at me with his lovely eyes. I place him between us and Sontje lies on her side, pushing her breast toward his open mouth.

He drinks like a drowning creature, eyes wild. He jerks his head back and forth like a frenzied animal until he closes them, in rapture.

I laugh. "He acts as if he's never eaten before."

"Yes. He has simple desires. Milk, sleep, a cleaning after his *poep*."

At that very moment, Ebel screws up his face and empties his bowels into the square of cotton cloth bound around his waist and legs.

I laugh at his apt timing.

"I will change him." I remember how because of Hlaska.

From somewhere beyond all the darkness of other memories, this other knowledge returns to me.

We prepare for sleep.

Little Ebel lies between us, his arms outstretched so he touches both of us. His fingers curl around a strand of my loose hair.

I listen to their breaths. Short puffs from Ebel, as though he labors at his sleep. Long exhalations from Sontje. She, too, sleeps hard, as she did on the *Leyden* when recovering from her fever.

For the first time since my marriage, I feel a lightness within. Joy? Contentment? More than contentment? I'm afraid of this sensation, for I know I will want it again, and lying in the night's stillness with the three of us together, I wish for some unknown, impossible power to anchor time as it is. Here.

The image of the De Graafs' *vanitas* painting comes to me. The smiling skull and its extinguished candle trailing a narrow streak of smoke.

Early ripe, early rot.

A shadowy, familiar sadness muddies my joy as I fall back asleep beside them.

"Jana."

Mattheus's crackling voice jars me from whatever dream I have entered.

I startle awake, and Ebel flings his little arms upward with a start, but settles back to sleep.

Sontje sits up, round-eyed and naked.

"He's just walked in," I whisper to her. "Hurry and get dressed. I'll keep him outside."

I pull on my blouse and skirt and thank our good fortune for remembering to close the thin, *sappanwood* door to the bedroom last night.

I open the door just enough to let myself through and walk to the entrance of the cottage, hoping Ebel will remain asleep.

"You're back early," I say, slowing my voice despite the stomping of my heart. I give Mattheus a rare kiss.

"We've met an impasse," Mattheus says with frustration. "The directors and sailors set to argue over every detail. The number of masts to use on vessels back to the homeland, the shape of the sails—square or triangles, how best to deal with shipworm, and what to use for ballast on the routes between our Asian ports." He sighs. "Important points to be sure—we've had a ship capsize because the sailors kept the ballast too light—but with all those hotheads in one meeting, the discussion stalled. Seemed a waste of time to stay, and I'm not the only one. A good many of us left today."

I wonder if Willem Brouwer is among them, and worry anew for Sontje.

"Well, it's good you're back early," I say, burying my disappointment. "I found some broken plaster around the back of the cottage. Can you look at it? We should have it fixed. And since you're still wearing your boots…" My mind jumps to whatever excuse I can use to lure Mattheus out of the cottage so Sontje can escape.

"I suppose I can," he says, winding his arm around my waist. "And you're right. Best to repair it now before the monsoons arrive. This soggy air ruins everything so quickly. The Company didn't think to observe the natives' houses, which hold up better than ours. They just wanted to build a miniature Amsterdam here without thought for the different climate. The canals keep silting over from the monsoons, some of the houses are sinking, even our ships fall apart if left out to port for too long." Mattheus seldom criticizes the Company, but today's trying events coax a rare complaint from him.

I lead him out the door, grateful for his interest in my hasty lure. "I'm also afraid of rats or scorpions getting in," I continue. "Aini said she found a scorpion in her hut last week, crawling in one of her earthen bowls. She keeps all her bowls and baskets overturned now." In truth, Aini said no such thing, but I once overheard the discussion at the market.

I hold Mattheus's hand and pull him around the cottage to the side away from the bedroom, and make a great effort showing him the plaster, speaking in a louder voice than usual, so Sontje knows to leave. Fortunately, the outside walls indeed show some wear.

As he looks over the house, I ask Mattheus questions about his trip—about the growing opium trade from China, about the argument over the type of sheathing for the vessels—pinewood, lead, or oak, and the method of careening for the *retourships'* repair. Topics I always enjoy hearing about, but feel especially relieved to learn of now. And Mattheus is eager to share his thoughts, enjoying, as men do, the opportunity to display their knowledge to us women.

I continue this prattle, listening for the sound of Sontje leaving.

Some long minutes pass, and at last I note the light grate of footfalls on the gravel path outside. The soft, trifling sound causes a flare of loss and emptiness.

I think I hear a single bleat from little Ebel, who is probably hungry again. But the sound could just as well be a passing *bulbul*'s cry.

*

Later that evening, when Mattheus comes for a late tea after his usual afternoon rest, he holds Sontje's black ribbon between his fingers. The sight of it causes me to panic, thinking of all we did in my marriage bed last night.

Like a disagreeable magpie, I wish to tear it from his thick fingers for myself.

"Is this yours?" he asks, handing it to me as he sits at our simple dining table where I've placed plates of dried figs, cheese, and sweetened rice biscuits. Mattheus covets his routines, and never veers from this afternoon repast.

He's not yet asked me about Aini and Candra, but their unexplained absence causes more worry, for I've not had time to make a story for them. "You don't often wear ribbons."

I tie the thin fabric around my braid, thinking to keep it as a reminder. "Yes, It's mine. I thought I'd lost it."

Mattheus nods, chewing on his biscuit. He studies me a moment, and I can't help but wonder at his thoughts.

Chapter 64

Months pass before I share time with Sontje and Ebel again, though we've both become regular churchgoers, meeting on Sundays with the other wives, enduring Falks's droning oration for the promise of a glance or a quick grasp of each other's hands afterward. And this way, I can hold Ebel, who reaches for me with an eagerness that warms me more each time.

Mattheus attends also, and I wonder if his presence owes to his suspicion or some other worry. I have observed older people making a habit of vigorous church attendance, perhaps feeling less distance from their own eventual end.

After today's service, as we mill about outside the church, Sontje leans toward me.

"Meet me tomorrow. Can you?" Her whisper tickles my ear.

Mattheus stands some paces away, chatting with Madaleen's husband, Tomas. Of late, Mattheus has become something of an expert on the proper timetables for voyages to Ambon, and other merchants and sailors seek him out for his knowledge. He stands taller with Tomas now, his bony shoulders set back, scratching his beaky nose in concentration.

In that short moment, free of others' watchfulness, Sontje brushes her hand against my hip, and squeezes.

"Come to my cottage." Her whisper sounds fierce as I hold Ebel, who I have grown to miss as much as Sontje herself. "We can walk."

"I have some orders for lace I must work on." Another shipment of women arrived two weeks ago, and now the Company commissions me to adorn one of their plain frocks for each woman's fast-approaching wedding day. My patterns become more complex, but Aini and Candra choose simpler patterns to finish the work quickly, thus helping me fulfill the Company orders.

"Surely you can take three hours off? And don't you want to spend time with Ebel? He smiles and laughs so much now."

I nuzzle Ebel's head, his floss-like, golden hair. He pulls at a strand of my own hair and I wince.

"Yes, of course," I say, kissing Ebel's cheek. "The work will wait for me, after all."

I wait until mid-morning to leave. I must be sure Mattheus won't return for some forgotten item—his compass or sheaf of papers or book of maps. He forgets these items with such regularity, I sometimes wonder if he does so purposefully, so he can check on my doings.

Once certain of his departure, I hurry to the other side of town, avoiding the public square where someone may see me, taking the smaller, crooked pathways closer to the rampart instead. The slaves use such footpaths, leaving the nicer, more finished interior walkways for us.

I arrive at the little gray cottage, which always saddens me for its dingy color and disrepair. At least now the doorstep is clean.

Three knocks on the door.

Sontje answers, holding Ebel on her hip. She smiles, milky and aglow despite her tired eyes.

She closes the door before embracing me, little Ebel between us. He pulls strands of both our loose hair.

"He looks happy to see you," Sontje says, freeing her fair locks from his warm fist. "As am I." She kisses my cheek, so hard I feel the wetness of her mouth upon my skin afterward.

A heaviness enters me when I see her, knowing that in hours, whatever we will share now will disappear, so I will be left wondering if it happened at all.

"I already feel the dread of having to leave." I kiss Ebel's head, inhaling his wild, milky smell.

"Don't think of it." Sontje kisses me again. "Let's enjoy these hours."

We take the footpath behind her cottage. Slaves rarely travel here, as the Company develops the area closer to the castle and port. The western side of the colony remains rough and unbuilt, though like the rest of the settlement, a thick rampart surrounds it. Mattheus says the wall protects against hostile Sundanese tribes, but Falks once said it's meant to discourage the tigers that roam freely through the forests. Perhaps the Reverend only wished to ensure that we remain locked inside. Sontje and I certainly saw nothing more than lizards the night we escaped to the forest.

"I've heard that they will soon build a school in old town," Sontje says. Ebel stares out from the nest of her arms, watching the flies and midges spring from the grasses as we walk, all lit up from the sunlight so that even they look beautiful.

"Yes, more churches, too. Mattheus says we'll be called for evening services often as more fleets set off."

"As though our prayers make a difference." Sontje's voice grows bitter. "I prayed on the *Leyden* more than anyone, and look at all that's happened to me."

I wrap my arm around her and Ebel pats my hand with his little fist, as though wishing it to stay there.

We walk in silence, and in the streaming sunlight, Ebel between us, I feel a glow encircling the three of us, as though we are the fairy people Helena and I made stories about. Ageless and beautiful, one with all growing things in the world. The waxy leaves of ficus trees shimmering overhead, the hidden sparrows and songbirds filling our easy silence, the droning bees inspecting the nearby flowers—I feel tethered to them all. Young and healthy and alive in a way I have never felt before.

But then I look over at Sontje, whose dress has slipped as she shifts Ebel from shoulder to shoulder. Another ugly purple blot creeps up from the collar of her dress, and a flash of anger replaces my brief joy.

"Is Willem beating you still?"

She sighs and readjusts Ebel, who protests at being carried over her other shoulder. "It's not worth speaking about, Jana. I've learned to endure it. As long as I receive the blows and not my son."

Ebel reaches for me and I take him, feeling full of a fury I can do nothing to diminish. Sontje stretches her arms overhead, now freed of her warm, heavy load.

"What provokes him?"

"Too much *arrak*," she says, of the drink the natives make in the *kampung*. "Or Ebel crying at night, or the sunshine too early, who can say? At least he is careful to keep his work hidden under my clothes."

"I could kill him." And for the first time, I feel I could, and can even imagine the satisfaction of pushing a slow dagger through Willem Brouwer's ruddy neck. I shiver thinking of it, and clear such bleak thoughts from my mind.

"He was most enraged when I came home with Ebel after staying with you."

"You said he came later." We met at church not long after and I asked her.

She shrugs. "I lied. No point in speaking of it. And I don't regret it. Nothing he does will make me regret being with you that night. I draw on that memory every hour. Every day. Of Ebel between us as we slept. Of how happy I was."

Sontje takes me to a clearing not far from the western rampart.

"We can't go over it on this side. They've built it tall," she says with sadness. "In every way, they keep us locked like doves."

I unfold the thin blanket we've brought with us. Sontje has packed a lunch—mangoes and papayas, dried figs, bread, and fresh cheese from the goats that survived a recent voyage. None of ours did on the *Leyden*.

I take Ebel on my lap, holding his little hands. He sits up now, and grabs at whatever he can. I bounce him on my outstretched legs. He laughs and grunts, wanting more.

"I wish we could raise him together," I say, and then regret my words. Why wish for impossible things? Even confessing it causes an ache in my chest—best not to imagine such a life, or I'll just want it more.

"I know," Sontje says. "I spend hours at night imagining us escaping from all this together with Ebel. Living out in the forest."

"Being mauled by tigers or speared by the natives, whose land we've stolen."

"Yes. Exactly that." We laugh a bitter laugh, which we learned on the *Leyden*.

We eat our lunch and pretend we have this life instead of our other ones, requiring services to our husbands, and the making of suppers and mid-suppers, and ordering about of slaves we wish we did not have. But in moments, I allow myself to imagine a different life—my little business to keep the three of us fed, our husbands somehow disappearing. Perhaps old age or illness. Or just continuing as we do now, but with less worry of being discovered. The possibility of such a life hovers just out of reach like the blue dragonfly drifting over us now.

"I hear Maritjen has amassed some thirty slaves," I say as I lean against Sontje, watching as Ebel waves a plucked violet back and forth in his hand. He examines the bright bloom, pulling it to his nose before a sneeze overtakes him, which seems to surprise him as well.

"I've only seen her at the market, but she came with only a few." Sontje's eyes twinkle. "Just one slave holding a parasol, and another carrying her hymn book, another for her cuspidor, and one more to carry the betel box itself."

"I'm sure she doesn't want us to envy her," I say. "Since she has always been so kind and modest." Little Ebel has dropped his violet and makes noises as though asking for it. I give it to him and kiss his plump cheek. "I've managed to avoid seeing her. But Mattheus mentioned her slaves. We Company Daughters have a growing reputation for laziness, apparently. I blame Maritjen for that."

"Agatha has at least as many." In the midday sunshine and stirring of air, Sontje glows, and her hair moves like white flames around her. Ethereal, like the Sontje of Amsterdam, but with more strength than she had in those distant days.

Later, I wish I had paid her this compliment, for it would have brought her happiness. But I often think of things to say after the moment for saying them has long passed.

"Well, that does not surprise me, either. Agatha always regretted her poverty," I say instead.

"Didn't you?" She kisses the top of my head. The gesture fills me with some deep sadness, for no one has ever kissed that part of me, not since I was a girl, and for a moment I miss my mother with a despair and hunger that I've not felt in many years, and wonder if she is alive, and if she thinks of me.

"I was too busy escaping from poverty to be ashamed of it," I say. "I only felt shame for what I needed to do to survive it. But even that I accept now."

"No sense being ashamed of surviving as you must," Sontje says. "Many wouldn't have, Jana." At this, her voice darkens. "I wouldn't."

"You've endured so much as well," I say, stroking her pretty hands.

"I did not always want to." Her voice is small with this admission.

I take her hand and press it to my lips.

She slides her index finger into my mouth. I gently suck. We laugh.

"Let's lie down on this blanket," she says, smiling again and smoothing down the fabric. The sun moves behind a thatch of banyan trees, and its light no longer causes my eyes to water. Ebel lies between us, growing sleepy for all his playing and looking about.

Sontje turns Ebel to his stomach and pats his back and sings him a song I've not heard before, a tune she has invented—about stars and birds and the waves of the sea, and wishing him good dreams. He falls into a slobbering slumber, his lips glisten in the light and his plump cheek spills upon the blanket as she covers him.

"Now," she says, and her eyes fix on me and my heart feels both heavy for the long time that may pass before we see each other again, and joyful for our closeness now.

She pulls me to her side of the blanket and we lie next to one another. Thready clouds and scattering seedlings float and catch the sunlight overhead.

I have not looked up at the sky in a long time.

She kisses my mouth.

"There is still more for us to do."

Chapter 65

Weeks pass after our meeting, and I do not see her, not even at church. Mattheus becomes ill from rotten fish and I busy myself nursing him back to health, bringing him fresh water and plain, sticking rice to settle his sick stomach. His age slows his recovery, and he remains weak for days after.

Then, Mattheus asks me to go with him on a week-long trip outside the colony to explore another outpost along the eastern coast of the island. We take a decorated carriage—Mattheus insists. We must assert our wealth to those we meet, both to properly represent our colony and ourselves. Though I dislike such displays, I enjoy the excursion, an excuse to see more of this place. Palm trees tower into the sky and bamboo groves form bright green walls flanking the narrow road for our carriage. We pass waterfalls flowing into small lakes, and the gentle sound of two waters meeting reminds me of the *Leyden,* its gentle sloshing, and of course, Sontje.

I think of what I will tell her of our journey—about the Company's plan to control the spice trades, compelling our exploration of these outposts, and about the Sundanese living in these forests who greet us with more warmth than we expect or deserve. The native women wear fine, richly dyed cloths woven with multicolored threads in pleasing designs I've not seen before. According to one of the Company men traveling with us, the recipes for their dyes are deeply held secrets—not even the native men know their ingredients. My lacework causes me to notice clothes and stitching now, and I find myself admiring the industry of the native people and the beauty and lightness of their fabrics. The heavy serge we use for our own dresses seems bulky and foolish in comparison.

At times, a glimpse of blue ocean appears from behind the forest canopy, its presence a comfort. The water's blue color matches the same brightness of the little house in Amsterdam that so often lightened my long days working for the De Graafs, and a curious, tugging sadness surfaces in me for that little house near Dam Center and its cheerful color, for I know I will not see it again.

I allow myself the luxury of daydreams, remembering when I first met Sontje, and had no time for such fanciful thoughts. As Mattheus holds my hand and our carriage jolts and pitches over the newly cleared, craggy roads through Batavia's forests, I imagine living with Sontje and Ebel. But guilt overcomes me, and I turn my thoughts to the colorful forest birds, the streaming sunlight, and strange animals hiding in the tree canopy as we travel in our Company carriage.

When we finally return to the house, Madaleen is there to greet us. I'm surprised to see her, since her husband prefers that she socialize with women of a higher standing who do not attempt paid work, and remain agreeable to the use of slaves.

Her expression worries me. Round-eyed and stricken, as I recall seeing her back on the *Leyden*.

"Madaleen, what is it?" I ask after she embraces me and greets Mattheus.

She whispers, and I'm not sure why.

"It's Sontje, Jana." Her pretty eyes grow wide, and a numbness enters me. Madaleen holds my arm. "Jana, she has taken ill."

I do not ask Mattheus for permission or even tell him when I'll return.

We hurry toward the western side, to Sontje's cottage. Inside me a buzzing sensation, as though I could drown in my own fear.

"Where is Ebel?" I ask Madaleen.

"The baby is with Dewa. Sontje's girl brought Dewa back to the house." Madaleen sees my worry. "He is fine. No fever."

"So, fever again?" I think back to the *Leyden*. She survived it then, so she will survive this. I feel some relief.

"Yes, but it's different. She complained of terrible pain some days ago—headache and a trembling even worse than on the ship. Said she felt as though flames passed through her legs and spread." Madaleen takes my hand. "Jana, I'm afraid. This is so much worse than on the *Leyden*. And Dewa offered some sort of tree bark to help early on, but Willem refused it. Said he wouldn't take advice from a heathen and so on. And Dewa says now it's too late. The bark only works when someone first becomes ill." Madaleen has that frightened look she wore so often on the *Leyden* and I think for all her wealth and slaves, she remains the orphaned girl she was when we first boarded in Amsterdam.

When we arrive at the cottage, Ebel cries for me from Dewa's arms, and I take him, and kiss his soft cheek.

I enter the dreary, dark bedroom with no furniture save for the pallet where Sontje lies. Not even a simple vase and flower or wall tapestry. A plain and cheerless space.

Her eyes are closed, her hair damp. Her skin is flushed with fever and she trembles so hard her teeth clack.

I give Ebel to Madaleen, afraid that whatever illness Sontje has he will catch if I give him to her. I recall Griet's parents and how her father gave the plague to her mother and they both died within the week.

"Sontje. I'm here." I hold her hand. Her eyelids open slowly.

"Ebel is well?" Her voice is a whisper.

"He is here."

Her tears roll into her hair.

"Jana, I'm so sick and it came so suddenly. I've never felt such pain and it only worsens." She trembles again, a great shaking shudder that moves her whole body.

Madaleen leaves with Dewa to find a wet nurse for Ebel, who is hungry and wanting his milk.

Sontje is pale, pale. Her lips losing their blush. Her hand is cold now. A ragged, chipped nail on her index finger, I only now notice. Sontje was the tidiest of us on the *Leyden* until her illness and the attack. In those first weeks on the ship, we marveled at how she managed to look so fresh despite the salty wind making our skin papery and our hair sticky and lank. A vertical scab on her middle finger above the knuckle—she must have scraped herself somehow. A loose board? A stone? The scar on her fourth finger from the blunt knife that cut her when she trimmed a loose thread from Madaleen's dress, back on the *Leyden*.

Her wrist bone protrudes like a giant pearl. I rub the bone with my thumb, absently, as I did during our last night on the *Leyden*, when I told her about Fader and how I learned to skin a deer.

The carcass still warm and smelling of blood.

She kissed me after hearing the story.

The panicked look never leaves her eyes. At least when she was ill on the *Leyden* her eyes disclosed a surprising, rigid defiance. And after her attacks, a lived-in weariness that only left when she birthed Ebel.

But now I see a Sontje I have never seen before, neither defiant nor weary. Simply waiting. Absent. I'm reminded of Helena in the cave, how quick she was to surrender, to leave me alone in the rainstorm, too afraid to wait.

"Talk to me, Jana..." Sontje whispers, clutching my hand, and pulling me out of my thoughts.

"Look at me so I know you are listening." She opens her gray eyes, fixes them on me. I can't read the thoughts behind them, and my ignorance disappoints me. As though I have failed her and our bond.

Madaleen is still with Dewa, so I speak freely. "We are in the water, back at the Cape." I squeeze her hand, recalling the cool water between my fingertips. "Your beautiful skin. You looked ghostly at night. Lovely. I wrap my legs around you and your arms hold me." I tell her my memories and in so doing, I'm there again.

I talk for hours it seems—recalling our days in Amsterdam, on the *Leyden*, and Ebel's birth. The click-woman, the cave, Sontje on my lips, on my fingers.

All the world. Her.

"Think of it, Sontje," I say, "The red markings glow on the cave walls. The three of us hold hands, just as the women in the paintings." I have been here before. Telling Helena, and now Sontje, my memories of them, as though I'm some sort of terrible, ominous mirror.

"You take him," she says in a voice I do not recognize, that sounds of surrender. "Willem told me after Ebel was born that he doesn't want Ebel. He can scarcely care for himself."

"Don't say that, Sontje." I kiss her damp forehead and blink back my own tears.

But her eyes lose focus and the light of her, that beam of warm sunshine that reminded me of apples and Helena and those short moments in childhood when happiness seemed a solemn requirement, suddenly dims.

Sontje, that tentacle of moon and light, the one to whom I gave all my blackest, most secret stories, and all I believe remained of my joy, goes very still.

She leaves this earth, and then I know I am again, alone.

Chapter 66

Madaleen arrives with the wet nurse soon after. She says she must return to Tomas, but weeps as she leaves. I am too blunt with my own grief to offer comfort beyond a distracted embrace. The wet nurse and Dewa walk with me back to the cottage in the darkness as I carry Ebel in my arms. Dewa knows the path better than I and I feel like a gaping wound. When I arrive home, I have no memory of having walked at all.

Sontje gone. Numbness and swirling. Disbelief. I hold Ebel. He, at least, sleeps peacefully.

Before leaving me before the cottage, Dewa passes her worn hands over Ebel's head, leaving what seems like a blessing in her light touch. She nods at me and walks toward the *kampung*, and I'm alone with Ebel. And afraid.

I open the door. Mattheus sits in his favorite chair, an uneven highbacked that soothes his surly back. His eyes look red and spent, like he has aged in these few hours. He holds a piece of parchment in his hand, perhaps some old Company ledger.

"I wondered if you'd return at all," he says at last, watching me in a way that causes my skin to prickle. "You left like a storm."

"She's gone." I can hardly speak the words, for the emptiness of her absence swallows me. The silence like lead between us.

"How?" he finally asks.

"Fever. Much worse than when she was on the *Leyden*, and that was bad enough. No idea what caused it." I feel I must say something, anything, to lighten the grim feeling of the room. "She suffered."

Mattheus nods and I wonder if he relishes this detail. "And Willem? Where was he?"

"Gone. Who knows where."

"The most irreputable settler in the colony," Mattheus says. "Unfortunate she ended up with such a man."

I hold Ebel close and he stirs in my arms. I'm not sure how to ask my question, but know I must.

"Mattheus."

He seems to expect what will follow, but wishes to hear me make the request, knowing the discomfort it causes me.

"Ebel has no one. Willem is unfit."

"That he is. But it's his child."

"Sontje asked me to take him." I nuzzle Ebel's warm head, smell the newness of his skin. Milk. Some unfamiliar wood smell, too. "Just before she died."

"Jana, Willem is his father."

"He doesn't want him. Sontje said so."

Mattheus smooths the parchment in his lap. A gesture to fill the space between us.

"You left me without even a goodbye. No time to say when you'd return or what I'd have for supper."

The smallness of his bitterness inflames me when I am so burdened by grief. That he expects me to pity him for suffering through one supper alone after I have lost Sontje. I think of so many other meals I've prepared for him, often tired or sick or too sad with longing for

Sontje, but I performed my duties anyway. I nearly laugh at his self-pity, but force myself to stay quiet. For Ebel.

"I'm sorry," I say, though I'm not.

Mattheus sits still again, leaves the paper on the table as I hold Ebel, sending silent pleas into the air for one last act of generosity from my husband. I regret wasting his generosity on my desire for a space at the market, but I did not know then I would need this favor. If I can't raise Ebel, he will end up in an orphanage, or with some bitter old widow, a stranger, when I have loved him as my own.

A long, exhausted sigh escapes Mattheus, like his very soul has tired of me. And indeed, he could exile me from his home, knowing all he does of Sontje and me. He glances again at the parchment on the table before speaking.

"He needs a father, even if he's an old *traag* like me," Mattheus growls, at last. He stands up, slower than ever, and walks to the bedroom before I can even form the words to thank him.

I stand in the room holding Ebel, listening to the boy breathe against me. My arms tremble from holding him for so long, all the way from Sontje's gray cottage to here. I wait for my heart to beat again, for it feels it has stopped.

And then I glance down at the parchment on the table, and a hollow feeling enters me again.

My practice parchment from months ago. Sontje's name, written again and again, in my own crooked hand.

Chapter 67

Two months have passed, and I wake before dawn, ignoring the fatigue weighing down my eyelids, the weariness burrowing into my bones. Ebel is hungry. A sharp ache hits my middle—I feel his hunger in myself. Sontje once said that with motherhood, some new voice entered her, distracting her from herself, forever connecting her to Ebel's needs. I understand it now. When he cries or screams, my own stomach feels swallowed.

I don't want him to wake up Mattheus, who sends long, deafening snores into the dark silence of our bedroom. I can't help but feel guilty for forcing my old husband to take someone else's infant after he's raised three grown children already, but the colony has no orphanage for Dutch children, and I would never agree to Ebel being sent to one. The few wives of the colonies are busy with their own babies. Mattheus asked Reverend Falks to discuss the matter of Ebel's care with Willem, and true to Sontje's prediction, Willem readily agreed to the arrangement, eager to be rid of his child.

With Falks's blessing, Mattheus took to Ebel quickly, and accepted him as his own. Perhaps he felt relieved that Ebel's mother was finally lost to me. Or he knew I would be grateful.

And I am.

I lift myself from the bed and go to Ebel's crib. He is wide awake, staring at me with Sontje's clear, gray eyes. His arms and legs jerk in excitement. I would laugh but I might wake Mattheus.

I gather Ebel up and his arms wrap around my neck. He grunts at me. At eight months, he is trying to talk.

"Shh, little one." I pat his back and he presses his wet mouth against my cheek. I take him into the kitchen. Aini will be here soon, but even her help provides little time for all I must do today.

I hold Ebel at my hip, though already my arm aches from this grip. Using my other hand, I peel a banana, digging my thumb into the fruit, and squeezing the ripe pulp into Ebel's bowl. I mash the banana with a fork. I'll have to return later for his milk.

Ebel grunts again, and drools onto my arm. Hungry.

"Almost done." I explain all that I do, naming each item I touch, each of my actions. Even when he sleeps I sometimes find myself speaking to him, then stop myself. How entirely motherhood swallows me. Quiet Jana becomes Jana who can't stop talking, who now converses with the laundry, the rosebushes, the wooden bowls as I stack them in the cupboard.

I place Ebel on the floor once we enter the main room. He craws into my lap, and I spoon banana into his mouth and kiss the back of his head. I wish I could sit still and enjoy this, but I have too much work to do.

"Finish up, Ebel, and then you can crawl a bit." He drools banana down his chin and I wipe him with my apron. His bottom is wet. All my movements feel slow because I'm so tired. Between lacemaking and caring for Ebel, and worrying about him, and missing his mother, I become so tired I can hardly sleep, for fear of never waking again.

The Councilor-General's wife has ordered me to embellish her church service dress. She wants a unique design, something no one else has. I have the collar and the ruff of one sleeve to finish, and the fabric squares lie close to me on the table, but I dare not work on them with Ebel so close. He trails a mess wherever he goes.

"Now for some milk." I wipe his mouth and neck, slick with banana.

I'm afraid to leave him alone in the sitting room, so I carry him to the kitchen again. He no longer uses a wet nurse, and can sip goat's milk from the feeding bottle Madaleen gave me. One of the slaves leaves us a bottle of goat milk in the morning, and I'm relieved when I see the bottle outside the kitchen door.

I pour the milk into Ebel's bottle with its tin spout. Ebel reaches for his milk, hands out, grasping.

"Uhh. Uhh," he says, wincing. In a moment, he will scream. I hurry to finish filling the bottle. My only desire is to prevent his piercing wail.

"Here, you hold it." I let him take the bottle in his hands. He puts his mouth on the spout, waiting for his milk.

"You must tip it to get the milk," I say, knowing he can't understand, but still speaking out of habit. "Let me sit down."

I nearly run back to the sitting room with him, plopping him on his back and feeding him his milk. He sucks at the bottle, slapping his hand against it. I'm reminded of his newborn days, when he would tap Sontje's breast while feeding. In the midst of my triumph at having avoided Ebel's screams, I ache for Sontje, wishing she could see him now, so fat and happy, slapping away at his bottle.

Sontje's was the third burial in the colony's new cemetery, though six stone markers stood for sailors lost in the voyage here, their bodies forfeited to the ocean. Reverend Falks delivered a paltry eulogy in his loud, sermonizing voice: "Sontje Brouwer was a dutiful Company Daughter, a beloved wife."

How I wished to correct him, my anger a flat stone in my chest.

She was sunlight and sadness and a thin, cold rod of iron, but only I would know this, and since women cannot speak at the colony funerals, I held Ebel in my arms and remembered her—lavender and wheat, the blue-gray shadows under her eyes. Butter. Salt. Iron. Her potted crocuses back in Amsterdam. The black shutter hanging loose.

I'm nearly finished with the lace collar when Mattheus enters the room. He rubs his eyes. Yawns.

"You've been awake some time?"

"Ebel was hungry before dawn and I must finish this lace." I nod toward the fabric.

"I feel tired just watching you work," Mattheus says, rubbing his sore elbow. "I don't know how you manage it all."

"Not much choice. The Councilor-General's wife is expecting her dress by Saturday and this is the most difficult lace I've made."

Mattheus picks up little Ebel, who pulls on Mattheus's long, fleshy earlobe. "Owa, little one. I might drop you." But Mattheus smiles. He looks over my shoulder, inspecting the fabric. "It's lovely, Jana. I'm sure she'll be very pleased. And your work will be a boon to my own presence at the Company. You keep the wives happy with your fine lace and the men have better gifts for their wives. You're a wonder."

I feel shy at his praise, and grateful too. He hugs Ebel close. "I agree, little one," he says. "Your mother has many gifts."

I smile at my stitching. A welcome warmth fills me. Aini will arrive shortly, and then I can finish the lace collar in peace. For

Mattheus's kindness, I will prepare him an *appeltaart* in the Walloon manner, boiling the apples in Rhenish wine, to serve for dessert later this evening.

Chapter 68

I missed sleep altogether for two days to finish the pieces. The Councilor-General's wife wore her dress to church, and everyone praised the delicate work on her sleeves and ruff. Even Maritjen made a great show of her admiration for the Councilor-General's wife, though Maritjen flatters all women higher in station than herself. She even ordered cuffs of her own, anxious to join the others in their praise of me. I wished I could tell Sontje. How she would have laughed.

With many new orders for my lace since then, I've earned enough to cover Ebel's needs and to provide money to Aini and Candra over the past weeks. Mattheus must know I pay them, but he says nothing, satisfied that his young wife makes him known within the Company, and his permissive approach earns him a reputation for being more than just an old man, wearing out his days in Batavia.

It is late in the evening after the following day, and Mattheus is not yet home. I have sung one of our old Dutch lullabies to Ebel, patting his back all the while, and placed him in his crib. My eyes feel tired and dry from my lacework today, since the flickering candle provides an unsteady light. In the passing months, I have found a new fondness for Mattheus, in his affection for Ebel, his pride in my growing business. I flinch less at his touch and the roughness of his lips against my cheek. Though I feel no desire for him—nothing resembling my feelings for Sontje—I enjoy the sweetness of our family, the welcome sameness of the day's routines. Perhaps all marriage is this way? A long stretch of grating tolerance that thaws into something like warmth, though I can't imagine Madam De Graaf ever discovered such tenderness for her own husband.

The hour passes and I listen as the wind throttles the nearby palms and rings our hanging outdoor bell. Mattheus's dinner will be cold. I try to ignore my disquiet. I reassure myself—I must expect such worry, having lost so many and so much.

A knock sounds on our little door, not the steady rapping I expect from Mattheus, but two gentle knocks. I walk to the entrance of our cottage.

A Mardijker stands at the door. This is what we call the Portuguese ex-slaves brought from India. They live separately from us and the Sundanese, so we rarely see them except at the market. But I recognize this man from the forest. Sometimes eating a banana under a tree. Other times, closing his eyes as though napping, even as he hums.

He carries Mattheus, gray-faced and limp.

My stomach lurches. "What happened?"

The Mardijker says nothing, just brings Mattheus inside and lays him on the floor. The Mardijker wears purple trousers, his toenails neatly trimmed despite three black nails on one foot, and then I'm ashamed to notice such things at this time. He straightens Mattheus's wig with surprising tenderness. Falks and Mattheus are the only ones who wear hair pieces, perhaps because they're the oldest in the colony.

Suddenly, I feel I'm elsewhere, watching. Thinking of how I lost Sontje. Helena. That familiar sensation of disbelief.

"What is this bruise?" I touch the blooming purple at Mattheus's temple.

The Mardijker opens his palm as though holding something within it, and dashes it against his head. He explains in Portuguese. A fallen rock or tree branch must have struck Mattheus, perhaps from the wind.

The man mutters a prayer. They are Christians and I understand a few words. The Lord's Prayer. The sweet smell of betel nut and bitter odor of smoke rise from the man.

I hold Mattheus's hand. Cold. I have no way of knowing how long he lay outside. I listen to his chest. Silence. Only the sound of the Mardijker's deep breaths beside me. A comfort though.

"Please get the Reverend. Tell him to bring the medic. Thank you." I can't leave Mattheus alone, not even with this man who saved him. I can't leave him with a stranger. And then Ebel is sleeping in the next room.

The Mardijker nods and rises, then lets himself out of the house.

I sit on the floor and hold Mattheus's hand. His loose skin drapes across the back of his hands, covered with sparse, white hair. When we first married, I looked for some part to love in him, and settled on his elegant hands, long-fingered like Sontje's, but with sturdier bones and knuckles. A vertical line through the middle of his littlest fingernail. He had smashed his hand in a drawer two days earlier.

"Owa!" he had said and put his finger in his mouth and I had smiled at the time, thinking how Ebel pulled his earlobes, and Mattheus said the same thing.

I'm not sure what to do, so I speak to him.

"The man who found you is calling on the Reverend," I explain to Mattheus, as if he hears me. "He will bring the medic." I have not seen a doctor in some time, so I'm not sure who it may be. His hand is very cold, unmoving, and I think of all the others I have lost. Their cold hands in mine, and a feeling of dread washes over me. I beg, as I have done before.

Please let him live.

Reverend Falks arrives looking old and tired with his wig askew, freshly roused from sleep. He brings the medic, a gaunt blonde man with an unkempt beard and weak chin. The Reverend is bent over now, and walks slowly from a recent fall and injured hip. The medic approaches Mattheus and bends his ear to his chest. He holds his limp wrist between his thumb and forefinger. The medic breathes loudly, as though he announces his good health to ridicule my husband's injury.

"I'm sorry," the younger man says, after his examination. "He is gone."

I sit very still, as though I'm on the *Leyden*, shifting back and forth on the sea.

The Reverend pats my hand. I see now his own discomfort with death, his fear. Such unease seems improper for a man of God.

I think back to the Reverend's eulogy for Sontje. Perhaps he will do better for Mattheus.

"Rest in Peace with our Great Father, Mattheus Haffner." Reverend Falks places his hands on Mattheus's forehead, and whispers a prayer I can't hear. The Mardijker bows his head, and for the rest of my days in Batavia I will greet him when he passes. This man I do not know now stamped into another of my losses.

The medic leaves to summon some slaves to remove Mattheus's body from the house.

He feared dying alone. It is why he married me in his old age, absurd as our joining appeared to other settlers. I hope he was with me at the moment of his death, but of course, I can't be sure.

Four slaves arrive some hours later, as I wait with Mattheus. The slaves lay Mattheus into a *suar* wood coffin, and place his wig on his head.

"No," I tell them, thinking the wig gives him a pitiful look. "I will keep it." One of the slaves hands the heavy wig to me, the inside patched with blood.

They remove his boots and belt, costly items that can be resold. Reverend Falks tucks a small Bible into the box before they cover the coffin with another thin slab of *suar* wood. They heave the box onto their brown shoulders to carry to the cemetery outside the compound. To prepare for the funeral.

And thus I am made a widow.

Chapter 69

No matter how many times I encounter death, it is always a surprise. A wolf. A windstorm. Moeder explained it to me once when I saw a dead squirrel, its tail separated from its body on the grass outside our house.

"What's wrong with it?" I asked.

"The life has gone out of it," Moeder replied.

I did not need to ask her more. I knew even then that I, too, would be like the squirrel someday, my life exiting me by some unknown circumstance. I imagined a glass bottle of some clear liquid, like water, but thicker. And for years, the fact of my own ending scared me. And then I thought, *well, for most of eternity, we are nothing.* Just space. We get only a little chance on earth, and then it's back to eternity, whether hell or heaven—and I never truly believed in either of them.

The night of Mattheus's death, I dreamt the wall behind the bed became a cave wall dripping with an ancient moisture. When I looked closely, small, translucent mice crawled upon it.

Wake yourself, I said.

And then I gazed at the cave walls, but my eyes remained closed.

Chapter 70

Months pass. Ebel walks now, in the jerking movements of a drunkard, his arms stretched out for balance. He laughs at the black-winged butterflies hovering over the rosebushes, with their white spots resembling eyes. He grabs at everything, his hands wishing to discover and understand. Aini, Candra, and I follow behind him, like ladies in waiting. Watching him exhausts me, and I have less time for my lace, but I remind myself that time is passing, and I must enjoy what I can.

Even so, my worries multiply. We have savings, but not enough. I sell the maps, the globe, the magnifying lens Mattheus held above one of the maps on the second day of our wedded life. "Take a look, Jana," he said, the letters suddenly stretched and visible and beautiful in the way light changes through a glade of trees because you see it differently than before. I could not help but exclaim in surprise. He laughed at my simplicity and kissed my forehead and that was the first moment I felt I could be married to such a man.

Next, the pearls. The four glass goblets. A small Nuremberg porcelain vase and a silver ewer and two candlesticks.

Without the protection of Mattheus's position at the Company and my status as a married woman, I have even fewer friends and can't count on others' charity. The settlers here are selfish and competitive. The burghers vie for the Company's favor, and young recruits from

Amsterdam arrive and upend whatever order has been established by the last burgher in charge. But what else can one expect? The promise of wealth is what brought us here. *Do not store up for yourselves treasures on earth, where moth and rust destroy.* But Reverend Falks never recites this verse, for no one would listen.

The claim to our cottage also troubles me. Two years must pass before the council can proclaim Mattheus's assets mine. The council sent letters to Mattheus's three children in Breda and Delft one week after his death, and I pray they do not receive them or do not care. His children could come forward and take the house, and then Ebel and I would have nothing. In my worst moments, I feel we are more entitled to this property than his heirs, who left him for me to nurse in his old age.

"Please, Great Fader," I begin each night. "Please let us not lose our home."

At times the gesture of prayer, palm against palm, thumbs pressed bone to bone, feels a contrivance. But nothing else protects us from that old beast. Poverty, again, claws at my door.

In my worries about money, I begin to lose the smaller aspects of my marriage to Mattheus. I no longer use his expressions—*De kippen zijn van de leg*—when people arrive from Amsterdam, only to complain about the laziness of the slaves here, the food, the humidity, or to recall with longing the elaborate water tournaments, fireworks, and masques of the homeland. I no longer use his words: *kwibus* or *houten claus*, to describe disagreeable people. Without his words, I become myself again, and yet a stained version, as though I now see myself through a greased glass.

I wake to small noises and fearful thoughts, sounds I would not hear at all if Mattheus were here beside me. I reassure myself. *Just some mice.*

Just a flowerpecker outside. Some drunkard singing in the distance. The wind. But my heart charges at these sounds. I think of escape routes, hiding places. Still planning for the darkest possibilities.

I have come to believe that once ignited, that feeling of being hunted never leaves.

When I can't sleep, I recite the Lord's Prayer, the recipe for *pannenkoeken*, the tired nursery rhyme of my childhood condemning me to the kitchen. *The girl plays with little things.* I repeat the words. Sometimes, sleep finally finds me just as the sun whitens the linseed drapes and then I know the rest of the day I will be irritable and tired. I will have to smile pleasantly when the lurching widower Nils, who lives in a nearby cottage, inquires how I'm doing as I water my rosebushes in the morning, as though waiting for me to admit defeat so he may sweep in and rescue me.

In such moments I wish I were a man. Mattheus always slept soundly. No fear of attacks or other abuses. At night, my mind remains a stampede of worries and what ifs. Memories that insist upon fading, leaving me lonelier, because while the memory of happiness can leave a dull shadow of loneliness, the full loss of those memories erases me from myself.

Sometimes I pray Mattheus's children have died in the plague.

Chapter 71

The letter arrives, just as I have allowed myself to feel some hope they might fail to respond. Reverend Falks delivers the document himself.

"I can read it for you," he says, for Falks is just as nosy as Maritjen, and must know I do not read well, since Mattheus passed before my reading lessons finished. "It's quite possible they will cede their claim to you. They're all grown and far from here, after all. It will be a nuisance to take his property over."

I allow him to read it for me, and Falks stands as straight as he can, even with his injured hip and curving back, knowing the importance of the words quilled on the parchment.

My heart beats hard in my chest. Ebel is so small to have lost so much already—even more than me. At his young age, I at least had my mother and a father, too. And two sisters and all the Bos to explore. I blink quickly, feeling my eyes sting with tears for my son.

Falks clears his throat as though preparing to deliver one of his sermons. "Well," he begins. "I'd hoped for better news. The family's representative will be arriving soon, and they will claim everything Mattheus owns."

Part Four

Chapter 72

Since receiving the notice from the Haffner family, I can't sleep longer than three hours. All night I wonder how I might convince them to give me the cottage, to at least beg some time to determine our plans.

But I also resent that I must beg for my own home. Mattheus spoke so little of his children, said they left him for their own fortunes, and didn't even see him off when he left. Gerrit, Paul, and Marc. I only know their names.

I bring Ebel with me to the market today so Aini and Candra can sew undisturbed. They work tirelessly on the lace and make their own patterns, eager to see how their sketches turn out in the lace. I, too, enjoyed seeing my visions for patterns becoming fabric, our little dreams turning real. But the work strains our eyes and fingers. Our elbows ache. We all work long hours so I may earn a little extra for whatever plan I must make for our future.

Ebel and I enter the *Nieuwe Markt* area, which expands week by week. Now, Muslim merchants crowd into the narrow spaces between the open-air stands selling teacups, porcelain vases, and weapons such as daggers and spears. Native women sell beans and cucumbers, peppers, and fruits from woven baskets. Slaves walk quietly behind the few

Dutch women braving this heat, carrying their owners' parasols and betel boxes. Even more female slaves wear our Dutch style of clothing now, and look awkward and weary in our many skirts in this sticking humid air and scalding sunshine. The old women still wear their simple *kebayas* and long skirts wrapped around their slim waists. They sit under nearby trees, selling melons and beans. Indians call out, announcing their wares: iron and tools, daggers, betel boxes, carpets, and bamboo spears.

Ebel stumbles alongside me as we approach my little stall. I have a basket of rolled bits of lace, and *brezels* almost as tasty as Adelheid's that I have learned to bake after many failed attempts. Unlike the other sellers at the market, who sell the newness of Batavia, I offer the homeland—our Dutch clothing and food, even if I'm not so fond of either of them.

"Let's try and sell all the *brezels* by midday," I tell Ebel as I cup the back of his blonde head in my hand. How snugly it fits in my palm, his hair as soft as rabbit fur. He takes my hand, squeezes it in his plump fist, and I recall Sontje's fingertips weaving through mine as we walked through the cave, as we waited for sleep to take us away from the sickening movements of the *Leyden* after the first storm. Small as he is, he has her long fingers. The same bird-like bones.

He allows me to play with his hair, busying himself with the task of clapping a mosquito away from me. He then stops and points to an antler beetle crawling across the dirt path, asking me its name. Ebel delights in Batavia's variety of insects. Beetles with hook-like pincers, black beetles with spikes all over their bodies, round beetles with iridescent spots, spiders of varying size and leg length. I sometimes find him kneeling in the grass outside the cottage, inspecting the insects, as I often did as a girl back in the Bos, and the memory of that time causes both sadness and joy, for the loss of my own childhood, and my enjoyment watching Ebel's.

I permit him to watch the beetle crossing and then we resume our walk to the stall. The market is busy today. Ebel holds hard to my hand now, pointing out and naming all he knows—clouds, sky, birds. We pass the native women selling melons, cucumbers, and the long beans they use in their cooking, but which have no place in our Dutch meals, though we have tried them once or twice. Merchants now have fixed stalls, but only the men. I'm content with my little space in the sun, with my basket of lace and *brezels* wrapped in linen.

The merchant in the stall next to me, Ajip, nods toward us. He offers Ebel a great, round orange, which Ebel takes into his hands and brings to his mouth, as though he may bite through its tough skin with his little teeth.

"It's too big, Ebel," I say, and thank Ajip.

"He grows fast," Ajip says in Portuguese. "Like my own son."

"Is he the same age?"

"A few years older. Walks and talks like a man already." Ajip smiles, proud of his boy.

A new group of Company Daughters approaches. I don't recall their names, though I should. My work swallows my time now. I avoid social gatherings, and the constant inquiries into my recent misfortunes.

"Jana Haffner?" A young man approaches. Someone I've not met before. His features are long and pointed—a sharp chin and nose, a face that stretches up and down and is narrow in its width. And still, something about him looks familiar.

"Yes?" I try and place him, worried he may know me from my Ringhouse days. Always the fear of being recognized when I encounter some new man. But he looks too young.

"I heard you sold at the market. Very unusual, no?" he asks. "Such work is reserved for the native merchants or guild members." I detect judgment in his statement, but stay quiet. Ebel presses his face into my skirts, leaving a dark ring on the fabric from his wet mouth. I wish the man would leave so I could talk to the women, ask them questions. Though I'm not much for conversation, I find that if I pay some compliment or make some other observation, the women will take a look at my lace, and feel more obliged to purchase it.

The man extends his hand in greeting, and then I know him. The same bony fingers and long hands. Panic clamps over my throat, and then he speaks.

"I'm Gerrit Haffner, your… stepson." He spits out this last word, as if wishing it could disappear.

I swallow and keep my face still, trying to conjure a kind reply. But Gerrit Haffner is too impatient for pleasantries.

A red burn has already appeared on his cheeks, his punishment for standing in the noon sun, and I feel some satisfaction for this blemish.

"Welcome to our colony," I say, not knowing how else to respond.

He nods, wipes the sweat from his long and narrow brow. "Yes, well. It was a long voyage to get here, and not much to see once I arrived. But I've come to claim our family's property, and thought it best to do so in person."

Chapter 73

Gerrit gives me one month to leave the cottage. I thank him for this generosity, packing away my bitterness along with our clothing. He wants nearly everything in the house—the furnishings, crockery, and silverware that Mattheus purchased after our wedding, even the linens on our beds. At least I sold the most expensive items, keeping what little I could for just this sort of circumstance. My life in the Bos and Amsterdam trained me well to distrust any certainty in good times. Short periods of calm end quicker than the next difficulty.

But in those earlier times I was alone. Only responsible for my own hunger. Now I have Ebel. And Gerrit, shrewd and curious, refuses to accept Ebel as his half-brother, and treats him as some lowborn stranger's child. He feels no obligation for my son and makes every delay to receiving his inheritance a great gesture of generosity and goodwill.

I'm spinning in my worries, unable to stop my dark thoughts. I bake more *brezels*, sew more lace, give up sleep altogether, wearing down our candles and then sitting outside to sew by moonlight. A rigid routine of work and selling at the market, and my sleeplessness, cause my impatience with Ebel. I scold him when he trips as we hurry to the market or spills his milk on the floor. And then I remember my vow to Sontje, and feel fresh waves of guilt and self-loathing.

"I'm sorry, Ebel," I tell him after chastising him for falling again as we return home from the market. I only sold two rolls of lace and must affix them to the woman's dress tonight, and all my thoughts rush to the list of tasks I must complete before sundown. "I'm doing too many things."

Ebel looks up at me with his great, round, gray eyes—Sontje's eyes.

"Don't be mad," he says, his eyes filling with tears.

I feel studied. In Ebel's expression I see Sontje's same curious gaze, as though Ebel wishes to understand but can't. Like Sontje asking me about my poverty in the Bos when I first met her.

I open the door to the cottage—now Gerrit's cottage, I can't help but think sourly—and imagine what to cook for supper. Aini and Candra sit on the floor sewing, though I've told them to use the chairs.

"Well, I have one sewing order for today," I tell them.

Aini nods and smiles at Ebel, who runs to her and sits in her lap.

He has not run into my lap in weeks, perhaps thinking I'm too busy for affection. A new sweep of guilt rises in me.

Aini kisses the top of his head and holds him close.

They are two shapes fitting together—key and lock, egg and nest. My chest tightens. I can't enjoy Ebel, lovely as he is. I'm nothing but worry and fear. A failure of a *moeder*.

My eyes sting and I wonder if some dust blows in through the window. I feel tightened, wrung like a wet petticoat. I'm unsure why I feel this echo of sadness when Ebel, at least, is content in Aini's arms.

And before I can cover my eyes, I begin to weep. It is a surprise to me, a sensation I have abandoned long ago. Hot tears drip off my cheeks and chin. I rub at them, ashamed, but more appear, and my cheeks burn with embarrassment.

Ebel stares at me, and Aini holds him closer.

Candra stands up from the floor.

"I'm sorry," I say, sniffling, flushing at the scene I'm making. "I don't know why... now."

Candra comes to me and pats my back. Makes sucking noises with her tongue like I'm a child in need of soothing. I hate the sound of my weeping, and that I require the comfort of her clicking tongue and gentle touch.

"I feel lost," I say, speaking before I can think. "I don't know what to do. The lace isn't enough. I have nothing but this house and soon it will be Gerrit's and I promised Sontje I would raise Ebel and I can't fail, but here I am. Failing." A fresh sob escapes from me. I think of all the other times I've felt hopeless, but somehow this feels worse. To lose those I love is terrible, but to break my promise to Sontje, to fail her blameless, beautiful son, guts me in a new way. I'm like the pitiful deer Fader butchered in the Bos all those years ago. Emptied.

Candra sucks her teeth again and rubs my back in long, slow circles, as my own mother once did when I was little. I sob again, thinking of Moeder, and remembering myself as that girl, before I knew the great breadth of losses I know now.

Chapter 74

Aini and Candra tell me they will sleep in the living room. I give them sheets that they fold into pallets, no need or desire for greater comfort, and I again envy them their simplicity and easy way with one another. They make us a supper of rice, fish, and their fried beans. They bathe Ebel, sing to him, put him to sleep, telling him their own traditional stories. I fear they are better mothers than me, than I will ever be.

Candra then makes me a dark tea and says it will help me sleep.

I lie down on my pallet, and listen to their low voices in the next room. Ebel sleeps on a pallet next to mine, his quiet, whispered breaths the loveliest sound I know. His hair becomes damp as he sleeps, as though the effort of slumber causes him to perspire.

I can't hear what the women say. Just whispering, but the sound comforts me. The tea appears to take effect and a dense sleep claims me, at last, releasing me from today's worries and all my failures, which I imagine stacked up in a tower like the plates I once carried from table to washtub back when I worked for Ebel's grandfather, kind Master Reynst.

I wake after sunrise, for the first time in months. Aini and Candra wait for me in the kitchen. Ebel runs to me, wraps his arms around my leg, and asks to be carried. I pick him up, smell his sleep-damp hair.

"Thank you," I tell them, still ashamed of yesterday's display. "I needed to sleep." I hug Ebel and set him back down.

Candra tells me to sit at the table, and Aini brings me a bowl of rice and vegetables.

"Eat," she commands, nodding toward the bowl.

I do as she asks, no longer simply filling the emptiness in my belly without thought for the meal, but tasting the sweetness of the cooked carrots and yams, the sourness of the basil. I chew the rice slowly, savoring how it yields against my teeth. Ebel runs back and forth in the cottage, showing us his speed, then drops down in front of me, spent from his activity. I heave him into my lap.

"We talked to our *kampung*," Candra says as I finish eating. The two women remain shy with me, and I with them, even though we have shared long days together. My discomfort with slavery causes me embarrassment, though now I depend on them too much to release them. I give them money, but feel guilty all the same—both for paying them when others do not, and for not paying them more.

"We want you to come with us. To show you," Candra continues. She speaks more often than Aini. Aini smiles more often, a smile that changes her face.

I know not to ask further. They look both shy and eager, and now I am curious also. I finish my bowl of rice, spooning bits into Ebel's ready mouth so I can finish breakfast quickly.

They take me through the *kampung*, and I recall all those months ago—more than a year now—when Dewa first brought me here. I've not visited the widows' *kampung* since. The Company discourages such mingling between the colonists and natives, except in the brothels on the outskirts, and no one speaks of that. Just as in Amsterdam, we Dutch rely on pretenses of order and virtue.

We walk past the long building where Dewa brought me, and well into a forested area where the footpath disappears. The air cools under the tree canopy and the sound of all human activity wanes against the birdsong and insects chattering.

I doubt even the colony knows of this place, well hidden in a clot of short, crowded trees. Even the trees are unknown to me. Great, oblong leaves hang from their branches with fat, irregular green fruit the size of our Dutch potatoes. The fruit produces an unpleasant smell and Ebel hides his face in my shoulder to avoid its odor.

We enter a second long hut, with open walls and a thatched roof woven so slats of space break into the ceiling, allowing streams of sunlight. The design impresses me; we Dutch did not think of it and our dwellings are often dark and stifling.

Inside, eight women work. Three weaving at looms, the others mixing great vats of some liquid.

"What is this?" I ask Candra.

She smiles and leads me to one of the women, not much older than me. I recognize her from when Dewa took me to the widow's *kampung*—long, sloping cheekbones and hair hanging in two braids to her elbows. She nods at me, seems to remember me also, and I watch as she works. She uses a loom whose beams sit in her lap and are attached by a long strap, and a flat stick to push down the rows of weaving. Her small, strong feet support the warp beam as she leans back in her chair. A hand's breadth of fabric lies at the bottom of her loom—a colorful pattern I've never seen before. The natives wear solid colors around the colony, not this ornate pattern of alternating colors in a geometric design.

"It's beautiful." I'm entranced watching her quick, flowing movements, so full of ease and sureness. She reminds me of Griet sewing her lace on the *Leyden*, unaware of the roll and toss of the ship as she worked, the same calm and joy in all her movements, and I think of the pleasure I have felt watching people doing work they understand and love. The cleanness of their dedication to a task. Sontje often praised my skills in cleaning, and indeed, I still find enjoyment in a well-scrubbed floor.

Even Ebel stops his squirming to watch the women stirring at the pots.

"They make color," Candra explains to him. Her Portuguese sounds shy and unsure, so different from the words she shares with the other slaves. We all sound different in other languages—I, too, am simpler in Portuguese, my thoughts limited to questions and simple commands. I wonder how differently I would know these women without my Dutch habits and speech, which rise like a hulking wall between us.

The women stir threads into the pots of dye, mixing them with long, wooden paddles.

"I always thought you dyed the cloth after weaving it." I recall seeing women in the *kampung* stirring finished cloth in dye baths during our walks with Reverend Falks when we first arrived here.

"Only for day clothes," Candra explains. "These are special clothes. For weddings and ceremonies."

Aini brings me a cloth, folded into a square. I open its panels as she and Candra watch. Indeed, all the women in the hut slow their work, as if waiting for my response.

The fabric is slick in my hands, softer than I imagined. I hold it in front of me.

The cloth seems alive, so full of design and color, almost as if moving. The pattern changes. At one moment, I see flowers, the next, open eyes. The red and gold weave both deepens and lightens at different points in the pattern, as though every shade of both colors exist somewhere in the threads.

I trace the design with my finger, trying to understand its lines. "I've never seen such a design." Ebel's grasp around my neck tightens, as though he, too is impressed by the cloth's quality.

Aini brings me a second cloth, smaller and patterned in shades of green. A simpler version of our lace edges the rectangular cloth. I smile, seeing Aini's familiar pattern of diamonds and leaves.

"You made this?" I ask.

Aini nods, shy and smiling.

"It looks like a table covering or place setting. It's lovely." My mind buzzes, fresh with ideas. Fabrics on our tables, hanging on the walls like the dusty old tapestries Madam De Graaf hung in her bedroom. But these are more vivid and full. Alive.

"You have more?"

"Yes," Aini replies. "More. For you. For buying."

"You want me to sell them? At the market?" My heart beats into my throat. How the women would exclaim over these unique patterns. Madaleen will like them—she has an eye for decorative items. Even the flowers in her house vases contain blooms I can't find anywhere else.

Aini smiles again. She looks as happy as she does when Ebel bounds into her arms in the morning. "Yes," she says. "We make them for you to sell. For you and Ebel."

Chapter 75

Madaleen invites me over for tea with the other *Leyden* women. I bring my fabrics and lace with me, hoping I may sell some of them, but also eager to see Madaleen. Since her marriage, I rarely see her outside of the market.

I'm nervous, afraid the other *Leyden* women will resent my attempts to sell them my goods, and I'm worried, as always, about money. One week remains before we must vacate the cottage, and Gerrit now makes a habit of passing the house every evening, often stopping to ask about the size of our land, my rosebushes, whether we have good soil for farming. I watch his shrewd face calculating and planning how best to squeeze money from his claim. My house. Ebel's house.

He offers me purchase of the cottage, but the price is beyond anything I can afford. Madaleen says I can stay in a room in her grand house, but I hate to rely on her charity.

I've been to Madaleen's *landhuizen* only once before, and this time she insists I see the entire grounds. When I first arrive at her property, she shows me her stately gardens with rows of potted plants, flower beds, and belvederes. Her fifty slaves keep the grounds looking like a European garden—the hedge rows neatly pruned, a fountain, and a vegetable garden. Her dining room dwarfs my sitting room, and its shining marble floors and ornate teakwood table remind me of the De Graafs'.

We enter the sitting room. I'm early, and the others have yet to arrive.

"You have an admirer, you know," Madaleen says, sitting ladylike and prim, pretending to be more grown than she is. On the *Leyden* she liked to curl up like a sleeping cat on the floor or her hammock, but she is less the young girl I met on the *Leyden.* Her steps grow heavier now—a baby grows in her, and I hide my sadness, that she must undergo childbirth when she is still a child herself.

"An admirer?" I can't imagine. The world of men has retreated so much to me, and I hardly miss it. "I'm still grieving." I do not tell her I mean for Sontje.

"Ebel needs a father." It is strange to hear her giving me advice, but she has a wisdom she lacked when we left Amsterdam. "Willem still refuses to see him?"

"Yes. He is lost. I can't even feel angry with him. He is either drunk at all times or muttering to himself about lions. And we have done well enough so far. It's only since Mattheus died that we are… challenged."

"Hmm." Madaleen raises her eyebrows, purses her lips. "Berend Oonstade is good with his hands. Was once a carpenter. He is starting off with the Company. Tomas says he's sharp."

"It feels too soon, and Ebel is so young."

"Of course. I'm simply saying it would make your life easier," Madaleen continues, ignoring my scowl. "And the others would stop whispering about you living alone. He has his own money. And you're still young, Jana."

"Ebel's lost too many people already, Madaleen. We've found a sort of peace." At this veiled reference to Sontje, Madaleen pauses. She pats my hand.

"I often dream about her," Madaleen's voice softens. "She was the sister I always wanted."

"I know." I feel no jealousy that Madaleen preferred Sontje to me. "I can hardly remember her face when I'm awake. I must look at Ebel to see her again." I pause, thinking of Madaleen's matchmaking desires. "Does it bother you? That I live alone?"

"It is unusual," Madaleen admits. "Are you not lonely?"

"I have been lonely for so long since Sontje passed, that I no longer notice the condition. I'm even protective of my loneliness now. It helps me see the world differently."

If Madaleen were Sontje, she would ask me how the world was different. But she is Madaleen, so she looks at her fine shoes and says nothing.

In the colonies we strive for sameness, to be an extension of Amsterdam. This is why Madaleen wishes me to marry. To be like all the others. The identical houses in the Herengracht. Every flower box filled with the same blooms, save Sontje's crocuses. Every shingle and shutter painted the same. But even then, I loved the most different house of them all, the blue one at Dam Centre.

Madaleen pats her hair down, wound in elaborate plaits that must have required the help of two slaves. "I do think you will like him."

For a moment, I see Madaleen as a little girl, whispering to her lost Drika. A pleading quality in her expression I thought had departed after marriage. I'm touched by her concern.

"I can't imagine another marriage. Try not to worry about me. I have been alone for so much of my life."

Madaleen nods. "Even me, Jana. I think when you lose so much early on, you are always a little lonely."

I do not wish to go down this path, reminding Madaleen of her own losses. I reach over to her as she sits next to me, and squeeze her hand just as the door knocker sounds.

*

One of Madaleen's slaves leads Catherina and Maritjen into the *zaal* where we sit. I feel more nervous now, clutching my basket of fabric with me, wondering when to show them my goods.

"You look well, Jana," Maritjen says with some reluctance as she enters. I stand to embrace her, her sour rose water scent filling my nose. "This place agrees with you, it seems. This sticky air and fish for breakfast every day tires me now. And the insects. Every day I get some new sting or welt from the swarms. Makes me long for our cold winters." Complaining about Batavia is a favored leisure activity, but I say nothing. Having slept out in the cold more than once, those Dutch winters feel forever sealed into my bones.

"Catherina, where is your sister?" I ask, noting Agatha's absence.

"You've not heard?" Madaleen says, when Catherina doesn't answer. "She's left with her husband to India."

One less possible customer for my fabrics, I can't help but think.

"She should be returning in a few months' time," Catherina says. "Not that it matters." She dresses handsomely, wearing a necklace with a rose-cut diamond and small diamond earrings. Her husband is rising quickly up the ranks of the V.O.C. Their household boasts some twenty slaves already.

"What do you mean?" I can't think of the sisters separately. On the *Leyden* I often fused their names together. Catherina-Agatha. We all did.

"We quarreled before she left." Catherina sits down next to me as a slave sets down the tea pot and an ornate porcelain set. Maritjen gazes at the delicate cups with approval. "She should have apologized before leaving."

"You'll mend things when she returns," Madaleen says. "At least you have some family here, unlike the rest of us, cobbling together families with these strange settlers." Bitterness enters into Madaleen's voice, and I feel some worry for Madaleen, despite her wealth.

"I hear you might soon have a beau," Catherina says to me, seeming eager to change the topic. Still, she appears more reserved and drawn than before, perhaps missing Agatha's agreements to steady her own opinions. "Berend Oonstade impresses many of the women since his arrival."

"I hear he is eager to marry," Maritjen says, reaching for one of Madaleen's sweetened seed biscuits. She's already eaten two.

I drink my tea, which tastes of flowers, though I can't name the bloom. Madaleen has a gift for surprising details, taking items we all use and improving them. Unlike the sameness in dress and hairstyle all the other women employ, she often wears her hair in a unique knot or arrangement. I take some pride in her subtle artistry. Sontje would as well.

"I'm too busy fretting over the loss of the cottage to his son, Gerrit Haffner, to worry about a beau." Madaleen winces at my reproach. I must contain my annoyance, or they will not want to see my fabrics.

"You need not worry about any of that if you remarry," Maritjen says, brushing crumbs from her fingers and onto Madaleen's tiled floor. "And a husband will provide some respectability."

"Yes. I haven't attended a wedding for months now," Catherina agrees.

"Nor have I." Madaleen nibbles one of her biscuits. "I miss wearing my better jewelry."

I bristle. Jana of Amsterdam would have kept her tongue, but I have no patience for such restraint now. "Why not have some other engagement? Why must we only wear our finery for weddings? As if marriage is the only event worthy of celebration?"

The porcelain cups clink in their saucers. Maritjen slurps her tea. Outside, Madaleen's slaves argue over some task.

"It's true," Madaleen says. "We should celebrate other things."

I feel the same curious fear I felt when I told Sontje about the Ringhouse. A desire to relieve the burden of my feelings while fearing the consequence of their release. But I'm less afraid now.

"I have decided," I say, placing my teacup on Madaleen's teakwood table, "that I will never again rely on a man for my fortune. I have no desire to be married. Not to Berend Oonstade or anyone else. Bought and sold like a *Lakenvelder*—did you know Albert took money for our weddings? That Willem Brouwer probably saved up for Sontje? And your husbands likely did as well?" I look to Madaleen and Catherina, who study the bright buckles on their fine shoes. "And I was bought and sold and used before we even arrived. As a brothel worker outside Amsterdam, and then as a house servant for some well-regarded Company minister who prodded and insulted me whenever possible."

The women stay silent, staring into their dainty teacups.

But I continue. "Only one person has shown me the kind of love I would seek, and I don't expect to have it again."

"Mattheus was indeed a good man," Maritjen says with relief, and primly makes the sign of the cross.

But her false piety inflames me further.

"Not Mattheus, though he was better than most." I see their curiosity. Even Madaleen looks up at me with her wide, watery eyes. I think her tea must be cold now.

"Sontje," I say, and the admission, her name, feels like a weight lifted from my shoulders. "I have never loved anyone more. She remains the best friend I had, and my only true confidante. And unless I find that again, I would just as well remain alone with Ebel."

Maritjen gasps.

I can't help but smile at her predictable response. "It's a fine thing to gossip about. The dead mother of my son is nothing but a moss-covered headstone in the forest now. I've spent most of my life in pursuit of respectability, and the one time I refused it, I finally felt free."

Madaleen blinks back her tears. "Even I miss her so, Jana. I sometimes speak to Sontje at night, after Tomas is asleep. It helps me somehow." She puts down her teacup and grasps my hand.

Catherina says nothing. When she finally speaks, her voice is so quiet I can hardly hear her.

"I should have said goodbye to Agatha. Every day I feel part of me is empty. Like I'm not myself at all anymore. I can't even recall the reason for our quarrel—some useless squabble between our husbands, that we felt obligated to continue. And now I don't know when she'll return."

Madaleen's servant comes to remove the tea tray and pastries as we sit, mired in our memories and sadness.

Even Maritjen knows better than to say anything.

"Well, now that we've settled the subject of marriage and why I will have no beau, Berend Oonstade or anyone else, I have something I wish to show you." I straighten myself in my chair. Take a deep breath and pick up my basket from Madaleen's gleaming floor. I place the basket on my lap, and think of Ebel, silently asking Sontje to send me more courage than I have. "It's a unique item. A blend of home and here."

The women stop their fidgeting, and look at me with interest. I lift out the stack of fabrics and place them on Madaleen's empty tea table, unfolding the cloths with care to reveal each new color, stitch, and weave. The swirling, tangled patterns, all fresh and unknown. The *Leyden* women stare, holding their breaths, as though the natives' wondrous, vivid fabrics are Batavia itself, just waiting in all innocence for their hungry exploration.

Chapter 76

In the end, Madaleen, Catherina, and Maritjen purchase all the pieces I've brought with me. Madaleen makes an order for a wall hanging. Maritjen requests a table covering. Catherina promises to ask her husband to help bring items to a larger market—perhaps for export.

Later that same day, Catherina comes to my stall at the market. Not only does her husband agree, but he orders the fabrics in a quantity I never imagined.

I return home from the market mid-morning, eager to see Aini and Candra, who are watching Ebel, to tell them of this news.

As I hurry home, my thoughts swirl, my heart quickens. Maybe we can keep the house. Gerrit pitied me, seeing me at the market two days earlier, said I could stay one more week. He softened only when I showed myself to be weak. I hated asking him, the flicker of triumph across his wolfish face.

But I can't think of that. I turn my attention to the orders, the possibility of reclaiming our home. Saving us.

"I have some news," I say, entering the house.

Aini and Candra sit on the floor with Ebel, teaching him a game of mimicry, so he follows their claps in number with his own. Always, they are able to concoct some game or another to keep him occupied. I struggle to think of such amusements, often relying on walks with him through the town instead.

The women stand up to listen to me, but I motion for them to stay as they are.

"Catherina's husband, Frederik, wants to export the fabrics," I begin to explain. "He thinks our Dutch will love them. We have some time," I add hastily, not wanting them to feel rushed. "We won't have another fleet for another three months. He said he would provide partial payment before then." I'm speaking too quickly. They will not understand. I'm anxious, thinking of the house, maybe even buying a larger one, with a garden for Ebel. My thoughts leap and skip like wild rabbits. "Can we go to there today?" I ask Aini, meaning the weaving house. "We can discuss how to do the work."

"I must make rice for baby," Candra says.

"And I must clean the floors." Aini looks at Candra and I can't read their faces. I do not think of it much. For the first time since meeting Gerrit, a welcome lightness enters me. I permit myself the small luxury of worrying less.

"After all that," I say. "We have more hours of sunlight left. And we have so much work to do."

When we arrive at the weavers' hut, the others surround us, offering to hold Ebel. One of the women, missing all but two teeth, gives Ebel a banana, which he gladly mashes with his little white teeth. Our Dutch require more visits before showing such warmth. I think of our teas and dinner parties. Everything planned in advance.

"Aini, can you explain?" I ask her. She hesitates a moment, perhaps unused to providing a service different from sweeping and cooking and feeding Ebel.

"The colony loves your work," I begin. "Thank you for sharing these fabrics with me. Everyone who saw them wanted them. I've received many orders for more. I can pay you a little for them," I add. Though I can't pay them too much, for I need the money for my own house, but even some money will be more than they've ever had. "I'd like to learn from you, also. Especially the dyes." The pigments they use surprised me with their richness and depth.

Aini translates in between. In her native language, she looks taller, her hands sweep out gracefully, reminding me of the long-tailed widow-birds I saw at the Cape. She becomes not Aini our slave, but herself, and I recall how I changed myself with my own employers— growing smaller, quieter, always wishing to disappear.

One of the older women interrupts. I can't understand what she says. She wears a long, white braid, coiled into a bun at the top of her head. Her forehead shines in the sunlight, a smooth dome despite her age. Her *kebaya* is neatly pleated, dyed indigo.

The women speak to each other, so I glance at the fabric on the looms. An indigo with gold, another woven of green threads in many shades. Madaleen would want this one.

Silence follows their burst of chatter.

Outside a crow calls out, cracking into the quiet of the room.

"Kaw!" Ebel answers, and the women laugh. He holds hard to my leg, embarrassed.

I imagine giving the money to Gerrit. The shock of his expression as I offer to buy the only house I've known since arriving here, other than our crude barracks when we first left the *Leyden*. The house where Sontje and I imagined a life for ourselves with Ebel, where we permitted ourselves to dream.

Perhaps Gerrit will be impressed by his stepmother. People sometimes surprise. Mattheus would be proud of me, and I feel a quick sting of longing for his approval.

"We should begin tomorrow," I say to Aini, thinking of who I must contact first—Catherina's husband or Gerrit.

Aini clasps her hands across her middle, as though embracing herself. I've seen her do this when Candra argues with her about some matter or another.

Her eyes look sad for a moment, then defiant, as she scans the other women's faces. She shakes her head slowly. "They say no," she says, her voice clear, and louder than I have heard it. "We do not want this. We gave you a gift, but our cloth is our own. Our dyes are our secrets. Only our women learn them. We can't teach you."

Chapter 77

I'm too stunned to speak. I stand, fixed to the dirt floor, until Ebel claps my knee with his chubby hand. I pick him up and smell his head, comforting myself.

I do not think anything, other than to leave. I walk out of the hut without Aini. Without Candra. Without saying goodbye. My belly feels twisted and sharp, reminding me of my hunger from my Amsterdam days.

I follow the overgrown footpath, tracing our steps back. The walk is long, and I'm holding Ebel, who grows heavier in my arms. He squirms and kicks, wanting to walk, but no, I will not put him down. I hold to him, like he is all I have in the world.

Because he is.

How green it is in this forest as we walk. My mind races with my next plans, but even with my upended, thickened thoughts, the emptying of my last efforts to save our house, I can't help but notice the richness of our surroundings. Great, leafy ferns spread out over the forest, as though gathering the ground. The brown trunks of trees teem with a rich, vibrant moss, the taller trees stretch up to the sky as if trying to grasp at the clouds, their smooth, white trunks all the more bracing against so many shades of green below. Perhaps the weaver of the green fabric I saw earlier in the hut meant to capture this landscape in her cloth.

The Bos comforted me in my childhood, and I seek such relief now. I can still feel Fader's strikes stinging my skin as I ran across the grass, looking for some tree to hide behind. No grass here, but I stop at one moss-covered tree whose branches stray outward in all directions, like a giant, outstretched hand. I touch the furred trunk. Cool. Wet.

I can beg the Company to let me return to Amsterdam, but the Company rarely permits a female to return. I could make a case for myself. Maybe I could take Ebel back with me. But Willem still lives here, and has more claim to Ebel than me, even if he does nothing for him. I could lose Ebel altogether.

And he is everything.

And if I were to return, then what? I would be a servant again, spending my remaining days wringing linens and scrubbing floors. What would Ebel do as I worked?

Ebel watches me from the clutch of my arms as I absently run my fingertips over the moss furring up the giant tree. He reaches out to do the same.

We stand under its branches, our hands outstretched, matching the tree we now stroke. Three open hands.

Asking.

I let Ebel walk on his own as we near the cottage. I will need to ask Madaleen for a room now, and the fear of owing her for her generosity, the fear of needing her charity, causes my gut to clench.

I think of Sontje, as I often do. I walk alongside Ebel, at his slow, doddering pace. Anger rises in me, at the *kampung* women, at Aini and Candra, at everyone. Fader, Moeder, Madame Aad, the brothel men, De Graaf, Mattheus, all these people who hurt me or left me to fend for myself.

But in the torrent of my self-pity, I think of Aini and Candra. What have I done for them? Given them loose coins to buy useless items—beads and bits of glass and tinsel. The Company brought slaves to build the bridges, canals, even the house where we live, just as the Company brought me here to satisfy their need for our civilizing ways. And despite the Company's efforts, so many of our Dutchmen take on the slaves as concubines, who are even more pliant than poor Dutch women cast out alone at sea for ten months. Then the men's half-*indische* children disappear into nearby villages, forgotten and lost.

Even Gerrit's claim to the house can be blamed on the Company, for abandoning its daughters to unknown men, for giving these men powers we will never have. And so we are all just left with little things. Bits of glass found in knotholes. Thread we coax and knot into lace for frocks too heavy for this climate. Buckled shoes, saffron, cinnamon, *sappanwood*. Tortoise shell combs to gather up our slave-braided hair.

My anger shifts. The women gave me their fabrics only out of generosity, and I allowed myself to become like the Company itself, expecting their labor instead of asking for it. I'm no better than Maritjen with her pageant of slaves and parasols, or Falks with his rattan stick to rap on the backs of exhausted slaves. I'm ashamed.

Just then, Ebel trips on a fallen branch and catches himself with his hands.

I resist the urge to gasp. "Good for you," I say instead. "We all fall. Now, you must get up."

He looks at me, perhaps expecting me to worry, to kiss his hurt knees. Instead, I smile, crouching down next to him under the giant tree whose fallen branch caused his tumble. Ebel turns his hands over to look at his palms, now pocked and dusted with crumbled leaves and red soil. His gray eyes turn to me, waiting for my reaction.

"Let's walk, my boy. Up."

"Yes, let's walk, my boy," Ebel laughs, mimicking me. He claps his hands together, as though extinguishing his pain. He pulls himself up and resumes his staggering path through the forest. Home, for a few more days at least, lies some distance ahead. I take Ebel's hand, the measure of Sontje's generosity to me. The chance to love someone when I thought I could not. I think of the tree we just passed, its outstretched hand, and find the beginning of an answer.

Chapter 78

Aini and Candra do not return to the cottage until the next morning. At first, I worry they will not arrive at all, and regret weighs on me for how I left the weavers' hut yesterday.

All night I think of how I may go forward. But for now, I pack my things—my Company frocks and Ebel's collection of seeds and rocks, and a few clothes. I sweep the floors, an unnecessary kindness to Gerrit, but I find the activity familiar and consoling. I dust the furnishings that will now belong to him, wrap our few clay bowls in linens. At least we have very little to move.

The door opens as I'm latching the trunk closed. Aini and Candra. They look around the house, long-faced. They look as sad as me.

I do not know what to say, not wishing to cause them more discomfort, and still feeling raw.

But Ebel, happily ignorant of our concerns, runs to Candra. He wraps his arms around her leg and asks to be carried. She lifts him up and whispers to him in her language, and hearing her soft, loving voice causes a thaw in my own awkward silence.

"I'm sorry." I stand and walk toward the two women. "I'm sorry for leaving."

Candra shrugs. Her wrinkled eyes show an unmistakable sadness.

"And you were all so generous with your beautiful fabrics." A choke of sadness rises in me, thinking of the woman weaving, her quick, gliding movements, and my covetous impulses to sell their art.

"We talked to the others," Candra says. Her Portuguese is better than mine, and she has even learned some of our Dutch words. I'm again surprised at the natives' sharpness, then embarrassed for my low estimation of them in the first place. "If we sell our fabrics, we want equal pay. And they want to learn the lace also." Her voice is steady, and I know even this offer is a gift to me. They do not need money the way we do, do not wish for fine villas in the hills or painted silk hand fans. And for a moment, I envy them.

"I'm happy to teach you, and yes, to pay you also," I say, stunned. I had abandoned any thought of selling the fabrics and instead felt clean relief that Aini and Candra had arrived at all, when I was so unsure they would.

Ebel presses his mouth to Candra's cheek and pulls on her stretched earlobe. She smiles. "And we will not share the secret of our dyes and colors. Those are our things."

"Of course. I do not wish to know the secrets, anyway," I reply, though of course I'm curious. But the women's generosity moves me beyond my desire to learn their secrets. "I was only thinking of moving now. And what to do next."

"Always, something to do next," Candra says, putting Ebel down and rubbing her arms. He grows heavier by the hour. A healthy, joyful boy. Sontje would be proud. "But sometimes we can rest. Sometimes we can sweep. Sometimes we can sing."

Aini giggles at her mother, a musical sound. "And we can make the lace. They all want to learn. I will show them how fast I am. Even faster than you," Aini says to Candra.

"Only because you are young," Candra replies, patting Ebel's soft head. "And still you have much to learn about slowness."

Chapter 79

That evening, I walk to Madaleen's *landhuizen* to ask her the favor of lodgings for a time. She offered earlier, but now, standing on the sweeping veranda of her grand house on the Tijgersgracht, where the wealthiest live, I feel timid. Afraid. So many doorsteps I have stood upon, waiting for others' charity. I grow weary of it.

Madaleen's slave, a young boy, opens the door, and motions for me to wait in the entrance as he summons his mistress. The entry dwarfs the sitting room of my cottage, and I feel very small inside it.

Madaleen arrives, looking flushed and pretty in her simple blue dress. "Jana." She embraces me, her arms biting into my ribs, she squeezes so hard. "I'm so happy to see you. But it is late. Are you unwell?" Her concerned expression causes in me a swell of love for this girl who cares for me despite all her new wealth and our different stations.

"I'm sorry, Madaleen. But Ebel and I must leave the cottage tomorrow. Gerrit is preparing the property to be sold. He gave us a bit more time, but we have nowhere to stay now." I look down at my hands, shy with my request.

"Whatever do you mean, Jana? You always have somewhere to stay—as long as I'm alive. I said so before. You and Ebel will stay here, with me and Tomas. This house is too big and quiet anyway, and I will love the company. Tomas is gone most of the day. It will be like our time on the *Leyden,* except no worms in the hardtack. Indeed, no hardtack at all. I never wish to eat that foul biscuit again. We can even play draughts." She laughs, knowing well how we despised the game by the end of our voyage.

"I feel low asking for your charity," I admit. "But I can't think what else to do for Ebel and me."

Madaleen takes my hand in hers. Small and warm. I remember how she held Drika close at all times, whispering to that tattered doll. "When I was on the *Leyden* with you—it seems so long ago now, doesn't it?—I was so lonely and afraid, and without you and Sontje, I think I may have died on that terrible boat." Her eyes shine in the candlelight of her lamps. "And I did nothing to help Sontje that night. I feel awful for that, like a black spot forever stains my own heart. So it will be a pleasure to finally pay you a kindness after so many you have paid me. A gift, really." She embraces me again. "I can't believe that awful Gerrit, though," she continues. "Mattheus would not like his son's greedy behavior one bit. He was a decent man."

"He was," I say, and mean it. "Thank you, Madaleen. It is not easy for me to ask you."

"Oh, I know. Sontje used to say that of you. Said it was your greatest weakness, in fact, that you can't ask anyone for much." Her eyes twinkle, seeing my surprise that she and Sontje would speak about me in this way. "But that is why I'm so happy to help you."

Chapter 80

Our room at Madaleen's grand house faces the west and offers great, rectangular windows through which we watch the sunset. Our bed is more comfortable than any I have slept in, and the room is cheerful and full of light during the day. In the evenings, a soothing orange glow enters the room, turns Ebel's white-blond hair orange, and he jumps into my lap while we watch the sun drift downward and into darkness.

During the days, Madaleen's slaves watch Ebel so I can go with Aini to the weavers' hut. The walk is far from Madaleen's house, but I enjoy being outdoors, taking care to touch the tree with its outstretched branches, feeling I owe it something for its guidance.

Aini and I speak little on our walks, but a friendly silence grows between us, as though we know each other well enough not to misjudge our silence for disfavor. It occurs to me that the true test of a friendship is the measure of silence that can grow between two people.

When we arrive to the hut in the mornings, the weavers are hard at work. They teach me their weaving technique, but I'm not skilled, often dropping the blade or forgetting to lean back enough to maintain the careful tension of the loom. Still, they are patient teachers and I make slow progress. The women ask me my opinion of colors and patterns and bring me their own lace to inspect. Like Aini, all the women are quick to learn lacemaking, and eager to try the more difficult patterns—diamonds, squares within squares, and small, intricate stars. Some of their crisp, fine work so resembles our Dutch snowflakes, I wonder if they have seen snow to create such patterns. But when I explain to them how bits of ice float down from the sky in Amsterdam, like their monsoon rains but quiet and slow, they laugh, believing I am telling them stories.

"No, it's true," I insist. "We must wear so many clothes to stay warm when it happens. Skirts and petticoats and shawls and mittens." They do not know what these words mean, but I try to describe them anyway. Remembering such chill causes me to shiver, recalling the ache in my wrists and hands after cleaning the floors in winter, and the numbness in my feet and my clouds of misty breaths after a long walk from Dam Centre. I remember feeling so sorry for myself, cold and struggling as I was. "It is so much better here," I tell the women, and then recall Tobias's old word for Batavia. "A paradise."

We remain busy—weaving, cutting, folding, sewing, joining pieces, couch stitching, drawing patterns in the floor with the long, notched bamboo sticks we use to stretch the fabric and prevent the warp's inward curve. The weavers rotate their tasks throughout the day to prevent boredom and I delight in all the movement around me, like a long, festive dance. I'm used to working alone, with only my thoughts to accompany my labor, but I know a different pleasure now—our collective work creates a kind of music and vigor that reminds me of the waves breaking against the hull of the *Leyden*, and then their retreat, like the silence that accompanies us during our more difficult tasks, broken, at last, by a question or joke or compliment that begins a burst of conversation or the exchange of a story I consider later as I make the long walk back to Madaleen's *landhuizen*, tired but satisfied, at the end of the long day.

*

After nearly a month of my daily visits to the weaving hut, we have amassed a good number of items: lace-edged wall tapestries, table, bed, and pillow coverings. Aini grows deft at making small handkerchiefs with lace edging, which Madaleen uses to accessorize our otherwise plain and somber dresses.

I have learned that the short clump of trees near the hut—the ones Ebel disliked for their foul smell—help to produce some of the pigments for the fabrics. But beyond that single ingredient, I know nothing of their dyes. And I do not ask or even wonder. Perhaps it is best not to be curious. Our settlers and the harm of their expansive curiosity—bringing slaves from their homelands to see how they would work, mimicking our city plans, full of canals and bridges, despite the change in climate and different flow of water—so much of Batavia now swarms with mosquitoes for such errors of our curiosity. Some questions are best left unanswered. And when I see a fresh indigo thread or finished woven piece sparkling with colors I think I've never before seen, I feel a shock of pleasure at all I do not understand about them. And this is a new feeling, the joy of not knowing. Like the God glass I once found in the trees of the Bos. I gave up wondering how those colored bits came to arrive in their knotholes, and instead allowed myself to wonder at the secret rightness of their presence, nestled in the darkness, just waiting for me to discover them.

Chapter 81

"Jana, they are all so lovely," Madaleen says as we arrange our work on her grand teakwood table. "The colors are so rich—and this lace! Griet would be so happy knowing you'd taught so many her craft."

Madaleen helps me fold the fabrics over the table, carefully pleating the longer tapestries over dining chairs. Her innate skills for arrangement and neatness impress me again, for I would not know how best to display our work, and it comes naturally to her. She has prepared her house so it looks ready for a grand party—the floors shine, every flower stands at attention. Even the slaves stand taller, ready for their tasks.

"You've gone to so much trouble for this," I say, looking at the loveliness of her house.

"It is no trouble at all. I'm happy for you, and so proud," she says, squeezing my hand. "I think Catherina's Frederik will be very interested in these pieces," Madaleen says. She is just as eager as the rest of us to see about expanding a market for our fabrics and lace. I'm again touched by her generosity and friendship. While other women in the settlement ridiculed my efforts, seeming to enjoy my misfortunes, Madaleen remains true in her kindness.

Catherina also. She convinced her husband to come to Madaleen's house, encouraging him to bring a few top merchants at the Company.

I'm surprised by Catherina's loyalty also, but I imagine grief inspires some measure of her kindness now. Agatha and her husband left some weeks ago for India, the sisters' quarrel still unresolved. Their ship was lost in a storm off the coast, nothing but the mast floating on the sea remained. Catherina's eyes have a new, sad shadow over them. I suspect not only for the loss of her beloved sister, but for the lost chance to mend their discord.

Catherina arrives with Frederik and three other merchants in the late afternoon.

I lead them to the dining room and the guests gaze at Madaleen's tasteful, uncluttered decorations, and I again think how fortunate I am for her friendship. She creates a welcome space best suited for showing our fabrics, so they stand out against the orderly, clean background like wildflowers in a grassy field.

Aini and Candra stand with me in the dining room, hands clasped behind their backs, chins high. They, too, look proud of our work, and carry themselves differently than Madaleen's slaves. How different work feels when its benefits flow directly to the person working, than when such service is imposed. A similar gladness entered me when I earned my first few guilders at Master Reynst's home—payment for labor I willingly performed and so unlike my toiling for Madam Aad, which I surrendered out of fear of her abuses.

But I shake my head to clear it of those foul memories.

The men amble around the table, stopping at different pieces, touching the fabrics, or tracing the fine lines of our lace.

"The colors. They are marvelous," Frederik says. "If we can learn their dyeing technique we could change the entire fashion of Europe."

"I'm sure my wife Gerta would wear this violet," one of the other merchants, Master Jansz, says. "So vivid. It's like gazing at a fresh painting."

"The pigments and dyes belong to the *kampung* women," I say, my heart beating hard. I worry I will offend them, but I wish to be clear with my promise to Aini and Candra. "But they will make the fabrics for us, whatever we wish. Certainly new frocks and shirts are possible."

Frederik nods thoughtfully, and I feel a flush of relief that he does not to pursue the matter of pigments further.

"I'm not much for fashion—Catherina chooses all my clothing." At this, Frederik beams at his wife and I witness the warmth between them, the suggestion that theirs is a happy marriage. A brief ache follows for all I have lost—Sontje and Mattheus—even as I'm happy for Catherina.

"You must have worked very hard to make so many pieces in such a short time," Master Jansz says, looking at one of the wall hangings—a geometric print Aini explained was taught to them by traders from India long ago.

"We all work hard. All day. The weaver women have great skill in all they do. They took to our lace so quickly."

Master Jansz pauses, still peering into the design. "Strange how the pattern feels familiar to me, reminds me of something in my childhood. Maybe a drawing I once made. Or a sky I saw as a young boy back in Rotterdam."

"Yes, their blues are very vibrant," Frederik adds. "Each cloth like a new world. More to explore. Extraordinary, really."

I glance at Candra, whose small, lined face remains impassive. I wonder how much she understands of our speech. The settlers usually speak Dutch with each other, thinking the natives and slaves do not understand, but I've been teaching the women and they surprise me with how much they learn and how quickly.

"Jana. I will talk to my partners," Frederik says. His dark eyes sparkle and a smile spreads across his handsome face. He is some years older than Catherina, but well-dressed and elegant in his bearing. Small wrinkles bracket his eyes when he smiles. "But if you and the weaver women can make more of these, I can't see why we should not sell them here and what's more, back in the homeland as well. I think we could bring gaiety enough to our people suffering through our gray and cheerless Dutch winters, no? It would be a service to them."

Madaleen claps in delight, and Catherina laughs.

"I think you have started quite a business for yourself and the widows," Frederik adds. "And I'm happy to help you with it."

Epilogue

Batavia, 1630

I watch as the *retourship* docks. The monsoon season brings us the next burghers, tradesmen, soldiers, and wives and then the ships return to the homeland with the new widows and their children, and families fattened well enough by Batavia's riches, now eager to reveal the fruit of their efforts back home.

I first began coming to the port to supervise the loading of our goods onto the ships for export, but it's become one of my favorite places to visit, like the docks of Amsterdam were when I was a hungry servant girl years ago. I still love the look of the water, and the beckoning horizon line reminding me of Sontje in my arms at night on the *Leyden*, and the click-woman waving goodbye as we left the Cape.

With the help of the *beguine* weavers, our little company has expanded. Thirty *kampung* widows now weave and embroider our fabrics—for wall hangings, place settings, bed linens, tablecloths, even clothing. Our lighter fabrics allow for richer colors and crisper pleating than the thick serge the Dutch traditionally use for their dresses.

I have kept my promise, and never asked about their pigments. When he is older, Ebel will inherit my stake in the company, if he also promises to protect their secret methods. He has grown into a sweet and thoughtful boy, strong and graceful like Sontje. He loves Batavia, the vastness of its creatures—the red-beaked rice birds and patterned finches, the furred moths, and brilliant green snakes during monsoon season. He draws small sketches of the native birds and insects in drawing books he keeps in a stack in his room. His protective nature and kindness earns him the natives' love. They dote on him, and like me, he says he will never again use slaves, whose populations from the outer colonies steadily swell.

Willem Brouwer died two months ago, having never uttered a word to his son. Probably dead from his own drinking, but who could know for certain? His last remaining slave discovered him in his crumbling cottage days later, rotting from the heat in the same house where Ebel lost his mother. Where I lost Sontje.

The passengers are exiting the *retourship* now, steadying themselves on the siderails of the pier. Sick and skinny. Sallow and crack-skinned. Some drop to their knees in gratitude. They never wish to look upon another ship. Dreaming of *brezels* and night swims and bluebell flowers they may never gather again to squeeze into a Delft vase. I recall my own wobbling steps down the same pier so many years ago, waiting for the earth to stop shifting like the sea.

Do not worry, I wish to say to these sick and suffering souls.

You will find other flowers to love.

One man squints and looks hard at me as he approaches from the dock, favoring his right leg, but I can't see him well in the sun's blinding glare.

"You," he says and gazes at me for a long moment. "You made it here. I somehow thought you had." Not until he is close do I notice the bright blue eyes.

He is bald now, and his skin more lined than before.

"Why are you here?" I ask, surprised by my own calm. Talking to him is like talking to a ghost of myself.

Tobias, my old friend from Amsterdam, smiles.

His eye teeth turn inward. I had forgotten.

"Over these years of working, it was this land that kept coming to me in my dreams. This is my last journey at sea. I wish to live out the rest of my days here. In Batavia."

I walk with him to the hold to gather his things. Tobias will stay in the Company barracks for a few weeks before purchasing a small plot of land. He has left Amsterdam with some fortune despite his undesirable background and now wishes to have a small garden and fruit trees, and do occasional shipping work for the Company.

"It does feel like such a living creature, doesn't it?" I think of the forest ferns with their great, outstretched leaves, and the blue sky that feels like a strong embrace by noon. The rainbow trees and clinging moss.

"Ay, it does, even after all these years. This land called out over the ocean for me, tempting me with its fruits and green things on the dreariest, gray days back in Amsterdam. My memories of Batavia felt like a fire to warm my hands over at the end of the day."

He tells me news of Amsterdam, the resurgence of plague, the exploration of New Netherland to the west, and ongoing skirmishes with Spanish naval forces, which captured an entire herring fleet off the Hebrides. All of it feels so distant here, under the blazing Batavian skies.

"I feel like I should keep up to date more," I say after hearing his stories.

"But why? None of it is good. Disease, violence, death. That's all it's ever been."

I tell him a little about myself. Arriving as a Company Daughter some ten years ago. Marrying Mattheus. Changes in the colony since those early days. I do not tell him about Ebel. Or Sontje.

I'm not ready to give him that.

"You've had a life in those ten years," he says with admiration when I tell him of my journey and Mattheus.

"Yes. Not often happy."

"Well, it rarely is if you've lived long enough. But that's better than the other option." He smiles, and the familiar wrinkles around his eyes cause in me a longing for the girl I was when we first met. How I struggled for every guilder and tormented myself over my feelings for Sontje. I was so determined and full of desire, unaware of all that lay ahead.

It is indeed a strange thing to miss one's struggles, and the adventure of simply being alive.

"It was you who first told me of Batavia," I confess as we continue our walk. "You told me about the mangoes." I feel nervous revealing to him the importance of his stories that night we first met. "And I wanted to try them so badly. To taste them for myself."

"You took a dangerous ten-month journey for some mangoes?" He laughs, and I don't correct him. It's a story for later times. "You are always a surprise, Miss Jana." He looks happy at my admission. "Ay, those mangoes haunted my own dreams for many years."

"I know where to find the best ones here," I say. "I can take you, if you like?"

"I would like that very much, Jana. Let us go then. Right now."

"Now? It's deep in the forest. You must be tired."

"Not so tired to give up the chance to taste a mango once again." He smiles, and when he does, I remember the man I met all those years ago.

We stop for tea at my cottage, and to drop off his few things. He compliments my simple home, its native furnishings, and tidy floors. I still use an old table Mattheus purchased after our wedding, now pitted with Ebel's fork marks. Gerrit gave it to me—the last of our marital wares, because no one else wanted it.

"I have so much to tell you, I'm not sure whether I should even bother to begin," Tobias says, taking a last draught of his tea.

"Well, since you've come here to live out the rest of your days, I suppose we have some time," I say, smiling. "But first, let us gather some mangoes."

The forest begins behind my bungalow. Ebel and I had cleared an area for gardening, but some space away from it, the grove of jungle trees emerges. We made a narrow footpath between our favorite trees, though the undergrowth is heavy and one must watch every step.

Tobias follows behind me as we enter the forest.

"Watch for the green snakes," I warn. "They can kill you with their bite."

He laughs. "How I love this place. So full of peril and beauty. More alive than any place I have known. It is a relief to be away from our cities, all noise and paved over with stones and horse *poep* at every turn."

He walks slower than me, limping a little. He explains later that he had an accident years ago that left one leg shorter than the other. But he never complains. Just another story to share. He touches the leaves of the spung and acacia trees with reverence, as though greeting old friends. I show him spider webs hanging from the branches, bright green beetles crawling on the underside of benth leaves. We stop and listen to the forest sounds, the screams of gibbons, hums and whispers, a loamy smell invading all.

"It's nothing like our forests, is it?" he asks, watching a slug traverse the trunk of a pink-flowering tree. "Like every corner of this place is full of new things."

"I bring my son Ebel here to watch all of it. The trees, the insects. They say dragons live in this jungle."

"And why not? It is a magical place. More magical than any other I have seen."

He doesn't ask me more about Ebel, who is with Candra visiting the weavers now. But I will tell him later, when it's time.

We reach a clearing after wading through the thick trees, waving away insects, pointing out the vivid, wild hibiscus flowers, clustering orchids, and unknown forest creatures along the way.

The tree sits at the center of the clearing. Glossy, waxen leaves, and full of yellow fruit.

"Some of these trees can be very old. The darker the leaves, the older it is," I explain. "This one's leaves are dark, though it is not very tall yet. Its fruit is the best. None of those tiresome threads that stick in your teeth. Dewa showed it to me long ago. The settlers don't come out this far. Just the natives and me."

Tobias stands paces away, looking at the tree, the sunlight on the tree. Me.

"I've always thought there should be a special word for the shadows tree branches make on whatever lies beneath them," he says.

"Shade, you mean?"

"No, that flickering quality. It's not shade exactly. Not covered enough. But it's beautiful. Half-light and half-darkness. Like the best of lives."

A quick shot of joy and sudden shyness as I dig the toe of my *klomp* into the damp, rich earth under the mango tree.

I lift my arm to touch a plump, yellow-orange mango overhead. The ripest on the tree.

"It looks as though you are touching the sun," Tobias says and smiles.

I stand up on my toes, stretching my arm to the branches.

I cup the golden fruit in my hand.

A Letter from Samantha

Hello,

First, thank you so very much for reading my debut novel *The Company Daughters*. I hope you enjoyed it and felt transported in reading it, as I felt in writing it. If you want to keep up to date with my latest releases, just sign up at the following link. I can promise that your email address will never be shared and you can unsubscribe at any time.

www.bookouture.com/samantha-rajaram

This novel was inspired by a footnote I came across while researching for another novel. The footnote mentioned how young, poor Dutch women were sent to Batavia in the early 1600s to marry Dutch settlers. I immediately imagined the conflicting emotions of terror and adventure these young women must have felt, and how the dual oppressions of gender and poverty ironically provided them with an experience usually denied to young women. I soon tracked down the book the footnote referenced, Jean Gelman Taylor's *The Social World of Batavia*, and became captivated by the Company Daughters, their social milieu, and the colonial culture of Java in the early 1600s. From there, my research took me abroad to Amsterdam's Rijksmuseum, where I spent hours looking at Dutch still-life paintings and furniture to understand the world Jana left behind. I read countless books and articles, wanting to learn who would undertake such a journey, and what might happen if two Company Daughters fell in love during the grueling ten-month journey to the new colony.

As a former lawyer who studied sex trafficking, I'm fascinated by the real-life implications of laws and policies on ordinary people. While that early Dutch policy isn't referred to as sex trafficking per se, I interpret it as such, since the women were so young, so poor, and had little power once sent out on their journey. Further, I wanted to explore how women in such circumstances might find ways to resist the oppression of colonialism, patriarchy, and early capitalism. (Historical scholarship often refers to the Dutch East Indies Company as the first multinational corporation). And since much of queer history provides examples of how members of the community found ways to transgress and resist political oppression, it made sense that Jana and Sontje's love might afford them unique, even radical, insights into their community.

Thank you again for spending time with this novel. If you enjoyed *The Company Daughters*, I would greatly appreciate a review, and of course, I would love to hear from you. My objective as a writer is to share stories of those ignored by history—stories of the poor, the dispossessed, the colonized. Reviews will help get my stories out to a wider audience.

Samantha

 @Samantha_Reader

 @samantha.r.reader

Glossary

arrak: type of hard alcohol derived from rice

boterkoek: butter cake

brezels: pretzels

havermout: hot cereal

hutspot: stew

jambless: oven

jenever: type of alcohol

kampung: village

klomps: Dutch wooden clogs

kulis: slaves

Lakenvelder: breed of cattle

meerkoets: coot—type of waterfowl

olykoeks: type of ring-shaped cake

passglass: type of drinking glass

rederijker: theater actor

roemer: large wine glass

sla: salad

stamppot: traditional Dutch dish made with mashed potatoes

stuivers: Dutch coins

volkorenbrood: wheat bread

zaal: salon or main room of a house

Acknowledgments

While *The Company Daughters* is a work of fiction, the policy of sending young women from the Netherlands to the Dutch East Indies is based on Jean Gelman Taylor's account of the Company Daughters' arrival in Batavia on the *Leyden* in 1622. On that first voyage, six girls traveled from Amsterdam. The group included young women named Maritjen and Madaleen. All other names I found elsewhere. Gelman Taylor's book *The Social World of Batavia* proved indispensable in writing this novel, as did her article "Meditations on a Portrait from Seventeenth-Century Batavia."

A number of other books helped me on this journey. For information about seventeenth-century Amsterdam: Simon Schama's *The Embarrassment of Riches,* Klaske Muizelaar and Derek Phillips' *Picturing Men and Women in the Dutch Golden Age,* and *The Sensible Cook* by Peter G. Rose. For information about the journey to Batavia: Stephen R. Bown's *Scurvy* and Mike Dash's *Batavia's Graveyard.* For information about Batavia itself: Ulbe Bosma and Remco Raben's *Being "Dutch" in the Indies.*

I consulted many research articles in writing this book, and found the following most helpful: Elise van Nederveen Meerkerk's "Threads of Imperialism", Marsely L. Kehoe's "Dutch Batavia: Exposing the Hierarchy of the Dutch Colonial City," Robert Parthesius's "The Shipping and Logistics in Operation" about the VOC shipping routes, James L. Cobban's "The Ephemeral Historic District in Jakarta," Pauline Dublin Milone's "Indische Culture, and its Relationship to Urban Life," and excerpts from Ruth Barnes and Mary Hunt Kahlenburg's *Five Centuries of Indonesian Textiles*. I could not have written this book without the brilliance of these and so many other scholars.

As a fiction writer, I have taken some liberties with the Dutch language to accommodate my stylistic preferences. Words like "Fader" and "klomps" are either anglicizations or more modern versions of Dutch words, for example. Other aspects of this period of history have been simplified or approximated as well. The real story of these women, and of this period of history, is far more complex than anything I could capture in a few hundred pages, and I invite readers to investigate further.

In the years it took for me to write this novel, I amassed a small army of supporters, helpers, and mentors—too many to name here, but I must recognize a handful of these wonderful, generous people. First, my agent Carrie Pestritto and editor Kathryn Taussig for their wisdom and kindness throughout this process. I am so grateful to you both. Pitch Wars provided me with a loving family of writers and the opportunity to sign with my agent. It also gave me my mentor, Carrie Callaghan—a beautiful human in every way. Thank you so much for mentoring me.

And to my many generous reader and writer friends: my extraordinary book friend Maria Dong, who cheered me on during the most grueling points of editing this novel. Also—Louis Jackson, Ava Reid, Deak Wooten, Cheryl Pon, Daniel Nazer, Lexi Pandell, Rachel Scheuring, and Birgit Bock-Luna, who provided feedback on early versions of the novel. My friends, mentors, and colleagues who encouraged and helped me in all sorts of ways: Sara Houghteling, Alec Nevala-Lee, Charles Ganansia, Mary Beth Henley, Karina Fitch, Punam Sarad, Lara Clements, Katie Bliss, Monica Crubezy, Steve Hugh Westenra, Kola Heyward-Rotimi, Rosa Cabrera, Melissa Danaczko, Richard Grove, Carolina de Robertis, Kavitha Rajaram, and my Chabot College family. *India Currents, Catamaran,* and the Wellstone Writing Retreat supported my work as well. Professor Matthias van Rossum shared his knowledge about slavery in seventeenth-century Batavia, and I was fortunate to be hosted in Amsterdam by Zorah and Peter Sopar.

I'm so happy to recognize my inspiring and courageous parents, to whom I've dedicated this book. Like Jana and Sontje, they braved their own adventure in immigrating to the U.S. nearly 50 years ago, for which I am so thankful. Thank you for your many sacrifices, and for always buying me books. And extra appreciation to my mother for reading this book before anyone else, and for loving it so much.

Finally, I am lucky indeed to be the mother of Esai, Sharad, and Tesni. They teach me every day to be better, to love more.

Made in United States
Troutdale, OR
06/14/2023

10612777R00217